ORDOWAHL

NINTH PRINCE OF NORDWEG

MANHOOD

ORDOWAHL

NINTH PRINCE OF NORDWEG

MANHOOD

Cover Design by Ana at Books-Design.com

ISBN: 978-0-9970326-6-6

First Published August 2019
Revised May 2024
        Words With a Mission (wordswithamission.com)

'Other work, also via Words With a Mission:
Genesis and Creatoion   May 2024
Ordowahl : Mate   August 2019
        Revised November 2024

BLOG
        oh-and-another-thing.blog

Dedication

Ruth Marguerite Hinrichs, 1923–2006
Joel Henry Hinrichs, Sr. 1919–2008

Beloved parents, you gave me more than I ever knew, and while I tried to thank you, there is always more to say. I loved you, I miss you, and, in time, may we be reunited at Jesus' feet.

Also to my astonishing late-career trophy wife Jody, a.k.a. JoAnn Glittenberg, RN, MA (Psych), MA PhD (Anthropology) etc. etc., a co-pioneer in the field of cross-cultural nursing, and an anthropologist with many publications.

Acknowledgments

This work owes much to a number of very able people. Reviewers include Atlanta Sheridan, Lt Col Ronald Geurts, Prof. Eva Edrich, Tammy Sherman, Steve Welle, Joe Berger, Jim Sherman and Kevin Chambless. To all of these and to my most beloved spouse JoAnn Elizabeth Kropp Hinrichs, muse, best friend, and true confidant, a.k.a. Jody Glittenberg, thank you, thank you, thank you.

Special Thanks

Many thanks to Rocky Mountain Fiction Writers meeting Thursdays at Debi's Bakery, Monica Pool owner / doyenne. Many thanks to the Aspen Grove writers group meeting Wednesday's at the Tattered Cover, Mark Lehnertz, buchmeister. And special thanks to Kevin Chambless who spoke truth with diplomacy.

My greatest thanks go to Lynnette Horner (Letter Perfect Writing and Editing Services,) without whose help this book would be a pale imitation of what you see before you.

Introduction

Look back at an age of old languages and simple truths, a period of tension, danger and war, of death by sword and subtler means, a time of mysterious powers, of mages white and black.

Prince Ordowahl, ninth and last son of Stegnwahl, King of Nordweg, towers over his brothers in body, mind and spirit. They refuse to let him disrupt their "orderly" contest to win their father's choice to succeed him on the Nordwesh throne. Ordowahl's coming-of-age is also the day politics and his own safety–thus his brothers' safety–demand that he leave the realm.

The prince is a devout, faithful Christian. This lends him a thoughtful nature. He strives for purity in thought and act. Ordowahl meets his violent age head on yet is gentle toward the weak, and (some of the time) meets wrath with temperance.

Once away from home Ordowahl has to learn what it means to be an adult. He finds Klarenz, a commoner with a knack for mastering any craft or trade, yet who finds himself driven from town to town because–-well, you'll have to read the story to see what curse he carries.

Embrace the Eleventh Century, the old, the formal, the cruel and harsh, the noble. A sonnet accompanies each chapter; find its meaning trying to bridge from what has taken place to what next shoe may drop. Come with me to a scene "long ago and far, far away"—but here in this galaxy, and grounded in earth and iron.

-Joel

PS: In the Ermsleben section you'll see some modern German. Middle German is a close cousin to Old English, and too big a stretch. Those able to read Beowulf in the original would be able to suss out Old

German. Neither intrudes upon our scenic wordscape.

CONTENTS

I sing of Ordowahl, now come of age.
In time of absent moon his mother bore
him, 'neath a darkened star pushed out on stage—
Prince Ordowahl is huge, quick, Christian—more?
    What omen hails the plain-spoke prince's start?
    What failure was it, brought a king to heel?
    What sons whose brother-hatred stoned his heart?
    What distant hope to help a king's soul heal?
Come with me now to track the hero's trail,
his royal-nurtured, tutored life expand.
Comes test on test to prove him strong or frail—
begin his trek alone—on rock, or sand?
    What started with an infant's outraged squall
    Is now a quest to meet, then master, all.

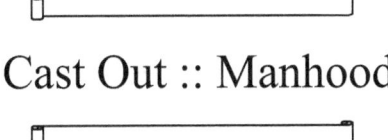

Cast Out :: Manhood

ANNO DOMINI MLXVIII (1068), 25 MAY

A coming of age rite celebrated the final day of each male's seventeenth year—today. On the morrow Ordo's birthday would start his adult life. Seventeen years of age and no longer a child.

His father, King Stegnwahl, still a proud **and** fearsome warrior, had gone from gold to silver at the temples. Silver lightened his beard. Piercing blue eyes looked out below bushy golden brows. The cloud-dappled May afternoon's sunlight made a craggy map across his weathered face. Light breezes interwove smells of roast meat **and** poured ale with the spring scents of new herbs **and** floral blossoms.

Twice a widower, Stegnwahl stood beside Magnhild, his third queen and Ordo's mother. She had come to him plow ox sized—if a bit fairer of face—and badger proud. From her marriage day, duty demanded that she finish raising Stegnwahl's eight stair-stepped sons. But when infant Ordo arrived, she saved all her love for him, thus held a portion of the blame for his brothers' sour natures. On reaching their own manhoods, they held small respect for either justice or righteous living. This came from many mistakes; more than a few were her own.

Stegnwahl was a hard man, but always fair. The qualities he valued most had not passed down to his first eight heirs, now making a semicircle behind him. The adults he had so far given

1

the world stood firm in will, solid in nature, cold of heart, and well beyond changing.

Ordo drew jealous enmity before he could speak in complete sentences. While Magnhild's special treatment sometimes fell more harshly on him than on his brothers, having a mother's love showed eight older, other-mothered brothers they would never have what Ordo owned by merely breathing in and breathing out.

From time to time Stegnwahl made it clear that he was not King David. Yet he might also say, "God has blessed me, alike to him, with many sons. And like David's, more than one of my sons aspires to take the throne after me. David chose Solomon. Who might become my Solomon?" The answer posed a tacit laurel. It grew the greener, year by year, on Ordo's brow.

His innate gifts—courage, wit, height, heft, sheer physical prowess—magnified his brothers' enmity. It grew as he did, year on year. This day a casual witness might mis-read the fresh state of Ordo's garments: one or two grass stains but no tears or mars. His face showed no marks. He moved with a dancer's lithe step, with none of the signs a man accumulates from protracted physical contests. Yet all present had seen him the prior day, He won every contest, plus a few held over and run this morning.

His opponents carried the sprains, bruises, grass stains and torn garments.

An eighteen inch deep pit wounded the center of the royal courtyard. Eighteen inches of dry-laid stone surrounded it. Passage into manhood required not winning—only surviving those contests. A new man could not affix "wahl" to his name unless he could step down into the pit, stand erect for an hour, then climb back out.

Ordo leapt in to bide the hour, hands joined lazily behind his back in the cloud-chased sunshine. He looked his father right in the Adam's apple; Stegnwahl's level gaze passed over Ordo's head. Behind the king, eight brothers' faces, plus four cousins who had also reached Manhood, showed an hour of blank stoicism. He'd bested each of them either yesterday or this morning.

Stegnwahl looked left and right past Ordowahl's head into the assembly—Magnhild's three almost-comely daughters, eight daughters-in-law, two dozen grandchildren, thirty or more of the top ranks of Nordweg's nobility, nearby thanes, and one or two braver town folk. He would, as king, perform this ceremony on a grandson come autumn after next. This Manhood held special significance, the last for a son of his own loins.

Stegnwahl motioned, a twitch of an index finger. Ordowahl sprang from the pit to block his father's view. The ceremony began.

"Nine sons, and the last completes his seventeenth year. This day he enters into Manhood. Today, Ordo, I dub you Ordowahl. I deem you a man. You may marry, you may come and go without let or hindrance, you may buy and sell lands and houses, you may do all that is lawful for a man to do." The ceremonial phrases rolled out. Eight brothers' faces stayed stoic. Magnhild beamed.

The rite concluded when Stegnwahl made a request of new man Ordowahl. "Give me the Latin of this: The Father of the righteous shall greatly rejoice; and he that begetteth a wise child shall have joy of him."

"Father, it is in the Proverbs of Solomon: exultat gaudio pater iusti qui sapientem genuit laetabitur in eo. No child, or man, is fully righteous, but I strive toward it. Thank you for my teachers. You stood first amongst them, whether or not you knew it."

Stegnwahl nodded. His point became clear—he had laid a second name on Ordowahl, "Solomon."

Nine royal men understood that implicit fact concerning the tenth, Ordowahl. *Everyone in this courtyard knows it. Yet even Solomon had to witness a brother's army before becoming king. I have no wish to war with my brothers.*

Overwhelming physical advantages and a razor-sharp mind became, on this day, unbreakable threads drawing Ordowahl toward death. Tomorrow would count him both an adult and a

3

friendless pauper. Springtime was a fair season, but the future bleak. His father naming him Solomon guaranteed eight older brothers' intention to end his life.

On the morrow he would waken, seventeen years past his day of birth, to the first day of his adulthood. Dawn would reduce childhood's shield to a dusty cobweb. To the end of this day only the vaporous protection afforded by honor and custom shielded him.

The participants went into the castle's large banquet hall. Lowborns who had stood outside the gate to overhear an event they understood as epochal now crowded into the courtyard to stand among savory aromas. Servants set up tables and piled food onto them. The nobles relaxed inside, beneath lofty beams spanning walls festooned with shields, swords, battle axes. A large altar stood at one end with a cross above it.

Toward late evening the indoor banquet dwindled to a drunken, belching cadre—a dozen nobles, several sons, Father Ewald, three carefully less drunken town elders, and ancient white mage Heorald.

In a quiet moment the king pulled Ordowahl into a rear corner. "Tell me your love for your brothers."

"Papa, I've seen my brothers reach Manhood. Most have wives and children—half my nieces and nephews seem more like cousins. I love all men as Jesus commands and I have a special love for my father, mother, and all their offspring." He hesitated.

"Yes," said Stegnwahl. "Go on."

"Yet, if I tell a truth, each brother makes loving him a hard thing. Each fears me in a way I cannot undo and shows me none of the kindness we are taught to pass between men, much less brothers born to the same father. Do I love them? Not well, Papa. Earnestly, but not well."

Stegnwahl's brows beetled. "Ordo—Ordowahl, do not spar with me."

"Papa, teach me how to answer your question. I sense no love from my brothers. They do not open their conversations to me. They want me gone and care not how. With effort, Father, I suppress such a mood in myself. Although we are nine strong men, after you the kingdom will need all of us and will be the stronger for each of us. I wish they felt that included me, but it's evident they do not. I am as I am. I fear no one by light of day and ask God to guard me when I cannot see. I love Nordweg, but I can not love this place."

The king gave him a slow nod. "God sets your fate before you, Ordowahl, but if it's here it is also brief. I can not hide the fact that I love you like David loved Solomon. I know your heart well and your brothers' hearts also." He paused in thought for a moment. "Final son, you are my chance to give Nordweg a proud and righteous king, but I command you to leave. Your mother and I must lose you; please make it a kind loss by giving us your farewell. Tell me that you will obey out of love more than fear."

Ordowahl's eyes went wide in surprise. His brothers' intent and plotting gave him a curious apprehension, not fear. He saw his father's fear, instead. Clasping his father's hands between his own, Ordowahl knelt and kissed the Royal signet ring. Then he rose up and left the hall. He did not look to left or right, but kept his ears and other senses sharp. *I am to be Solomon—yet for now I feel like Joseph sold down to Egypt. Joseph was not his own master; at least I still have that much.*

Becoming man shreds childhood's safety. Death
will trouble Ordo should he linger. Life
lies elsewhere. Kinfolk help him catch his breath
while wends he wayward, shuns both realm and knife.
    Did dad say Ordo is his Solomon?
    That name now dooms the best he's bred, to flee.
    What planning did he fail, what unbegun
    precautions, outcomes, did he not foresee?
Unblessed, alone, Prince Ordowahl sets out
to make the wider world his home. So much
to learn, so innocent, naïve, devout –
arms wide to fate and God's protective touch.
    Might cross a mountain, follow stream to mouth?
    Let's guess that on his way he wanders south.

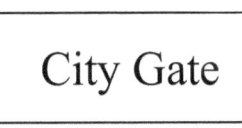

City Gate

New man Ordowahl, astride Hammerfoot and leading one mule, trekked southward down the length of Nordweg. Many relatives along his journey to realm's edge had welcomed him. Uncles, cousins, and progressively distant relations celebrated each visit on his way. They understood his grim lot. Their kindness salved the salted wound of his brothers' curse.

Their hospitality helped preserve the small gift of two gold coins he'd received from white mage Heorald before setting out. His genteel poverty included one mule. Its burden of armor, flour, bacon, and a hundred smaller items would make his trek comfortable.

Twenty green, happy days brought him to a mountain pass. On the far side he spent fifteen gray-minded days trekking down the mountains, along a stream, past small farms, and finally along a river. All of this was Viking land and Viking folk eyed him every part of the way, but left him alone.

Only deep bitterness leavened his new loneliness—that and the unrelenting company of a small flock of jackdaws. He didn't look back on his father's kingdom, nor his murder-bent brothers. He let flowing water lead him to the sea.

*__*__*__*

The rumble of distant surf and the strange, new smell of salt air raised his spirits. The road curved into a pine grove, trees rooted in sandy soil. Another small turn in the road and a low hum of conversation rose up. He caught the welcome smells of a town. Inescapable aromas of sweat and dung, too common to notice while amid them. Savory cooking, wood fires, the coal-stink of a blacksmith's forge, the odors and noise of livestock— coming around a third, sharper bend he encountered a massive wall and a heavy gate of large timbers bound with broad iron.

How odd is that? he mused to himself as he approached it. *This forest not only hides attackers from the town, it also provides them means for real mischief. The folly of leaving such a supply of firewood and a few heavy timbers for battering rams and ladders, abutting a town wall? This is as remarkable as the constant cacophony of jackdaws. Those thieving birds have followed me from the battlements of Father's castle. Do they warn the town that a stranger approaches?*

Behind the wall a town carried out its business. The massive gate creaked open just enough for a good-sized Viking to slip out before it shut behind him. A low-set helmet suggested that the man's skull had its same conical shape. A reddish beard, rounded to a point, mirrored the helmet's outline. Mail overlaid a tunic and pantaloons made by weaving together wide leather strips. He held a sword at the ready and stared at Ordowahl as though sizing up the largest roach ever to disrespect his town. "Hooy there! Stranger! Dismount! Explain yourself!"

What do I find in the world, but people more like my brothers? Is the wide world as hate-filled as my family? An angry rumble rose up from the pit of his lungs.

The Viking picked up a rock and hurled it, striking the mule's pack. Ordowahl quieted the beast while mount Hammerfoot fidgeted, ready for a possible attack. Smells of male anger and conflict roused him.

Outwardly calm, more so than a new man should be, Ordowahl dismounted and paced forward. He did his best to seem curious. It never paid to disclose yourself so soon. A regal manner said he'd ignore affront from a mere sword-holding peasant.

"I am Ordowahl, youngest son of Stegnwahl, King of

Nordweg. I seek the far side of the earth. My journey has brought me here. Can we establish good faith?"

The guard spat. "Verminous Nordwesh speech makes a stench. This is no place for you nor any of your dung-begotten kin. Show me your back, man-child, and return to your heroGodless shit hole of a land."

This put not only Nordweg but Christianity under insult. His gathering anger exploded. Pagan or no, such a thing announced a wish to die. Ordowahl's face, not counting eyes gone deadly flat, still aped polite curiosity. He kept his slow stride toward the guard. "I am Ordowahl, free knight. I seek the far side of the earth. My journey has brought me here. Can we—"

"**Are you daft**?" shouted the guard. "I heard you the first time."

Without breaking stride he said, "I wasn't sure about that. Thank you for hearing. But now you must learn to listen." On "listen" Ordowahl bolted forward. Two great strides closed the distance. Wearing plain travel garments and no armor, he also hadn't bothered to draw his knife.

The guard just had time to brace his sword toward the prince's midsection.

Ordowahl feinted right then plunged left, past the sword's point. An outflung forearm took the guard at the collarbone and sent him wheeling backward—the man hit the gate fully inverted and face-on. He sagged to the ground. Ordowahl curled his shoulder to absorb his own impact; the gate became a double-struck drum, "B-boom!"

The fellow lay in a quiet heap. Ordowahl picked up his sword and banged it hilt-first on the gate. He noticed a half-height door sized for a child or small woman, but not an armed man. The guard's consequence, lying stunned and inert, seemed fair. The town still had to satisfy the real insult. Focusing his wrath he shouted, "Hooy the town!" His voice, when the fight was on him, was bigger even than he was. He drew a breath, tightened a flat belly, relaxed his throat, and poured out a great roar of challenge.

"HOOY THE TOWN! Shall your man lie here? Might I throw him over this row of sticks and stones you call a wall?"

Silence.

Three kicks at the small door jammed it and sent booms across the whole town. Then a jackdaw flew down toward Ordowahl's face.

A reflexive flick of the wrist split it—the guard's sword was much lighter, hence faster, than his own. Ordowahl stared at the bird. Its two pieces seemed to wriggle like halves of a worm. A tiny mew of disgust came from the beak, in a voice that sounded very old and part-human. The hairs on the back of Ordowahl's neck bristled. *What sort of sorcery is this?*

A sudden flock of jackdaws curled down on him from behind. Ordowahl covered his face and peeked between two fingers. He flicked the sword back and forth as though the birds distracted him from quiet thoughts. His outward calm belied barely-contained rage. In the span of five breaths the ground acquired a coat of feathers and gore.

Half the flock had fallen. The rest fled to roost in a nearby pine. Their calls resembled speech, but standing unarmored beneath a turreted wall was no time to hear a flocking lecture. Anything could fall on him. He peered upward, to see a plummeting barrage of stones.

He leapt away and ran toward Hammerfoot. The placid mule hadn't moved, but Hammerfoot reared up.

Ordowahl counted two deep bruises and a handful of lesser ones, plus a bleeding scalp—no real damage. *So I* and *this Viking town are enemies* and *the day is more than half-gone.* Ordowahl pondered what to do when one side of the town gate creaked ajar.

The guard uttered feeble groans and lay where he had fallen. One or two of the rocks had landed on him, which didn't help. An arm snaked out, grabbed the wretch by his boot and dragged him out of sight.

The gate eased shut, but a trumpet sounded before Ordowahl could remount Hammerfoot. The gate surged wide.

Turning to look, he saw a dumpy, smallish but very proud man stroll out. He wore rich leather trimmed with fur. *Can he be master of this town, perhaps a Viking king?* His chest bore an elaborate gold and silver image—of a jackdaw. *I begin to understand the jackdaws that have followed me from the day I left,* and *the flock just now. Will I hear their odd voice again when this fellow speaks?*

Ten men in leather-and-mail-and-conical-helmet came next, five on each side. Nothing about them seemed organized, but they exuded grim purpose and glared at Ordowahl.

The time had passed for a relaxed countenance; in fact, his face hurt from the effort at staying flat. He settled for a cold eye-to-eye look at this "king."

The man halted a few feet from Ordowahl. His men moved forward. They closed the arc around him with one Viking near Hammerfoot and another with his hand on the mule's halter.

The king spoke, in a suave, cultured voice. "I greet you, Prince Ordowahl of Nordweg. I am King Ingvik. I see you've relieved Saeth of his little toad-sticker." The dumpy fellow exuded the smell of a plucked chicken but also an air of polite calm. He wore his expression like a mask. For the moment this king, a man of middle age with no physical presence, dropped the mask and showed Ordowahl a blank face.

The prince reflected that a man of many masks, including that chilling air of detachment, had an effective tool. Unslaked anger blinded him to the risks, the surprises a king might pose, dumpy or not.

The king continued, "Am I to understand that you've come from Nordweg?" He made the word sound as though it were an honorable and pleasant realm. He wore a perfunctory smile.

"Indeed. I am Ordowahl, ninth and youngest son of Stegnwahl, king of Nordweg. I journey through the wide world and wish to go well beyond this place. I forgive your gatekeeper's insult and ask the hospitality of your town, that I can lodge here for a night." *Father God, this man has already dissuaded me from the insult to Christ* and *dulled my anger.*

"Ordowahl…" mused the king to himself. The trailing edge of his voice reminded Ordowahl of the mew of disgust from the first bisected bird—that and the "speech" of the half-flock, even now perched on the pine tree. Again he ignored the thought and focused on the king.

"Ordowahl…I say, yes, I believe I saw your christening. Lovely ceremony. Do tell me, is there still a mage in your father's household, quite old he'd be by now?"

"He is Heorald. He taught me much and saw me depart not a month ago. He is, as you say, quite old, but still strong and well. Do you know him?"

"Enough of this chit-chat. Be my guest this evening and for as long as you care to stay. As to my poor guard's little sharp thing, there, do you think you could hand it to one of my men? They'll clean the mess off it—quite a picture, you with one hand over your face and bits of bird flying"—a wince—"everywhere. And poor Saeth may wish to have it again some day."

He looked straight at the king. "If it's all the same to you, I fancy keeping it. Poor Saeth, as you say, will see it again and I'll be happy to clean it myself before returning it." Ordowahl eyed each guard in turn. All managed to glower and threaten, but none could sustain his gaze. "Shall we?"

The prince-errant, all seventeen years of him, realized too late how foolish it was to go into a walled town under heavy guard. *At least they have more reason for ransom than murder. Father God, forgive my carelessness. Should I do some other thing?* Anticipate crimes just short of murder? Things such as those he didn't fear. Let them try what they would. He was Ordowahl, the Huge. He stared down at the peaks of ten brass helmets.

The king shrugged, nodded in the direction of the town gate and led the way. Ordowahl followed between his two animals. Awareness that the town might hold real danger sharpened every sense. He dared not enjoy it.

The final pair of guards still flanked them. Five abreast, they approached the gate. Even flung wide it would only pass

City Gate

Ordowahl and his two animals. The trailing guards paused to close the circle behind them. The gate swung shut.

Some pesky scouts those jackdaws proved to be;
not quite alone though outcast, trekking south,
and this—the jackdaws dog my path to see
me raptured by their dumpy master's mouth.
    Colliding oddities—tree-shrouded walls,
    Insults to visitors, the pompous king,
    a jackdaw on his chest as though it calls
    a brainless blare, "Let praises ever ring!"
"My brilliant mind, my lightning wit"—and what?
A pompous dumpling waves away my sense.
I tread his trap, all caution under-cut
by bland-masked face, suave voice, impure pretense!
    The afternoon is drawing on—the night?
    Do I plan head and heart to disunite?

Joust

The town's smells and noises felt familiar. A cooking spice smelled different; but something set him on edge. *I've never seen a town this large. Is this what Heorald called a city?* The townsfolk showed an odd, compressed wariness. Banter and noise filled every Nordwesh town but this place felt stiff. No one looked him in the eye, yet the faces he wasn't looking at seemed to scour him with hunger. The prince, always huge but now also foreign, felt more than usually self-conscious.

Shouts of praise fell on the king, but they sounded rehearsed. *What king wants rehearsed acclaims? If he earns them, he owns them. Who doesn't understand this simple thing? What Honor can there be in pretense?* Scorn altered, soured, his anger. But again he held his peace.

They arrived at a huge empty area, as though someone had razed an original town to use its stones for part of a wall around this one. In the leveled space he found a pagan version of a jousting pitch. No signs of cross or saint—just ornaments of bone, leather, wood, feather and horn. They reminded him of what he saw in the first Viking structure he'd seen, a ceremonial hut close below the mountain pass that led out of the Nordwesh realm. A noise pulled him back into the present.

"Young Ordowahl!" said the king. "We find the custom of

jousting novel and wish to master it. I've arranged a small tutorial. I pray you, accommodate our exercise."

"King, making space for a jousting pitch within these walls shows that your interest is strong. I will tour the stables I see on the far side then examine the jousting track, the rail, the arms makers—you seem to have most of it well in place."

"In time, young Prince, in time. For now we hope for a show of skill. Our best," he said while nodding at the ten guards, "are eager to try a joust this afternoon. The sun is halfway down the sky, but much daylight remains."

"King, I have armor but no lance and have no squire to assist me."

"Tut, tut, young fellow, tut, tut." He turned to a member of his guard. "Braewen!"

"Yes, Sire!"

"You're last and will squire the young prince for now."

"Sire!" He turned to face Ordowahl and nodded at the far side of the field opposite the armorers' tents, near some stables.

"This way," he said and took the reins of Ordowahl's pack mule. On the way to their kitting-up place he asked, in clipped but civil tones, "How do you wish me to arm you?"

"I'll use a padded leather tunic and leggings, chain mail, and a chain mail hood. I'll also remount better from a stepping-block. You have those, don't you?"

"Of course! And I see leather and mail packed on the mule. Someone who knows knots must have done that. We're seafaring folk and your knots-man must be a worthy fellow."

Thanks to my brothers, who showed me a few knots and "delegated" all of that to me while I was yet a child. Father God, do You reap where You did not sow?

Good sun still shone in the western sky when Ordowahl sat astride Hammerfoot in his leather and chain mail. The charger knew the smells of leather and iron. He began to fidget and prance. Ordowahl didn't feel the warmth of a June day. Instead, the oddness of every detail around him set his teeth on edge. Men mastered their fear. He was a man.

He leaned forward to whisper into his mount's ear, "Ssooo, sooooo, hussa hussa boy, hussa ssssoooo." He patted him along the neck and the stallion settled into a state of sharp watchfulness.

At least one of us trusts what will come next. "What are we to use for lance and shield?" he asked the Viking, Braewen. "My two shields remain packed on the mule."

"For practices we use lances and shields made of white pine. There can be splinters, but we use soft wood in practice to avoid breaking too many bones."

"An interesting idea. I am happy to play it out. Ten, did you say?"

"Yes and I'm tenth. After five or six runs, if you're still on your horse and able, I must prepare for my trial with you. Wyllen is first. He'll probably take my place to assist you."

How often my brothers would use sly words to confuse and *worry me. Here, it is the same—I am ready.* "Let me select lance and shield then take me into position."

"Yes, over there behind you."

Ordowahl scanned the loose stack of lances and chose the third largest, which seemed suitable for light practice. Braewen handed it up.

Ordowahl took a close look and noticed the start of a crack. He'd have to press his thumb near a visible knot to guard the crack from spreading. The shields also looked inferior, but the second largest seemed workable. "Now to the jousting run?"

A rail ran between two lanes of hoof-churned earth. It showed few signs of weather, as though built this spring. Fresh dirt, evenly raked, restored both sides of the rail to a level surface. At the center, where their lances should meet, the raked area on his side looked both wider and very smooth.

How could I expect pagans not to lay a trap? Yet if I were to abandon Honor and *act the pagan, where else would I have put it? Father God in Heaven, guard my spirit. You call us to love our enemies. Especially when that is difficult.* He whispered again in Hammerfoot's ear. "Sssooo, husssa, big fella, do you have a jump in you? Can we leap over a pitfall trap?" Ordowahl knew his mount well. The first several jumps would be certain. The last few might pose a problem. *No matter—go forward.*

A trumpet pipped out a `ready` note. At the far end of the track a mounted horseman, the one called Wyllen, raised his lance. Ordowahl raised his, then both lances lowered by degrees. When the lances came level the trumpet blared the charge. Both horses leaped forward. Despite Ordowahl's bulk the immense Hammerfoot carried him with eager grace.

Their lances now made delicate up-down bobs with each rider's rise and fall in his saddle. Ordowahl's lance crept over to intercept the oncoming rider. Right arms held the lances, braced close against the body. Left hands held both shield and reins.

The other rider sat well enough, but no better than a Nordwesh nine-year-old. *Don't lose focus! Ride through this and leap their damnable pit!*

At the point of impact Ordowahl thought the other fellow's lance went low—o*dd, as though he expected me to fall, or worse gore Hammerfoot*—but Hammerfoot caught his signal to leap, and went high. Hoof prints bracketed the area he had suspected and the other fellow, Wyllen, lost his seat when Ordowahl's lance struck him.

Ordowahl focused his gaze backward, at the downed man, while Hammerfoot slowed to a canter. *King or no, Ingvik is evil.* And *did that shield break? No! Never use a soft shield. Children carve toys from soft pine.* Ordowahl set his scorn aside and noticed that his lance was half its original length.

A guard stood at the end of the pitch. "Wyllen got up," he said and sounded relieved. "How fare you?"

"Well enough," said Ordowahl, "but I'll need another lance. This one failed on its first try."

As though he had expected this, the man motioned back toward the lances at the other end of the track.

Ordowahl walked Hammerfoot back along the track. The ominous smoothness of the dirt Hammerfoot leapt over gave him a shudder. Scant un-smoothed room lay between the great indentations of the leap and the deep hoof prints where he landed. Hammerfoot needed to bracket that area just so, not to break through on one end or the other of the hidden pit. *Father God in Heaven, help me now.* His anger chilled to ice.

Once returned to the far end he indicated a lance for Braewen to hand up from the stack. This one also seemed ready to crack. But if he gripped it at a certain spot it should serve. The trumpet started the next trial.

Again the opposing lance dipped just when he urged Hammerfoot to leap the too-smooth place. Again the other fellow fell and again Ordowahl's lance broke. *Do I scorn the ignorant? Certainly not—one learns by seeing a mistake and countering it. But while the second man should have seen Hammerfoot glide above the smooth-raked ground, he sent his lance low, the same as Wyllen. Surely he hoped I'd fall into their pit.* Ordowahl's icy resolve warmed a bit.

Seven more passes aped the first two. Nine unhorsed riders, nine broken lances, nine leaps over the suspected pit. Light work with his shield deflected each opposing lance at the moment of impact. After the first two Ordowahl had also glanced around to catch Ingvik watching. Where was he? After the fifth pass Ordowahl found him. *The tiny turd-king hides behind a bale of hay.* Just then Ingvik seemed to notice that Ordowahl had spotted him. He strutted out, calm and round as a pie on a table. He took a seat opposite the place their lances usually met.

Watch yourself, Ordowahl thought. *This is too easy. They don't ride well* and *have no real idea of how to joust, but careful is as careful does. Damn them* and *damn their pit. Hammerfoot seems to have found its far edge on that last jump.* Ordowahl looked back at the place where Hammerfoot had landed oddly; and saw a too-deep hole where one hoof had dug in.

As Wyllen, the first rider, prepared him for the tenth joust, he sounded too serene. "Well done, Prince. It's plain you have much to teach us. But here comes Braewen. He's watched you closely and we'll end the trials once he's had a go."

I hear an odd certainty. They are at least true to form. With a sinking feeling in his gut he understood when he saw Braewen's lance. Its tip looked like a sawyer's blade, with teeth the size of cats' ears. White pine would no more than give it something to bite. Deflecting those bright teeth would be like deflecting a knife with your neck.

And Ingvik? I don't care what smile he may wear, it is about to vanish. Fuming, Ordowahl reversed his grip on the shield. The barbed lance would seize it the way a hound's teeth grip a hare's head. Perhaps the shield might take the lance point with it. "Hammerfoot," he whispered. "My fine stallion, I pray he doesn't poke you with that thing!" And *Father in heaven, I pray we have a tenth leap in us.*

Lances lowered, trumpet blare: Hammerfoot surged forward, eager to do real harm, but nine prior runs with a short walk between each had taken the stallion to his limit.

Braewen was close. His lance point held steady and well on course to strike Ordowahl in mid-chest. Ordowahl's lance bore down a tenth time. Hammerfoot made a straining leap from the near edge of the pit.

Braewen's lance would have grazed the stallion's neck, but Ordowahl's shield was there to meet it, held forward from his body. The lance's tip ripped into the shield, drove through and jerked it from Ordowahl's backward grip.

Steel teeth protruding through the soft pine grabbed Ordowahl's mail. It twisted him half out of the saddle but he managed to stay upright while the barbed lance flopped onto the track.

Hammerfoot's rear hooves sank into the pit's far edge and the stallion landed on his knees. Ordowahl leapt from the saddle; he watched Hammerfoot thrash once then rise up.

Nobody noticed. Braewen lay on the ground with five feet of Ordowahl's lance showing on the battle side of his shield. Splinters had come through the other side. A few more splinters, bloody ones, stuck out of his mail tunic.

Attendants stationed at the midpoint on both sides of the rail had run to him. Ordowahl noticed that the ones on his side left no footprints across that wide, smooth area. But they peeked at the holes Hammerfoot had left, as they passed near them.

Ordowahl walked Hammerfoot to the far end of the track and circled back toward Braewen, who had managed to sit up. The splinters hadn't gone deep but would leave scars. Attendants hoisted him to his feet.

The man struggled to lift an arm to salute Ordowahl. "The sprites of summer smile on you, young Prince." And he smiled.

Braewen's was the first open face Ordowahl had seen since leaving the Nordwesh realm. He said nothing to cloud Braewen's smile. Returning it was the most he felt he could do. He pushed his outrage at their assault on his charger into a calming spot in the center of his being. Heorald's teaching aided him, even when hatred blanketed any recall of Father Ewald's Catholic instruction.

I am in danger of hellfire for not finding forgiveness in my heart. Even one who insults Christ has Christ's forgiveness, if he asks—so who am I to withhold it? No—what angers me is fear. What may come at me next from the depravity I find in Ingvik's behavior? Father God in Heaven, guard me from myself and from Ingvik! I can't guess at his real purpose.

*__*__*__*

The king's suave gentility made a quiet eye of calm amid a raucous pagan feast. Ordowahl felt as though the injuries planned for him had merely been put off, not defeated.

Everyone in sight was male. No women served or even appeared. Their absence seemed logical—no jealousies, no distractions, nothing but feasting and fighting. Disgust remained, left over from the afternoon's unbroken skein of fraud and trickery. Yet Ordowahl asked himself why he ate the king's food and drank the king's odd-tasting wine. *At home I would spew this out of my mouth. What is it about Ingvik that keeps me from that?*

Over the din of clinking tankards, shouts, boasts, jests, and artless singing, the king's voice always came through, while Ordowahl marveled at his knack for conversation.

"I say, young fellow, you acquitted yourself well today. You handled everything we threw at you with such ease. That mage of yours must be a wonderful tutor. I almost wish him here in Sea Loving Land."

Heorald! Does Ingvik want you here for his own purposes? Dear tutor, I find myself able to think only in direct terms. You would shame me. I've exceeded honesty, given answers which omit nothing.

Ingvik was learning a good deal while Ordowahl got nothing in return. He emerged from his recrimination to manage a question of his own. "Almost?"

"Very sharp!" said the king. "I say 'almost' because I have a report that he nears his end, no longer holds the honed edge he had when he molded a child into the young man who shares my table."

Ordowahl could feel the king fishing this time and didn't rise to the bait.

"Come," said Ingvik, "your cup is still half full. Drink, my friend!" The king raised his cup and drained it. Each time he set it on the table a steward filled it from an ornate gold pitcher.

Ordowahl picked up his own cup. He raised it to his face and pretended to drink but only wet the wispy hairs that might, in a year or two, form a mustache.

He set it down. A second server made a play with his gleaming silver pitcher. He dribbled out a spoonful of whatever it was.

The taste was unlike anything Ordowahl had experienced before—sweet, biting, yet with a bitter undertone that ruined the result.

"Lad, you insult me! To refuse a man's drink, his gift, is to call him someone of no account. Surely Nordweg does not wish to offend its good neighbor Sea Loving Land!" King Ingvik's voice had a knife's sharp edge.

Ordowahl felt, for the first time since early childhood, a sense of unease that had no bottom to it. His prayer for help had brought no sense of peace. The odd drink sat like so much vinegar in his stomach.

No matter the vats of ale and casks of Nordwesh wine he had poured through himself, he had no head for Ingvik's potion.

He sat up, erect. "I do apologize, King Ingvik. The day's exertions plus your food and drink, they tax me. I am done. You must shame me for my debt. I cannot return the good company I receive. In truth, I'm very near sleep. I cannot make sense of what I say." *That should hold him.*

The king nodded to himself. Ordowahl thought he could see another mask emerge, this one a wide smile.

Ingvik rose and helped Ordowahl to stand. *How can he have such strength?* Ingvik pulled aside the drapery behind them to expose a hallway.

Three steps took him to a bedchamber. It held an enormous bed, already turned down, with bedding of a quality enjoyed by the wealthiest and highest born. Several candles burned on a small bedside table.

As soon as Ordowahl made it through the doorway he heard it shut behind him. When the door closed he heard a muffled clink, as though a latch had been set, but found it impossible to care. He tripped and sprawled across the bed.

Such feckless fighters dwell in Ingvik's realm,
such flimsy shields and lances that they use.
Cede pride to jackdaw's master? Underwhelm
the prince, their king too wretched to excuse.
    He plays at laying deadly traps, then sops
    his jousters' tutor with fey druggish drink,
    plies Ordowahl with questions, stops
    when prince discovers that he cannot think.
Inebriated, off his feet, and locked
away, this faith-filled Christian dare not sleep.
No priest to hear confession? God's not mocked,
e'en when his child has dug himself in deep.
    Ord's bolted in, drunk, graceless on a bed.
    What might the dark night pour upon his head?

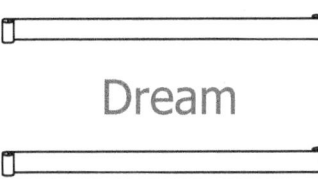

Dream

Ordowahl sagged off the bed. He undressed while sitting on the floor and rolled over to kneel. *Our Father in heaven, holy be your name.* ... He recited the rest of the pater noster then added his thoughts.

Father, guard me now. I've gone blindly into a place which I didn't know and *find here things that I do not understand. Did my father raise me up a fool? Did Heorald?*

May it please you, Father, forgive my incaution. May it please you, Father, send a guard of angels this night. May it please you, Father, protect my parents and *Father Ewald, who gave me Christian instruction* and *allowed me free access to his Bible,* and *Master Heorald.*

And *may it please you, Father, let me come through this night. Let me pass through this place. Help me continue the journey You've prepared for me. Amen,* and *Amen.*

Ordowahl looked around the room. Someone had unpacked his animals and brought in the few things he'd need now and in the morning—water, soap, a razor, fresh clothing. *A razor?* He smiled.

Saeth's sword was not there. Ordowahl realized that no matter where it had been at the start of the joust, he hadn't seen it since. Worse, his knife—something no man of arms would be without except when in bed with a woman, sometimes even

25

then—was not on his belt and was not in the room.

He blew out the candle; the scent of unburned wax filled his nose as he crawled onto the bed. Sleep flattened him like Hammerfoot trampling a tuft of grass. Deep, anxious dreams came. His drugged state did nothing to hold them off. His body felt bound with leaden chains. Which part of the night it was, Ordowahl could not tell, but one dream seemed utterly real.

A distant form resembling Heorald called his name. Ordowahl watched his anxious pacing, his pleading face reciting numbers. A thousand jackdaws drowned him out; Ordowahl tried to read his lips.

The king accosted him. "Ordowahl! I'm over here. Your host calls you. Here are some questions for you. Answer me, which is merrier, a troll under the bridge when a goat walks over it, or a large lad who knocks over a few smaller men?"

Ordowahl held his peace.

"I see you've lost that one. Score a round for me. Two more, best three out of five, what is your wager? Give me your heart, lad and I'll be kind with it. But make it a contest. Gladden me with a combat of wits. You may prevail, but if not my appetite will be the greater and you'll lose more than your heart!"

"Does the goat have horns?" asked Ordowahl.

The king's warm enjoyment poured out.

In his sleep the prince felt lulled, soporific. A sudden shout from Heorald startled both prince and king. The king's concentration wavered.

"Troll!" the mage had cried and "Troll!" Ordowahl responded. "A troll is always hungry. Does the goat encourage him? That is not merry, for merry is content. Pay me!"

King Ingvik paused. "We'll call that one a draw."

"Fie!" said Ordowahl. "Be gone, fake."

"Tut, tut, boy, tut, tut," answered the king. "Names must be accurate. A fake I am not, nor a troll. Trolls may not be merry, but neither are you, little goat. Draw it is and dull your horns. Now back to the game. What is your wager?"

Heorald shouted again, from the distance.

The king turned away from Ordowahl. He spat out a phrase in an ancient tongue. Heorald vanished like the flame of a candle in the wind. Ingvik's curse left a sulfurous smell.

This is a dream! Yet, do not cower. "A fool may argue with a fool forever, Ingvik. Can't Sea Loving Land wage words that are more than steam and dripping vapors? Are names to be accurate?"

The king exuded wronged dignity. His image in the dream swelled into rage, then cooled. "So you are intent on losing? I assure you, boy, I'm utterly out of the habit, myself. It hasn't happened in, well, much too long a time to worry about now." His words snapped like a whip's crack.

"The first can be a draw only if I accept the name 'goat.' If names must be accurate, the goat on the bridge is content else he'd not go there."

The Ingvik figure in the dream seemed to gloat. Ordowahl realized he'd won early, with four rounds left. He had to split them two-and-two with the crafty king, else forfeit—what? "Ingvik, speak to me again. Tell me the cost if I might lose. Tell me the cost to you if I win."

Ingvik smiled. "What is a man's heart? In fact, let that be the second round. Who best can tell what a man's heart is wins the round."

"Since you proposed the second question, put forward your answer where I may chew upon it and reply."

"You assign me all the risk. Tut, tut, boy, that is not how the game goes."

"So *you* forfeit. Give me your heart."

"Ha haaa! Lad, to stay atop the hill of state, to master the ebb and flow of Fate's tides, one's heart is top-heavy ballast. At the bottom of a king's being there can be no heart. At the top of him only a cool head. Between them, Sirrah, stretches naught but steel. I leave and forfeit nothing." Raucous chirping of a thousand jackdaws eddied in Ingvik's wake.

Ordowahl sat upright in bed: a rooster crowed. He knew the night had passed. His knife lay on the bedside table. *Father God,*

I give thanks for your angel and *for Heorald's white mage company. Whether that was a mere dream, or not, I give you thanks for Heorald as much as for Father Ewald.*

——*—*

The morning meal consisted of steamed fish, pickled apples and coarse-ground grain boiled in what had to be seawater. Fresh water to drink and no silver or gold pitchers. Platters of almonds provided something to give texture and flavor to the mush.

Ordowahl observed Ingvik, from the side. The dumpy king seemed preoccupied. *Does my enemy battle an inner rage? Did Heorald help me against him last night?*

Ingvik turned to confer with a series of aides. Each trembled, showing the king more than simple due deference. *They seem to fear a wretched fate if any detail goes amiss.* He suppressed a small shudder at the thought. His first observation inside the town came back to him, the forced accolades. *The stick he uses becomes plain. Father God, in truth Ingvik has no heart. His inner steel seems stretched to a cutting wire this morning. I fear him the more because he confuses me—what I do not understand can inspire terror. Guide me! Forgive my fear, Father, for I trust in You for everything.*

At one point the king gave Ordowahl an odd look. "Well, young Prince, your evening ended quickly. I hope that your night passed well?"

He steeled himself to show only a calm demeanor. "I had a stimulating dream, perhaps from eating and drinking more than I should have. I find my Nordwesh tastes are simpler than your own." *Father in heaven above, help me hold my head level, show Ingvik nothing. How I despise him—Father, forgive my hatred of another man.*

With no comment or visible reaction, King Ingvik rose to his feet. The entire dining chamber came to abrupt and silent attention.

"Make preparations today, for we sail early tomorrow! The tide will begin to ebb half an hour before dawn." He turned to Ordowahl. "Young Prince, the far side of the sea awaits you.

I've already had your gear packed. By tomorrow your animals will be rested and ready to go aboard my longboat. Please don't fret over poor Saeth. He's already received his sword. And in a way, he cleaned it himself."

What a calm picture he draws of Saeth "cleaning the sword himself." Steel, indeed. How like my brothers. I managed to survive them while a child. To survive Ingvik will take God's help. Look how he strews murder with one hand yet beckons with the other. And carry me across the wide sea? I told poor Saeth I wanted to reach the farther shore, and I know what is supposed to lie there. Yet I am captive like a bird in a cage. For being Royal I am at least worth more alive than dead. That much can slow my anxious heart.

*___*___*___*

The day passed in silence. Bread, greens both cold and cooked, and salt fish sat close to hand but without a mealtime. Ordowahl spent the day asking himself why he wanted to take his charger and mule out onto the heaving ocean. *Vikings don't have horsemanship to go with their sailing. Will Hammerfoot* and *the mule even reach the far side without winding up tossed into the sea? Should I try to escape?* He pondered the question in the still of his heart. He waited through the tense day for an idea, a plan to form.

His worry faded hour by hour. By sunset his sense of risk also dimmed. *Father in heaven, help me see what task You have set ahead of me. Surely You have brought me to this place. Should I remain a captive? Successful flight would cost me the mule* and *its load. You have me here for your ends; lead me forward.* He fell into a restless sleep. Dreams of maelstroming jackdaws plagued him.

Entrapped in dream-drilled night a second time,
and this without mage-tutor Heorald,
the naïve prince slaws jackdaw hordes to grime
while thrashing fuzzy blankets 'til they're bald.
    Yes, magery is real—this Ingvik, black,
    commands his Viking men like slaves: "Obey!"
    "What power did I dodge? What's Ingvik's lack?
    Dear Father God in heaven, guard my way.
Praise God for having helped my good white mage.
Praise God for giving life and breath to me.
Praise God for Father Ewald, called *me* sage.
Praise God for health and wit, such as may be.
    But I am rooted here and motionless.
    God grant me insight. What's my faith's success?

Deep

Two hours before sunrise Ingvik ushered Ordowahl down to the shore. A line of torches on poles aided the decent moonlight. He could see three longboats and well over a hundred men.

No prince of Nordweg would let himself show fear, nor even admit it to himself. But Ordowahl felt deep, icy unrest. He'd bobbed about in little boats on little lakes. He'd had one foot on a dock and the other on a boat. He knew about capsizing. Lake boats were toys next to a Viking longboat.

This beach had no wharf to tie up to. Gray-green waves rolled up, some as high as he, throwing foamy water far up the shore. New smells assaulted him—wet weathered wood, the piney resin of fresh caulking, the odd stink of a seasoned longboat, equal parts rotted food, piss, old fish bones, and mold.

"Hooy, Prince!" A voice called to him and he twisted his neck around to spot the man. "We want to load your animals but they've never been afloat. We'll need you to guide them."

Ordowahl went along the beach to where a Viking stood, straining to control Hammerfoot. Another stood by the mule. Ordowahl eyed them and went to Hammerfoot. He asked the man, "My friend, do you have some cloth to tie over their heads? A blindfold will help. What a horse or mule doesn't see moving can't startle it."

"Eh?" the man said. He had something more to do. All the

men were like bees—busy and purposeful. "Oh—yah, sure, I'll get you something." A few minutes passed. The man returned with two tunics and some light rope. "Will these do?"

Ordowahl used them to make soft blindfolds for the horse and mule.

"Hussa, big boy, come with me, big fella" he whispered in Hammerfoot's ear and led the stallion to a ramp of layered planking. It rose up from the sandy beach to the longboat's timbered rim. Guiding the stallion step by step up the ramp, he saw that the longboat's deck had an opening down the center—it must have supplied the boards for the ramp.

He stepped down onto the remaining deck, between large chests. He guided Hammerfoot's forelegs down first onto the chests. He eased him down to the narrow deck, then along that to a place where his enormous mount could stand at ease.

Behind him the Viking who had been handling the mule knew enough not to pull but to lead. He shifted the blindfold so the mule could see to follow him. The mule scented both Ordowahl and Hammerfoot somewhere ahead. It plodded up the ramp, stepped onto the chest as though it were commonplace then onto the deck.

At once waiting Vikings retrieved the planks and laid them across the hull's ribbing to serve as a lower deck. They motioned for Ordowahl to get his animals down into this lower, safer place. When he was done the mule's ears and Hammerfoot's withers showed over the edge of the longboat. Blindfolds left them content while they sniffed at the new scents and angled their ears to the noises all around them.

Ordowahl peered down the longboat. Every oar had a chest by it. Each man must have his own to sit on while propelling the thing. Oars jutted out on both sides. A yellowed mast, once a lofty spruce, stuck up from the center. A sail big enough to cover houses hung from a sturdy horizontal beam. Thick ropes seemed to run everywhere.

Men jostled about, tossing up and stowing bundles that could have held anything—food, tents, cooking ware, trade goods, bedding. They were not going out just for a day. Then he noticed the shields and swords hanging from the hull beside each chest.

A pit opened beneath him. *Father in heaven, help me now. Is this a Viking raid? Might I abet murder* and *theft? Father, You helped me at the gate. You kept me through their treacherous joust. Your servant Heorald was with me in that dream like the angels with Daniel in the lions' den. But am I now entrapped? Is Your hand in this? What use do You have for me?*

He hoped as he had never hoped before that he would not besmirch the honor of Nordweg nor his Christian faith.

He watched while Ingvik stepped on the knee of one man, the bent back of another, the shoulder of a third to board the longboat. The round little fellow went to sit at the high end, still grounded on the beach.

I thought Vikings were proud, yet he humiliates them without a glance. What ugly hold does he have on his people? The dream returned to him. It limned the obvious fear he had instilled in all those around him. *When it became clear that I must leave, Heorald let slip that black mages might appear on my travels. This Ingvik puffed him from the dream like a sleepy woman blows out a candle. He must be one of them—a black mage.* Seventeen years old and royal, he shuddered.

The sea end of the longboat bobbed up and down with each breaking wave. The continual motion began to agitate Hammerfoot. The mule came close to panic, so Ordowahl went down into the boat's lower part, to be with them. A few soothing pats, the scent of him, and gentle words calmed them, a little. The tide's growing ebb saw a few men haul a stone from the sea; it weighed as much as a man. Women and boys on shore pushed the longboat into the waves.

Ordowahl climbed back onto the deck past men busy rowing to sit beside Ingvik. *If in the presence of danger, seek it out. Keep it in constant view.*

The king looked askance at Ordowahl, who realized that he wasn't expected to share the Royal Bench. Ingvik overlooked the misunderstanding. "So, I see you've managed your beasts;

that will help. We'll be at sea until early tomorrow morning. You could have spent the summer going around the long way, but tomorrow you'll go ashore with us. That should please you."

"I have much to learn," Ordowahl replied. "What is the name of the place we will visit?"

"We don't bother with that sort of thing," the king said. "We show up, do a little trading, and move on. We visit a great many such places. But don't you fret, it's in the same southerly direction that brought you to Sea Loving Land. Now that I think of it there is one thing you can do for us."

"And what is that?" *Is this a raiding trip?* A sense of his own stupid *naïveté'* overwhelmed him. *Make the best of it. Father God in heaven, what have I done?* "How can a young man who's never seen the ocean be useful to a king with a hundred fifty men and three longboats?"

"Oh, it should be simple for one such as you. When we arrive we'll haul the longboats up on shore, same as when we boarded. But all my men are eager to go 'trading,' as you say, and the boats will be poorly tended. If you were to stay with the boats, keep an eye on them for the span of a morning, I could spare several of my tradesmen who would much rather go and haggle."

Ordowahl felt momentary relief, and wanted to scoff at the idea—a Nordwesh prince guarding trading vessels. "I think I can manage that," he said. "Trading is a good way to make your way in the world, I suppose." *Father God, I lie with a plain face to shield the skeptic in me. He lies about sailing merely to trade! Father in heaven, educate my simpleness. I see the insult but not a way to avenge it. As he is my enemy I must love him. Guide me, Father God. Teach me.* He breathed the way Heorald had taught: deep, slow, long. In . . . Out . . . In . . . Out . . . Peace began to still his anger.

The wind came from a front quarter. But looking at the billowing sail, their speed into the wind across heaving water astonished him.

White mage Heorald's lengthy tutoring returned to him.

Heorald taught Stegnwahl's sons about the world around them. His lessons included not only the heathen Arabs' remarkably practical numbering system but also their medicine and astronomy. He encouraged close observation to understand changes in the weather, to understand people by their choices and fakeries, and much more.

Ordowahl knew that an hour's heartbeats at rest amounted to two thousand five hundred. Heorald had required him to learn this. Now he held off helpless worry by counting oar sweeps against his pulse. This proved difficult, but after several trials he estimated sixty oar sweeps per each hundred heartbeats. Sixty times twenty-five gave an hour's oar sweeps: an hour held one thousand five hundred of them.

The decimal numbering system used by the Arabs made mental arithmetic simple. Knowing their rate, he looked at the curling wakes of the oars on the face of the sea. Each oar's swirl, each oar print rippling outward on the waving sea, glimpsed by the moon and early dawn, came twenty feet after the one before. He discounted the fact that the sea itself might have a current, which would be small compared to the ship's progress across it.

Multiplying strokes per hour times feet per stroke gave him thirty thousand feet across the sea in an hour's time. Since they'd already been at sea for an hour and since a mile was about five thousand feet, they had come six miles. The mental distraction had helped Ordowahl suppress the dread of betraying his Savior by abetting pagans about to do murder.

Curiosity gripped him. He'd never seen anything that far off; what did six miles look like? Dawn had just broken. He stood up to look left, right, ahead, behind. The land was visible, but a blur. Thinking and counting had stilled his mind, so also blocked out the undulation of the longboat across the rolling sea. There was no other reference but the waves. The waves went on, and on, and...

At once he felt dizzy, then nauseous. One hand clamped to his mouth, he leapt the short distance to the edge where he spewed out what felt like his last five meals, one at a time, into the rushing waters.

The green salt sea flashed by, but out of reach to grasp a handful to rinse his mouth. Ordowahl stood, teetering, when the dregs of another meal spewed out. His mouth and throat felt putrid and raw, his belly a tight knot. He hoped that none would come out his nose.

He waited. After perhaps ten minutes he managed to teeter back to where King Ingvik sat.

The king motioned toward a bucket and rag. In a few minutes Ordowahl had washed the collar of his tunic and rinsed his mouth. Bit by bit the sourness diminished. The king told him to drink the fresh water in sips; that helped.

He tried sitting with eyes open, eyes closed, eyes focused on the sail, the mast, the drum-banger who set the oarsmen's pace, all to little avail. Now, wretched in body and mood, he used Heorald's mind-clearing exercise. He became a stone, withdrew into himself. Ordowahl moved very little, only enough to endure the journey. Heavy folds of dread over Ingvik's many foul deceptions strapped him to the bench.

To clear his mind more he moved to another of Heorald's disciplines, awareness. In front of the king sat two men. One banged a drum to set the beat. Another seemed intent on a pin sticking up from a round disk floating in a large bowl, hanging by three long strings. They let the bowl glide to and fro. The water in it stayed calm, unlike the undulating waves they traveled across.

This man held one end of a long, narrow beam that stuck out over the longboat's trailing end. Occasional small shifts on the beam, to left or right, seemed to keep the vessel pointed just so, to keep the pin's shadow steady on the disk. From time to time the man would measure the sun's height in the sky with his outstretched palm and thumb, then adjust where he kept the pin's shadow on the disk.

Ordowahl roused from his torpor once. He asked Ingvik about the trailing beam. "What is that called?" he asked, and got back a gruff "Rudder."

Deep

*___*___*___*

Ingvik seemed to disappear into his own thoughts across the afternoon. Ordowahl did his best to stay both calm and alert. Out in the middle of an endless sea he could do nothing but watch the men row or the steersman order occasional changes in the sail. It could swing from one side to the other as the boat's direction shifted. Over time their zig-zag path appeared to even out to a southeasterly course.

At dusk Ordowahl knew, from the long days of early summer, that the men had rowed at a relaxed but steady pace for sixteen hours, broken for an hour at midday to eat and rest. Even burdened by nausea, he marveled. Three longboats had gone fifteen leagues, their wake three parallel tracks across the deep, on the strength of a steady breeze and one hundred fifty Viking backs. A good week's journey along a single course.

In the fading daylight a watcher at the top of the mast called out. He had seen land and a village. The drumbeat stopped: the crew pulled in their oars. They lowered the sails. The king rose up as though he had been poised for this moment.

Ingvik shooed Ordowahl away. "Young fellow, we must have this place to discuss our trading venture. I'm sure you understand. Perhaps you're able to take a bite of bread—just ask someone." He shooed Ordowahl away.

The watcher saw the shore so we're close. And even though I'm just inconvenient chattel, I may be worth keeping alive, amongst one hundred fifty Viking swordsmen. Father God, do You want your Christian child to be humble? I yield to You, if never to that demonic toad Ingvik.

The king gave orders: "You others lash up alongside. The moon will be highest an hour before dawn. Steersman, set a sea anchor. We will drift until then."

The drummer relayed instructions to the crew, telling one man to watch four hours, another the next four. The crews furled their sails while pulling down the crossbeams. The sails and crossbeams used most of the available deck space. They crowded Hammerfoot and mule on both sides. The steersman made a small shift. Now they paused. In the waning moonlight the crew roused the animals up onto the deck, to stow the sail below.

They shared a cold supper of bread and pickled fish. All those not on watch pulled open their sea chests, got out rough bedding and lay down to sleep.

Ordowahl checked his animals. They had laid down on the folded sail to accept their predicament as well as a dumb beast might. The slow, steady rhythm of the sea seemed to soothe them. He got small buckets of fresh water for his animals then lay down between them to sleep as well as he could.

When the second watch ended the watcher roused the crew. Their quiet stirring woke Ordowahl into moist, chill moonlight on a bobbing sea. He saw them return packed bedding to their sea chests then check their swords and shields. They ate a solid meal of bread, water and dried fish, then relieved themselves with naked cheeks perched over the edge of the boat.

The shame of guarding Viking boats during a raid hammered his soul even more than it scoured his dignity. Honor shouted, "Do not make your word a lie. You have no room to negotiate your lot." *If Heorald could see this! I am glad he cannot, for I have created my predicament by abandoning both caution and thought. Soon I stand guard while pagans do theft and murder. I have increased the peril of peaceful folk about to suffer a Viking raid.*

"Young knight," said Ingvik. Ordowahl fumed at the demotion. "I see that you understand our purpose. We're here to take some very stingy people by surprise and get from them what is rightfully ours."

He slapped Ordowahl across the middle of his back, smiled and moved to the side of the longboat. Three vessels bobbed on the waves, roped together.

"Any attempt to interfere will lead to great pain; do not stir from the company of the six stout men I will leave behind to guard you. In fact, I foresee no reason not to bring you back with us when we return. Your value has to be great."

Deep

Ordowahl, his belly on fire, set a calm face. *If I survive this day there will be many years to look back, to make amends to Nordweg, to take vengeance on Ingvik, to glim my thousand small errors. Father God, guide me. While I assist pitiless violence, you have already seen every step I will take. You knew every word I would utter before I was planted in my mother's womb. Lend me wisdom, Father. Teach me better judgment. Amen.*

Ingvik convened a council of war. Ordowahl thought he heard them discuss current, tide, bay, beach, and the like. Because Viking speech had many different words for each of these, he could only guess. But the gist of the plan was clear. The council ended. Ingvik addressed the entire group, "We must find our prey. The tide crests soon and we must beach ourselves early on the ebb."

Each boat untied from the others. The men perched on their sea chests and resumed rowing, but this time the drummer only spoke his gruff cadence, "Ho! Sweep! Dig! Deep! Land! Come! Women! Weep! Ho! Sweep!" The almost ecstatic chant began to rise in pitch and pace.

Three longboats moved forward, Without sails their speed was less. Ordowahl guessed that the ocean's current had carried them along the coast during the night. They didn't know their position relative to any landmark.

Perhaps half an hour before dawn they heard surf breaking and saw white foam in the moonlight. From the top of the one remaining mast a watchman called down a few terse directions; he had seen a village. The steersman made a small shift.

Ordowahl rode in the central longboat, with no billowing sails to snap in the wind or make them visible against the sky. The king's crew would not let their extra cargo delay them. Each longboat sprang into a sudden race along the shore, close to the breaking waves. The navigator took soundings, until he was sure of the sea bottom—a bottom with channels meant rip tides and cross currents, which could disrupt a clean landing.

A quiet but intense command spurred one hundred fifty

oarsmen, each straining to drive his longboat toward the beach. The closer they got, the louder the surf roared until the boats sliced across crashing water.

The drummer's hoarse chant timed their final lunge to ride a large, breaking wave. It propelled them up and over the previous wave's retreat and drove each longboat up onto the sand.

All the men leaped out, half of them splashing waist deep through returning surf to run to the beach. Burly men pulled on thick ropes to drag each boat further onto the beach.

Even while seated at the end bobbing in the surf, Ordowahl knew the longboat would be hard to budge before the next high tide. Three men in each one heaved a large anchor stone over the seaward end then pulled its rope taut.

The moon sat high in the sky. The sun would appear in another quarter hour. Ordowahl stared at the tense anchor ropes as though they bound his soul. He wondered what the first rays of sun would reveal.

What action might he, captive, undertake?
Six guards to hold him while the rest go fight.
The target is a Christian town. Forsake
the town, or oath—which one does God make right?
 His sense of honor shames his promised task—
 withstand some angry Christians, should they come?
 But, what is honor if a black mage ask?
 Guard Vikings from their victims? Odium!
How satisfy his pledge yet also Christ?
Berating self as foolish child, as knave:
one hundred fifty men Valhalla-viced,
and none but he to help them to their grave.
 Regardless the above, he prays for heart
 to finish what the Vikings went to start.

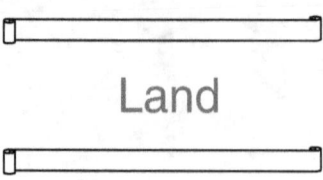

Land

Hammerfoot and the mule, without their blindfolds, lurched op onto the deck and leapt into the retreating surf with the crew. Their packs plus Hammerfoot's saddle and harness had burdened them since the prior morning. They found hard sand and dashed up to shiver on the shore. King Ingvik and Ordowahl came last off the command longboat. The sky held a two-thirds waning moon, which would set at midday.

Ordowahl carried water buckets and grain to his animals, whispered soothing noises into their ears, breathed on them, and gave each a friendly rub. He didn't hide a grim face from them but left their burdens in place.

Ingvik said, "Quite a good pair of animals you have there, young knight. Your mage has prepared you well and your father gave you from his best. I salute you and your kin. Oh and by the way, I will count it a small service—a barely sufficient reply to my generosity—that you remain by the boats long enough to repel any upset locals. You did give me your word earlier. I want to be sure it's still good."

Stone faced and composure recovered, Ordowahl nodded assent at his lying captor in the wan moonlight. He agonized. *A thoughtless promise. Even if to a pagan, it is still my word* and *I that gave it. So I stand rear guard on a pagan assault. Not just that, but from the men's talk this is a Christian town. The raid would happen the same without me, but I am here. Shame is my lot, that I am close by while horror unfolds. Father God, how can I stop the slaughter?*

Behind a slack face, being held captive to return in a boat too laden with plunder to hold Hammerfoot and mule compounded his sense of outraged honor at the pillage of a Christian town. His pulse slammed at his temples. Everything he saw had a reddish tinge. Sense enough remained, at least, to keep him from slaying the king.

Ingvik turned to the two other boat captains and said something to them, too softly for Ordowahl to overhear. He saw them nod with smiles and furtive looks in his direction then dart their gaze back toward Ingvik.

Ingvik plans a ransom?. But he is leaving. A moment's rapture almost lifted Ordowahl off his feet. Blood rage compressed to a small fire in the pit of his stomach. His heart went icy, hard behind a placid mask.

Being left in the company of a mere half-dozen armed men didn't impress Ordowahl. He watched the raiding party trot up the beach toward the town a half-mile distant. They strove for silence but the occasional clank of sword on shield gave them away. Their scent blowing ahead of them announced them to the town's dogs, which began to bark. Ordowahl watched until they faded down he lengthy shore.

Father God, I trust You to see me through this. I sit in a trap. The constant pulse of the surf might hide the sound of battle coming from the Christian village. He tried to calm himself. *What now? How do I lull six armed killers while I plan an escape? My older brothers deserve thanks for training me to battle superior numbers, to dissemble, to hide thoughts from enemies. A noble's duty is to hide his thoughts from his kingdom's enemies. Can I dull Viking senses? What do I have to lose?*

*__*__*__*

Gold tinged the horizon as seven men sat around a new fire. They heard the start of a pitched battle in the distance. The surf's punctuated roar did not hide it.

Ordowahl masked his concern: "What do you make of that?" he asked, motioning down the beach with a flick of his head.

"I guess the distance at under a half-thousand paces. We're hearing a fight," said Volden. "The dogs warned the townspeople, and they chose to resist. Nothing makes a Viking happier than that. If I say so myself, young knight, even though you didn't have the good fortune to have a Viking mother and a Viking father, your spirit makes it seem that you could have."

He went on. "Of course, the fighting has only raised the spirits of our men. In the end it will go much worse for the town. We'd have been content to burn a few barns and take away three boatloads of plunder, but battle means casualties. To send our fallen warriors to Heroes Hall we'll need much more and when we send them we'll burn all the town. Yes, it will go hard on the few who live through this day." The Viking spoke what was to him a matter of simple fact. He gave no false sympathy because, while they had fought, they weren't Warriors, so wouldn't die as Heroes.

Father God, did You send me to rescue the many Christian souls about to die not far from here? Free me, Father. "I am, as you say, a fighter," said Ordowahl. But I never imagined taking a life. As you say, I am not a Viking." *But now I will take lives. To withhold is not to lie.*

Volden smiled; he patted Ordowahl's arm. "We understand, young knight. There's no shame in that. We saw you in the joust. You are a fighter. That is praise when a Viking says it." The other Vikings nodded their encouragement.

Bowing his head, Ordowahl prayed. *So, Father God, what man price do You set here? My weapons lie tied on the mule. My fingers tremble. I'll spend an hour undoing those knots. My bare hands are good against bare hands but the town calls me!*

A sidelong glance showed him Volden's knife, sheathed at his waist. He caught Volden's eye and looked down at the knife. Volden offered it to Ordowahl, handle first.

"This is truly fine workmanship, Volden." He examined the

hilt, looked down the blade, felt its edge with his thumb. Blood lust in blossomed in his belly. Time slowed to a crawl. *Thank you, Father. I escape, or die here* He hefted its weight in his hand.

Now! He whipped the knife up beneath Volden's chin, spine-deep, and leapt across the fire. He flattened the Viking sitting opposite him with a kick, bent down to slice that man's neck as well. The other four rose up in haste. One pulled his own knife to do battle while the other three went to retrieve their swords, stacked against the nearest longboat. The Viking who stayed to fight fell dead into the fire. His knife twitched in the smoke.

Three Vikings now circled Ordowahl, their swords waving like stiff silver snakes that sprayed moving glints of the rising sun. His reach plus a knife would be nothing against them.

"Young Knight!" said Rolf. "You fight well. You take lives well. These dead are now Heroes. They will enter Valhalla this day. And you will be wherever it is you go at death. It's your turn to die. Fight us with courage!" Three Vikings praised him by waiting to see how he would die.

I can't call Hammerfoot. He could trample one or two but those swords make that a bad idea. The mule? Hardly. What can I find that is long.

Smoke drew his eye back to the man in the fire. He had tripped on an odd piece of wood that stuck out, one end cold, the other burning.

Ordowahl discarded Volden's knife. The log was too big around for even Ordowahl's hand to grip it well. He used both hands to seize the log's cold end.

Rolf stood to the left. Ordowahl decided to attack him last and went for the man on his right. He feinted as if to go outside him then drove the firewood up into his belly; the man fell hard. Ordowahl broke the flaming end over his skull.

The next Viking was already within a step when Ordowahl snatched up the fallen man's sword. Rolf, a stride farther, moved to get his own angle of attack. Ordowahl's sword moved much faster than the middle man's. He yanked it from an opened belly and faced Rolf.

"King Ingvik warned us to be wary of you, young knight. You have kingship in you, to gull six Vikings into quiet trust. Now I face you alone. It is my honor." At the word "honor" Rolf launched a slicing upswing, aiming to split Ordowahl at the crotch.

Ordowahl's parry didn't prevent a painful slice on his inner thigh, but he raised his own sword under Rolf's arm. Once again, he watched someone bleed out. He stared in horror at the man's final twitch.

While tying a slice of Rolf's bloody tunic around his thigh he prayed. *Father God, I have murdered two men* and *slain four in battle. Six lives against mine burden me. Yet they ease the shame of trusting lies. Evil never produces good unless You reap it. Did You move Volden to hand me his knife? Have I reduced my shame?*

Ordowahl looked up the beach, toward billowing smoke and agonized cries. *Please forgive me if I have sinned. But **now**, Father, unleash me. I am become Your answer, Your vengeance, blooded. Send me to rescue what lives I can. Amen.*

In holy dedication to defend
the Christian town, he begs God for the might
to block their pillage, and at last to mend
his will, his foolish hunt to find the right.
    But how can one be-razored blade carve, whole,
    a dozen-dozen steel-edged warring men?
    A moment's thought, find shape for what his role
    must be to fit God's purpose, ink God's pen.
His blood already flows, God's ink? Prepare
to bet his body 'gainst a gross of men.
He seethes, heart hot, to make himself death's glare,
and yet, heart cold, to slay and slay again.
    Slay whom? Go slice the Vikings, one and all,
    to guard God's people—make this sword a wall.

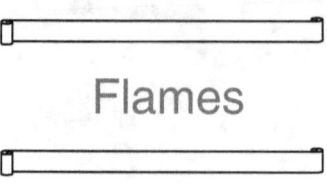

Flames

A breeze blew in off the sea, carrying its scent and salt spray. Six bodies sprawled around him in bloody poses of unnatural death. The iron-like smell of blood made Ordowahl queasy, plus the stench of burning hair from the Viking dropped across the fire. He went to the placid mule to undo its bindings, but trembling fingers slick with half-dried blood made that impossible.

Stallion Hammerfoot rose up on hind legs to paw at the air, anxious to join the distant battle. Ordowahl went to pull Rolf's knife from his belt. Like Volden's it had a razor edge. He sliced through the mule's bindings to retrieve sword and shield. For now he would abandon the rest. A beacon of black smoke beckoned to him in the early morning sky.

He turned Hammerfoot toward he town, but looked back.

Three vital Viking longboats sat above the surf, each with one end still bobbing in the water. The sight froze him.

He leapt off the stallion and tied the drag rope of the nearest one to his saddle. He coaxed his mount to lean forward into the load and pull it alongside the middle longboat. The other took scant minutes. He drove Hammerfoot to his utmost to do the work quickly, lest more townspeople die. The mule's strength went unused. The frightened animal brayed its distress from a place close to the small tub of water.

Three longboats lay together making one long woodpile. The driftwood fire continued to blaze. Two unburned sticks served as tongs to toss flaming wood onto the closest longboat. It smoldered at once. If it went the rest would follow. The smell of scorched sailcloth wafted over him.

Man and horse still suffered from the day-night voyage. But Hammerfoot's urge to share his master's war rage overflowed. The prince leapt back astride his steed. A lust to fight drove them across the trampled beach sand. They gave no thought to the mule,. It backed away from the fire before returning to the half-full water bucket.

Viking footprints churned along the beach and up a rocky escarpment that occluded one side of the town's shoreline. Townspeople had gathered at the top to stage a defense. Several dead Vikings lay there.

These valiant townsmen fought, and died. By now the smell of blood was commonplace and faded. He refused to think of the vultures that would come. A dozen dead townspeople lay akimbo, reminiscent of his own six victims. A trail littered with corpses led downward into the town through green tangles of foliage. These wounds were from behind; none of the fallen were Vikings. *It is one thing to die in combat, another to fall to murder.* Blood-and-ice rage drew him past several still-moving, moaning forms.

At the edge of town thatched roofs sent up smoke lit from beneath by tongues of fire. Even though the town was built with rock and mortar, thatch covered everything but the church. Many roofs had already burned and fallen in.

If they expected to carry away three boatloads of plunder, they were mistaken. Nothing survives here but angels and vermin. Father God, send an angel to guide me now. Several deep, calming breaths helped narrow his focus.

Nothing moved. The uproar emanating from the center of town had already abated; Ordowahl despaired that the battle had ended before he could reach it. He led Hammerfoot between two huts. One lay open to the sky, filled with smoldering ash. On the other's doorstep a man and wife lay dead, akimbo like life-size puppets, splashed not with paint but blood. Noxious smoke made the air heavy. A toddler's gashed remains lay inside one doorway.

He advanced toward the sounds of Viking laughter, women's screams. He stopped to take stock at the town square. Many survivors huddled in terror: non-combatants made malleable slaves. Female survivors had immediate carnal value. A group of them cowered in one corner of the square. Vikings not occupied in looting or herding the men occupied themselves with rape.

Some of the Vikings shepherded able-bodied males carrying bundles toward the seashore end of the town square. An occasional group of men would emerge from the smoke, cross the square, lay their burdens down then turn back toward the smoke.

The shrieks, the wailing, the crackling of burning roofs, the groans of the near-dead and the hooting Vikings made speech impossible. In the center a low stone fountain that yesterday sourced fresh water, gossip, and laundry, today made a tub for Ingvik. He luxuriated with buttocks, legs and feet soaking in the water, arms draped over the fountain's edge.

No plan came to Ordowahl's mind short of a suicidal rush; something held him back from that.

A furtive movement off to his right caught his eye: a robed figure with a large hunting bow. No, three priests filled the space between two huts, all pointing across the square. He turned; four more of them stood, also with long bows, in a narrow space on the far side. Ordowahl exulted. *Thank you, Father! This town won't die! Thank You for Your gift, your angels in human form!*

With a wordless bellow of rage he toe-jabbed Hammerfoot. The stallion sprang into his jousting charge. No padded leather, no mail, no lance—but he seized one greatest joy, to carry Ordowahl and share his master's ferocity.

No one had heard him over the shrieking din. Seven bowmen leaped into the open before any Viking understood his danger.

Ordowahl galloped clockwise around the packed dirt of the

square, his right arm to the inside. Deaf to the shrieking din, he lopped off four Viking heads before the rest recognized the horseman as an enemy.

Seven bows at close range made a merciless crossfire that felled more Vikings. The bowmen seemed methodical, patient, but Ordowahl didn't puzzle over that. The priests were God's angels. He and they had killing to do.

The Vikings realized that these few enemies were cutting them down like herbs in a hedgerow, yet they were unable to reach the archers to fight back.

Ordowahl raced through each knot of Vikings he could see, hewing off an arm or a hand or a head, whipping his long sword from side to side like a steel wand. He took no thought that a priest's arrow might find him. By now the standing Vikings each held a sword. His still-whole left leg took three cuts, one of them well into the muscle. Hammerfoot jumped as though he wanted to dislodge his rider, yet each time put a Viking near Ordowahl where his sword could deal a quick slice.

Ordowahl realized that he and Hammerfoot made too-good targets for Viking archers, who had raced to find their bows. He guided his steed back the way they had come in. For the time being battle-rage filled his veins and stopped up his wounds.

He saw four groups of eight to ten Vikings each slip out of the square, to take the archer priests from behind. Ordowahl went to find the lane holding the nearest set of them. He yearned to intercept the Vikings he had seen split off.

In such tight quarters, among burning huts and narrow winding lanes, Hammerfoot would still be easy prey. Ordowahl dismounted. He whispered, "Mule!" at the horse. Turning his charger away from the square he slapped him hard on the rump. The stallion, beginning to foam with sweat, with no rider or purpose, trotted back the way he had come.

Ordowahl gripped his shield, shook the blood off his dripping sword, and began to walk, limited to short strides, to find marauders. The first narrow lane hid the trio of archers. When an arrow pierced his shield he knew they were ready for an attack from behind. He set off, limping through narrow lines, to find others.

He soon met a group of Vikings with Wyllen in command. Only a warrior's bloody purpose passed between them.

Ordowahl hacked arms off the closest two and bludgeoned anyone he could reach with his shield. One tried to crawl under. He stomped on a waving sword and sliced off another arm.

Wyllen led three others around to find the far end of the narrow lane, but by the time they came up behind Ordowahl, their companions had all become Heroes.

"Heroes!" he snorted. On sheer impulse he leapt at them and killed two more. Wyllen and the one remaining other Viking ducked inside a house. Ordowahl didn't wait for them to come back out. He left to seek out the next group.

He found a red-mottled clot of bodies spilling from the lane holding the second set of archers. He called out in Latin, "Salve et vale, amici (Health and welcome, friends.)" An answering bit of Latin doggerel told him they were still full of fight. He returned to the first group; more bodies, more Latin encouragement.

Four Viking parties but three indeterminate clumps of bodies—no matter, Ordowahl understood that they no longer wandered the town's lanes. He went back to the square. Odors of blood, char, fear, the stench of spilled bowels, smelled like a curse flung at heaven.

All Vikings still in the square lay dead or dying. King Ingvik had watched the entire spectacle from his spot in the fountain. He rose with solemn dignity and clapped his hands.

"I applaud you, Ordowahl. You show the makings of a king. I pray it does not shred your life as it has shredded mine. But you'll get no ransom for me." He took a small dagger from his belt, tilted his head back as if to shave but instead sliced open his throat. His remains collapsed into the fountain. Flies billowed out. A cloud of them buzzed around the square then drifted off into the smoke.

Ordowahl stepped closer. Despite the stench his mouth

gaped open. The king's body was a dried husk. Behind the jackdaw motif on his jacket lay maggot-swarmed ribs. The sulfurous reek of pork offal left a fortnight in a warm, dank place bloomed out. Even against the background of battle's stinks, Ingvik's remains made it difficult not to vomit. His corpse fouled the town's water source.

Two priests rushed to the fountain, lifted out the maggot-crawling remains, and ran to hurl them into the sea at the open side of the square. The rest gathered by the fountain. All of the priests used cupped hands to splash water and bits of Ingvik's remains, both crusty and gooey, out onto the ground, until the water washed them down to the shore's edge. A slow trickle replenished the fountain. In time it would again hold clean water.

The priests made the sign of the cross, whispered amongst themselves, then sat down to wring out their soaked garments.

The sudden silence made Ordowahl's ears ring. A deep fatigue overtook him. He staggered to keep his balance while moving away from that stench. *Father God in Heaven, what was that? What evil did You send me against? How close to hell have I come? No scripture ventures beyond the witch of Endor, who doomed Saul by waking Samuel. What does this portend? How does this damn, or dedicate, your use of me? For that matter, what have the priests made of this?* Ingvik's banal evil, his casual cruelty, made it impossible to wonder about white mage Heorald, or about what it could mean to be any kind of mage.

"Did I just see that?" Ordowahl cries out,
but only in his mind. The sober peace
in his and priests' demeanor helps the town
folk doubt their widened eyes, their fear release.
   Ord knew that Ingvik held an odd black pow'r
   but had no notion why he ceded life.
   He mentioned "shredded" life – had that last hour
   come over him by way of Volden's knife?
Mage Heorald was white, and Ingvik black.
What could a life of magery entail?
Both priest and Scripture said "demoniac,"
without regard to nature, dark or pale.
   The battle's done, for Ordowahl a first.
   So, had he done his Christian best, or worst?

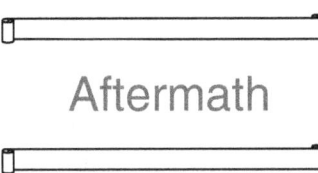

Aftermath

The silence made Ordowahl wonder whether he had gone deaf. He looked at the archer-priests; each had a sword embroidered on his habit, over the heart. Then a bit of Latin reached him, "Te morituri salutamus!"

How odd, Ordowahl thought. *"We who are about to die salute you."* He turned. *But it was the Vikings* and *their King who had died, were already dead. Did you note the king's fate?* His legs began to throb. He absentmindedly looked at his own clotting blood. It had run down into both boots. *I will deal with that later.* Ingvik's suicide and satanic remains would haunt Ordowahl the rest of his life.

The priests turned to Ordowahl and spoke as though nothing had happened.

They know what God has allowed here, but do not care to share it with a man not of the Cloth. They refuse an open reaction to what can only be a work of blackest evil. I will follow their example, for now.

His Latin was good, but fatigue dropped him into Nordwesh. He asked the closest one, "Do you know Father Ewald of Nordweg?"

Nothing.

He greeted them in Latin. One of the robed priests brightened. He ran to give Ordowahl a powerful hug, one

55

possible only with an archer's upper body.

"My boy! You must be Ordowahl! How fitting. Yes, Father Ewald and I were novitiates together. He has often written to me about Nordweg. You figured in many of his letters. I ask you now, Prince Ordowahl, if you choose to confess to me, please reach an Amen before meal time has come and gone."

His gushing remark splashed against the pall of death. Ordowahl saw it dissipate the man's pent-up sense of horror and understood. One of the townspeople came up to the group and spoke in his own vernacular, trusting that at least one of the priests would understand him.

"Good my fathers, good my knight, God be praised for rescuing us from slavery and further death. Fathers, the priest of this town is one of the dead. We will need many burial masses said. Our children are scattered and we fear that dozens of Vikings have gone away. They will surely come back because a fire has destroyed their boats. They can't leave, thus we fear them the more."

Ordowahl felt constricting shame for having burned those three massive longboats. The time spent on that had also wasted townsfolks' lives. How many more would die of their injuries? Thoughtless ignorance! It embarrassed him into close-mouthed, wet-eyed silence. All eyes now stared at the group of warriors who had staved off annihilation. No one noticed the grief up there on the largest face.

Then one of the archer-priests delivered a sermonette in that area's dialect:

"People of Shortharbor, we are part of a new order, Priests of Arms. By God's grace we had planned to visit your town this morning. Night found us half a league away. This morning's pillar of smoke brought us to you."

The crowd stood in silence as though torn between gratitude and anger that they had not arrived sooner.

"God has delivered these Vikings into our hands. What He has begun today He will complete soon enough. Those who have gone to God this day only sleep. They will awaken at Jesus' feet.

There He will wipe away their tears. Spend your own tears on the pain of those injured who survive today. Pray for their healing."

Ordowahl suddenly felt the bruises, an odd sprain in his belly, the burning ache of slices on both legs.

"God does not call us to live where there is no accident, injury or pain. He only calls us to use each day to His glory. His love is for our souls, our hearts. His comfort is always at hand.

"Give thanks that your lives continue. While God's will is beyond our understanding, His joy increases each time we give thanks—at all times and in all places, in all circumstances, and always for our salvation."

The dialect differed from Viking speech as much as that differed from Ordowahl's. Yet as the priest spoke of peace and healing, the exhausted prince began to understand the idiom from similar words and phrases.

The priest who had corresponded with Father Ewald said, "Young Prince, we are more than merely curious about you. I am Father Emil. Over supper tonight I hope that you will tell us your story. First we must care for the dying and bind up the wounded—including you, I noticed. I understand you have a good head for battlefield medicine?"

Ordowahl felt too tired to stand, especially on wounded legs, and too dazed to recite his own name much less examine his guilt for rash arson. But having something important to do revived him. He drew a deep breath. "Yes, of course. I mean, yes I will."

The able-bodied carried in the living and all the dead from the escarpment and from all parts of the town. Numb, they set about sorting the dead, victim from Viking. They cleaned out what space could be made habitable, scavenged clothing off the dead to make bandages for the living. They carried the survivors to makeshift beds.

Through the long afternoon Ordowahl, priests of arms and the able bodied tended to the injured. The priests also said last rites over many. Whether Christian or Viking, it made no matter—when the fighting was done their calling was to heal and to minister. Only God could judge.

Able-bodied women washed cloth free of dirt and blood, boiled it, slapped the moisture out of it on whatever was handy and took the still steaming material for use as soon as it had begun to cool. Other women salvaged unspoiled foodstuffs. Slaughtered livestock was in oversupply. They cracked some of the spilled grain. They labored to boil up a thick soup reinforced by newly butchered flesh. Some savory herbs had survived the chaos. The aroma of meat, bay, onion, and too-early produce from their gardens lifted each weary soul. At mid-afternoon they paused to drink, rest, and eat.

The agonies of the injured, the disquieting stenches of blood, piss, shit and vomit which dead and dying bodies release began to diminish until only groans from within the sheltering church disturbed the quiet. A tiny breeze helped dispel the stinks.

A few women began to make an evening meal. Midsummer's Night, the shortest of the year, began. They sat down, as best they were able, to a quiet supper in the town square's deep shadows.

"Let me tell you about Father Ewald," said Father Emil. "No, let me tell Father Ewald about you, my prince. I thought him a windy fellow, a loose braggart. Then I saw you ride that stallion around the square today. Now I can tell him he was too poor a poet. Imagine! An avenging angel, twice the size of a mortal man, screaming in Nordwesh, wielding the most terrifying sword on God's earth."

The other priests echoed his amazed half-belief. Ordowahl's throbbing legs pulled his attention away from Father Emil's glowing report.

"Riding through a tangled mess of people jammed into the square, his mount nimbly leaping this one, dodging that one—slicing Vikings apart as though they were suspended on butchers' hooks, never touching any other person save perhaps to push them out of the way with a toe. Drive fear into Hell's demons, you could. You kept the Vikings confused and inside the square long enough for us to give them God's Present Answer to pillage and savagery."

Ordowahl hung his head. Father Emil's remarks gave him unbearable discomfort. He mumbled, "If it please you, I did only what God gave me the means to do. But I also burned those boats--"

Father Emil stared hard then asked, "You accomplished that, too?" Looking around the table at his fellow priests he said, "As Jesus forgives me, as God loves me, I wish I could have seen it. Young Prince, you trapped every mother's son of them. Yes they will be a trial, but really! Brothers," he continued, scanning the table again, "Brothers, we will not see the like of this again."

The villagers gained much of their living from the sea. Some of them laughed, but all of them understood what the fire had destroyed.

He turned back to Ordowahl. "My prince, each of my good Brothers is a seafaring man. Your wonderful deed also hurt them to the quick, turning three vital longboats to ash in a single blaze, hull to hull, reduced to the grandest pile of embers anyone is likely to see in a lifetime of looking."

One of the townspeople came to stand behind Ordowahl's shoulder. The priests could see that he wanted to say something. "What is on your mind, my child?" asked the closest one.

Ordowahl turned to look at the man. Two halter ropes dangled in his hand. By flickering firelight, under a starry but so far moonless sky, Ordowahl saw two familiar large shapes behind him. "Hammerfoot! My pack mule!" He leapt up, his legs in agony and his whole body filled with aches. He grabbed their lead ropes.

The man addressed Ordowahl. "I saw you mounted. Then I saw you afoot. When we were carrying the dead back to the square I saw a Viking try to grab this one's lead rope. You'll find him amongst the Viking dead, without a face. I know a bit about livestock and managed to gain the stallion's trust. But when I tried to lead him back to town he dragged me to the shore as though he were walking a puppy."

Ordowahl would have smiled at the comparison any other time. This left him dumbfounded.

"Those boats, far down the beach, sent flame and a pillar of smoke up to God like a kingdom's incense. A mule stood on the shore, packed but with the bindings sliced. Your stallion dragged me to the mule. I tied his load back together as best I could. These two very fine animals came with me to the grazing commons hill-ward from town. Now I bring them so you will know they are safe."

Ordowahl stroked Hammerfoot's matted mane. "Without these animals, my friend, I would be lame and poor. You have restored me. I can't thank you enough, good my rescuer. What is your name?"

"I am called Klarenz," the man said. It struck Ordowahl then. Klarenz had used flawless Nordwesh. *Where did* he *come from?* Fatigue and wounds stilled his question.

That night all the uninjured slept in the open. Dawn's skewed light made the town square look worse than Ordowahl remembered it. He had shared his bedding, stallion and mule's saddle blankets, his second set of clothes, and his foul weather gear to cover the sleeping. Each piece of it came back to him in careful hands, with a shy smile of thanks.

The morning meal consisted of more meat-and-grain stew. No hen was laying. He knew that for a time all eggs would stay under the surviving hens until new flocks could replace the old.

As to goats, pigs, and sheep, that simplicity didn't exist. Half the town's animals lay dead. Salted meat and sausage would soon reach over-supply. Replenishing herds would take years. Replenishing people would take generations.

Broad daylight stares in disbelief at what
blind acts of war can make man do to man.
Receding smoke discloses war as slut
whose rounded heels pull down whoe'er she can.
    Dark daylong carnage takes a toll so deep—
    a lifetime's moisture can't unbake burned clay.
    A shuddered agony relieved by sleep—
    rebuilding starts the moment sun brings day.
A man named Klarenz caught Ord's mule and steed.
He brought them to the prince, and spoke in clear,
good Nordwesh. Ordowahl then failed to read
between the lines, he heard but didn't hear.
    The chaos that sprang up, the carnage, plus
    the jumbled, ended lives? God's calculus.

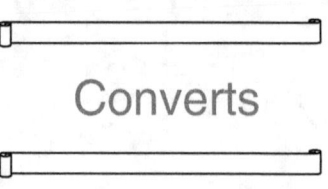

Converts

SUMMER

Encounters with stranded Vikings punctuated the first several days, forcing the archer priests to stand guard on the penned-in livestock. At last a starving Viking came in with a flag of truce. The priests and village elders questioned him. At length, they struck a bargain.

Twenty-two Vikings remained. They took survival as an omen and accepted the Christian faith. They forswore violence and did acts of obeisance in the town square. Each man chose his own act. One stood bare backed while each raped woman, a total of fourteen, gave him three lashes with a thick, soaked reed; those left angry welts, even when swung by a woman. Four others took ten strokes, each from a different man. The rest selected lesser stripes, save five who were nearly starved. They took one week on a water-only diet. Each man also asked a priest to carve the sign of the cross into his forehead, and add tattooing around it.

A few of the townsmen wanted to make them eunuchs to answer the rapes, also to resolve any question of intermarriage. Ordowahl wished them well figuring *that* out. After a loud discussion they agreed that the newly Christian Vikings could remain intact.

As converts and forgiven sinners, they worked harder than anyone else.

Ordowahl chose to remain in the town since bandages stiffened both healing legs. He joined a party, mostly Vikings, cutting reeds to re-thatch roofs. Even though youngest among them, he led the work party. It gave him a chance to observe foreign men's behavior. He strove to intuit once-Viking minds. Across ten days of cutting reeds, drying them, and re-thatching roofs, he sounded them out on Ingvik's black magery. "How could a Viking submit to Ingvik's insulting treatment?" he asked on the first day, at noon.

Feldun, a middle-aged fellow with calm eyes and a leathery face, replied. "Prince, you haven't seen him fight. A Viking does not cower before any man—he was no man among men. He was Loki at times, Thor at others, and demanded that we treat him as we would treat Odin."

"I am puzzled," said Ordowahl. "If so Godlike, why would he have ended his life instead of killing me and the seven archer priests? None of us suffered anything from him."

"Prince, we argued about that for days before choosing to surrender to Christians and accept the Christian beliefs." Several of the other men murmured assent. One or two sounded less than convinced that they'd made the right choice.

"If you disagree," asked Ordowahl, "is it because Ingvik was a false Odin?"

A younger man named Ahrwelf spoke up. A still-scrubby beard belied his burly build. "Yah! Odin showed him to be a fake. This Christ teaches us that fighting is bad. What a stupid thing that is!"

Half a dozen growls shut him up. "Prince," said Feldun, "We have decided this amongst ourselves. We saw you fight! Ahrwelf learns slowly," and he glared at the man.

After that Ordowahl asked them questions then answered theirs—about being a man, a Viking, and then a Christian. "You learned from boyhood to be fighters."

Feldun rose to his knees. "Prince, being a fighter is the height of manhood. A man who will not fight is not a man and deserves only contempt." His gestures illustrated the point; his matter-of-fact tone said that he still believed that. He would always believe it.

Ordowahl replied, "This is a hard truth. Amongst Christians there are times when a man must fight, but a man must also choose when to fight and when to give way. I ask you this—if a man who is strong enough, brave enough, known to fight, gives gentle treatment to one who is weaker, may even choose not to avenge some insult, is he still a man?"

Feldun paused in thought. Finally, "No. A man who endures insult from anyone, large or small, surrenders his manhood." Several others in the group murmured their agreement.

"Then," said Ordowahl, "such a man allows others to choose when and whom he must fight. He surrenders that choice to others such that a deliberate ruse can steal his manhood. Have you seen that happen?"

A man named Ruloff spoke up. "Prince, I have seen jarls do this—urge on a small man to provoke the jarl's enemy, who replies. Then the jarl sinks a knife or axe into the man when he rises to avenge the insult. The jarl says that he is merely protecting the innocent fellow."

Another added, "My wife shames me in front of others; but I simply urge her to become a Shield Maiden; that way I can swat her down as she deserves."

Several chuckles endorsed that idea. A fourth man said, "I don't wait. A woman who disputes anything her man says has asked out loud for a good cuffing."

Ordowahl looked at the man in feigned surprise. "So, a woman must always cower in fear of her man's anger? Is this how your father treated your mother?"

A few nodded, yes.

Ordowahl answered, "Christians are men. They also follow Christ, who preached peace. He even said that if a man strikes your cheek, you should turn the other cheek so he can strike there as well." He gave every man a stern look. "Strike me and I may avoid you in the future, but I will make the choice of when to fight. You cannot make that choice for me."

From a spot somewhere behind Ordowahl Ahrwelf said, "Prince, then you can never fight. A man hits you in the face yet you wait for him to hit you a second time? You confess to being a pussy. Finish growing your beard, pull your teeth, and you'll be the best pussy possible."

Their laughter was loud and ribald. Ordowahl laughed along with them. "I tell you a truth. If the man who tolerates abuse forgets the words of Christ he will descend to a being like a dog or an ox." He gave each of them a knowing look, daring them to dispute him. "No, a man who chooses when to fight is always a man. If a larger, stronger man makes an insulting remark, isn't he drunk? Or isn't he a bully? Never let a drunkard or a bully choose your actions. A man chooses his own actions, even when he risks letting others think him weak."

The Vikings stayed silent.

"I could have been fearful that Ahrwelf believed his remark about being a pussy—and you with him. If he were to come at me with a fist, I would let him. If he were to come at me with a knife, I would take it away from h—"

A soft footfall behind him—a knife went through his tunic, into his right shoulder blade. Ordowahl had heard the footstep so responded without thought, ducking down, and avoided a deeper wound. The man tumbled over his shoulder. Ordowahl's two hands seized his head and pulled, laying him supine in front of the prince. Before the pain of his injury bloomed, Ordowahl grabbed the hand still holding the knife. He broke the man's wrist.

Ahrwelf looked back and upward at a scowling, giant face. Ordowahl pressed his left hand onto Ahrwelf's neck. He bent down to put his face nose to nose, only to receive a wad of sputum. Ahrwelf used his good hand to strike at Ordowahl's head. The prince closed his hand around Ahrwelf's neck until the man stopped struggling.

"Viking friends, tell me how other Vikings would judge this fellow's actions." Ahrwelf's face was purple; Ordowahl loosened his grip.

Meanwhile Klarenz, who seemed never to stray too far from Ordowahl, had pulled a bag of light medical supplies from somewhere. Ordowahl rose to his knees and lifted his arms long enough to let Klarenz remove his tunic. Klarenz began to treat the injury. He ignored Ahrwelf's evident distress as the fellow began to breathe again.

"Prince," said Feldun, "Ahrwelf is known to act rashly, also for being none too bright. He seemed confused by your teaching and responded the only way he knew."

"I see," said Ordowahl while folding his arms and drooping his head to give Klarenz better access to the wound. "But, tell me, while you were Vikings, what would a man in my position have done?"

"Killed him." It was a chorus.

"This will be a difficult lesson," Ordowahl replied. "In my father's realm we live very much as you do. But when a man loses his life, it falls to his family to seek the life of the man who took his."

Feldun nodded, as did several others. "We value the right of the winner of a fair fight to live. His opponent goes to Valhalla; we honor that kind of death."

Ordowahl raised his head to nod; Klarenz touched Ordowahl's ear, bending his head away from the wound. With the prince's back stretched smooth he was able to wash and clean the cut.

Ordowahl replied, "That makes Christian living difficult, so we try not to kill anyone unless he truly deserves it, such as for shaming either his family or someone else's."

Klarenz seemed to hesitate for a moment; his usually deft hand jerked. Ordowahl chose to ignore it.

"But, Prince, if you let a man hit you twice, you still didn't let Ahrwelf stab you a second time."

"Yes! Striking with the fist is an insult. I chose to live. Then I chose not to kill the man who sought my life."

"Arrrhhh!" mumbled Ahrwelf. He tried to sit up. "My attack has come to nothing. You didn't let me die in a fight, else my soul would have reached Valhalla."

Klarenz moved Ordowahl's head back to vertical and applied an aromatic salve to the sides of the wound, "This should make it sting less." He used a needle and thread to sew the wound shut.

Still stoic to Klarenz's ministrations, Ordowahl continued. "We'll talk of Valhalla another day, Ahrwelf. Christ, who helped me defeat all of you not ten days ago, has made a far better place than that for his believers. Even though my man Klarenz has bandaged your handiwork, I will be one-armed for a short while. You, I choose to forgive. You have no need to fear me. This is the way Christians ought to answer injury, with the hot coals of forgiveness burning an enemy's heart."

Ahrwelf scowled. "Hot coals my ass," he said. "You're a pussy. I have disabled you and will kill you when I see the chance."

Ordowahl broke his jaw with a flick of his good hand. "Ahrwelf, if I must answer injury with injury, so be it." But he spoke to a man who for a second time was beyond hearing. "You deal with him, my friends. Try to keep him from dying, which could happen if he attacks me again. And remind him to listen closely to Klarenz. Good fellow," turning to Klarenz, "thank you for your healing art—Ahrwelf needs you now even more than I do."

While Klarenz tried to hide a frown of disgust, Ordowahl motioned them all to return to work; their midday meal was done.

They went back to cutting and drying materials to re-thatch the burned roofs.

"Klarenz, I'll need a little help from time to time. Right now, try to help Ahrwelf, because I did break his jaw." Ordowahl rose to oversee the men in their work.

Showing them the truth of God's power in weakness versus Odin's power in strength has become a test. It had been strength, after all, that made them take to Christianity. May they choose to understand my patience with Ahrwelf as another way to show strength. He saw the former Vikings committing themselves to learn the Christian way of life. He saw them work for the good of Shortharbor village with the energy of warriors, and made no secret of admiring them for it.

A practical democracy expects
the prince to work 'longside the rest. Until
he heals he leads the Christ-ian-elects
who mend the town that once they tried to kill.
    Fief Klarenz tends that scabby back and limbs,
    he nurses Ordowahl to help him knit.
    While Odin's faith and Christ are antonyms,
    Prince Ordowahl and "shy" are opposite.
The summer moves along and August heat
oppresses, as it always does. Amassing
winter stores begins. They'll need to meet
the needs of all the town; it's an impasse.
    Departing time will be there when the town
    is back to right-side up from upside-down.

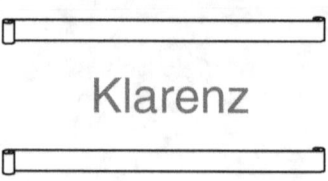

Klarenz

The weight of summer came on—hottest days, warmest nights, little relief from biting flies and gnats, though tempered by sea breezes. A few times Ordowahl thought back to the swarm of flies that had billowed out of Ingvik's remains. Had that happened? Was it related to the strange dream, the contest with Ingvik? Every detail lived in vivid memory, but he tried not to dwell on it. The priests had seen those maggoty bones, had cleansed the fountain—after which they had said nothing. He couldn't bring himself to discuss the memory with them.

The town, with the descriptive name Shortharbor, began to feel like home. Each evening Klarenz placed himself near Ordowahl. Their conversations tended toward question-answer: "Klarenz, teach me more of this town's speech. Since leaving home I have lacked for someone to speak with."

"Prince," Klarenz had replied, "A week's travel brings a noticeable shift in speech. Do you wish to travel to the end of the earth? I can help for a time, but there are limits."

"Tell me about that," Ordowahl would say. Klarenz admitted to fluency in seven regional dialects plus a useful grasp of five more. They spanned a range that included Nordweg, with two in a direction Klarenz described as "away from the sea." What puzzled him was, what had happened early in Klarenz's life to drive him away? Why else would he say so little about them?

Which one of them might be his home village?

In time Ordowahl had mastered enough of the local vocabulary to converse with the townsfolk. He also learned quite a bit about Klarenz.

"So, tell me about tinkering," or "So, tell me more about stonecutting," or "Tell me more about the cookery south of here," or …

Klarenz never seemed to run short of skills for Ordowahl to quiz him on.

"So, tell me more about this knack you have with…" Ordowahl said, evening by evening. In time the question was "…knack with girls." Klarenz realized he'd included a leading remark describing some particular place he'd visited, and he tried to shift the discussion.

A town made of stone houses with thatched roofs and simple interiors, no matter how badly burned, takes a measurable time to clean. Finding new reeds, saplings, branches, and withes for thatch, making new cots and tables, weaving new blankets, throwing new pottery, tinking damaged pots back to a serviceable state—the myriad domestic details all had their time and place.

By late August the townspeople had no further need to repair or rebuild. They were more concerned with accumulating food to carry them through the winter. The seafaring priests helped bring in many loads of fish to preserve, but this also was a need the town would fill on its own.

Ordowahl needed to put something in perspective. *On my way out of Nordweg I learned about the way of a man with a woman; my close-cousin hosted me for almost a week, and sent a fertile widow to my room. She, and certainly he, wanted my "royal blood" for her child. She managed to teach me things no boy would imagine. As a so-called New Man I was to leave seed in her – I have no idea whether she bore a child. But she left in me the 'seed' of knowing the joy of a woman. How can a man give praise, and not receive?*

Other opportunities followed that one, as I moved farther and farther from the castle. At least I kept myself to barren or unattached women. One, only one, did I refuse, because she was my host's daughter and wanted to get herself a royal husband. He smiled. *Pert, attractive, and possessed of a very strong will. Nanneke, I wish you well, and your husband, whoever he may be, a stronger will than yours.*

He also sensed it was time to depart. *Father God in Heaven, You brought me through trials. Now, I feel no purpose here. Where is the wide world I went to find? It's not in this small place.* He decided that, although perturbed by Klarenz's disastrous behavior around women, he should add the fellow to his journey. "What say you move on with me, Klarenz?" he asked on the last night before leaving.

"What say, indeed, Prince? I think this place, with its splints and bandages mostly gone, has a restored future. I am ready to find mine somewhere else."

"So, tell me why you haven't settled down," Ordowahl asked as they sat outside in the early dark, waiting for the moon to rise and the air to chill. He had made yet another set of sad, fond good-byes already—his burden several times over while exiting his father's realm. Once again he would leave at daybreak.

"What, me? Settle down? Why ever for?" replied Klarenz. He seemed lost in thought for a minute.

"You've been here how long then? What age have you, thirty years? A bit more? Master of many trades that each take an ordinary man seven to ten years to gain journeyman status, much less master? You are a most curious fellow, Klarenz."

The man looked wounded. Ordowahl had used tact but called him a fraud. "See here, honored Prince, I confess much on Saturday before Sunday Mass, but neither untruth nor exaggeration are on the list. Ask anyone about that."

In fact Ordowahl *had* inquired. Klarenz arrived at the first turn of winter into early spring, with mastery of multiple hard-to-find skills. If it involved cloth, wood, small metal, antler, leather, bone, stone, food, what-have-you, Klarenz was its master. He was even quite the wordsmith.

Klarenz's voice, on the other hand, stood at a disadvantage to an asthmatic goat. But subtle rhymes and startling puns made that irrelevant.

And in so small a place as a seaside fishing town, nobody failed to notice how his sweet honeyed words had won him frequent amours. If the Vikings hadn't come, he might have run into the Priests of Arms on his way out of town, perhaps with a coat of tar.

Ordowahl drew in a deep breath to prepare for frank speech with a man who was part wretch, part wonder. "I know you well, Klarenz from your language lessons; also from listening to the local folk."

Klarenz's face went slack. His ears and neck turned red. Cold sweat broke out on his face. Words deserted him—a rarity.

"Indeed," said Ordowahl. *Surely Klarenz is the damnable ass who, three years ago, broke Elspet's heart.* Elspet, older than the prince by six years, had been his consoler, his "aunt," his one source of comfort when the rest of the world seemed mad. Cold, ugly memories broke his heart—her stoic acceptance when a vagabond tinker's too-intimate attentions betrayed her. His blood ran cold.

He paused. She'd said nothing, she told him later, for fear that he would bring the wretch back, at considerable risk of damage to said wretch. The pause lengthened.

At last, his pulse smoother and his heart deadly, he spoke. "I am highborn, a son of Stegnwahl, King of Nordweg. You speak my own language fluently. I wonder what I could learn about you if I went back." Another pause. "In fact I think you knew who I was before Priest of Arms Emil did. That is of no consequence. Here, then, is something of real weight." His face went flat, not so much as a twitch of muscle, his Honor face.

"I, Ordowahl, ninth son of Stegnwahl, King of Nordweg, do hereby accept your liege loyalty, in fee simple, from now until the day one of us passes from life, or until I grant you freedman status within the realm of Nordweg. In return I offer full pardon on behalf of the Royal House of Nordweg for any and all offenses which you may have committed while on Nordwesh soil, up to but not including insult or abuse of the royal household."

Klarenz rose to his feet. He stood mute, looking neither to right nor left. Standing by the fountain, in near-dark, he cringed as if hoping that no one could overhear.

Ordowahl stayed seated and lifted his gaze to hit Klarenz eye-to-eye. "By accepting this pardon you thereby pledge your fealty and service, in fee simple, from now until the day one of us passes from life, or until I grant you freedman status within the lands of Nordweg. You will receive a bondman's earmark at my hand. If you decline then we must part company. If I ever encounter you again I may prove your crime or crimes, thereby also exact due penalty." *Father in heaven, as yet I can find no forgiveness for Klarenz. His offense is against someone far away. Please shepherd me toward kindness regarding this strange fellow.*

Klarenz and Ordowahl stared at each other for two agonized, tense minutes.

Klarenz lifted his shoulders to face Ordowahl. "Liege Lord Ordowahl, your kindness is great. I accept your mercy. I offer my loyal service to you. I pray that at all times and in all ways you find my service worthy."

He offered Ordowahl the left side of his head.

Ordowahl unsheathed his knife. As neatly as possible, without haste, he used its point to drill a small hole in Klarenz's earlobe then threaded a slender leather thong through it. This marked Klarenz as his bondman. For a few moments blood from Klarenz's ear dripped down the frayed, ancient, absorbent leather.

"You should understand how I got this thong now looped through your ear. It once belonged to a dear friend of mine, a thane's eldest daughter. She was like an elder sister to me. When she had a maiden's pink of beauty someone broke her heart. That fellow gave her a trinket—an astonishing thing, made of tinker's lead, some silver and bits of semiprecious stone. It showed mastery of not one but several rare arts."

Klarenz displayed no recognition.

I think he's frozen in fear. And *rightly so.* "Even though it was beautiful, she could not bear to keep it. She gave it to me. All I have left of it is this leather string, which once hung around her neck. The trinket could not hold a boy's attention, but the thong always seemed to have a use. I kept it for her sake. Find something fitting to loop through your ear then discard this one final part of that accursed trinket. Strive, Klarenz, never to remind me again of such things. I will pretend that you did not break that beautiful heart." He departed, leaving Klarenz alone by the fountain.

Klarenz stared after him, mute and unmoving.

Two days before, the seven priests at arms had departed along the coast. They headed away from the longboats' charred, sea-washed remains.

This day at dawn Ordowahl stood by the fountain in the town square, to say his own good-bye. "My friends, our time together must end. You face a hard winter. I am a young man not connected to home or inheritance, with a wide world to explore. I give you my blessing, as I go."

Shortharbor's head elder stood in front of the gathered townsfolk, to bid their defender farewell. "Please accept this horse, Prince. We will honor you in song and story for ages to come. God keep you well and guard you on your travels." It was a brief speech, but from the center of his affections. He ended with throwing his arms around the prince.

"Thank you for such a costly present; your need for this gelding is great. It is fitting that each time I put a load on its back I will remember you and pray for your continued well-being."

Secrets like Klarenz's new ear insignia don't exist in towns. Whatever had passed between them the prior night, they knew from Klarenz's bloodied ear that it had surprised him. They sensed an unseen but certain justice.

Ordowahl set him on the horse and they rode through the square and away from the sea. Everyone pretended to ignore the change. A tacit understanding ("…that fellow surely earned his new station…") oozed through their last farewells in the late August dawn.

Prince Ordowahl and bondman Klarenz go
on south along the Danemark land until—
Good question. Ord has little need to know
the way to Klarenz's first domicile.
    While Klarenz is a fascinating source
    of fact and fancy, ready with a tale,
    his history, his story, stayed a horse
    of hidden color, gave no small'st detail.
The sight of harvests on their way evokes
warm feelings. God has prospered Christian folk.
The soreness in his legs and back still pokes—
he's sure he'll soon again become like oak.
    Some problem lies ahead, but what it means
    is slight, for God is good. He intervenes.

Homecoming

EARLY OCTOBER

The odd pair reached a huge river. Hammaborg's fortified castle sat on the far side of a wet, wave-tossed mile. "Klarenz, I have seen the ocean, but this expanse of fresh water still surprises me." It didn't occur to him that such a frank confession elevated Klarenz above bondman status.

Klarenz said, "Liege my lord, if it please you, is there some way we could spend one more night on open ground?"

Sun low in the west, the level bank of an impassable river, under trees plus good grass for the animals, invited them to camp. Ordowahl turned to look at him. "I see. For a half-dozen weeks I've trained you to sleep in the open; now you wish to do me one better. Do you tremble to return—or do you ask me to evaluate your new expertise?"

"Liege my lord, you've taught me much by your most excellent example. No, Liege my lord, before we go into Hammaborg I need to explain my history there. I don't want anything to take you by surprise."

"Surprise, is it? Klarenz, I am more than happy to spend another night of peace under God's starry ceiling, with subtle evening scents carried on caressing nighttime breezes, to waken clear eyed then wash my face in its coat of dew."

"Liege my lord—"

"Another thing, Klarenz."

"Yes, Liege my lord?"

"Endless repetitions of 'Liege my lord' vex me. It's accurate, but dispense with it."

"Yes, Liege."

"And that's too formal. It will do until I find a better. Now, proceed."

"Liege, since the time I became, as they say, able to rise to an occasion, I have never been without a woman. I don't boast. Everywhere I go an inescapable magic blooms in women's eyes and I can't suppress the like in mine. Conflict always follows. Soon I must leave that place. Liege—Lord—Prince, I don't choose to do what I always wind up doing." He looked at Ordowahl, pleading for belief.

Paul said something like that, somewhere in his letter to the Christians in Rome! Ordowahl stared at him, but with open curiosity.

"Other men, strong self-governing men for the most part, don't evoke the same response in a woman that seems inevitable whenever I speak to one. Liege, please pity me. I am capable of great discipline in everything but women. I have no roots. I've never found a place with only one woman who may smile back with no others to cloud my vision. I always become layered in intimacies, thus always alone."

Ordowahl had heard the wild gamut of male boasting. Klarenz spoke none of its themes. From the townspeople's stories about him, what his bondman had said was simple truth. "Klarenz, I believe you. It is a great problem. You must solve it. In fact I'll guess that you were least in control of it in the first city you were driven from."

"Liege..."

Ordowahl sighed. "Liege will do."

Klarenz nodded. "Liege, you found me out for what I am, yet show me the kindness of a priest. Thank you. I left Hammaborg shoved down into a cask freshly emptied of vinegar. It happened to be the only way to avoid an ugly end. The fellow who put me there had his own reasons to see me dead before the lid of that cask finally came off. He wanted to stop up the bung hole but couldn't find the cork."

"Yet with that behind you, vinegar brings you no fear. It's basic to any decent diet. I've seen you cook, Klarenz. No one would ever suspect that a cask of it took you so near death, while keeping you from an uglier one."

"Fourteen years have passed. I've grown a hand taller and added creases to my face, but I'll still be known."

Ordowahl stared at him. He itemized the broad forehead, narrow chin, prominent Adam's apple, the striking greenish-hazel eyes.

"Yes, Klarenz, you would be recognized on your deathbed, much less while still hearty. But as soon as your voice exceeds a whisper—a reedy tenor and nasal rasp mark you from thirty paces."

Klarenz tried to look hurt but couldn't. "Liege, you see my situation. There are old injuries. Some say that time repays all wounds . If so I have much owing. Let me hope that time has healed others' hurts. But when we go through the town tomorrow, you will—forgive me, Liege, you never go anywhere without getting many strange looks. Perhaps I can hide in your shadow."

"Indeed, Klarenz. But at noon there are few shadows. You'll be seen soon enough." *What scale of injury brought that heavy a comeuppance? A vinegar barrel, indeed!*

*___*___*___*

The morning meal was their usual fare—last night's leftovers wrapped in simple flatbread made in the precious iron skillet. "Bondman, what do you think of sweet cream, fresh butter on soft bread, and berry jam?"

Klarenz had rehearsed his answer. Ordowahl asked this question every day. Each morning he required a new answer.

"Liege, I believe they exist in the center of Hammaborg, but in very short supply. If we want any ourselves, that house beside the road might have some."

Ordowahl replied, "That is the house of the ferryman. I see

him returning from the town. His passengers may have come to greet me." *Surely tales of the Vikings* and *the pyre of longboats have raised questions.* He preened. So the idea that a commoner might interest them even more? *Preposterous. It will be good to enjoy the company of a fellow highborn.*

Klarenz turned to get a better look across the wide, slow river. The approaching vessel was a raft large enough to transport six mounted men. The ferryman with two, no—three assistants rowed with long even strokes.

An incoming tide made them point the raft seaward to keep a direct course toward the landing. The passengers, all armed, studied Ordowahl.

Klarenz said, "I am glad that they carry no badge or insignia of a jackdaw. Liege, your stories made a dark impression on me. And I wonder whether I know enough of my own story to tell it correctly."

"Eh?" *Is this wretch their purpose?* "You cheated death twice that day. Evidently death may be returning for a third try at you." Ordowahl stood at rest, arms folded, feet slightly apart, facing the landing. He strove to calm himself. *Wretch first, last, and perhaps forever? What scale of injury, indeed?*

Klarenz broke camp while they were waiting. The soldiers didn't hurry after landing. They walked their horses over toward Ordowahl. Klarenz stood close behind him but off to one side. The soldiers halted a polite distance from the prince but it became clear from their stares that Ordowahl held no value. The apparent leader spoke to Klarenz.

Ordowahl had been absorbing lessons in Hammaborgish. He understood enough of what was said. When the fellow reached a point where Klarenz might reply Ordowahl held up a blocking hand. Using quiet, precise Latin he said, "This man is mine. He is my bondservant. He answers to no one other than to me. If he has an unpaid debt I may decide to satisfy it, or not, depending on whether I believe it is a true one."

The lead man shrugged. No one in the party understood any Latin, but they knew it by its sounds. They also knew that people who spoke it, especially with calm, utter command, would only deal with the highest authority. Moreover, a fellow of this size and in prime condition made use of force stupid. Stories had come down from the north; Ordowahl could see it on their faces. *At least that part is true,* he consoled himself.

"Please, Knight, follow me to the prince of this town," he replied. His accent was thick but his Latin was fair, as though he had memorized a few handy phrases.

Good God! Is this a death escort? Ordowahl spoke to Klarenz in Nordwesh. "I see that you had more to tell me. When did you think it might be wise to describe your history here more fully, Klarenz? I understood that you had helped a few young girls enter into womanhood. You didn't say that one of them was highborn. How else do I understand six men-at-arms?" He didn't wait for an answer.

Ordowahl mounted Hammerfoot. He motioned for Klarenz to mount his horse and lead the mule. *Death it may be—a grotesque one at that. Father God, I know You use me in Your way. Is this a time to exert myself to shield this amazing wright, also a wretched corrupter of women's virtue?*

Ordowahl astride Hammerfoot displaced two of the men; Klarenz and mule displaced two more. Four soldiers remained on the river's northern bank. The ferryman and rowers looked at Ordowahl and Hammerfoot with both mistrust and awe. But then so did most strangers.

The lead man occupied a place at a front corner of the ferry with the other man diagonally across, aft. Neither said a word, but Ordowahl inferred that Klarenz was a phoenix, long since burnt and flown, returning to ashes fourteen years cold but newly warm.

It dawns on Ord that Klarenz has more tale
in him than "I am cursed by too much tail."
How else explain the pomp: is he a Holy Grail
too precious to let slip, nor granted bail?
    The polished trim and force of arms that take
    the two of them declares a truth. The sin
    was far too great, that near-death gaol-break
    was not salvation—hear this bulletin!
"Who dares to drag a prince in such a way?
Suppose I kill these soldiers and take o'er
the raft, return? In less than half a day
whoever sent them sends a hundred more.
    I see no single step that I can take,
    nor might I doze when I must be awake."

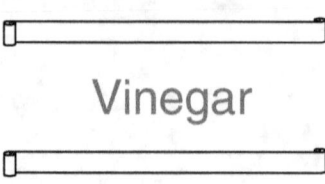

Vinegar

Ordowahl endured the ferry ride to Hammaborg in tense silence. Watching Klarenz tremble, he pondered the implication of their sizable escort. He didn't fool himself that only having two guards while crossing the wide water was any sort of reprieve.

The far landing came into view, plus six more mounted men-at-arms. Ordowahl watched Klarenz's demeanor dive toward panic. A stern gesture kept him from leaping into the river.

The lead man from the first set used elaborate military courtesy to invite Ordowahl to alight from the ferry. He screamed something clipped at the receiving party, which formed two opposing columns of three. All six sat on fine horses. Their flawless harness sported gleaming buckles. He barked another odd syllable; they wheeled their mounts to face away from the ferry, with room between for three riders, single file.

Ordowahl accepted the invitation to head the procession. The man-at-arms in charge put himself between the first pair of the receiving party. *How odd that I lead but don't know the way, and they look ready to kidnap Klarenz.*

Klarenz wound up behind the lead man, boxed in by soldiers on each side, two more behind them, with the mule between. The last man came off the ferry to take position behind the mule.

He closed the lock on Klarenz, who got the bored disdain due a cheap criminal, the sort who might not see another dawn. None of the soldiers deigned to notice sweating, trembling Klarenz.

A throng of people gaped at them. They had followed the procession down to the ferry landing, saw it make its slow way over and back. Some pointed at Klarenz, as though they recognized him despite the years.

Ordowahl pondered anew how grave a sin Klarenz might have committed—just how high up was his illicit paramour? There was nothing for it now but to stay alert. Behind an impassive mask Ordowahl studied the crowd for clues. The Viking town was one thing; Hammaborg was beyond easy understanding. The mounted armed guards also posed a threat far greater than Ingvik's foot soldiers.

People lined the streets, ten deep in places. There was no need to puzzle out their route. The way led between large buildings with few windows out onto a broad square. They crossed it to pause, in pomp and protocol, before a massive wall with an open gate. Fifteen-foot-high, foot-thick slices of oak, wide iron bands—a palace gate, in truth.

Ordowahl put Hammerfoot into a delicate sidestep to give the lead back to the head man-at-arms. The fellow put fingers to lips and whistled.

A trumpeter stepped into the open gateway. He raised his horn and produced a crisp, martial sequence. The head man-at-arms motioned Ordowahl to advance beside him. The entire party proceeded at a stolid, formal half-pace.

Klarenz tried his best to follow suit, but his usual command of any skill deserted him. He showed himself a despairing fool.

Grand marble stairs rose to a broad front entrance. A man of early middle age stood at the top. He wore rich velvet of pearl gray. He extended a hand and beckoned Ordowahl to come up. Ordowahl dismounted. Handing Hammerfoot's reins to the lead man he ascended steps wide enough to dwarf his shod foot. To show decorum he ascended one step at a time, when it would have been more natural to glide up by twos.

The lead man-at-arms led the stallion around the side of the palace, presumably to the stables. Ordowahl watched the party follow, around a corner and out of sight.

Ordowahl paused two steps below the top to give the nobleman a polite gaze. In Latin polished by the Priests of Arms he said, "Good my host, I ask the privilege of a meeting with you." *My father has the same look of utter command. Other men see it* and *fear him, but for good reason. This man is a puzzle. Even though I am royal, he will require utmost care. Father God in Heaven, help me rescue my most curious bondman, perhaps even myself. Might I be hung for bringing Klarenz here? He is a base-born wretch, yet I cannot escape the feeling that he is important to my purpose. Father, I pray that means Yours, too.*

While he was thinking, the nobleman said, "Prince, you bring me a surprising gift. Please come inside." Both faces held flat, noncommittal stares.

The nobleman led him through an imposing doorway into a large front room. Rich tapestries draped the walls. A stiff, dignified elderly servant in formal livery led them into a small study lined with book-filled shelves. Ordowahl had never seen more than twenty books in his life. He tried to keep surprised awe off his face when he noticed shelves covering each wall. He sat in a chair while the prince sat down facing him. *Surprise gift? That term for Klarenz is a knife with a razor's edge. God help you, Klarenz—likely you're in chains by now.*

"I've heard much of you, Prince, which is my advantage. I believe you are called Ordowahl, am I not correct? Your home is Nordweg and you are ninth son of King Stegnwahl."

Nice easy start. "Yes, all this is so. I grew from child to man in the castle of Nordweg. While I am proud of it, this is far more imposing. May I learn, if it's not presumptuous, your name and title?"

"I am Prince Euwart IV, son of Prince Euwart III, of Hammaborg. I tender allegiance to Henry IV, who rules the Holy Roman Empire, and to no other. Hammaborg is an ancient, proud city with many neighbors. We have shelter from ocean

86

storms but also full access to the sea. We are a city of merchants and craftsmen. Many of our common folk live in greater comfort than some of the highborn with whom they do business. We are quite content with this."

Prince Euwart paused. "Not to be blunt, Ordowahl—please call me Euwart, here in private, it is simpler that way—I find grave discomfort in your arrival. You've had the incredible bad luck—I'm sure there's no other explanation"—a raised eyebrow told Ordowahl that Prince Euwart didn't believe it—"to bring us the single most wretched individual in this City's memory, which is long and precise. Would you like to understand the difficulty your Klarenz has put you in?"

"Of course," Ordowahl agreed. *Better to assume little and hope for much.* "I would be very sad to lose his services. The fellow seems to have a thousand talents. But if I understand you, acquiring his services has brought me his burdens, too. Please tell me more."

"If Klarenz had ruined *my* sister, both of you would, right now, be turning on a spit above a slow fire."

"Interesting," Ordowahl admitted. *Indeed, fascinating. Reference to an action not taken is often hollow, but nonetheless he draws a dire picture.*

"Your youth would not have been a valid excuse, Ordowahl. Not knowing the extent of Klarenz's crime is inexcusable for someone aspiring to lead men. I'll guess that, as a ninth son, you've been 'led' all your life by eight older brothers. No matter: you are highborn. Your destiny is to lead. It's no stretch of the imagination to guess that your otherwise impeccable wit, manners, and as I'm told impressive martial abilities made you an untenable member of your father's household."

How subtle—patronizing yet with no open disrespect. "Yes, Euwart, as in all else you are correct. But to the nut of the matter, Klarenz harmed a highborn woman? I failed to read that in him prior to your men crossing the river. I have to thank Father God in Heaven plus my guardian angel that the woman was not kin to you."

"Indeed so, Ordowahl, indeed. Your debt of thanks extends to me, as well. It has been difficult to restrain news of Klarenz's arrival in this area. Both of you owe a large debt for that alone, because the woman was—is—very high in the nobility, with a living brother. Discretion should prevent you ever venturing westward from here. Your safety is assured while you are a guest of this city and a guest in this Haus. When and if you might choose to leave, I urge you not to go west. We do understand each other?"

"Fully, my esteemed host. We do. A thousand questions beg to approach your ear and it seems unlikely I'll get an answer from Klarenz. Perhaps I can earn the right to one or two if I answer any questions you may have?"

Prince Euwart allowed himself the hint of a smile. "Yes, as a matter of fact, I do. Did Klarenz happen to mention how he escaped?"

"I did hear a detail or two but do not wish to harm the man or men who launched Klarenz on a path that met mine."

The prince didn't smile, but nodded. Ordowahl had posed a condition, which was his option, without a blunt "no." He knew better than to assume he could.

"Well said, Prince. I give my pardon, as long as the act was not in itself criminal."

Ordowahl could not help smiling. "The thought of Klarenz crammed into a barrel recently emptied of vinegar, with the lid on, makes me smile," he said. "Klarenz hoped that the fellow would not stop up the bung hole. It seems he'd given him reason to do that."

The prince nodded, stone faced. He steepled his fingers. "That would be the owner of a simple inn. The high quality of the food he served his guests moved the wealthier merchants and tradespeople to demand that he let them buy meals there! A fellow named Fridoric."

Ordowahl absorbed this detail.

"While Klarenz served in Fridoric's kitchen, I'm told its table rivaled my own. People tend to exaggerate, but the stories persisted. The high noble woman in question, the one Klarenz sullied"—his face looked sour, as though the thing had happened in recent days—"let herself be persuaded. She went there at midday many times too many. She was, as you can guess, also empty-headed."

"I see." In fact Ordowahl didn't "see" but suspected that the persuadable woman had had a very close connection to Prince Euwart. Very close, yet not a sister. The implication stunned him.

"You do begin to see," said the prince. "Your face, young prince, gives you away. I should warn you that success in life requires you to control that face. Its striking contours don't hide your thoughts well—yet."

Ordowahl struggled for words, which he seldom had to do. He looked at Euwart. "A persuadable woman linked by marriage can be a deficit of enormous consequence."

The prince made a small nod. "You learn," he said. "On the surface of things Klarenz spoiled the honor, the good name of this Haus, Rechtmann, also my bride's family, the very noble Haus Tannhaueffig. In the end I prospered, no credit whatsoever to him. My Haus was freed from a princess-to-be whose tenure as First Lady of Hammaborg would have been a constant irritant. She who is mother to my children proved a far better choice. She is younger sister to the first, who now tats the alphabet onto pillows for the clergy, an honored Sister of the Order of Comforts, in Bremen, her home city."

He continued, "My princess is wise, strong, faithful. Not only did the City of Hammaborg receive a far better First Lady, it also received a second dowry. She does, by the way, know that you brought Klarenz back here. When you see her, you will witness great discretion behind the kindness of her smile. Don't be misled; she would smile with bright joy to see Klarenz gradually dismembered, his 'member' first."

Euwart's tight smile suggested that he shared his wife's animus—but not toward a scion of the king of Nordweg, especially one of such unusual proportion. Finding that hint of mercy left Ordowahl on edge—he saw it as a dire left-handed compliment.

Euwart continued. "You understand how the feelings of sisters are as pronounced as those of brothers. Might I feel common gratitude to Klarenz?" he asked the air. "No more than to any other commoner who has brought good commerce to the City. On the other hand, the 'tool' he used to bring this good result is something he would do well to part with."

Ordowahl tried not to visualize that.

"I am not vindictive, but the people of my city enjoy an occasional test of fortitude. They'll be sure to imagine something most worthy, if I let them." His dead-pan face hinted that he'd enjoy it, as well.

"I see. Euwart, I understand your right to dispose of Klarenz, or any part of him you may choose. It behooves me to propose a bargain that would let me keep the rest of him in good spirits. But since I find myself a rootless pauper, nothing comes to mind."

The prince held him in a cool gaze. "You of course have time to think of a suitable exchange," he said. "A prince has all he can use of everything there is, yet never enough. In fact he never actually has everything there is. We will talk of this again."

A cry of hideous torment sounded from far away. Ordowahl tried not to pay it any notice. Euwart looked over his shoulder and said, "Stay as you are, please, Prince. I've a small matter to settle."

Several minutes passed while the pitiable agonies continued. *That has to be Klarenz. He needs me even more than I need him.* The noise tapered; after several tense minutes, it stopped.

When the prince returned he said with a smile, "No harm done. Now I'll have my Hausmeister show you to a room. Feel free to inhabit that room—in fact this entire floor of the house— as if you have always lived here. For the time being I deem you a valued guest. I hope to see you again at the evening meal." And he left.

Vinegar

At least Klarenz isn't receiving torment any longer. But his lot is still wretched. Nothing good will come from that—what can I do now? Think, Ordo, think hard.

Fief Klarenz lies in foetid dungeon dank.
His master Ordowahl seems not to care—
he owes or will owe Euwart gifts to thank
his host for patience re "that sad affair."
    Yon day when Ordowahl owed Klarenz all
    his wealth, for guarding horse and mule, is past.
    Prince now is far from bond-man's reach and call,
    Ord's conscience muted by his royal caste.
Prince Ordo deemed him mere, a wretched turd.
He'd ruined Elspet, or at least her heart.
So many brides un-virgin'd. How absurd
to worry now. But lose him? Not so smart.
    Prince Ordowahl must weigh his chances; how
    to get him safe, past Euwart's angry Frau.

Game

Ordowahl enjoyed keeping noble company. He missed the close camaraderie with Klarenz—the fellow was remarkably well-versed in anything not related to books. An idle week passed, then two. Ordowahl began to develop a small clientele of young men who sought him out for training in martial arts.

It was easy to guess that Klarenz clung to hope in a foul basement beneath the guards' barracks. It could only be that chains bound him to a stone floor in a tiny cell, without so much as a bench or blanket. He might receive bread and water once a day. Sanitation would be up to him. The stench of an occupied dungeon is beyond inference—imagination by itself is mercifully incomplete.

Poor wretch, the prince thought to himself multiple times per day. *Not just my dearest "auntie" Elspet but a tangle of hearts spanning fourteen busy years? I won't even guess at how many times he's had to flee. Has a priest explained this passage to him, in the Book of Numbers? "You have sinned against the Lord: and be sure your sin will find you out." Its first meaning is that you must not take a sin to your grave unconfessed. And the second is the other side of an ominous coin: now that your sin is found out, the grave's hungry mouth awaits your body to chew on. Yet, in the eyes of God every man sins, so has no right to pass judgment on any other man. Klarenz is beloved to God—*

93

and passably good company.

Ordowahl at last found his wits. "Prince Euwart," he said one morning at table, "let me propose a wager." *Successful, powerful men either despise the unknown, or relish it. I wonder whether this Euwart is both shrewd* and *accustomed to weighing risk.*

"Really. Tell me more. No doubt this concerns that wretched cook's assistant, Klarenz."

At least he didn't call him a seducer of noble women—"Yes it does. I daresay you might profit by letting him see the sun, bathe in the river, and begin to cook in your own kitchen."

"I am not amused, Ordowahl. Please assure me that your sense of humor is as underdeveloped as your beard."

Nothing good will come from that line of conversation so try something else. "Let me compete against Hammaborg's best, in some competition worthy of the name. If I should lose, I cede any and all interest in Klarenz, who came here as my bondman. Until we arrived he was my fief."

Euwart raised an eyebrow. He deemed Ordowahl's claim on Klarenz's person to be moot. "Taking fief from a wretch, Prince, you got nothing in the first place."

"But if I should prevail," continued Ordowahl, "I will take both Klarenz and Hammaborg's champion. My retinue needs to grow. This would cement our loyalty, one to the other, no matter which way the matter comes out."

Ordowahl watched Euwart's face freeze. *Much worse than a frown. But I know the ploy I'm using.*

"So, Ordowahl, if I understand you, the outcome of some contest of manly skill either grants a vengeance that is already mine, or loses me both the just vengeance and the services of a valued champion. Do I understand you? If your loyalty toward me might result, it would lie lower than a crude familiarity. I truly misunderstand you, Ordowahl."

"As you say it, Euwart, I've weighed my scant stock too heavily. If you have patience, let me propose something more modest."

Euwart raised an eyebrow again.

Ask for too much then appear to retreat, while still asking much: the haggler's art. Surely Euwart knows it.

Prince Euwart peered at Ordowahl. "Klarenz whole or Klarenz dead— publicly, formally, and slowly. As I mentioned, my people appreciate that sort of display. What say you to that?"

Euwart also knows the art of asking much. "The prospect will demand my utmost. But the chance to regain Klarenz whole requires me to agree."

"Whole, I suppose, if you happen to win. Now the challenge: you proposed a contest, so I will give the terms."

Ordowahl asked himself, *Will he propose something with even odds, or not?* "Please continue. I am of course eager to hear your terms." *Have I given him free rein?*

The prince smiled. "Yes, my young prince, you begin to learn." He thought for a moment. "Tell me which of your abilities we might use as a basis for the match. What are your greatest skills? And which of your skills are indifferent? Trust binds highborns together. Without it, loss always ensues. We depend on each other at this moment. No good can come when frankness departs."

I don't see bluster in him, but if I withhold a truth, he may want to ruin me. I have no doubt he could. "Euwart, you know me well already. I've won outright every competition of arms, of whatever sort, from the age of sixteen, a year ago. I sat unarmed amongst six Vikings. In a few minutes' time I used the knife of one and the sword of another to kill them all. In a few minutes more my stallion pulled their longboats together on the beach, where I set them ablaze."

The prince interrupted. "That part I hadn't heard, but your galloping untouched through a throng of Vikings while laying the lot of them waste—please tell me I heard rightly?"

"I was well mounted—you've seen my horse. They were afoot. By surprising them I was able to cut down a good number, yet I carry scars on both legs. There were also seven Priests of Arms with long bows. Yes, I shed more blood than I'd seen spilt before in my life. Each of seven armed priests took more Viking lives than I did. God was with us that day."

"And is God with you now, helping you to defend an adulterous wretch whose act amounted to treason against his sovereign prince?"

Father God, let me speak only Your truths, with Your wisdom, not my own. "Euwart, noble prince, God's ways are beyond our understanding. I know only that He has brought me to this place. I know that I admire Klarenz's many skills. I understand him as someone who is, at least now, no longer a simple wretch. Can I guess that the rash seventeen-year-old copy of him didn't even know who it was he had fornicated with? Be that as it may, my interest is to retain the services of a man of amazing skills, his lack of discretion notwithstanding."

Euwart's face stayed immobile. *For him, Klarenz's indiscretion has to be impassably negative.*

Euwart softened his stare. "I at least admire your clarity, Ordowahl. Even so you want to sew black and white into a quilt of a thousand shades. If I propose any contest of arms, you'll annihilate half a platoon to preserve one wretch. There is no profit there, nor any sport. Indoor games? Hardly. Riddles? Perhaps. We must exchange a few after supper—I'm always looking for new ones."

Ordowahl thought, *He's trying to lead me off the topic.*

"Or, should the wretch ever find the light of day," Euwart continued, "he could share some from his own store. Common folk sometimes own uncommon riddles."

"Hmm. Euwart, hear me with kindness. Would you let Klarenz defend himself?"

Euwart narrowed his eyes into an icy cold stare. "Elevate a commoner, and a foul one at that, to share in a contest between nobles? How can that succeed? I miss your point completely."

"Prince, Klarenz has a true gift for rhymes, puns, and verse. Let me propose that he must praise you better than the City's best. Suppose Klarenz meets a champion of the City in a contest. I've had the use of him for a short while; I believe him sent to me by God's hand."

Euwart's face stayed frozen.

"While my bondman is a commoner with no standing, for sport let him engage a champion of the City who is also a commoner. His loss, as you make clear, is his loss. If he might outdo the City's champion in some way that brings praise upon this noble Haus, what then?"

Euwart had been holding his breath. Now he relaxed. "Ordowahl, you continue to surprise me. Pray share your thoughts. How, indeed, might this knavish wag bring true praise to Haus Rechtmann? Managing that will take more skill than I had thought God would grant a mortal."

"Klarenz's ability as, what you say, a 'knavish wag,' would be well remembered. Let me suggest that the entire City compete to make a new paean to Hammaborg. Who wins that contest will be Champion. Then let there be a duel of song pitting him against Klarenz. For instance, suppose a simple list of words, not knowable in advance. Let the two of them spend an afternoon in the town square, under close observation."

Euwart kept his gaze in an eye-to-eye lock with Ordowahl.

"Give each pen, ink, and paper to scribe a song of praise to this Haus. Then let each sing his song. Let the better song win. Need I remind you that Klarenz's voice is unfit for music? So if he produces the better, the truer, the more beautiful praise, let him win what you see fit to award him. He will have made, as it were, a token restitution for his crime."

Euwart's face relaxed. He looked away to give the matter several moments' consideration. "You are, young prince, already adroit. I will think on this. You will learn my decision tomorrow. Now leave me to my thoughts."

Ordowahl rose. With a polite nod he stepped away from the table. *Did I actually move Euwart in a direction that will save Klarenz? Father God, I can't tell. What is a song to Euwart, against the indelible stain Klarenz left on two noble families?*

*__*__*__*

Behind the prince's retreating back Euwart mused that if

Klarenz's song were the least bit insincere or second best, he would mete out whatever fate he wished, likely brief—no more than an hour or two, but fiery and specific. He might even invite his brother-in-law. On second thought, Prince Euwart put a firm *No* to that.

He ruminated further, visualizing the effect the first contest might have, then the second. Nothing guaranteed success to either one, but at worst it should give the City something to talk about over the coming winter. Fourteen years on, his own need to punish Klarenz had faded, but Rigomonde still wanted grotesque vengeance on her niece's father.

The prince must guess at what he doesn't know.
While circumspect in youth, his father's hand
protected him, a hidden status quo.
In Hammaborg he's put his feet on sand.
 His awkward try to free his randy fief
 has borne a fruit – but is it ripe, and sweet?
 All hinges on the prince's wan belief
 that Klarenz' wit will stave off dread defeat.
It's in the hands of God—Ord's own are slow.
Fair Rigomonde's polished smile? He found
it hard to glim her face in carnal glow.
But here's the day, and Klarenz—is he sound?
 Man's justice is as justice does; his fief's
 own faults are many—virtued, his motifs?

Clean

Later that day Prince Euwart found Ordowahl in the stable yard, currying his stallion by himself after a good run.

"Ordowahl," he said, "my stable servants must smile to see a prince do their work, especially dealing with an intact stallion of such spirit and size."

Ordowahl turned to look at Euwart. "Thank you, Prince Euwart. I heard the town crier this morning."

"Your Hammaborgish improves, Ordowahl. Have you learned your way around our City?"

"It's quite amazing. I have viewed several of your merchants' shipping warehouses. Some of those goods have come vast distances, only to go on to even more distant places. The scale of it staggers the imagination."

"To us it's quite normal, you know. Have you given any further thought to some sort of gift? After granting your astonishing request, I'm sure that you will surprise me." Euwart looked straight at Ordowahl, expressing an unspoken "and *in a happy way.*"

"I wrack my brain, Euwart. But there is one thing,"

"Isn't there always? How may I extend the courtesy of Hammaborg even further?"

"My bondman has endured the onset of cold weather in your dungeon. If he is to acquit himself in a public contest, please allow me to restore him with soap, water, unsoiled clothing, decent food."

"Allow you? You are my guest. It is simple hospitality to have done this already. You'll find him in the bedchamber next to yours. It even has a window. But you must keep him there. He won't be praising the town, so he has no need to see how it may have changed since his grievous youth. And I have a strong need for him not to be seen. You surely understand that much."

"Of course. He is under my parole. He will come out only on the day of his trial."

"Good. You may go to him now. I imagine the two of you have much to discuss." The prince left. His brusqueness reinforced the feeling that forgiveness for Klarenz's sin still lay far off.

It is my duty in this bargain to make Euwart a remarkable gift. For that I will consult my master of the material arts. He ran up the stairs and down the first hall to Klarenz's room.

"Bless you, Princess," he said to the First Lady of the City of Hammaborg, as she emerged from it.

She seemed flustered but hid it behind a cold, piercing gaze. "Prince! Your wretched man has caused irreparable harm, yet now my Christian soul depends on forgiving him. I still find that impossible. Moreover, I also depend on your discretion. In my experience, depending on others to be discreet usually finds some way to fail. I hope, Prince Ordowahl, that your discretion about seeing me at Klarenz's door is as reliable as your head is thick." She turned a prim shoulder and went to descend the stairs.

What a relief! The impassable gulf separating highborn from commoner couldn't tame this happy sense of a reprieve. Ordowahl tapped on the closed door. *Klarenz is free! I can't wait to see how he is.*

"Please, dear Princess Rigomonde, please believe me," came a familiar voice, muffled by the closed door.

"I will not," said Ordowahl. "And you have the name wrong too."

The door crept open. Smells of soap and wet hair met him. Klarenz's beard looked trim, his hair neat. A table held scissors, a basin, and a pile of cut hair. He stood there, wearing clean clothes from his pack. They hung loose; his imprisonment had taken him down to a pale, lank shell. He stared back in disbelief and bowed to invite his liege into the room.

"Well, Klarenz. I believe your atonement is easing, even considering that your conquest had been given in troth to Euwart IV, son of reigning Prince Euwart III."

"Liege! Where do I start? There were three. Each wanted to have me to herself; none were virgin. Two were the daughters of wealthy merchants and a third played the traveling friend. Deep in the middle of the night Fridoric comes to pull me from under the stairs, tosses me out of my bedroll. He drags me out the door by one ear."

Ordowahl shrugged. *Pain and insult are commonplace. Given the background of Klarenz's offense, it seems kind so far.*

"Liege, that ear still pains me! We wind up behind the inn. That's when he tells me to jump onto a cart and climb into a barrel. He is cursing under his breath the whole time—and he was fluent. You've heard this part—the barrel still damp from its load of vinegar—I don't fit. The barrel is lying on its side. He shoves me in feet first, doubles me up, then slams the lid in place. If my nose hadn't been near the bung hole I would have gone to the next world."

"That must have been a hardship," Ordowahl admitted.

"He whispered through the hole that the cork had fallen, he couldn't see it in the dark and didn't dare light a candle to find it. He wanted to bung the barrel shut then roll me into the river. I lost consciousness., and awoke at the bottom of a steep-sided glen, spread-eagle across a little stream with full sun in my eyes. The barrel had broken against a rock."

"What was the season? Did you freeze?"

"Early summer, which was my good fortune. And nothing broke but the barrel. An ancient crone came to me in the middle afternoon. She said the noise of the barrel breaking startled her, but she didn't spy me until well after midday. It was a week before I could draw breath enough to walk. Many more weeks passed before I could breathe deeply."

"She did get you back to a healthy state, though?"

"She was a sweet old dear, Liege—the grandmother I never had. She saved me from a slow death in the open. I don't know how, but the two of us made it all the way up the slope to her hut. She nursed me back to health."

Ordowahl nodded.

"Liege, I tried to repay her, but she was like an angel from heaven. God seemed to be saving me for something, though I've never guessed what. Before leaving I managed to chop her a winter-worth of firewood—she fussed that I would make her lazy! So, now I understand what made her cackle so to see me leave. She told me to stay away from rich women. Liege, I never guessed how rich!"

"In other words," said Ordowahl, "Princess Rigomonde has heard your story just now but doesn't believe you. I'm not surprised."

"I suppose. But it's true! What can I say? And another thing, Liege—she swore me to secrecy, but I assume you saw her leave—she told me her penance for failing to forgive a Christian who has asked for forgiveness was to wash me, put me into clean clothing, and barber me. Liege, many women have seen me with my breeches loosened. She isn't the first to reach in, but she is the only one who reached in with a wet cloth to pummel me."

Ordowahl struggled not to laugh. Looking at Klarenz, he could see the liveliness begin to return. "Klarenz, tell me your state of mind. Weeks of suffering have come close to killing your body—do you have any injuries from that? Has your spirit taken an injury? Do you despair of ever living free again?"

Klarenz took careful stock. He patted his buttocks, arms, legs, head, miming the effort to find an injury. He shook his head vigorously front to back then side to side. "Liege? Everything still seems to work. And now that the Princess has groomed me, well—I've been mistreated so often, Liege, that it's simply my lot in life. I feel as confident as any other wretch might, who sees the light of day. But, now that I think about it, why would the First Lady of Hammaborg wash and barber me?"

"Her penance for failing to offer you Christian forgiveness. You heard her say as much, although you may not repeat that to anyone."

"Forgiveness? That a noble would need to show any kindness to a wretched commoner? Bless the priest that persuaded her."

"Tell me what you know about your future."

Klarenz looked puzzled.

"So you don't know."

"Know? Liege, I don't know anything."

"Try to guess, from Princess Rigomonde, how things stand. On the one hand, you're getting better treatment. On the other hand, you are a long way from living to the pains of old age."

Klarenz's face pinched into a frown.

"To begin, a contest will soon choose a champion poet of Hammaborg. All of the City buzzes with excitement. On the day of All Hallows Eve, a few days hence, the prince, the abbot, and the head of the Merchants' Guild will hear the works of all local residents, excluding any named Klarenz. They will compete to praise the City. The prince will make the final decision. He will choose the one who has made the best praise song. Then comes the interesting part."

"Yes, Liege, go on. What is the interesting part?" His voiced quavered.

"The following afternoon, after High Mass of All Saints Day, again in the town square, the champion poet will meet one Klarenz, formerly of this City. They will spend an hour, each writing a praise song to the prince."

"Liege? Do I have to praise the man who threw me into a dungeon?"

"You do. Not only that, but you are to praise the man whose first betrothed bore your child. That scandal still comes up in off-hand conversation. Poor Fridoric came close to being run out of town when he couldn't produce your body. You, Klarenz, must sing a lovelier praise song than one written by Hammaborg's champion poet."

"And if I fail…" Klarenz's voice trailed off.

Ordowahl was silent for a moment. Klarenz understood his silence.

"You're such a witty fellow, Klarenz. But you are a wag. Sincerity and your wit are like vinegar and oil: marvelous together, but they don't mix well."

"Yes, Liege."

"You're also very clever, Klarenz. You'll see your way through this, but I haven't gotten to the second part."

Klarenz staggered back and sat hard on the bed.

"I can see you still feel cooped up. But you cannot leave this room for any reason until you go out to defend yourself with a song. Stay here, sleep in comfort, eat well and tell me more about sweet cream, fresh butter on soft bread, and berry jam. Once you win forgiveness for a song, there's yet another part. I will need you to become a blacksmith, but we'll have the entire winter to worry about that."

"Blacksmith. I'll be an apprentice again." Klarenz fell silent.

"Meanwhile, Mr. Oily Vinegar Poet, let's discuss your plan to out-praise the champion poet of Hammaborg. In fact, Klarenz, it's my plan. I value you too much to see you go to waste. Now: let us kneel, you beside me. Address our Father in heaven. You're learning the value of that, I am sure. He has brought you to me, in such a way as to find out the sins of your youth and, with His help, put them to rest."

Klarenz began the Our Father, but let Ordowahl carry their petition to God by himself. He still didn't trust his right to speak to the Almighty with his liege within earshot, doubly so when his life hung in precarious balance.

How odd—Prince Euwart has to have a heart
like Christ's to blot this commoner's offense.
On t'other hand, forgiveness isn't carte
blanche, it's up to Klarenz to sing sense.
    Did God send Ordowahl to help this man?
    Does God need Klarenz, or does Ordowahl?
    What pride on prince's part to think he can
    move mount'nous circumstance by protocol?
Forgiveness, said and done, is better to
provide than to receive. It eases pain
to balm the sinner who offended you.
Ord asks, is Rigomonde's peace the gain?
    Whatever happens, Ordowahl hopes God
    will keep all parties sound, above the sod.

Verse

On the morning of the contest Princess Rigomonde made it clear to her husband that she had no wish to see a champion crowned. "Keeping a calm face would be a great bore," she told him, "but doing so while anticipating that wretch Klarenz's possible reprieve is beyond me. I know what you will announce after today's contest but do not care to hear it."

He looked at her with a trace of pity; yet his mind was firm.

Hers was, too. "On the morrow my duty is clear; but please excuse me today."

Late that afternoon Ordowahl stood outside Klarenz's chamber door. *Vagabond, yet a wondrous fellow. I can't help admiring him, even though his life's aim is vacant. Twenty times or more he's had to flee, yet he holds such an even temper. Father God, help both of us to keep him alive!* He held a piece of paper covered in writing. Without a knock he entered the room. "Here is the champion poet's winning verse." He gave it to Klarenz, who returned a curious look.

Klarenz held it to his expert nose and sighed. "I see that it's finely scribed. Both paper and ink smell fresh."

"Aha! Here is a skill my bondman does not own. Soon enough, Klarenz, I'll have you able to write out your many songs. But for now I will read this to you. The tune had something to do with a pine tree:

O Hammaborg, O Hammaborg, how rich and sweet your
river.
O Hammaborg, O Hammaborg, how rich and sweet your
river.
It ever flows and brings us trade,
We prosper when the ships unlade.
O Hammaborg, O Hammaborg, how rich and sweet your
river.

O Hammaborg, O Hammaborg, good fortune smiles upon
you.
O Hammaborg, O Hammaborg, good fortune smiles upon
you.
How rich your docks, your stores and barns,
How packed with goods, with wools and yarns.
O Hammaborg, O Hammaborg, good fortune smiles upon
you.

O Hammaborg, O Hammaborg, you are the best of cities!
O Hammaborg, O Hammaborg, you are the best of cities!
You swell my heart with civic pride,
I evermore will here abide.
O Hammaborg, O Hammaborg, you are the best of cities!

"The prince made something of a flourish when he
announced the prize: 'Good innkeeper Fridoric, good citizens of
the City of Hammaborg,' he said, 'these games are not yet
complete. I've admitted to residence in this City a wise woman
from the far North, Frau Klarenze.' What do you think of that?"

Klarenz's blank look showed him unable to form an opinion,
as though the idea were too foreign.

"He went on to say, 'Moreover, she will meet our new
champion poet. They will compete to discover which can best
praise the reigning House of Hammaborg.' Your turn is
tomorrow at noon, Klarenz—or I should say, Frau Klarenze. I'm

sure you'll have no trouble looking the part. Now, Klarenz, what can you tell me about this man Fridoric?"

Klarenz stared. "If I defeat him, it will be a partial repayment for the vinegar barrel. But he didn't kill me, Liege. If he loses, what becomes of him?"

"The prince is not bloodthirsty, Klarenz. Well, we'll see about *your* case." His face went grim for a moment. "But if you win, no harm will come to Fridoric. When the prince announced tomorrow's second contest, it gave Fridoric a smile. And Fridoric has never met the aged Frau Klarenze. She is not only a wonderful poet but also nearly mute, though I hear she is a great wit."

Ordowahl paused to let that sink in. "Fridoric will indicate a tune for his verse, then the church cantor will sing it. The crowd will cheer, the prince will smile his thanks. When you hand up your work, a woman will sing it. Fitting, don't you think, dear respected Frau Klarenze?"

Klarenz nodded. "Fridoric's tune refers to pines cut down at the winter solstice then decorated with candles for Christ's Mass, which comes three or four days after."

"That is also a Nordwesh custom. But pay attention, Klarenz. Do I need to emphasize that your verse must not only win the contest, it must do so with strength, with honor. It must deliver the purer, the clearer, the kinder praise."

"Liege, this is the point where I may fail. You know me."

"Yes, Klarenz, I do know you. Now listen to me. You will praise the prince, with all the vigor of your considerable mind. You will also have an opportunity to poke a little fun at Fridoric. That is why he will go first. You've seen his work. You know the man from close experience."

"Yes, Liege. And it's no surprise that he's the Champion Poet. Fridoric spins rhymes very ably."

"All the better. You, Klarenz, will guess at how Fridoric might use the assigned words—oh, didn't I tell you? There will be a random draw of ten ordinary words. You must use each word twice."

Klarenz nodded. His interest was growing.

"Your piece will make his sound clumsy, or ineffective, or even inappropriate. It will, when sung by a woman, give sweet, direct praise. Be sure your tune is one a pure churchwoman can sing. Can you accomplish this?"

"Liege, I will, or I'll die trying." His face quivered when he understood how accurate a metaphor that was.

"Good, Klarenz. Tomorrow you'll have real sunshine in your eyes."

*__*__*__*

The contest platform remained at the center of the square, with the same trio of political, ecclesiastical, and commercial leaders a before: Prince Euwart, Abbot Einselmann, and Theodor Schlach, head of the Council of Guilds. In front of them sat Princess Rigomonde, quiet and starchy, with her two children.

Daughter Ana, age ten, rose. She stepped to a small table. Wearing a grave expression she wrote one word on a slip of paper. She folded it twice and dropped it into a basket. She continued until there were twenty-five slips.

Son Euwart V, age seven, went to the basket. He fished out ten slips, one at a time. He unfolded each one and handed it to the Town Crier, who spoke it aloud in his official Crier's voice, then tacked it onto a placard visible to the crowd.

Fridoric wore his finest pumpkin colored tunic. Frau Klarenze, in an enormous hooded cloak of now-faded but once dark green velvet, sat next to him at one of two small tables just below the platform. An even larger crowd had come out this Holy Day to see the mysterious Frau Klarenze.

The prince rose; the crowd hushed. "The wise woman of the north, Frau Klarenze, sits before you. Beside her is your new Champion Poet, innkeeper Fridoric."

Fridoric rose and made a small bow. The aged Frau seemed unsure of herself but managed to rise enough to perform a nervous curtsey.

"Frau Klarenze and our Champion Poet will each write a

song to celebrate the beneficent reign of the House of Rechtmann. They will devote specific attention to the Lady of that House, Princess Rigomonde."

This took Klarenz by surprise. Heavy face makeup made it difficult to smile or change expression, which was a good thing. He began to re-think Fridoric. Klarenz asked himself, *How might my old master shape praises for Princess Rigomonde?* He didn't need a fresh look at the words. Both he and Frau Klarenze were illiterate, and had memorized them:

blue	**berry**	**bird**	**flower**	**sun**
shower	**rain**	**river**	**good**	**evil**

To assist the venerable Frau Klarenze, Frau Hilde Schlach took a seat beside her. She looked proud to be part of the spectacle—doubly proud to function as a literate woman. She would copy out each word the good but aged, voiceless Frau Klarenze would whisper into her ear.

An hour's duration depends on one's point of view. To Klarenz, the shadow cast by a prominent sundial set up for the occasion seemed to race ahead of him. Tens of minutes passed before either Fridoric or Frau Klarenze seemed to do more than fidget. Then a word here, a word there, a crossing out, and "More paper, please," from Fridoric.

Frau Schlach displayed quiet respect. To assist an elder woman of wit—God help us, the Frau was said to have great wit? That held her patient attention.

When a quarter of the hour remained Frau Klarenze appeared to stir. She whispered to the waiting woman.

Frau Schlach smiled and wrote a title at the top of her paper. Then, word by careful word, three verses took form. Frau Klarenze nodded. The song was complete. Frau Schlach put down her quill and relaxed.

Those at the front of the crowd could see tender pride on the good Frau's face, but Frau Klarenze's expression looked neither tender, nor happy, nor relaxed—merely wrinkled with age. And it never changed.

Fridoric continued to redraft. The shadow touched the hour line, but he wasn't finished. "One moment, please!" He waved, inked a final word, and jumped up. He passed his paper to the robed cantor, who ascended three steps to the platform, stage front.

After a look and a nod, the singer bent over to confer with Fridoric then struck a pose to sing:

O FAIREST LADY

O fairest lady of the land, your eyes of _blue_ are loveliest.
O fairest lady of the land, your cheeks are _berry_ red and blest.
The _birds_ show envy for your voice, and _flowers_ vie to be your choice.
O fairest lady of the land, the _sun_ gives warmth at your command.

O fairest lady of the land, now _shower_ us with your _good_ smile,
O fairest lady of the land, _rain_ down your cheer and us beguile.
Your kindness like a _river_ flows, so blest your will on us bestowed,
O fairest lady of the land, no _evil_ comes from your soft hand.

O fairest lady of the land, the skies are _blue_ when you appear.
O fairest lady of the land, A _berry_'s sweetness strikes the ear.
A _bird_ in flight or bee on _flower_ can't outdo your beauty's power,
O fairest lady of the land, the _sun_ comes up at your command!

O fairest lady of the land, if wind or _shower_ might come by,
O fairest lady of the land, _rain_'s but a pause in weather dry.
If _river_ rise or if it fall, _good_ Lady you can comfort all.
O fairest lady of the land, no _evil_ comes past your soft hand.

The crowd cheered. They applauded Princess Rigomonde, who smiled with noble restraint. No one could have guessed the mixed dread and disgust piling up behind those sweet eyes.

The wife of the head of the town musicians' guild approached the Frauen Klarenze und Schlach to accept their tidy paper.

She scanned it. With a smile she mounted the steps to the platform. She turned to face the crowd. They knew her voice to be sweetly lyrical. A hush fell as she began to sing. The tune was a plainsong chant often used at the matins Mass:

O FAIREST LADY

O fairest lady of the Land, do we who sit in awe beneath your throne
Compare your grace to *bird* or bee or *flower*'s *blue*? Does your face own
Our hearts, or does your kindness sing us love? Both *good* and *evil* weave
Each life, yet here our God did bring you for our *good*, we all believe.

Your grace a *river*, yet a *sun* that shines away what *evil* may
Appear, *rain*s joy on every one within your husband's realm, so say
We all who've felt your gracious hand. Is joy a *berry* or a *bird*?
And if it were, joy's *shower*s land on us who drink your every word.

Your prudence is a mix like *sun* and *rain*; it *shower*s when you bless.
Your wisdom's fruit is *berry*, run to tart, yet *river*'s strong caress.
How modest, Princess Rigomonde, *blue* of eye with sky-wide Christian soul!
Your smile? It *flower*s down on who may need it most, makes white from coal.

A few tittered when the first line seemed to echo Fridoric's, but mothers shushed teenage sons so they could hear the song better.

The dulcet female voice became the only sound in the entire square. When she finished, the crowd called out for her to repeat the song. Prince Euwart nodded. She did so into rapt silence.

Then the Frauen Schlach und Klarenze rose. They turned to make a full curtsey to Princess Rigomonde, who allowed herself a very, very small smile. Prince Euwart managed to look pleased; he asked the musicians' guild leader's wife to sing the piece a third time.

Again the crowd applauded. The prince nodded at Frau Klarenze, still standing in front of the platform, turning her inscrutable gaze on Princess Rigomonde.

"Hammaborg, this is a happy day," the prince began.

The crowd noticed their prince addressing them. They gave him their full attention.

"Hammaborg, this is a happy day," he said again. "Once upon a time there was a grievous event in the life of this city, which rose from a tragic misunderstanding. When you mix an ignorant wag with a foolish young woman, omit her name, omit her connections? The destiny of a commoner may collide with that of a prince."

No one seemed to understand what the prince had in mind, but the crowd listened in polite silence.

"Just such a collision happened here, fourteen years ago."

The audience began to buzz with excitement. "Look, that Klarenz fellow came with the huge foreigner—what *is* this?!"

"None can refuse to forgive yet stand before God."

They quieted, if only a little.

"What appeared to be a gross criminal offense was in fact something less. An ignorant youth swived a young woman he didn't know, thereby destroying her future as First Lady of Hammaborg."

The crowd went silent then resumed its buzz.

"Hear me!"

The prince looked stern then beckoned behind him.

Ordowahl got up; the crowd gasped. He'd been sitting in a low slouch so that his presence on the platform wasn't a distraction. Now the tiptop of Prince Euwart's head came even with Ordowahl's shoulder.

"Not long ago this young man arrived here, Prince Ordowahl of Nordweg. If you've seen him, you haven't forgotten him."

A smattering of chuckles plus a few cries of "Hear! Hear!"

"He brought with him a bondman, a vagabond wretch of a

thousand interesting crafts. The bondman felt apprehensive, because fourteen years earlier he was left for dead on a mountainside, never learning why."

The crowd's noise changed. There were gasps, stifled guffaws, expressions of astonished surprise.

"My Princess Rigomonde was, of all of us, most directly, deeply wounded. Yet she is also, as I am, very much richer and happier, all from that wretched event. My dear?"

Princess Rigomonde rose to stand beside Ordowahl. She waved Frau Klarenze up onto the platform. "My dear Frau," she said when Klarenz stood next to her, "Please tell me your background. Where are you from? What have you been doing these past fourteen years?"

Slowly at first, the crowd's noise began to swell. Prince Euwart raised both arms. He lowered them to quiet the crowd once more.

"Klarenz," said Princess Rigomonde, "Thank you. I am finally able to forgive your sin against my sister, against me, and against the man who is now my blessed husband."

Puzzled silence lasted only until she reached up to remove Klarenz's wig.

Klarenz himself peeled off the thin layer of wrinkled muslin pasted onto his face then undid the binding on his woman's overcoat to let it fall.

Fridoric vaulted onto the platform and put Klarenz into a crushing hug. "You misery! You nearly closed my inn; now you've returned to mock my song. But welcome, old friend. I have missed you!"

The crowd's noise made it impossible for anyone else to hear that, but Klarenz struggled within Fridoric's bear hug to return the affection.

Ordowahl wrenched Klarenz out of Fridoric's huge arms and hoisted him to his shoulder for all to see. He spoke up into Klarenz's ear. "The people got their spectacle, Klarenz. I'm happy you managed to live through it." *I'm more relieved than I can say.*

——*—*

Klarenz sat at the dining table that night, instead of standing against the wall behind his master.

"So, Ordowahl," the prince said, "We were discussing steel? Steel swords are commonplace. I've seen fine steel knives before, a few too costly for anything but ceremonial use."

"That's right, Euwart. I've discussed this with Klarenz over the last day or two. He's given the matter a little thought."

"Highnesses, if I may speak?"

"Yes you may, Klarenz. What is it?"

"Prince Rechtmann, I've heard a thing or two about making knife steel. If I apprentice myself to an ironworker for a time, I believe I can learn enough to make an entire sword, not of ordinary steel, but of truest knife steel. A sword that will bend but not break yet hold its edge at least as well as any knife you've ever held in your hand. I've heard tales of such swords, Ulfbehrt by name, in legends passed down through many storytellers. I aspire to make such a one for you."

"Your sins are legend, Klarenz, but boasting doesn't lurk amongst them. I trust it won't inject itself any time soon?"

"Prince," said Klarenz. "I owe much to everyone at this table. I am ready, as Ordowahl's bondman, to make something that will honor him when he presents it to you as a gift. I pray that it will please you well."

"In that case, Klarenz, pay a visit to Herr und Frau Schlach. I'll give you a letter. They will provide whatever you need to do that. Rigomonde, Ordowahl, please excuse me. Duties of state, you know."

Fief Klarenz—not just bold, but full of zeal.
Hard-won forgiveness and the chance to learn
another trade—he now can study steel.
But first fief Klarenz has to "learn the burn."
    To learn a craft he's never seen before,
    fresh freed from chains his sins returned him to,
    fief Klarenz's sponge-brain will soak up lore.
    Have two plus two? He'll give you twenty-two.
Prince Ordo needs a noble gift of steel.
Well, what's so noble 'bout a metal gift?
Fief Klarenz, modest to the end, can "feel"
the making of a sword both strong and swift.
    It will not break, will freely bend yet never
    take a set, and will a moth's wing sever.

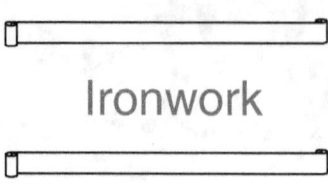

Ironwork

The morning following Klarenz's reprieve Ordowahl gave him the first of many physical training sessions. Poor Klarenz sagged from the start, even though the morning was still fresh. "Liege, I feared death in that dungeon. Even its stench seemed welcome in contrast to dying, yet here you show me a new death."

Ordowahl had taken Klarenz to a side yard on the castle grounds for a few simple exercises. "That's it! Twice more. Steady, steady…here, I've got it…keep at it,…done!"

Klarenz sighed and sat on the ground. He had been doing deep knee bends while holding a sack of sand high over his head. The smell of fresh outdoor air, zesty with the cold of early November, renewed his sense of hope.

Ordowahl said, "Down on your belly, Klarenz!" The light bag of sand came down onto Klarenz's shoulders for "enhanced" push-ups. Each time Ordowahl let him stop he took the bag so that Klarenz could breathe.

"Air is life, Klarenz! Deep, full breathing!"

After warming up legs, arms, torso, shoulders, and neck, it was time for a slow trot. Real running would come later.

Klarenz's first sessions took twenty to thirty minutes, twice a day. Later in the week this became three. After that week he passed through the initial soreness. His safety when away from

Ordowahl, however, seemed as diminished as his vigor. More than once Ordowahl overheard a voice mutter in passing, "What a piece of work that asshole was, to do what he did and come back plain as day, not to mention think he'd escape unpunished. If I had the means…"

*__*__*__*

Six weeks of steady work and good food got Klarenz fit enough, in Ordowahl's studied opinion. Five weeks of freezing idleness and wretched food took five weeks of intense conditioning to repair, plus one for good measure.

Late on a bright Sunday afternoon in mid December they trudged across the square on new snow pressed down to an icy lacework of footprints. They climbed the steps to the imposing Schlach house. Ordowahl used the ornate brass knocker.

Herr Schlach came to the door. When he saw Klarenz his scowl cowed the bondman. "Herr Nordweg, you are welcome in my home, always. But what might it be that requires this other fellow to keep you company?" He struggled to keep a civil face.

Is it that his daughter was one of Klarenz's three eager swivemaids? Ordowahl said nothing but reached into his jacket to retrieve Prince Euwart's letter. "The esteemed prince has encouraged me to ask a favor," he said, handing the stiff piece of folded paper to Herr Schlach.

The good Herr examined the wax seal, broke it, unfolded the letter, and read it. "I see. I cannot refuse such a small request, no matter that it asks me to be reminded daily of this rootless vagabond and what he did."

He sighed. "Please come in." He paused. "Both of you."

Herr Schlach retreated into the house. Ordowahl followed him, and Klarenz tiptoed in as though a full footprint would be rude.

The three of them made a stiff group near a small table in the richly paneled entryway. Hallways led off in multiple directions. The smell of baking made the house fragrant.

"I see that your bondman fancies himself ready to apprentice to my ironmaster. At an age when most men of any merit have become journeymen and husbands with families?" He sighed again.

"Yes, I have an ironwork half a league upriver. It makes a lot of smoke, and Frau Schlach hates the soot, so I moved it there. Yon Klarenz hardly looks the part—ironworkers tend to be heavy and very strong—but he is, as a favor to my esteemed prince, welcome to apprentice."

Frau Schlach came into the small entry. Her expression was sour. They followed her into a parlor. "Perhaps you recall our daughter, Treudel." She stood beside a woman of middling years and still attractive.

Klarenz peered at her. He recognized one of the "two rich girls" about his own age. He'd forgotten her name—Treudel Schlach! He shrank in on himself; Next to her stood a girl with an odd, angular face atop a scrawny neck.

Treudel eyed Klarenz with cool distrust. "This, Klarenz, is Bertrice. Bertrice, you may look upon your father."

She paused while thirteen-year-old Bertrice gave Klarenz a momentary glance of bored detachment.

"Good day to you, Klarenz," said Treudel. Three Schlach women returned to the inner rooms of the house.

The next day at quitting time—two hours after December's late dusk—Ordowahl stood outside the ironwork stable to greet Klarenz. The way back to town ran through wooded hillside country. On that first ride back, Klarenz remarked that while the work was difficult, the constant standing was the hardest part of all.

"You'll not care to accompany me on a run then?" Ordowahl asked him. "Mind, while your body feels weary, you still need to spend at least a quarter hour gasping for breath, with your heart pounding. Every day. Or you'll grow old before your time."

Klarenz forced a smile. Ordowahl tended to repeat himself.

Halfway back to the City Ordowahl turned off where the path went through a copse of trees. "It's dark. There is no course to run out here. We'd startle people if we ran through the City at night, so we will run standing still."

They dismounted, laid their horses' reins across a tree limb and began to run in place.

"Tell me about your first day," said Ordowahl. "I want a full report. Your moods and what someone else said to you, and what you said back, don't interest me."

Klarenz's breath was even. Six weeks of good training had served him well. His feeling of fatigue began to lift. "Liege, I learned right off to stuff tiny bits of rag into my ears, because the noise there is deafening. We're too good to buy Swedish iron and turn it into steel. We make steel directly from ores and coal instead."

"Why does iron come from Sweden?"

"I don't know. The Swedes make a lot of soft, high-quality iron, but Herr Schlach would rather start from raw materials. We make steel directly without going through the soft iron stage."

"What's the difference?"

"Liege, that hides in the foundry master's head. Iron is soft, at least in comparison to steel; steel is much harder. But some steel is so hard you can't do anything with it. Color is one way to tell. Cold iron is gray, while cold steel is slightly bluish. When it's too blue it's useless, even beyond salvage."

"So you've already learned that much. I'm impressed. Are you breathing hard yet?"

"I...think...so," Klarenz puffed.

"Good. A quarter hour more; then we can go eat supper."

It became a ritual. Each evening, sooty and weary, Klarenz followed Ordowahl back toward the City. At some point they would leave the path to run in place.

Day by day Klarenz gained understanding of how Herr Schlach's ironwork turned fool's gold, mined ore, and coal into raw iron. While jogging in place he did his best to tutor Ordowahl. If the details of managing the operation were easy to communicate, only hands-on experience would help his liege gain more than a smattering of what Klarenz was learning about steel.

"Tell me again: soot turns iron to steel?" Ordowahl sounded

perplexed.

"Liege, we put the raw mixture into a furnace, light it, then use a bellows to push air through it. When the fuel is gone we find a mix in the pit—some metal, some slag. We hammer the metal—in fact, the river turns a wheel that does the actual work. An interesting set of protruding arms along the shaft raise and drop huge hammers. We use tongs to hold the raw metal under the hammers while the metal flattens out. Slag isn't metal, so it tends to get knocked off. There is a separate charcoal hearth with its own bellows to get the raw metal red-hot again. We hammer it flat, bend it double, reheat it, hammer it flat, many times. Eventually Herr Meinz, the foundry master, declares the result steel. We go from ore to steel."

"What happens in Sweden?"

"Liege, the same thing happens in Sweden. But they get the exact same dull color every time without using carbon. That's iron. Herr Meinz has an eye for the significant detail. For one thing, he stops the initial burn before all the fuel is used up."

"And why doesn't he just use less fuel?"

"Liege, you'd laugh if I told you. He says that the black of fuel turns gray iron into blue steel. No fuel left, no blue in the metal."

"Klarenz, I have to take that on faith. Do you?"

"Liege, I see it happen. The results differ slightly from one batch to the next one. Herr Meinz always writes down how much weight of this, how much of that, what colors dance in the flame, how many birds fly overhead, even what he ate at midday for all I know."

"Well, Klarenz. When do you think you might gain a step on Herr Meinz?"

"It's the Mass of the Resurrection of Christ this Sunday, Liege. Ask me again on May Day."

*___*___*___*

Herr Schlach noticed Ordowahl leaving Mass one workday morning. He spoke to the prince to admit that Klarenz was learning so much, so fast that he might soon outclass Master

Meinz.

"Even though he ruined my Treudel—left me a homely granddaughter to boot —he has been a fine addition to my ironwork. It will be a sad day if I ever lose him. Even those townsfolk who wanted to do him harm have come to accept him."

Klarenz walked behind them, trying to remain invisible.

"I see. What makes you think of losing him? I haven't planned to take him anywhere."

"Yah, you will. He has his head full of Damascus, for one thing. And he knows you're likely to go somewhere new rather than settle here."

"He does, does he? What is this 'Damascus' you mention?" Ordowahl was amused but curious. *Klarenz always displays discretion, now that he's unable to cross paths with women. But what is this?*

"You do know of the Holy Land? The followers of Mahomet occupy it. They've spread their Christ-denial by sword and fire over a vast area. Yet they have also learned much. Their medicine, their understanding of the skies. Their metalworking—all are said to be great wonders."

Herr Schlach shook his head. "How God in heaven could permit them to surpass Aristotle plagues me. But they use an odd way of numbering, with a mark reserved for nothing. What preposterous humbug! How can you rely on a system that uses a something to denote nothing—the idea is so absurd it defies itself! Roman numerals work well already, and that's the end of it as far as I am concerned."

Herr Schlach paused for a moment. "Now, as I was saying, Damascus is one of their supposed Great Cities, and the metalworkers there make a kind of steel that can take a blow that would break a harder blade or put a permanent kink in a softer one but stays sharp at least as well as our sharpest weapon. And your Klarenz has been talking for some weeks now about going there. God keep him, Herr Nordweg, I'm close to fondness toward him—a little bit more and I might actually worry."

They parted on reaching his house. Ordowahl proceeded across the square into the castle courtyard where Klarenz saddled their mounts for the trip to the ironwork. He had to fight the urge to cuff Klarenz; such a thing was beneath him. An inflection of rasp in his voice was enough.

"Why do I have to learn these things from Herr Schlach? I discover that you've scheduled me to leave Hammaborg by the end of spring, perhaps to travel beyond the Holy Land to Damascus where you might apprentice alongside a Mahometan swordsmith? Here I thought you'd have made me a fine sword in time to present it to Prince Euwart before I leave. Tell me more."

"Liege, I don't have an excuse. When Herr Schlach asks you a question, you'd better find him an answer. So I say whatever comes to mind."

"Just like wooing a young woman? Say whatever comes to mind?"

Klarenz looked dismayed. "Liege, it has never been anything like that. I don't know where to start on that subject, but it has not escaped my notice that never, since you took my pledge of fief, have I been alone in the company of a woman save once, and she only wanted to bruise me. Why else might I, a lowly foundry apprentice, live in a castle yet sleep alone, across a wall from the prince of Nordweg?"

Ordowahl let himself smile. In addition to an uncanny knack for acquiring new abilities, Klarenz was a decent fellow. "We should make time to discuss that, Klarenz. In fact, you might offer me a lecture on matters that involve women. I must hear you at length. But not now."

Klarenz offered a glum nod.

"I don't mind your revealing what's on my mind when you speak with someone I trust, such as Herr Schlach. But this kind of thing can put me at an unexpected disadvantage. Do I act toward you as though we are brothers, or friends? Even though I am fonder of you than I care to admit, you must remind yourself to limit discussions of my thoughts to times when no one else is nearby. At no other time should you ever pretend to know my intentions, or plans. How is it that you didn't realize this?"

Klarenz hung his head. "Liege, please forgive me. I realize that we are now and ever will be bondservant and master. Your affection for me is so great a blessing that I can't bear to think of losing it. For my part, Liege, I would sooner die than disappoint you."

"Well, don't die without first asking permission, Klarenz. Or for that matter, don't do much of anything without being certain of your liege lord's good will in the matter."

As all true geniuses find out, a rough
beginning harms one's credibility.
Prince Ordowahl, uncouth (not couth enough)
should learn more civic sensitivity.
    He's quick, we'll give him that, but also young.
    What difficulties might he conjure up?
    We're talking of the prince, not fief—who hung
    himself a noose with "mistress buttercup."
That crime is washed away and partially
atoned, if Klarenz makes a sword that's good.
Who comes up short in this exchange? Who'd be
more prone than whom to show his babyhood?
    Prince Ordowahl at least is trying hard.
    We'll see if he can not confuse his bard.

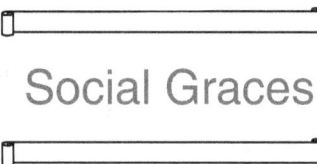

Social Graces

"Young Prince!" said Rigomonde early one day while the servants cleared away the remains of the morning meal. "Young Prince, your value to our City will increase if you place yourself under my care. To the people of Hammaborg you are a rustic. That won't do, so I have engaged a tutor who will instruct you in social graces and customs. You will learn dancing steps and conversational protocols. In time you may return this favor by instructing us in some of the dancing steps that are peculiar to Nordweg."

Ordowahl considered this for a moment. He felt puzzled, but didn't object. "Princess Rigomonde, I won't be reluctant to take instruction alongside young Euwart V. My father King Stegnwahl of Nordweg gave each of his sons tutoring in genteel behavior. A traveling dance master taught us comportment when we were old enough to represent Father well amongst his subjects."

She nodded.

"We learned Nordwesh social protocols, such as the art of sensing what may be asked of us with at least a semblance of grace. We find that useful when deciding whether a man's statement is an insult, or instead our own momentary misunderstanding. Honor is sacred, but so also is peace in someone's house."

She nodded. "I do understand the value of maintaining both honor and peace. I also smile at your willingness to learn, Prince Nordweg. As you say, there is a semblance of grace in your intuition. But you won't need to learn alongside Euwart V. I will call on Ermintrude Frau Helmbloch, who is very presentable She will take you on as a, shall we say, project?"

Ordowahl had been a "project" before. He wondered who, Frau Helmbloch or Princess Rigomonde, had first presented the idea to the other.

Father, forgive me for being presumptuous. Let me hear Your will always. Keep me from conflating it with my own.

"I understand the necessity of preparing for an introduction to Hammaborgish society, Princess. Thank you." *So this is what it feels like to be an uninvolved adult, with no enemies yet with others going out of their way to make me a part of their circle.* He couldn't help wearing a smile.

*__*__*__*

His tutor was pretty, in a wholesome way—also half again his age. Frau Helmbloch reinforced the point by inviting Ordowahl to share in a family supper.

She did not include Klarenz. Her commission concerned Prince Nordweg, not his controversial servant. Klarenz would stay within the castle walls while Ordowahl was learning to pass for a civilized young Hammaborgian man.

"Good evening, Frau Helmbloch," said Ordowahl when she greeted him at the door. "Your kindness in asking me into the sanctum of your home honors me."

She led him to a cozy kitchen, to seat him at the supper table. Several candles lit the room. He examined the serving dishes—platters of cold roast pork, slices of several kinds of sausage, a loaf of heavy bread, jams, cheeses, a dish of pickled vegetables, a pitcher of watered wine.

"Come, dear family. Meet our guest!" She stood at one end of the table. As if on cue three children entered and took seats at the table. The children stair-stepped from an eldest daughter to a son to a younger son. A robust–looking man of perhaps forty years came behind them.

"I introduce our guest to you, dear husband," she said. "My beloved Herr, Einar Helmbloch, this is Ordowahl, Prince of Nordweg. I will be spending time tutoring him until he will no longer embarrass us with his too-simple Nordwesh mannerisms." She looked at Ordowahl with a gimlet eye to see how he reacted to blunt speech. The pupil–tutor relation had begun.

Einar gave Ordowahl a quiet smile to let him know that Ermintrude could be a handful toward those not in her close friendship. "I am pleased to make your acquaintance, Prince. I trust that your tenure as my Ermintrude's pupil will be fruitful and not take up overmuch of your time."

He offered his hand to Ordowahl. His handshake was firm; Ordowahl recognized from Herr Einar Helmbloch's grip that he showed no awe for Ordowahl's size, but also knew better than to force a trial-by-squeeze. Einar impressed Ordowahl with his uncomplicated confidence. It promised a calm, stalwart friendship.

Ermintrude took over. "One of our customs, Ordowahl, is that children are to be seen but not made part of adult conversation."

"Thank you, Ermintrude. If I may, I was about to remark that you and Herr Einar have produced children who will become very fine adults."

"Thank you, my pupil. Here is another lesson: to you I am Lady Ermintrude. I will address you familiarly as my pupil Ordowahl, until such time as I consider you ready to mingle in Hammaborgish society. When we get you to that point—that includes an ability to mingle properly amongst all people from the lowest to the highest—you will become Prince Nordweg once again. Am I clear?"

Ordowahl smiled, suppressing an urge to laugh with delight. "Yes, Lady Ermintrude. I am happy to absorb your wise, patient instruction. Now, Lady Ermintrude, please explain the protocols of a family supper."

Smiling, she gave a set speech on the order in which those at table reached for items, passed them, and ate. She recounted the specific phrases to use, placement of dishes and flatware, of salt, pepper, and other condiments, the ways to serve drink, how one could conclude a supper by excusing oneself from the table. Good manners showed respect for the meal and for all participants—when to attach food to fork, when to invite others to take more food before adding to one's dish, and so on. Complex-seeming rules built a comfortable interaction founded on quiet respect.

Her children sat through the discussion with quietly bored expressions. Ordowahl understood at once that this was not a novel experience for them, but remembered Lady Ermintrude's instruction: children in Hammaborg were discussed only among close family members, and not spoken to. He wanted to congratulate them, or at least their parents, for so much patience in children so young, but knew better.

Doing his best to abide by each of the lady's dicta, Ordowahl managed to enjoy the supper. At the time to excuse himself from the table Ordowahl missed the exact phrasing. Instead of "Herr Helmbloch, Frau Helmbloch, I am happy to have eaten such a fine supper," he used "Herr Einar" and "Lady Ermintrude."

She looked at him.

"Ordowahl, you already impress me with an ability to recall so much, so quickly. But it's 'Herr Helmbloch und Frau Helmbloch.' We'll have to invite you to supper at least once more, to be sure that you've learned everything." She raised an eyebrow at Herr Helmbloch, who showed relaxed contentment.

"My friend Prince Ordowahl," he said, "it has been our pleasure to have you as a guest. But your speed at absorbing, as you say, Hammaborgish customs may reduce these pleasant suppers to a very few. I trust that we will find a way to see you more often than my Frau requires."

Lady Ermintrude gave her husband a submissive nod. "Yes, Herr Einar, I will be pleased to honor your wish."

——*—*

The morning meal was ending. A plate now emptied of fried bacon topped the stack when the serving girl removed the platters of food. After Prince Euwart took his leave, Rigomonde spoke. "This afternoon, Prince Nordweg, Frau Ermintrude Helmbloch will be your partner at a caroling. Do you have this kind of thing in Nordweg?"

"Princess Rigomonde, I regret that I am not familiar with the term. Please tell me something about a caroling."

"You've seen it happen here several times already, Ordowahl. Do you recall long chains of adults in festive garb, dancing in the square in front of the church? They sometimes circle the church, or simply wind about."

"Yes, Princess, I understand you now. In Nordweg we have a slightly different way of dancing. But as you do here, we link arms or hold hands. We sing; we follow a leader who weaves his way through the town. It can become very confusing but always great fun, such as when he leads the line back through itself. We also vie to be the most agile leaper, best singer or storyteller to lead the dance—it warms us up when the weather is chilly, I will say that."

"I see," said Rigomonde. "Perhaps you would like to teach us more of your leaping and storytelling?"

"I do not wish, Princess Rigomonde, to become a spectacle or pretend to teach while I am still a student. But at a more appropriate time, yes, it would be my pleasure to demonstrate what Nordwesh folk enjoy."

"Ja. Well, we also have room for leaping and singing. Despite yon wretch Klarenz's voice." She aimed a stiff smile at Klarenz, whose place had returned to standing against the wall behind his liege.

Klarenz stiffened a bit then relaxed.

She continued. "I am told that, despite Klarenz's uniquely unqualified voice, he often led children's dances when he was young. More than a few of the older folk look forward to having him lead the commoners' revelries."

"Princess Rigomonde, in Nordweg these caroling chains

sometimes begin with highborn folk but then include town elders, followed by the common folk. Nobody watches from the edges of the square, because everyone dances. I can guess that thousands of people in one chain would take half of a feast day to organize and set in motion."

"My prince, have no concern for the difficulties of a large city such as this one. We do manage to get by. Simply prepare yourself for a festive, active day. Prince Euwart has laid on a feast for the town, which means a great crowd. Whatever do you do in Nordweg to get everyone into the dance? Don't you give them food and drink?"

"Because we are so small compared to this great city, Princess, we all dance, then we all feast and drink, and then we all come back to dance, holding hands on both sides but with meat in one fist and a mug in the other. It becomes hilarious by the end of the afternoon."

Rigomonde gave him a polite smile. "Hilarity is as hilarity does. Our own common folk wind up doing the same. They strive for some decorum, though not always with complete success. Eh, my bard?"

Klarenz could tell that his penance might be eternal, in Rigomonde's eyes. He did his best to smile. "Yes, my esteemed Princess Hammaborg, but we do strive to improve."

Her smile thinned. "Certainly," she said, then reached over to pat his hand. "Certainly; it is welcomed."

He blushed.

——*—*

"Take my hand like this, Ordowahl," said Frau Ermintrude.

Klarenz, a continual observer of people and customs, looked on with carefully disguised interest.

Ordowahl held her fingers between his thumb and two fingers. "Am I so heavy? Please, Ordowahl, lighten your grip. I won't slip away from you, I promise. Now, hold the hand of— who is that behind you? Yes, Treudel Schlach. Here, Treudel, have you met Prince Nordweg?" Her face stayed innocent, as though Treudel's involvement with the prince's bondman hadn't crossed her mind.

Treudel stiffened; she held herself erect. With polite reserve she said, "I am not sure that we've been publicly introduced, Prince Nordweg. I am Treudel, daughter of Theodor and Hilde Schlach. I am pleased to make your acquaintance."

Ordowahl recalled encountering Treudel and her daughter Bertrice in the Schlach house parlor. Her history with Klarenz was an open book, but she held out her hand with a courteous smile.

Frau Ermintrude nodded at her with kind approval. "Now, Ordowahl, observe the pattern your feet should make as we dance. The step is simple so you should learn it as quickly as you do other things."

She demonstrated which foot went where, and when, through an intricate pattern of steps.

Ordowahl released both ladies' hands and stepped to the side.

He practiced the sequence with short steps, then the steps for turning a corner.

"I see you can make a fine dancer, Ordowahl. Very nice. Now, the exchange of hands. We always keep the right hand forward, so when the line reverses it is necessary to release each partner's hand, pivot, and join hands again. When this happens we—let me show you."

She tugged free of Ordowahl's hand, with a small frown to show him his grip was still too strong. She stepped to the side to demonstrate, including a half-twist when both feet were off the ground, and landed with athletic ease. Then she demonstrated a turn to the other side.

"This happens when the leader adds 'Turn about, *now!*' in the middle of his song. I'm sure you will learn to pay as much attention to him as you do to your fair companions, Ordowahl."

"I see, Lady Ermintrude. I see."

Treudel gave him an odd look—both loathing and grudging admiration in it—then took his hand. "Where is the leader of the dance?" she asked.

Again the prince is inadept, but he,
like Klarenz, learns apace. His social ken
has needed polish—coarsened as it be
by comp'ny kept with busy Viking men.
    But pride, it goeth oft before a fall.
    We see the modest prince believing he
    will stand the test of Hammaborg. It all
    will hinge on random opportunity.
Behind this soft façade his promise rests
on Klarenz, 'prentice at the ironwork.
Fief Klarenz works on Ordo's gift, he nests
within his craft, intensity his quirk.
    Our Klarenz is a spy, who picks the brain
    of masters, scouting steel's surreal terrain.

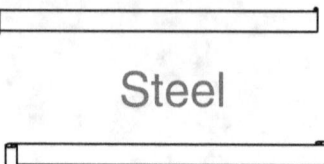

Steel

Winter faded into spring, letting nightfall come later each day. By late April it coincided with the end of the work day. Each evening prince and bondman took a cross country run. Both men looked forward to the freedom of motion. Their conversations also expanded to odd topics.

"Liege, can you imagine why folk believe that iron drives away unholy spirits?"

"I haven't given it a thought, Klarenz. Does it involve swordsmithing?"

"I see it like this: iron is a great mystery, because we can't make it pure by melting—we can't get it to melt. If we found a way to do that, then perhaps either the slag or the iron would float to the top. But no matter how often we heat the iron, no matter how hard we hammer it, there is still slag within. We drive out the slag, bit by ever tinier bit—but always some remains. We need to explain this to ourselves, so we believe that iron possesses other mysteries beyond defeating our attempts to make it pure. You see, ignoring the fact that it is never pure, it must be able to defeat other things as easily as it defeats us. And what are those things? Why, if you say it defeats something you've never even seen, there you are!"

"There I am—but where? There I am where?"

"You've explained iron's power, Liege. It chases away

136

certain evils so well that we never see them, which means we love it. Instead of hating it for remaining slightly impure, we love and respect it."

Does Klarenz see any comparison of iron to a woman? "Hmm. Love and respect for something in God's creation is good, I suppose. But is there really a risk that we might hate iron for its eternal resistance to our arts? What if it could melt, and flow like lead or gold or copper?"

Klarenz chuckled. "An interesting thought, Liege. Flow? After you spend some time with Master Meinz, you'll believe that to be impossible. He can get bright steel to yield to a good hammer the way a fist might reshape cold candle wax, but no more."

"Let me guess. You've found a way to melt iron."

"No, liege, I have not. What I've overheard is more interesting. What do you know about the ancient Ulfbehrt swords?"

"Have I heard of them? Klarenz, they're a revered legend—swords which bend but don't break yet also keep a keen edge. The best iron from any foundry anywhere you can reach in a year's travel is made from ores, a coal fire, and repeated pounding. The purest iron is soft in that it bends but does not spring back. If you make it into steel it becomes harder. It holds an edge better. It may bend—but is always prone to break. The Ulfbehrt swords were said to bend, a lot, but never to break."

"Then where, Liege, have they gone?"

"Klarenz, they were prizes, owned by great warriors. They were often buried with their owners or lost when a boat was upset in treacherous waters—in short, if they ever were, such things are not now."

"And, Liege, where did they come from?"

"That, Klarenz, isn't something I ever learned."

"Liege, I believe I've heard enough pieces of different tales, right there in Master Meinz's ironwork, to answer that question and maybe one or two others."

"Indeed! You've found the location of the Ulfbehrt sword

works? Klarenz, many places claim that. Many of them make steel today. None of them produce anything like the mythical Ulfbehrt."

"Liege, to find is not the same as to understand."

"You remind me of my tutor Heorald. Did you ever meet him while you were sojourning in Nordweg?"

Klarenz paused. The usual "something" had happened in Nordweg, which had forced him into fiefdom under Ordowahl, prince and ninth son of King Stegnwahl of Nordweg.

"Liege?"

"Heorald. He was Father's mage. He taught all my brothers, and me, many things that don't appear in books. One of his lessons was precisely what you said: To discover and to understand are often different."

Bowing his head, Klarenz demurred.

"Liege, before it was that I met you, I consorted with all manner of common folk but never came near to a king's court."

"I see. That is no matter now, Klarenz. Explain yourself. Tell me how finding a place which claims to produce Ulfbehrt swords yet can't make a good one helps understand how to make them today?"

"It's this way, Liege. I believe these swords were made with steel that came from far to the east. Do we trade today with people far to the east? Long ago we did—I haven't heard that we do any more. That might explain the lack of those swords. I've heard it said, as a joke, that people in the east were so backward they made steel in mud pies that yielded lumps the size of a large man's fist. Some of them still had mud-crockery sticking to them, in fact. Standing next to an open hearth which we feed with shovels makes little mud pies seem unmanly, Liege."

Ordowahl could not keep the cynicism from his voice. "And what conclusion does that suggest?"

Klarenz squared his shoulders. "Liege, thought has taken me down many pathways. There is, of course, more to the tangle of legends. I struggle to make sense of them—a few ideas—they may have made clay containers. Start with a small clay pot, add good iron ore and some soot, seal it up and bake your pie."

"I see. Klarenz, you make yourself impossible to believe, but something tells me you know more than you can explain to someone else—and you the poet. So, tell me how you would, as you say, bake steel. Also tell me why no one else has tried this."

"Liege, even though a hearth is hot beyond your imagining, think as if you were a hearth."

"Go on."

"When you wear a hat, you are warmer than when you don't. In summer, the hat has to let the air go through, else you bake. In winter, you cover your head to endure the cold."

"So hearths have heads?"

"Indeed! Liege, a hearth is like a head sliced open right above the eyes. It's fortunate that a hearth doesn't have to think! Now tell me what will happen if we make a hearth with a hat on it."

"Klarenz, the poor hat would become a cinder before you half had it fastened down."

"And if the hearth is made of stone, why not its hat?"

"What? If your hearth is covered over, how do you get anything into it?"

"You build a new hearth each time, with a load of fuel around its mud pie jars. Wrap that in brick, including a top covering, then light the fire."

"You seem to have an image in your mind that fits all these pieces together. Don't bother drawing me any pictures, Klarenz. Someone might see it lying about. They would think us both mad."

"Liege? You don't think of me like that?"

"No, Klarenz. I am always alert, yet often surprised. This has nothing to do with women or vinegar, so I hope for an agreeable outcome."

"Liege, I may be ready to recapture this method. Herr Schlach controls the Guild of Manufactories, also the Council of Guilds. Master Meinz tells me to stay on good terms with Herr Schlach. Do you know how likely that is?"

"Klarenz, the good Herr Schlach loves your work. Why can't you share your secret with him?"

"Two reasons, Liege. First, Master Meinz would sooner expose his chest and pretend to wet nurse his grandchild at the cathedral door than let an apprentice of six months outdo him. Second, if he observes me succeeding at what I do, he will make a thousand swords as good as the one you intend for Prince Euwart."

"So all of Christendom will continue to use weapons inferior to Damascus steel? Is that also true?"

"Liege, God guards Christendom against the Mahometans. I have to guard you against Herr Schlach."

"Klarenz, Herr Schlach and I have only good will between us."

"That may be so. I'll wager making Ulfbehrt steel will be so tricky that the making of it will surrender to me alone. Perhaps no one else will get the knack for it."

"You seldom boast, so why does this sound like boasting? After all, it was done in the east long, long ago, with no help from you."

"Liege, my word has always been good. I feel this in my bones. Iron is so difficult to master that I'm not sure I will master it in years, much less a single season."

"I've seen the light of understanding on your face when you talk about making steel, Klarenz. I believe you will do it. So now let me think like a highborn. I'm beginning to agree with you about doing this where no one else can watch. Let us suppose that Herr Schlach tells Master Meinz to give you free use of whatever coal, ore, furnaces, hearths, tools, billows, tongs, buckets, what-have-you in his ironwork. And let us suppose that Master Meinz is a decent, kind fellow who won't work against you behind your back."

"For the sake of this discussion, Liege. We could suppose such things."

"Now let the good Herr Schlach see you finishing a hundred mud pie jars, enough to begin an armory with your 'new

Ulfbehrt' swords. Businessman at heart, he'd bring Prince Euwart with him if, for instance, he wanted you to stay right here in Hammaborg. You would remain here the rest of your life. Treudel would permit you to marry her, I'm thinking. What say you?"

"Liege, the important point is that I wouldn't, couldn't continue as your fief."

"You are right, Klarenz. God sent me away from Nordweg. In time He may guide me back. I want you with me then. I give you my peace with regard to the town thane's daughter, she whose heart you may have broken, she who gave me the trinket—you know which trinket I mean. When I left home, Klarenz, she was happy, a wife, and mother to a fat baby girl. You will be with me when I go back there. That is a promise I make to myself."

*__*__*__*

Ordowahl sat across from Herr Schlach at a table in a small room at the hall of the Council of Guilds. Herr Schlach had provided a plate of cheeses and mugs of ale. Three candles provided plenty of light.

"My good friend, Herr Schlach," Ordowahl began, "I hope that my fief Klarenz has been useful to you these past six months."

"Indeed, Prince Ordowahl, he has. I suppose that I must lose him?"

"In a sense, Herr Schlach, in a sense."

"And what sense might that be? Something that requires you to come to see me here at the hall of the Council of Guilds?"

"Yes. To be brief, Herr Schlach, I wish to set Klarenz up in a small iron manufactory of his own, where he will make a small amount of something quite different from anything that leaves the docks of Hammaborg."

"I see. And what might be so different about it? I assure you that, whatever it is, he would be able to make much more of it where he is. And he would earn you as his fief holder some wealth making this, whatever it is, in my ironwork. How can he set up an entire manufactory on his own?"

"As always, Herr Schlach, you see matters just as they are. What Klarenz has in mind would divert much from your current business. You supply steel and iron goods to many. For a time they would see less of your ware than before. Other suppliers might pull that trade away from you. There might also be difficulties with Master Meinz. He would see Klarenz doing things he didn't learn from the good Master—you of all people understand how temperamental a master craftsman can be."

Herr Schlach nodded.

He doesn't appear to value anything new. Klarenz is going to stay on as my fief! "So, my friend, after hearing Klarenz out, I've decided to set him up with a small workshop where he can perform his special work. That is why I come here to the Council of Guilds."

An eyebrow went up.

"Herr Schlach, as I understand it, anyone may make whatever he wants. To sell his wares he must obtain membership in a guild. He must obey its rules. I am here to inform the Council that Klarenz will be working in steel yet not for sale to any customer. So, you see, I don't pretend to complicate the prosperity of any trade or any commerce flowing through Hammaborg. I pledge that I will not sell any goods, nor provide them for sale by any agent."

"I am astonished. Losing Klarenz is something I've come to accept, yet having him turn aside from commerce—that feels sinful. Yet, so be it! I thank you, Prince Nordweg, for coming to the Council and stating your intentions for Klarenz."

He and Ordowahl stood. They shook hands.

"Prince, we are most of all interested in the prosperity of Hammaborg. If you change your mind such as to help make this City even more a center of trade and industry, you will of course be welcomed here. I confess, Prince, that I'll miss seeing my granddaughter's vagabond father. Ach, it even sorrows me that she doesn't and won't care."

"Indeed, my good friend. That is a pity. Please convey my

respects to Frau Schlach."

*__*__*__*

Ordowahl and Euwart were about to rise from a brief noon meal. "A thousand fire bricks?" Euwart thought for a moment. "Those will take a month to make. Can you pay fifteen skilled laborers a month's wage each? Then rent the kiln? You'll need to find two heavy wagons, drivers with draft horses, a crew of woodsmen to harvest trees already dead and dried—good luck finding those anywhere close by—plus men to mix the clay, mold the bricks, make the charcoal, and operate the kiln. Count on a similar effort of at least a month to build your furnace then erect some sort of shelter around it."

"I've accepted modest fees training highborn men of this area in martial arts, Euwart. I believe that you may be almost as happy to have me doing that as to have the gift I've alluded to. They seem to have gained from comparing Nordwesh technique to their own. For that matter, so have I. Yes, I can fund it.

"And I see," continued Ordowahl, "that Theodor Schlach's ironwork sits on the bank of the river, where the current drives a water wheel. Is there, somewhere nearby, another good riverbank spot where a strong current flows right at the edge?"

"That is Theodor Schlach's good fortune, Ordowahl. Currents eat riverbanks, slide them downstream. This makes the river shallow at its banks. Half-eaten banks also tend to slow the current. That is why most of the current runs in the middle, where it is deepest. Herr Schlach found a stone outcrop on a bend where the river challenges the bank but can't move it. He managed to place a waterwheel there. If you're looking for something like that, your outlay for men and materials will double or more. Even then you need to hunt for a suitable spot."

"Yes, Euwart, one must make do with what God has provided. But Klarenz is an amazing fellow. He must have worked this all out ahead of time. Did I tell you what he intends? He thinks he can make Ulfbehrt steel, something that hasn't been done in many generations."

"Ordowahl, I always find myself taking what that fellow

says with one grain of salt—then he returns two. If he claims he can do a thing, he always does it. I pray that this time is no different, but I will believe this when I see it and not before."

Prince Ordowahl can now relax—his fief
claims he can manufacture slagless steel.
As Frau E's pupil, boredom has relief.
Time spent in tutelage has its appeal.
    Without a hurry to grow wise and lacking
    any odd demands that he perform,
    Prince Ordowahl is picking up the knack
    of living like a royal, sweet new norm.
So, what of Christian duty? Does he pray,
do penance for his sins? He's sure he does,
entrained from mother's knee. But this cachet
descends to rote, intensity to buzz.
    What happened to the matter in his walks
    with God? He has no problems, thus no talks.

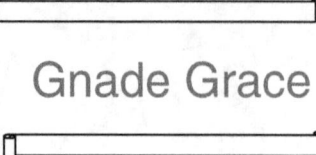

Gnade Grace

One late July dusk Ordowahl took a quiet walk through the main square. A woman called out to him.

"Mein Herr Prince?"

Ordowahl turned around. Among the lowborn, a girl's parents tended to choose her spouse. She needed to show them due deference in their choice. That meant she couldn't show interest in the many handsome young swains who might seek to distract her.

Hammaborg differed—an unmarried young woman of either the wealthy or the highborn had freedom to strike up a conversation with an unmarried man. He returned a polite "Jawohl meine Jungfrau? And what is your name, young one?"

She pouted. "Young virgin, am I!" and, with a coquettish pivot, presented herself in a way that showed off her figure. "I am not all that young, you know, Prince. My parents have named me Gnade, which in Nordwesh is 'Grace.' I'd feel flattered to be called that."

"I shall. Do your parents have a husband waiting to claim you, or are you simply passing the time until they do?"

"Mein Herr Prince! You ask the most pointed questions. Did you think me so simple as that?" She pirouetted and stalked away.

Ordowahl knew better than to gaze after her. He had learned

146

that much while still in Nordweg, so he didn't see her turn, look at him over a bare shoulder and frown.

Wealthy young women had apparent freedom to develop a social life. An ideal Frau, while showing submission to her Herr's overwhelming authority, could entertain a man's guests with a certain flirtatious panache, to create a happy impression.

Happy is as happy does; moneyed commoners learned in childhood that their special place brought them forgiveness for acts which wouldn't find permission beforehand. This simple truth softened Ordowahl's stuffy morals.

Since his manhood day he had come to appreciate women very, very much. Each time, he used a figment of circumstance—barrenness or widowhood—to excuse carnal enjoyment of someone he would know only in passing and always lowborn. It didn't occur to him to compare his surrenders to lust with Klarenz's – the gulf between them was too great.

Ordowahl made an earnest prayer.

Father in heaven, I confess to you and *not to a chatty priest that I am drawn to this young woman, Grace. Please help me to keep her out of my thoughts, because I don't sense that you've placed her in my life in any important way. Whatever comes to pass, I know You will bring about Your own intent. Help me to see, Father. Help me to keep this saucy* and *very appealing young woman at arm's length! It was easy to endure one celibate night with Nanneke of the red hair* and *violet eyes. Her father, my second-cousin Kleywehl, was anxious that I remain circumspect. She entrapped me into allowing her to sleep, naked, in my bed on the last night before I entered Viking lands. A full conversation with Grace? Father, help me. Amen.*

Caroling time returned on a warm day in early August, when summer's first harvest broke the annual fast. The main square buzzed with people. They ate, drank, rested, and caroled with happy abandon. One of them was Gnade Grace.

"Meine Jungfrau Grace," Ordowahl said. He evaluated her pout-turned-smile. She was approachable; she also seemed to lack an educated mind. He prayed again:

Father, forgive me for judging her. I challenge the situation, Father. She has an odd hold on my attention; help me govern it.

"You are such a tease, my prince! Tell me, does this dress make me look old enough that you will call me something more adult than 'Jungfrau'?"

"How should I know? I see that it's in the style of an unmarried woman It is in fact somewhat more daring than those around us. Tell me, if you will, how you differentiate daring as opposed to adult?"

"Such a pompous question! Really, Herr Prince, are you testing me before asking my parents? I assure you, I am bespoke. Rejoice with me, Herr Prince."

She frowned. "He is older than my father, has children older than I am. He was even so ill from wine that he couldn't journey here a month ago, when he was supposed to visit. But Mutter und Vater tell me he will be a warm, loving husband. He will leave me considerable wealth—after turning everything over to his original heirs. Such a monstrosity, Herr Prince! Am I required to honor my parents' judgment? I do. But I don't look forward to anything good from following it. Humor me, Herr Prince. Give me a smile and the arm of a pleasant companion for the time being."

Her story moved Ordowahl. It didn't occur to him to examine any detail of it, so he offered his arm.

She took it, pulling his elbow sideways into a generous bosom. He was too delighted to notice his caution fading. "Mein Herr Prince, thank you so much! Let us celebrate our new arrangement, shall we? The prince serves very good wine."

They were between rounds of caroling; Ordowahl was not just hungry, he was thirsty. "Wine satisfies some of a man's thirst," he said, "and there is water for the other." He winked at her. She went to the table with a backward smile at him.

"Here is a fine flagon, Herr Prince." She handed him a large, full goblet while taking tiny sips from a little mug. "Enjoy the day, my lovely Herr Prince. Show us some Nordwesh leaping."

Ermintrude Helmbloch approached. "Please do show us, Prince Ordowahl."

The official form of address announced that she had promoted him to adulthood. He also noted the skeptical look on her face and wondered what that look meant, coming from her. He was alert and, so far, sober. He sensed that she considered him,, so far, marginally acceptable. Had she dared him to prove her either correct or sadly wrong?

"My good tutor, Frau Helmbloch, the idea interests me. First I would like to do this in the Hammaborgish manner. I see many Hammaborgish examples here in the town square. Permit me to join in with them."

He handed his goblet to Gnade Grace and went toward the leaping, cavorting young men showing their prowess. They quickly formed a ring around this recent arrival, recognized at once as the celebrated Prince Nordweg.

"Cheer this royal on, my friends! Watch that scissor-kick at the top of his leap. He leaps higher, farther, yet more smoothly than any of us."

"I watch and agree," said another. "Look at his flip and half turn—go up looking south, get his head looking east when inverted and land facing north! And then back again!"

Several voices made a chorus. They chanted in time with the piper piping the carol to watch Ordowahl demonstrate his understanding of the Hammaborgish style. "Will he tire?" one finally asked. Ordowahl had been at work and was beginning to sweat. His face flushed bright red.

One of them called out, "Prince Nordweg, can you show us how this is done in the Nordwesh style?"

Without stopping, which was the questioner's real intent, Ordowahl moved into a new style. The ring of admirers buzzed as they critiqued the Nordwesh form's variations on pirouettes, flips and mid-air spins.

Finally a panting, perspiring Ordowahl stopped to rest. Walking back to Ermintrude and Grace, he used a cloth from his pocket to wipe the sweat from his hair and flaming-red face.

"Thank you, Frau Ermintrude, for your invitation." He accepted the flagon of wine from Grace.

She asked him in a little girl's voice, "Herr Prince, did I not invite you first? Have you forgotten me in the glow of your Tutor Aunt, Frau Helmbloch?"

Ordowahl glanced at Ermintrude, who shook her head slightly and stepped back. "Why, yes, Grace, you did do that. Thank you."

Partly mollified, Grace once again pulled Ordowahl's arm to her bosom.

With the flagon in his other hand Ordowahl drank two large gulps. Even watered, the wine was heady. He knew he would need to be careful and guard his senses.

"Let's go back to the caroling!" urged Grace. She drank a few last drops from her mug and winked at Ordowahl. "Your own isn't empty, Herr Prince, but I am not sure I can help you with it."

Ordowahl drank deeply a second time then set the half-full flagon on the hard surface of the square. "I am ready to carol," he said and led her over to the front end of the line. "Klarenz!" he called out.

His fief was braying a raucous, artfully lewd ditty in a voice with clear diction, carrying power, and nothing remotely pleasant about it. The carolers loved his performance.

"Now, Herr Prince, it's more fun at the other end. Look, the other leapers are there, too—see how they welcome you!"

Ordowahl observed that they appeared to be welcoming both, mainly with a happy eye on the Frauelein. "If it makes my Frauelein happy, I will do it," he said. She towed him toward vibrant hilarity.

*__*__*__*

The following day at the morning meal Rigomonde gave him a sharp look. "I see, Prince Ordowahl, that you've made a new friend."

"Yes, Princess Rigomonde?"

"Her name is Gnade, or to you Grace. To many her name is

Comfort, or whatever euphemism you may imagine for a young woman whose experience in the marital embrace is, shall we say, current, catholic, and robust?"

"I thank you, Princess. I surmised as much. I presume that the standards limiting the behavior of a wealthy young woman are looser than those for lowborns? Could that have something to do with it?"

"Ordowahl?" she asked with a raised brow. "Do you construct an apology for her behavior? Has she comforted you, too?"

"She has not."

The direct question put Ordowahl on the defensive, and he felt unable to make a better answer. These ran through his head:

Princess, you mistake me.

Princess, while we agree on much, you misjudge me.

Princess, my own standards of behavior are as strict as yours.

Yes, I've appeared to encourage Grace. No, I don't intend to justify my actions to you, or even to myself.

Ordowahl dwelt on his last answer for the rest of the day.

Klarenz went early to bed. Working in the foundry required a lot of deep sleep, which left Ordowahl time to himself in the evening. In the town square the stars were bright. A sliver of waning moon sat low over the western horizon.

"Guten Abend, Herr Prince Nordweg, do you secretly scorn me?" The voice came from right beside him.

"Gnade, Grace, Guten Abend. No, I do not. How have I made you think that?"

"Is that all you do, think? When are you going to show me your, what can I say, your affection?" She flattened her hands on his stomach then slipped them downward under his belt to massage his belly.

"I see. Affection is not only a matter of time, smiles, conversation, and small gifts. It also somehow involves our bodies?" He made himself sound innocent to see her response.

"Bodies!" she whispered, exulting. With a firm grasp on his

belt she towed him off the square, down a side lane, into a nook in some tall shrubbery.

The moon didn't reach them. Ordowahl sensed that the ground held a soft carpet of last year's leaves. For a moment all he heard was a quiet, busy rustling then the sound of a dress falling. The next moment her hands had undone his belt.

"Grace? What are you doing?" *She must have had a lot of practice to understand a man's belt well enough to unbuckle one as heavy as mine.* "Tell me more about these 'bodies.' Do you mean yours and mine?"

"Dear Prince, I am making love with you. Do you love me? For I love you very much."

Ordowahl remembered his brothers teaching that this is what a man says when he wants to enjoy a woman. "Are you telling me this just so that you can enjoy my body?"

"Such talk! Prince, we've spent so much time together, what else am I going to believe?"

His pants fell to his ankles; Grace tested his erection. "Yes, good! Osculetur me osculo oris sui quia meliora sunt ubera tua vino, or, 'Let him kiss me with the kiss of his mouth: for thy breasts are better than wine."

"The opening words of Solomon's Song."

Mute, she tugged his hand downward to wrap his fingers under the furry softness below her waist. She bent his fingers to make a small support then wriggled onto the tiny seat. Her voice became a ragged whisper: "Hold me upright. Lift me up, Ordowahl, lift me up so I can kiss your face. Raise me, carry my weight, bring me up to you."

He waggled his middle finger between moist lower lips; she quivered. Cupping his other hand under her bottom, he lifted her high off the ground.

She placed hands on his shoulders. He raised her until he could press his face against each taut-nippled breast then eased her back down so they could kiss. "You are a gift, Grace."

"Hush, Herr Prince, lest they hear us." She didn't bother being silent, herself.

*Hmm Klarenz, you would've admired the sight. So now what do I do? Am I merely a momentary male organ that she can use at will? The price a man pays for intimacy with a woman depends on what he has. The lowborn of this city have nothing so likely pay nothing. I have, what?—*and *whatever she might think that is, she will make a demand on it.*

He prayed, again. *Father, I have fooled myself. I am stupid. I don't know how to repent, because I haven't found a way out, I don't have a way to stop wanting her. Until that happens I will not find a way to persuade her to break away. Please help me, Father. Help me to govern myself.*

I ignored the obvious, discounted her ability to plan. Please keep me safe according to your perfect will.

*__*__*__*

Coming back from Klarenz's new workshop at the end of an early August day, they were about to dismount for an hour's light running.

"Klarenz, good my fief, speak wisdom to me from your experience."

"Liege?"

"You've often entertained the affections of more than one woman at a time. In fact when only seventeen you had three competing for you."

Klarenz frowned. "Liege, your kindness is always close, yet I don't feel that right now. What have I done to remind you of that terrible time?"

"Ha, ha! Not terrible then, Klarenz—that wasn't my point. I have more women chasing me than I want. I need one of them to lose interest. Please review what you did, if anything, when this was a problem for you."

"Oh, liege, I am so captive to a woman's closeness, at least the most basic kind. Yet once or twice I did choose to steer one away. Liege, you have only one. The town is amused by your dalliance. Her parents, in fact, are thinking on how to get you to come to them to ask to marry their daughter."

Ordowahl sighed. "That is nothing I want. I understand your

loneliness. Would you like to distract her? I could make that a requirement, in fact. No– the thought paints me in my own mind, and everyone else's, as a coward, weak."

It was Klarenz's turn to say nothing. Ordowahl's confessed insufficiency stunned him.

"Anyone can have a soft or foolish thought when under a woman's spell, Klarenz. If you think of something fitting for a highborn which will end Frauelein Grace's pursuit, please tell me about it. Now!—let's pursue a four-legged fox, eh, instead of a two-legged vixen. It's also time to re-devote myself to training the poor wretches hereabouts in the ways of war and men. Let's go!"

A Frauelein plunders Ordo's Christian poise
And Lady Rigomonde calls him cheap.
Grace counsels him, "Be quiet!"—then makes noise.
Prince Ordo falls, and doesn't know how deep.
    He hasn't paid attention to his fief.
    That focus has to change. His host remains
    ungifted, naught to validate belief
    that young Prince Ordo's taking any pains.
He spends his days as tutor teaching men
the arts of arms, his evenings perhaps
in Grace's charmed embrace, again, again.
Unversed in eros, he lets care collapse.
    Prince Ordo dumbly dodges cupid's darts,
    though Klarenz fell to fiefdom breaking hearts.

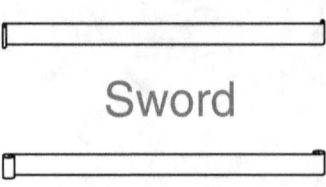

Sword

After a week's absence Ordowahl paid an unannounced visit to Klarenz's modest ironwork. "Speak to me of mud pies, Klarenz. I've left you to yourself for a time. Have you found a way to make steel yet?"

"Liege, it wasn't simple. I've baked many hundreds of mud pies, ten or twenty at a time. Only in the last handful of days have I found anything useful. I add various things beyond mere soot, to make each one different. Bits of glass, chalk, river sands. Some proved useful. Like seems to attract like, so I am searching out which things to add, as well the proportions for each, to draw out all of the slag. Each day when I tear open the furnace to break open the mud pies in it I find more of interest. Often I find a still-glowing, yellow-hot lump of steel."

"Introduce me to your assistants, Klarenz."

"Liege, this is Brutus." He indicated a tall, robust man of heavy build.

"Brutus has lost the gift of speech. He still manages to make himself understood if one pays attention."

Brutus made a smiling bow to Ordowahl. His voice was smooth, and unintelligible. He clearly was honored to meet the prince.

"And this is Hanryk."

"Muh Prinzz," said Hanryk. He was between Klarenz and

Brutus in height, no brighter than a seven- or eight-year-old child, but massive and well-formed.

"Brutus, Hanryk." Ordowahl acknowledged them.

"I understand, Klarenz. You've hired men who are very able, yet unlikely to divulge any information about what you are doing here."

Brutus protested—it was clear he felt as though Ordowahl had questioned their loyalty. Ordowahl smiled approval at them.

"You are without doubt the right men for what Klarenz is doing here," he said to comfort them. "Now, Klarenz, speak to me of mud pies. How well do your pies compare to Herr Schlach's ironwork?"

"Liege. Each bake requires half a day to set up. We light it off then tear down yesterday's bake in the second half of the day. Sometimes I can reach a conclusion about it right then. Usually I work on it the next day while Brutus and Hanryk build the new bake. Six bakes in a good week. This is a gain when you consider that my methods result in more steel per week's time. I also have closer control of the blueness. No pounding soot in or pounding slag out. All that is not steel appears to seep out into the clay walls of the mud pie. Each lump is uniformly blue all the way through. That blueness is what I will vary to make swords."

"Vary? You mean, in making a sword that is both durable and has a hard edge?"

"Yah. Less blue in the steel makes it durable; more blue keeps a hard edge."

"So far we have two types of iron yet one sword. So, which is it?"

"Liege, it is both. You understand a sword as a thin, wide blade of hard steel. I will put a blade of medium steel on either side of the hard blade, perhaps two even milder, more durable blades on the outside of those."

"Thin or not, laying five blades on top of each other would still make a very thick sword, would it not?"

"Yet if I start with a short one then work it to be much longer and thinner, Liege, it will take any proportion I choose."

"So you will be hammering after all."

"Liege, I actually look forward to it!"

*__*__*__*

Two weeks passed. The rare passer-by would hear ten or a dozen resounding hammer strokes, a pause, another volley, continuing from morning until evening.

When Ordowahl visited the ironwork he could identify nothing particular about the glowing object Klarenz was working on. He took it for a sword blank in an early stage.

Ordowahl left Klarenz to his work to devote his own time to training other highborn men in martial arts. He'd been doing that ever since the snows had gone. His Hammaborgish was now fluent. More to the point, it had moved him to re-examine his own behavior as a highborn.

The same way that learning Latin and Greek in his youth had clarified so much about his own language, observing the small behavioral tics of a new set of highborns had clarified much about the ways men dealt with each other. Ordowahl found a new ease at intuiting the differences from one fellow to the next, how each would respond to praise, to criticism, or to questions.

He knew for a fact that certain attributes—speed, strength, sharp vision—could not be taught, only enhanced. Many more subtle things could be learned whole: how to assess an opponent, how to study him, how to guess his next move, how to disguise one's own intentions.

He admired the fact that, as a teacher of men, he could put himself above personal matters. When he refused to discuss Gnade Grace, the questions died.

Then there was training the body to respond before the mind did, in endless drills until each stroke, each step, each smooth twist of the body preceded thought.

Ordowahl realized that Mage Heorald had made him into an observer, and of himself as well as others. One more easily figured something out, understood it, after paying attention while experiencing it, then reflecting on the memory afterward.

He had always paid close attention to little things. That had helped him reach uncanny skill in military arts even before his Manhood day. Highborn folk came to Hammaborg from increasing distances. They had heard about Ordowahl as an instructor even more than as a giant, and he always had several men to tutor.

One day a pupil made an unguarded remark. "Prince Nordweg, have you picked up any of the scandals of this place? I have a cousin twice removed whose aunt came here fifteen years ago and was ruined!"

Euwart did his best to keep the news of Klarenz from escaping the city. Am I going to ruin that? "Do tell! Yes, I heard something about that myself. You never know what fate may hand you when you travel to a distant place." He waited a moment to see whether the student would continue with that topic. Changing the subject too soon would be as unwise as not changing it at all.

"Distant!" said the student. "How distant are you from your home? And what odd things has fate handed you?"

"Oho!" Ordowahl said, showing a wolfish grin. "Six dead Vikings, a rescued town seventy leagues northward from here? And now, students to discipline. Up your sword and shield. Show me your best feint-and-attack!"

*__*__*__*

Weeks devoted to tutoring kept Ordowahl away from Klarenz's steelworks. He came back at the end of an October afternoon to find Klarenz firing many swords in a coal-fed hearth of sufficient length to heat an entire sword. At least a dozen lay in the fire. Brutus tended it, taking care to keep the flame bright while Hanryk cranked a huge bellows.

Klarenz picked up a sword blank that glowed bright yellow-orange to examine it.

"Klarenz! Tell me what I'm looking at."

"Ah, Liege!" Klarenz turned to Ordowahl and gestured at Hanryk to slow the bellows for a time. He pulled up a stool. "Sit with me if it please you, Liege. I've been trying many variations.

Here are fourteen sword blanks. A few of them may actually be good."

"Only a few? Yet I see all of them are in the hearth at once. Which ones are good, which not?"

"I will need an expert swordsman to help me learn that, Liege. Let me explain them!" Klarenz jumped up, pulled out the sword he'd been examining, and plunged it into a tall, slender cask of melted beef fat. Flame spewed upward. The scent of roasting masked the stink of coal. After a long moment the flames died away. Klarenz counted to five then pulled out the sword. He laid it on a bench. "Ah! No clinky-pingy sound. It didn't crack." He looked pleased with himself.

"That seemed to be a deliberate, calculated act, Klarenz."

"Quenching a sword, Liege, must be done when the metal is at a specific heat, which its color tells you. That hardens the sword. Yet, if done more than two or three times, the metal becomes useless, the ruin of much hard work. This blank was ready for the quench. It is still very hot to the touch, yet safe for a close look."

Ordowahl surveyed the blank. He had seen armorers' unfinished work before; perhaps the sight of a half-made sword was something foreign to Klarenz. He knew that Herr Schlach produced a few swords. Most of his output was nails, cooking spits, andirons, horseshoe blanks, iron hoops for wagon wheels and barrels, plus dozens of other domestic items that were easier to make than good weapons.

"Klarenz, have you ever worked with an armorer?"

"Liege, I've eaten many a midday meal picking the brains of Herr Schlach's swordsmith. I learned what I needed to."

"Yet I've seen sword smithies in Nordweg and some of the unfinished goods they had in them. This doesn't look familiar. Even fresh out of the fire, it's as smooth as if you've spent days putting it to a grindstone."

"Liege, I never got a close look at Master Schmidt's work. Can't be helped. I listened to him while he worked, to learn what he had to teach. Then I did him one better."

Ordowahl sighed. "Do you ever tire of people doubting you, Klarenz? Each new idea sounds impossible, or sometimes inane. For instance, besting a master based on chat."

Klarenz tried to smile.

"Liege, a highborn's doubt is like a horse sitting down on me. The horse gets up every time and sometimes may even give me a ride on his back, if you will take the metaphor. Each time, the doubt becomes happiness and pride. Of course, Liege, I get weary of the horse that continually comes to sit on me."

Ordowahl shook his head and sighed. "Yes, Klarenz. I believe that you will surpass Master Schmidt the same as you've surpassed Master Meinz. Now describe your new ideas and remember to give your listener time to absorb them at his own pace, one by one."

"Yes indeed, Liege! First, a sword with only one sharp edge will be lighter than one with two. If I simply leave off the second edge the sword will still be stiff and strong, as well as lighter. The few times I've seen you at sword practice I've noticed that often just one edge of your sword strikes the target. You may grip it either way, but once you've gripped it, the same edge almost always goes forward."

Ordowahl frowned. *Both sides of a sword can't get equal use. Blows sent forward have full strength while backhanded blows are always weaker.*

"Second, having only one edge lets me shape it into a curve. Consider this, Liege. At table, a knife with a slightly curved edge cuts better than a straight one. Why? The curved knife is more likely to slide through the meat. It cuts a slice. When you pull it toward you, you rock it to accentuate the slicing effect."

Ordowahl nodded. He imagined himself slicing meat with a curved knife.

"So, Liege, if you attack with a curved sword, its edge has a bias as it strikes. This means it will slice while driving through its target. Also, Damascus swords all curve. After much thought I believe that is the reason."

"Klarenz! You poke sword making in the eye two different

ways. Swords are straight, with two edges. Swords have a groove down the center, which also makes the sword lighter without losing strength. Tell me again why a bent one-edged sword will be a better weapon."

"Then there's the third difference, Liege."

Ordowahl raised his eyebrows in a patient, "please tell me more" look.

"When a weapon cuts, you don't want its sides to drag. The weapon should be polished until you can see yourself in it. To be that slippery, it must be a mirror."

"Klarenz! Am I supposed to pause, preen, examine my face in its mirror surface before wielding it? Now you have left your senses!"

"Please give me your patience, Liege. It must own such a gloss that it *could* be a mirror. That way, when you wield it in combat, it will glide through whatever it strikes like a carving knife through butter."

"I'm still struggling with the image of using a lady's dressing table implement as a weapon, Klarenz. As always, you will silence those who doubt you. I believe you will prove that shiny swords outdo plain ones."

"Thank you, Liege. So far I've told you something that applies to every sword here. Now let me tell you why there are so many of them."

"Please do, Klarenz. I'm still struck by the way you're about to poke poor Master Schmidt in all three of his eyes. So tell me why there are so many swords?"

"Liege, I made many versions to be sure that at least one is good enough. Some of these began as three layers of steel, some as five. I have several of each. I will make both straight and curved weapons from each type."

"I see. Can I work out each one's lineage just by looking at them, or does each one carry a special mark?"

"I've marked them, Liege. The Ulfbehrt swords were supposed to have an inlay of gray steel, hammer welded into the blade up near the hilt when its shaping was complete, prior to the quench. I've done the same to mark each blade. The mark is difficult to see now. When the sword is complete it will be distinct."

"Mirror!" Ordowahl mused. "If your aim is to make it slippery to the touch, why not oil it?"

"That's easy enough, Liege. We can see what each blade does when it's merely smooth enough to gleam, again when it has a polish. Would you like to place a small wager on the outcome?"

Ordowahl couldn't suppress a grin. "Klarenz, nobody ever gets past you. That day may come, good my fief. When it does I pray to be there myself, to offer you a mug of ale and a kind face. Until then, good my fief, I exult to have access to a craftsman who beggars earthly description."

"Klarenz, you left off making steel to focus on hammering out swords for six weeks now. When I talked to Master Schmidt—" Klarenz flinched, "—he said he thought you'd spend a week or more on each sword. Yet you have fourteen, each one ready to be made smooth and sharp." *Father in heaven, thank you for the gift of this plain man who assumes little. He makes the incredible seem commonplace.*

"Liege, I know you didn't tell him much, but the thought of the two of you discussing swords—I don't know what to say."

"That's easy then, Klarenz, don't say it. I think I understand the horse sitting on you that you mentioned a while ago."

"Sorry, Liege! I am truly sorry! The image of Master Schmidt—Liege, he's no dummy!"

"How well I know that, Klarenz. He may have learned a thing or two at our expense. How does that compare to you picking his brain for half a year? Put your mind at peace, good my fief. He assumes that your efforts have produced multiple blades. That would be simple common sense. He also told me that Herr Schlach is fascinated by the fact that your slag pile seems to consist of broken pottery. He is envious of your technique. In fact, his whole shop is experimenting with clay."

Klarenz mused for a moment.

"He'd naturally do that. I hope he doesn't ruin his prosperity chasing after something he's very, very unlikely to achieve. So, Liege, he realizes I'm working on multiple swords. Does he understand anything about what might make them special?"

"Well, as long as no one suggests combining varieties of steel into one weapon, he may not think of it himself."

"How many swords does he think I'm making?"

"You've been at it a month and a half, so he's used six fingers doing the arithmetic."

"Liege, don't demean him. Master Schmidt has a good head."

"Of course you're right, Klarenz. He has had to guess at the number. He thinks four would be an impressive gift for Prince Euwart."

"Indeed! Knowing our purpose, he pictures us achieving it the same way he would. Now, Liege, let me show you where we are." Klarenz turned to look past his workbench, to demonstrate yet another innovation.

"Here is my sword press. Each sword comes from the fire bright yellow-orange and relatively soft. Each hammer-blow leaves a low spot. Can't be helped. I wanted to think of something special to keep the layers smooth inside each of the swords."

"You didn't mention the smoothness of this sword."

"Right, Liege. I also need them to get longer without spreading out. I'm not ready to pull them, though the idea is tempting. Did you peer into the hearth to see how much the blanks resemble each other?"

"I did. They seemed too free of the uneven surface every sword blank acquires from constant pounding. Yet I heard your constant pounding, too."

"Yes, Liege. If Master Schmidt were to sneak by he'd wonder what we were up to. Brutus, Hanryk, and I swing sledge hammers, not mallets—all three of us at once."

"I see. Do you each hit the blank on a different spot?"

"We don't hit the blank at all."

Ordowahl's eyebrows rose. "What do you hit?"

Klarenz glowed. "Liege, I made bottom and top mold halves such that when a sword reaches full length and proper thinness, the halves will meet. We have to pry them apart before the whole thing welds into one boar pig, if you will."

Ordowahl looked at a flat metal object embedded in a bed of oak boles cut to the same height, held together with long bolts. It was the sight of this steel forming table face that amazed him.

A narrow, two-foot-long groove ran down its center, three fat fingers wide. The inch-deep trough had vertical sides the color of a sword's blade, but far too smooth. It reminded Ordowahl of the surface of Prince Euwart's finest silver serving tray.

"Klarenz? You made this?"

Klarenz basked. "Liege, it is the female half of the mold. The beater stands next to it. The hot, soft blank goes in. The male half goes down on top of it. Then we strike."

He motioned toward his assistants. They raised a massive piece of steel that had leaned against the forming table.

Ordowahl saw another very regular work face, this time with a raised portion that looked like an exact fit for the mold.

The external face showed heavy wear from long hammering.

"So the softened blank goes in. The top mold comes down. The three of you strike it with sledge hammers. I would guess that the blank cools almost at once, though. Doesn't it?"

"That's the way of it, Liege. I built the mold halves with very, very hard steel on the inner faces, soft iron on the outside. I put it to use once I had some steel to make into sword blanks. With fourteen in the fire, there is always a hot one ready for the mold. In fact, we have to splash water on the mold from time to time. I also had to choose which side of the blank would taper to an edge. The other becomes the back. With fourteen blanks, it has been necessary to form eighteen edges."

"Eighteen?"

"Yes, Liege. I made four traditional blades with two edges and a center groove. The ordinary method of forming an edge is to beat on one side of the blank so it gets thinner, then grind some of it away. With the mold I only needed to add edge and fuller blanks to the mold to do accomplish the same thing."

Klarenz nodded to Brutus, who had been following the conversation. A broad smile formed as he picked up two long, narrow, wedge-shaped pieces. He showed them to Ordowahl.

"So! One of these goes under the blank, one goes over it before the mold comes down. After several trips back and forth, the blank has an actual edge."

"That's the idea, Liege. The three-layer and five-layer blanks tended to squeeze all the layers very thin at the edge. Each morning when the blanks are cold Brutus and Hanryk do grind off a portion of the outermost layer. The finished edge consists entirely of hard steel from the center of the blade."

Ordowahl took a close look at the blanks. "Aha!" he said. "Klarenz, this one is straight! In fact, they all are straight! Your mold is straight and your blades are straight."

"Right you are, Liege. What do you think might happen to heated steel? How difficult would it be to add a bit of curve, before the hardening quench?"

Unchallenged by the ease of this good life,
Ord shows his awe when Klarenz masters steel.
Prince Ordo studies other men—but wife?
He's "milked the cow" yet thinks of Grace piece-meal.
    Sweet Gnade Grace has fallen from his view.
    So is he gone from hers? He doesn't know.
    What might be next, between them? Something new?
    So smart, and yet he glims no "quid-pro-quo."
Across so short a time, half-dozen weeks,
the dancing and romancing pass him by.
He takes her smiles and sex, and never speaks
to her in honeyed words, "My butterfly."
    We've seen him talking metal with his fief;
    So, Gnade Grace—mere sexual relief?

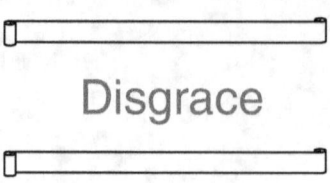

Disgrace

August and September came and went, giving way to October when he heard, "Mein Herr Prince?"

Ordowahl sensed the ice in her voice. When he turned around he saw it in her face. "Gnade Grace, how are you?"

"You have to ask! We are lovers, you and I. We are bound to each other in God's eyes, if not yet in the eyes of Hammaborg. It wounds me, mein Herr Prince, that you even ask. I feel betrayed. I feel cast aside. Where are the hugs, the smiles, the many kisses and nakednesses we've shared?"

"Gnade? I can only say the things I have to say in a frank manner. It was wonderful, at first, to have you come to me to offer your naked embrace. I admit this. It was wonderful. I remember the joyful abandon. Then it stopped being wonderful, because each time we came together, it began with you coming to me."

"Yes!" She was shouting. "Yes! *I* had to come to *you*! Do you realize how undignified that is? We are lovers, you and I. Yet do you bring me gifts? I bring you the gift of myself, and you seem, if I dare say this, you seem to accept me as Hammaborg's gift to you, which you are free to enjoy as publicly as possible!"

"I see. Yet when I stopped sharing you in public, as you put it, the only result is that you've become unhappy. The open sharing didn't upset you. Rather, ending the public display caused your anger. Tell me I am wrong."

She fumed. "Wrong? Of course you are wrong. I've never met a man who seemed so able to be right, then I find that he, I mean you, turned out to be just like every other man!"

"That, Gnade, is what has been bothering me. You've had many men. When will you move on to the next one, or the next dozen for that matter?"

Stunned disbelief blanked her face; she dissolved into tears. "Ordowahl," she sobbed, "How absolutely unkind, how unfair! If you took me, you took me. Once you had me, I was yours. Do you now call me lurid names? Beloved idiot, please don't insult me in such a tawdry, desperate way." She threw herself onto him.

Ordowahl didn't move. He didn't wrap arms around her or yield a consoling smile.

"Gnade, when you became mine, so to speak, it was plain that you had belonged to other men before me. In fact, as I've put your history together, I doubt your ability to number the men to whom you've belonged already. If by some personal failure I were to take you to wife, perhaps the only way I could guarantee your body's loyalty to mine would be to wear you inside my belt. What would you think of that?"

She pushed away from him, pounding on his belly with all her might.

"Ouch! You make my fists hurt! The more time I spend around you, the more injury I receive. Ordowahl, I demand that you respect my situation. Give me the honor I am due. We made Christian love. Now, at this moment, the three of us—you, I, and our developing infant—yes, I am pregnant—are on the verge of something wonderful. Aren't you thrilled to know that we have a child? I treasure the tiny thing growing inside me. How can you not bend down this instant, put your ear to my womb to hear the new heartbeat!"

Ordowahl frowned. "Gnade, I know the timing of these things. If, as you say, my child grows in your womb, it's still so tiny that even you may not feel the first fluttering of life, much less imagine to hear its heartbeat."

"Highness, Prince, you may belittle and disregard me if you wish. But what I say is true. Now as for your habit of quoting Holy Scripture, measure yourself by what Saint Paulus said in his first letter to the Kirche in Corinth:
'Know ye not that your bodies are the members of Christ? Shall I then take the members of Christ and make them the members of a harlot? God forbid. What? Know ye not, that he which is joined to a harlot, is one body?'"

She gleamed at him. "Ordowahl, we are one body, and God has blessed our union. The bond between us two is rewarded by God, sanctified by this gift. Now you simply must see that the right thing to do here is not to run from me. I am yours, you are mine. We now have a son, or perhaps a daughter," she said with coy dimples, "which, you will see, is your firstborn. The gift of this child will bless your life."

His eyes went flat and he drew one calming breath, hiding inner turmoil at hearing a lie. "If I understand you, being named a harlot doesn't trouble you? Thus you expect me to join with the bodies of an unguessable line of other men as well. Tell me that I understand you, because I hear you telling me to become enjoined with all of the able-bodied men of this town, all the noble men who have visited Hammaborg since you became able to, er, 'comfort' men, plus visiting sailors and acrobats? I believe, Gnade, that I am not first with you. You also aren't first with me. Which of those women should I be wed to? The tangle of bodies which you describe includes them as well. How many other men would take you to wife?"

Gnade's face froze. She would not try a second round of tears. For the moment she had run out of answers. She recovered. "Such impoverished untruths!" Her voice became a scream. "How dare you attack the virtue of a woman you've been intimate with on so many occasions! You have used me, you have gotten me with child! You are Klarenz's wretched apprentice and a horrible ass!"

She stalked away.

The town square, which she had chosen for this encounter, now held a growing audience.

Ordowahl looked at them with a question in his eyes, as if to ask, "Did you see that as I saw it? She is daft!"

As one, the townspeople showed him grim tolerance—he was, after all, nobility. What he read behind those noncommittal faces astonished him.

Everyone's view of Gnade was kind. She was one of theirs. Since she was pregnant (how else?) noble or not his plain duty was to give the child his name by taking Gnade to wife. He could see that they imagined only one outcome—Gnade's.

*___*___*___*

Ordowahl knew there would be a repercussion, so used what he hoped would be tact. He moved out of the palace. The next day a knock sounded on the door of his rented room. He got up from eating supper to answer it.

"Stay seated, Klarenz, this can only be for me."

He opened the door. It was Rigomonde. A burly footman stood beside her. Behind them in the lane was a magnificent coach and driver. One or two passersby made a point of not staring.

"Good evening, Prince Ordowahl."

"Please come in, Princess Rechtmann," Ordowahl said with as much formality as he could. "Shall I send my fief Klarenz outside while we chat?"

She stepped inside; the footman shut the door behind her. "He may stay, Prince. While this is between nobles, I doubt he will learn anything new. His opinion is of no consequence in the first place. You surprise me, showing concern for a wretched servant."

Ordowahl stared for a moment then regained his composure. "If you please, Princess, my furnishings are modest. Can you sit down with me? To chat, at least? I would not be so bold as to ask you to share my humble meal."

"I am told, Prince, that you enjoy passable food. I can smell something good, in fact. I didn't visit for small talk over a snack."

Ordowahl went down onto one knee to speak face to face. "Please help me to use your time well, Princess. How can I serve you?"

"You can help me, Prince, to understand things which cause great unhappiness in this City, in the household of poor Gnade's parents, and in the palace. We are astonished that you have brought things to this state. How did this happen? Did you decide that your responsibility to uphold a prince's higher standard of self control was void when far from home?"

She looked at him, eye to eye. "Did you decide that making yourself a pariah thus no longer fit for Hammaborg was worth the passing lusts that Gnade promoted in you? Did you forget your position as a stranger in this City? Despite Gnade's shortcomings, we find her a winsome human being. We are very fond of her. She is, when not under the duress of her carnal pastimes, a very kind young woman. Everyone loves her."

What Rigomonde said was true, as far as it went.

"Now," she continued, "where you are concerned, we carefully admire this or that yet fear you for your size and great martial ability. To be truthful, your worth in our City ends there."

Ordowahl looked at the floor. He had suspected as much, for his station in Hammaborg.

"How did you think we would react when you chose to deny your responsibility as a father? Really, Ordowahl, noble young men leave many bastards behind them. It is done. Not, however, amongst those with Gnade's high standing in our City's life. You may answer me now, but I will only allow you a few minutes, then I must go. Speak to me."

"Princess, you understand much. I have little to add. I failed to govern my lust. I have no excuse. My behavior, my frequent acceptance of Gnade's naked embrace, shames me. I believe that, if she is with child, it isn't mine. To me she is—was— someone who needed me. That plus her effect of such animal joy, erased my better judgment. The rest has been an unpleasant surprise."

Rigomonde failed to suppress a sneer.

He ignored it. "That is what I have to say, Princess. Much of your criticism is accurate. I am at fault. If she turns out not to be pregnant, this situation will be simple. Is that not so? If there is a child and if I am its father, then I will of course adopt and raise it. Under no circumstance will I compound my fault by joining the brood mare of Hammaborg to the Royal House of Nordweg."

He looked at Rigomonde, until she dropped her eyes.

"Thank you, Prince, for your point of view," she said, and stalked out.

He turned to give Klarenz a questioning look. "Good my fief, you see me at my lowest. I have sinned, yet cannot find solid footing for surrendering to Lady Rigomonde."

Klarenz could only shrug.

*__*__*__*

The next afternoon the sun, low in the western sky, made it difficult to see well. Ordowahl and a half -dozen healthy young men, all in full armor, were practicing the arts of war.

Klarenz, off to the side among many other footmen, knew what they would ask about. *Liege, sometimes your brilliance overawes me, and sometimes you play the simple fool.*

Ordowahl began his lesson. "Men, you must learn to read shadows when your opponent has a low sun at his back, such as early in the morning or late in the afternoon. Tell me how you might handle this situation, Egeno."

"Prince, tell me how you might handle your own situation!" His other pupils laughed. "I would," Egeno continued, "with the Grace of sunlight in my eyes, embrace the light." Their laughter increased.

Ordowahl ignored the banter. "Well said, Egeno. Move out of your opponent's shadow to put the sunlight as far behind you as you can."

"And your lovely sunlight, Prince. How far behind you have you managed to move her?" Louder laughter. Egeno added,

"Prince, all of the men who've had Gnade's expert, vigorous comfort find her a happy companion. We keep her friendship. This City's people do love her. So what if she has her hooks into you, Prince? So what if she won't let go? Please understand that your predicament is humorous, to us. We don't scorn you but find your situation, well, it makes us laugh."

Ordowahl looked at all of his pupils. "My friends, I do see your point of view. My own laughter is impossible. Now let's use your time, also mine since you are paying for it, on martial arts, rather than marital inartfulness."

They chuckled, and got back to business.

*__*__*__*

That evening, another rap at the door. Klarenz had begun to prepare supper. Ordowahl opened the door himself and a different footman handed him a written message.

MY DEAR PRINCE NORDWEG, I HAVE HEARD OUT MY PRINCESS RIGOMONDE'S ANGER AT YOUR FRANK AND, SHALL I SAY, HARDLY REPENTANT ANSWER WHEN SHE VISITED YOU YESTERDAY.

PLEASE MAKE ME THE GIFT OF YOUR TIME SO THAT WE MAY DISCUSS THIS FURTHER.

I HAVE SENT A COACH. I ASK YOU TO RETURN IN IT AS SOON AS YOU ARE CLOTHED IN A MANNER SUITABLE FOR A DISCUSSION BETWEEN PRINCES.

"Klarenz, my supper must wait. Feed yourself. When I return I may not, or more likely will, be hungry." Without bothering to do more than slap his clothing to remove any traces of leaves, grass, and dust that may have come through his leather-and-mail armor, Ordowahl left.

He found Euwart waiting at the top of the castle steps. "Thank you for your promptness, Prince Nordweg. It compliments you." Euwart's grim face showed that he interpreted Ordowahl's quick arrival as failure to make any effort to dress up.

"Please tell the Lady Rechtmann, Prince Euwart, that I considered frankness appropriate and truth, as it appears to me at any rate, to carry no insult."

"Interesting that you would use that word, Prince Nordweg. By failing to keep yourself chaste, you've shown this City—its prince in particular—that you value a naked cunt more than your good name, more than your noble rank."

Still two steps below the threshold, Ordowahl looked Euwart in the eye. He was surprised to find the answering stare intimidating. *He reminds me that I am an isolated presence here, now also past unwanted, to indefensible. I cannot argue that.* "Prince Rechtmann, it is beyond dispute that I misjudged the woman owning the cunt. Yes, I have placed House Nordweg into disrespect. I am grateful to you for your attention."

"Don't be! You've managed to upset the City—my City. When it's upset, I must act. I first sent Princess Rigomonde to you. While you admit fault, you don't appear to understand the gravity of your offense, both upon Gnade and her very esteemed parents, thus on the City and therefore on me."

"Herr Rechtmann, you are correct. As an outsider I did not understand what I found here. I failed to anticipate the unpleasant consequences you describe. Yet, speaking as prince of a noble House and son of the king of a powerful realm, I ask leave to present these circumstances to you in my own light. I ask you to hear me without prejudice."

Euwart dropped some of the stiffness from his face. "Come this way," he said, leading Ordowahl in and back to the book-stuffed library. A servant followed them to light several candles. The smell of burning wax and the flickering flames seemed to settle the mood into one of reflection. "Please, Prince, you are, so far, a guest. Sit down with me. Present your case."

Each took a chair, settled back into it and crossed his legs. Genteel behaviors fostered a superficial mood of quiet tact.

Once again Ordowahl felt awe at the wealth of learning stored on the room's many full shelves. He began, "Simply put, Prince, I failed to grasp the complexity of a place that has three sorts of people, not two. Nordweg doesn't have Hammaborg's concentrated industry and commerce. Thus it has no lowborn who are also wealthy, hence powerful. I have deep regret for not understanding both that they aren't really lowborn and how to behave toward them."

He continued, "Second, Prince, when my bondman Klarenz—if I may be so frank—made a highborn young woman pregnant, he almost lost his life, and twice at that. The fact that she was not a virgin when he first laid eyes on her is not at issue—rather, the fact that the honor of House Rechtmann, and of the City of Hammaborg, had been compromised."

He waited for Euwart to betray a reaction; there was none. He continued. "Yet I understand from Lady Rechtmann and from you, Prince Rechtmann, that you believe it appropriate for House Nordweg to sacrifice a potential future king to take as wife and future queen a lowborn woman comparable to Klarenz in her careless promiscuity. Have I made my point?"

Euwart quoted, "Brood mare of Hammaborg?"

"Or 'a tool he would do well to be without'?"

"You continually surprise me, Prince Nordweg. We will not, I hope, need to discuss this further. While you haven't moved my own opinion on any matter, including that wretched fellow's tool, I comprehend your statements. Noble houses either compromise or risk deadly conflict."

Euwart steepled his fingers. "My compromise will be to endure the unaltered consequences to Gnade and to Hammaborg. I suggest that yours will be to leave—soon."

"Thank you, Prince Rechtmann." Ordowahl stood and bowed. He exited the library and walked alone through the entrance hall, out of the castle, and back to his rented room. He ignored the many stares along the way.

Forgive me, Father. I cannot find Christian admiration or love for that man. I recognize that he is acting exactly as he must. Yet I am not ready to show him the broken and *contrite heart that I bring to you. My guilt is before You always. Why do I refuse to show it to him? Amen.*

The townspeople continued to see Ordowahl as a flagrant scoundrel. They knew that Gnade enjoyed herself with many. Her time of such enjoyment seldom lasted very long, and her manner showed such pleasant equanimity that they overlooked her youthful "vigor."

Ordowahl had been the first man ever to tire of her before she tired of him. That shocked them. A true prince would either have shown the discretion to stay away from her nakedness, or honored the fact that she adored him, not cast her aside after casual use. With a little luck she might have once again grown bored. Didn't he understand at least this much? Even if not, he could do far worse. She had everyone's good will, decent beauty, was nobody's fool, and lastly, most importantly, carried a child.

His.

*__*__*__*

"What was for supper, Klarenz?"

"It's waiting for you, Liege. Surely Prince Rechtmann didn't waste time persuading you, nor did he let you waste his time, either. Neither of you have moved the other's thinking. At least each has heard the other and made a truce."

"Your frankness, Klarenz, to speak of your liege lord with such calm analysis, is offset by your insight. I marvel at you. Promise me to stay healthy and close by."

They sat on two modest chairs at a small table. This furniture plus two beds almost filled the room. They ate. Ordowahl was convinced that he now, in this rented hovel, had better food than was served in the castle. Food was one thing. Understanding others was much more important.

"Klarenz, it is clear that I need to learn from this situation. Tell me, with freedom as a tutor instructing a backward student, what you've seen that I have not."

"Liege, you had to have seen her coming. Is this a new thing to you, that you haven't had women throwing themselves on you since before the time you had a tool to use with them?"

"Well, Klarenz, no. Until the day I left my home in

Nordweg, what you describe did not happen. Go on."

"Hmmm. Yes, I've seen you around young women. You actually appear blind to them. This is a pity! Well enough then, you didn't understand that when Gnade approached you she was interested in you as a swive-mate, or at least a behind-a-bush fuck, or whatever. Liege, I didn't tell you what I observed. I regret that. Even then, pupil-Liege, after she first achieved intimacy with you—in the bushes, of all places!—you could have turned her aside."

"That is hindsight, Klarenz. In fact I considered how, and failed!"

"You may understand this as hindsight. To me it was obvious at once. Yes, I lay sleeping in bed at the time, and the next day all of Hammaborg knew your 'secret.' You also asked me how to deal with her, long after you had made swiving a habit. I didn't find a way to say it, Liege. The longer you continued, the more deeply enmeshed you became."

"Supposing I had the self-governance to turn her aside after that first, what, moonlight romp: what then?"

"Liege, her pattern says that she'd have moved on. Soon enough I could have pointed out her newest partner in rut. You'd have been publicly free of her."

"Tell me this then, tutor-fief. How is it that she has never become pregnant before, yet seems to be now, so soon after she has begun 'comforting' me?"

"Ah! Pupil-liege, there are herbs which, if taken at the right moment, will prevent pregnancy. It is my sorry fault that I haven't carried them with me, Liege. Be that as it may, over-use of them is known to interfere with a woman's becoming pregnant later on."

"Yet she appears pregnant now."

"Count with me, liege, the weeks of your dalliance."

"Klarenz, that sum is nine and one-half."

"Yet, I am told with some authority from a midwife I shared great comforts with several years ago, that from rut to lying-in takes three-quarters of a year. She told me the ways in which a woman knows that she is with child, chiefly that her monthly flow does not happen. That is at two to three weeks: you've had ten. So there has certainly been time. She told me that a woman becomes visibly pregnant after fifteen to seventeen weeks. The sign is subtle, a barely noticeable prominence of the belly. At about that time her teats begin to grow larger. At nine months, well, I'm sure you've seen that often enough."

"Indeed, Klarenz. So five months spans the time from just-visible swelling to impending birth."

"Now, Liege, bear with me. Four months is seventeen weeks, and you've had at most ten. From the moment she begins to look as though she may be pregnant, count back seventeen weeks, no less. In my judgment it's likely that she decided to keep an unexpected child in order to safeguard her ability to bear children in the first place. More importantly, Liege, she likely used it to collect the best possible husband."

"So, tutor-fief, I learn that I've been swindled by someone well beloved by the City of Hammaborg and have made a habit of not taking the right step."

"Yes. In so many words, yes. You've told me how much you've learned to admire women, in your very recent experiences of them. I understand you better now, pupil-Liege. Your limited understanding has come from few encounters, with few women. Moreover, those women were also unlike most of their sex. Now everyone shows you open disgust. They want you to quit this place. Nobody expects you to surrender to Gnade, no matter how much they seem to harp on that. They just want you to leave."

"Indeed, Klarenz—Herr Schlach no longer wants you to return to his foundry. He stopped me on the way out of Mass this morning to make it clear that, while a prince can do as he pleases, the City of Hammaborg will be a happier place once it can forget it knew me. To her credit, Ermintrude Helmbloch tried to cheer me up. She is a remarkable individual, Klarenz. She was my tutor again—'Keep a calm outward appearance; ignore any unkindnesses that you may encounter.' I already

agreed with her on that, as a matter of fact. Her charity meant a
lot to me."

His tenure at an end, Ord's pride is all
that's left. His pupils still take lessons but
the one accept'ble plan for Ordowahl
is "Klarenz finds a way to crack this nut."
    Grace-Gnade shamed him in the public square
    And Rigomonde shamed him to his face.
    Prince Euwart showered scorn on Ord's affair;
    that gift he's waited for? Ord holds one ace.
One ray of hope, his tutor knows his heart.
She bids him persevere until it's done.
So what else can a young man do? His part.
He's royal while the sky has moon and sun.
    Prince Ordowahl has failed this time around.
    Fief Klarenz up; his liege must go to ground.

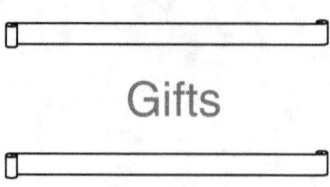

Gifts

Ordowahl, exercising Hammerfoot, rode toward Klarenz's ironwork. The wet chill of a cloudy mid-December day set a lid on his spirits. *I hope that he is near to completing Euwart's gift—his impatience to see me gone would irritate me almost as much as my brothers' did. I can't blame him. Yet, turn tail, run like a cur? Impossible! So let me see what my miracle craftsman, God's undeserved gift, has made.*

Haze dimmed the near-winter sun. Inside the ironwork the forge sat cold. Instead several tens of candles, an extravagance, lit the area where Hanryk, Brutus, and Klarenz shared the work of polishing the blades, none of which had handles yet.

"Liege, do you have any idea how hard it is to polish a blade?— polish it to a mirror sheen, while avoiding its razor edge?"

"Klarenz? I don't remember the last time I heard you complain."

"Yah, I guess. Even though I didn't have a workable idea, it seemed I could finish in a reasonable amount of time."

"And what do you call reasonable?"

"If a sword in Master Schmidt's end of the shop takes a week, from rough iron to finished weapon, how long should it take to give one a good polish?"

"Ask yourself, Klarenz, how long it takes to polish a mirror.

182

I've heard of brass mirrors. Brass is much softer than steel."

"Yes, Liege, it is. Even with you keeping me apart from other people the way a mother hen shoos ducklings from water, I found a mirror polisher. He gave me a lot to think about."

Ordowahl smiled. "So, you've been polishing steel with your mind?"

"Of course I know about honing stones. Very fine ones come from a place fifty or more leagues south and west of here."

"I see. West, hence you're not eager to travel there to get any."

"Hammaborg is a trading city, Liege. Everything useful comes here. Let me show you my polishing area." He went over to a low table with a soft cloth draped across it.

A blade lay on the table, plus several flat, off-yellow stones on a leather pad. A few stained pieces of cloth and small bowls of water, rust, ash, and fine river silt completed the kit.

"Rust? Dirt?"

"Yah. They polish steel. The problem comes when you try to make them into a fine powder. Did you know that the best mortar and pestle wear away when you try to reduce these in it?"

"So you're telling me that if I want to hollow out a mortar and reduce a pestle, rust and ash are the things to use."

"Right! Liege, I considered making new pies of too-blue steel, until I located some useful lumps in a corner."

"So if they're too hard to work then there's no way to form them into pestle and mortar? Or is there?"

"It was a close thing, Liege. Putting them back into plain clay then breaking down the oven at its hottest—Liege, you have no idea what hot is until you've tried that—I got both pieces malleable enough to form into useful shapes."

Ordowahl noticed two odd-looking lumps of metal on a corner of Klarenz's workbench. "Your mortar and pestle? Klarenz, I am beginning to think you can solve anything."

"Thank you, Liege. Now to the real issue. With an everyday granite grindstone Master Schmidt can bring a blade to a useful condition in a day, maybe two. That mold over there"—he waved toward the forming bench—"gave me blanks that were already close, with no work marks to grind away. I only needed to reduce the whole edge to one fine, smooth state."

Ordowahl looked around. He saw that the half-dozen blades still unsheathed already looked finished. "Brutus and Hanryk have helped you with this?"

"Liege, you'd be surprised. I taught them to make long, even strokes against the grindstone to make a fine edge. They have the knack. These first blades are both straight and knife sharp."

"And?"

"To reach a final good polish and bring each edge to true razor sharpness, add hilts, and make good sheathes has taken three months so far. Don't frown, so, Liege. Please trust me on this. I'll hold back one straight sword, knife-sharp, not polished. Then we can compare the effect of that one to what a polished, razor-sharp blade can do."

Ten days passed. Under a gray winter sky in air chilled by a drizzle, a proud mood proved elusive. All around them, denuded trees made a spotty forest with areas of holly and tall dead grass. A still-warm beef carcass, intact with horns, hoofs, and hide, lay on mottled snow and dun-colored leaves at the foot of a tall oak.

"This has to be more than the waste of a good beef, Klarenz. What do you have in mind?"

"Liege, this tree has a stout branch ten feet up with nothing beneath it. I will dangle the carcass from this limb on a good rope. Brutus, Hanryk." Klarenz motioned at his two assistants.

They tied a rope to the hind hooves of the animal. Klarenz tossed its other end over the limb. With Klarenz pushing from below, Brutus and Hanryk hoisted the five-hundred-pound carcass until it swung free of the ground, and tied the rope securely around the trunk.

"Liege, please show me what a decently sharp sword can do." Klarenz retrieved the plain sword from a bundle holding several with a mirror finish.

Ordowahl examined the hilt, pommel, hand guard, and blade. "Nice fuller, Klarenz. If Master Schmidt could see the symmetry of your blood-groove down the shaft of this sword, he would call you a worthy apprentice."

Klarenz took the faint praise in stride. He couldn't recall coming off second best in any comparison. He held his tongue.

"Liege, can you swing this sword through the ribs into the spine of this animal?"

"I'm not sure. Striking this sort of target isn't something I've done before, Klarenz. God in heaven knows how many different strokes a swordsman learns. This is a very basic one. Yet, a whole beef!"

He took the sword in both hands, waggled it to get its feel, and stepped in front of the dangling carcass. He drew the sword back, held a half-breath, tensed, and took the cleanest yet most forceful swing he could. The blade sank far into the animal. He severed two ribs and embedded the blade into the spine. Blood trickled out of the carcass where the sword had gone in.

After several good heaves at the blade he pulled it back out. "Klarenz, I thought I might put a kink in this thing or break it trying to pull it out. When I look along the blade, it is unharmed. Good my fief, I am proud of you."

"Thank you, Liege. Now, I will take a turn." Klarenz pulled a gleaming blade from the bundle. It was oddly curved, with only one sharp edge. While he was not a swordsman and nowhere near Ordowahl's size, working as a smith had made him strong.

Ordowahl saw the glitter of a mirror finish along the entire blade. "Let me see that," he said, taking it from Klarenz. He poised a thumb to feel its edge. Klarenz gasped. Brutus and Hanryk both made strangled noises; Ordowahl paused to look at them.

"Liege!" Klarenz pleaded. He stooped to pick up a dried grass stem, and ran it along the blade's edge. The grass seemed to slice through the blade, until Ordowahl realized that the blade was still there while half the frond had fallen to the ground. Klarenz held up his half for Ordowahl to examine.

"It's as though a razor cut it!"

"Now, Liege, it's my turn." Klarenz took the weapon and repeated what he had seen: waggle the sword to get its heft and feel, draw back, then strike with controlled force.

He struck the carcass through the shoulder, a foot below Ordowahl's slice. He, too, buried the curved, gleaming blade into the spine.

"Ach, mein Gott in Himmel!" Ordowahl studied the way Klarenz extracted the sword, cleaned it, and laid it back in the bundle. He knelt to look at what the sword had done.

"Klarenz! Why was that sword so much sharper? Why aren't all swords made that sharp?"

"Liege, nobody bothers to polish them, so the edge can never challenge a razor's sharpness. Swords can be knife sharp. Yet even an Ulfbehrt could not take, nor hold, this kind of edge, for one thing because any steel that can survive shocks is too soft."

"So, hard steel and polish leave, what?—an edge you could shave with?"

"At least that sharp, Liege. At least that sharp and very hard. For someone with your reach, just the blade is an inch over two and one-half feet long."

"I see. How much of that was polish, how much hardness of the edge; how much was due to the curve?"

Klarenz knelt by a second bundle. He unrolled both of them. "I brought all of the swords, Liege." Twelve swords lay there, each in a snug leather sheath. "The sword you swung first is the only one I didn't polish. You noticed that it has only a stone-ground edge."

"Klarenz, nobody gets past you! The first sword was passable, yet other than its toughness, it is not a gift for Prince Euwart. Let me see the others. So, good my swordsmith—more than good, my fief—tell me about these."

One by one Klarenz removed each sword from its sheath. He looked at small marks of different-colored steel near each sword's hilt.

"Klarenz, I see your markings. None of them speak to me."

Klarenz examined each mark and described how it was

made—three layers, five, plus a few that he had doubled once, twice, or several times.

Ordowahl used each to strike the dangling remains: none failed to take a full slice.

"Klarenz, we might ruin a hundred beeves to learn the different natures of these swords. We will carry the meat back to Fridoric. What the slices fell on won't hurt the meat. If there's a decent roast or steak in here I'll ask Fridoric to hold it back for the four of us."

Klarenz cleaned the bloody blades with care to preserve their bright sheen then returned each to its sheath. Brutus and Hanryk loaded the strangely even slices back into the wagon. The two of them seemed to gloat. Ordowahl guessed that he was the only one surprised by their swords.

"That was clever, Klarenz. Set up the show by letting me cut half a slice then cut the same yourself. Made your cut through a shoulder! We must do that for Prince Euwart—and you will take the first cut again, not I."

"Liege, we understand how gifts work. I'm sure he will enjoy this one. Which sword do you think will please him best?"

"I'm thinking, Klarenz. He is a risk taker, so a curved sword might work well. Better yet, I'll give him two that are straight and have two edges and two that are curved."

*__*__*__*

"Ah, Nordweg. It's not good to see you, again. Come into the library with me. You may or may not be interested to know that Gnade's child will have a man to act as its father. I am told that the child should be born in the middle of January."

"Euwart, that may give your city some relief—my use of her is too recent to be its father."

"Perhaps you are not the father after all, which is just as well, because you won't return and try to seize the child from its mother. Now: Where will this demonstration take place?"

"Klarenz and I are prepared and have brought my gift. If the whole City sees what Klarenz's work can do, there is the likelihood that he will be forced to spend the rest of his life here making hundreds of them, eventually thousands."

"Ordowahl, you are too frank! You invite me to condemn you now to losing Klarenz and, as you suggest, see me set him up as master of a new guild."

"Yet I know you, Prince. You gave a promise that Klarenz will remain my fief, that he will go with me wherever I choose to go. So instead I propose a private place. If there is a ceiling, it should rise at least ten feet from the floor. You might choose potential allies whom you'd like to impress."

Euwart's smile was thin. "I believe that can be arranged.

"I'll need some kind of scaffold to suspend one or more fresh beeves above the ground."

"Also easy to arrange. So, you are going to display your gift's prowess against a dead foe."

"It's easier to see what it can do when nothing distracts the eye. I will not use the sword, Prince. First, Klarenz will take a sword he has made in the normal fashion. You will see it as a decent weapon, no less, no more. He will strike a beef first."

Prince Euwart nodded. "Then I suppose I will use a "special" sword, the better to understand how advanced it is. Is this correct?"

"Just so. From our private demonstration, you will gauge whether or not a public one should follow."

Euwart lifted a small bell and rang it. A servant standing outside the small room, just outside Ordowahl's sight, stepped forward. "Yes, Sire?"

"Send someone to locate Klarenz, and hang a fresh beef from a scaffold."

The servant had heard their conversation; he went immediately to do as asked. In moments Klarenz stood with them in the library, since he had come with Ordowahl.

"Klarenz, it's good to see you again. Lay your weapons on this table."

Klarenz placed his bundle on the table, which was barely large enough. He untied its leather cords and unrolled the fine, tanned leather wrapping to reveal five swords. He unsheathed each one.

The first was ordinary while the other four shone, two of standard, dual-edged form and two curved with a single edge. Each sword after the first looked as though smoothed by an angel's finger, with a polish so brilliant it was possible to count eyelashes in its reflection.

Conversation died, while Euwart stood over the table and examined each piece of Klarenz's art. "I must say, Nordweg, when you present a gift you make it look like one. I won't expect such a sheen to outlive a rough outing. Even so it is beautiful."

Klarenz looked at Ordowahl, who nodded. He offered up the ordinary sword, hilt first. Ordowahl said, "My Prince, I ask you whether this simple sword is at least ordinary."

Euwart examined it, hefted its weight, studied its workmanship, tested its edge, and put it back.

"Yes, Klarenz, you could pass yourself off as another Master Schmidt—in fact, this sword is more evenly crafted than most I have seen. You will show me what this sword can do. I don't expect to be surprised. I do want to see you use the thing."

Klarenz re-tied the bundle, and five more tense, silent minutes passed. When the servant returned, Euwart led them through the back part of the castle. They emerged in a small courtyard, where a beef hung, as asked.

"We must have privacy." Euwart said over his shoulder to the servant. "Complete privacy. See to it." He nodded toward a table at the side of the small courtyard, and Klarenz re-displayed the gifts.

Euwart looked at Klarenz. "Let me see you use your own sword."

Klarenz bowed and picked up the sword and stepped to the carcass. He twisted his torso, took a swing, and severed a rib.

"Lad, that was a goodly stroke. Ordowahl, I imagine that you will strike much farther into the animal than this?"

Ordowahl took the sword from Klarenz and, as he had before, buried it into the animal's spine.

Euwart steeled himself. The sight was a shock, no matter how often he'd seen Ordowahl teach military drill. He watched Ordowahl struggle to pull the blade back out and nodded when he saw that it had not been harmed.

"Prince, please choose one of the gift blades. Be careful with the edge. Klarenz assures me it is a true razor, if also a bit larger than one you might shave with."

Euwart picked up one of the two-edged blades and took a stance in front of the beef. He hefted the blade, gripped the hilt with both hands, and drew back.

"Please, Highness, if I may!" Klarenz trembled at the thought of interrupting the Royal House of Hammaborg; Prince Euwart just looked at him to see what he wanted to say.

"Prince, please consider your balance, in case the blade carries through the entire carcass. Please, Your Grace, I don't wish to be impertinent."

Euwart frowned. He drew the sword back again. Ordowahl could see that he was more relaxed. He would not rely on the beef to keep him erect by stopping the blade, since the blade might somehow fly out the other side. He swung, with force.

Severed through the shoulders, the head dropped onto the paved courtyard.

Euwart studied the fallen head for a moment, waggled the blade and gave it a closer look. "Nordweg, I must consider whether even to accept your gift. This weapon might destroy the current balance of military force. Whoever has a thousand of these will soon use them!"

"We understand this alike, Prince. I aspire to your accepting one or more of these swords as trophies. What they can do will be hidden. I know your ability to keep secrets. To have these high on a wall in your castle would be my great honor."

"Perhaps. A sword mounted on a wall would be a symbol, not a threat."

"Did you notice that two swords are curved?"

"Please explain that to me. Why did you bring me something so misshapen?"

"Perhaps if Klarenz could show you."

Klarenz picked up a curved sword, stood in front of the beef, and swung into the ribs. The hind legs and rump swayed while a clean slice of the animal lay atop the head.

Euwart stepped closer to inspect the sword, keeping his hands to himself as though it were satanic. He turned back to Ordowahl. In a trembling voice he said, "No, Nordweg, no. This weapon would seem an insult. It is too different. Anyone who has seen its power would find it impossible to leave alone. This is a secret you must help me to keep. Promise me you'll never use this unGodly thing within a hundred leagues of here. And never permit Klarenz to make another!" He wiped his face with both hands, to smoothe it free of tension.

Klarenz cleaned the three used blades. He sheathed the two straight swords that Prince Euwart found acceptable then bundled up the curved swords and the plain one.

"I mean this." Euwart's voice became ragged. "You must leave here as soon as you can. Your usefulness to House Rechtmann and to Hammaborg has ended. Your continued presence is no longer tenable. I wish you well, young Prince. While you have much to master, starting with yourself, I sense that you will become useful to your father's kingdom, if not to another lying somewhere ahead of you. In time you will know, and I will not. Go far from here and do not return. Godspeed!"

With rust and dirt and finest honing stone,
with careful finger down the slicing brim,
he made each razored mirror worth a throne,
full thirteen deadly blades: bright, gleaming, grim.
    The implication upsets Euwart's sense
    of history, of war, of politics.
    Blades such as these could scatter then condense
    the realms of Europe just like kindling sticks.
Ord rescued Klarenz from the torturer's fire,
killed all that animus to bring a sword
from this ingenious fief. It can inspire
deep awe—its greatness cuts their friendship's cord.
    Prince Ordowahl has squandered his good will.
    "Just go, be't fare thee well or fare thee ill."

Wintertrek

"Liege, it grieves me to see your workshop destroyed."

"A year ago you were apprenticed to Master Meinz; you chatted betimes with Master Schmidt. Now you've gone far past both and made many swords, if taking more time than Master Schmidt would have taken. Yet each of them, even the ordinary one, is far better than anything he will ever produce. The workshop is gone, Klarenz. We go toward whatever new adventure God has set out for us. I suspect the workshop would be difficult to load into a wagon."

"Liege, ever since dicing with death in that vinegar barrel, I've come to a place, been at peace, learned the dialect and the local arts, yet afterward been driven out with curses. Now we are both loose and in winter. What month is this, Liege?"

"What was that tune? Fridoric used it for both of his songs. It was about an evergreen, I think."

"Yah, it is sung at the eve of the Mass of Christ, and comes three days after the turn of the sun, when the days become longer again."

"We sang that yesterday."

"Yah."

"Today is the Mass of Christ. Nine fortnights from tomorrow will bring the first day in May."

"Ah, the promise of summer! Liege, the present is bleak."

"Tell me, Klarenz, about other times you've found yourself thrust onto the road like this. How many were in good weather, how many in bad?"

He paused in thought. "First let me count—Liege, I stopped counting at a dozen, ten years ago. In fact, our stay in Hammaborg lasted more than twice as long as any I've had before now."

"So, Klarenz. You learn much in each new place yet never learn how to become one with it, nor how to join in."

Klarenz searched Ordowahl's face for a sign of teasing. "Liege, that hurts."

"It should, Klarenz. It hurts me as well. All the while you were becoming one with various women and, as you might say, 'joining in' with them, you failed to form any public bond of brotherhood, or citizenship, or comity—with anyone aside, that is, from several members at once of the gentler sex."

"Far be it from me to ask whether my liege lord has judged me." Klarenz pouted.

Ordowahl changed the subject. "Good my fief, there is no bad weather, only bad clothing. In Nordweg that is winter's watchword."

"Clothes, yah, Liege. Clothing we have. Prince Euwart destroyed our memory with one hand and showed us kindness with the other."

"The better to help us travel far. Look to your good cheer, Klarenz! An unhappy heart often finds ways to enlarge its sorrow. God has blessed me with a man of untold talents. Through you, our Father in heaven has armed me with many astonishing swords. He has given me a fief. When your mood smiles, a companion as well. Look to your good countenance, Klarenz. Contentedness will follow."

Klarenz's grump lasted an entire week. They pointed themselves always south and camped in the open. Euwart had given Ordowahl a second mule to carry sufficient gear without a wagon. Klarenz had suggested taking a large sheet of sailcloth for a makeshift tent against sleet, snow, and blowing wind.

"Liege, you are always right. Even three days trapped below this carved-out stream bank under our sailcloth roof can't keep me downcast. We and the beasts have been warm enough, but if I never smell another horse turd it will still be too soon. Do you think we can make passage through the snow, now that the sun shines and the air is empty?"

"Say, Klarenz, what do you think of fresh butter on hot biscuits, sausage gravy, and fried eggs?" This had become Ordowahl's new morning query.

"Liege, I'd like to find a place where I can make them myself."

The two men scaled the near-vertical stream bank and freed their sailcloth roof from the anchoring rocks. They struck off its heavy ice crust, shook it well and stretched it between trees to catch the low winter sun. The cold, dry air cleaned their noses of dank smells.

The horses and mules found their own way up the stream bank and grazed. After an hour spent cooking and re-packing gear, Ordowahl and Klarenz re-folded the ice-free sailcloth, loaded it on a mule, saddled the horses, and resumed their southward trek.

"Klarenz, I heard repeated foolish talk amongst some of the highborn who live in this direction. They alluded to a black knight."

"Liege, amongst the very few highborn folk I've met, you and Prince Euwart aren't the kind to make foolish talk. So, with respect, why does foolish talk make good conversation?"

"Amongst the very many lowborn folk I've met, you aren't the kind to make foolish talk. Don't you think I might have a purpose in bringing up an odd topic?"

"Forgive me, Liege."

"At first their talk did sound foolish, yet enough of them mentioned it and with matching details, that I believe a truth hides in it. I only wish I knew which part was truth and which not."

"Liege, do you remember the jackdaws that King Ingvik

kept?"

"Yes."

"What's that over there?"

Ordowahl looked where Klarenz pointed. The bare limbs of one tree held four ravens. "Those aren't jackdaws, good my fief."

"They're ravens, yet I've seen them following us since we left Hammaborg. Liege, ravens go south in late fall and return in spring. It's hardly spring yet." He shivered.

Ordowahl looked at them. He said nothing.

After nearly three weeks' travel Ordowahl selected a thicket of saplings on a hillside just above a farmer's field to set up camp. Each night he kept the party far from any farmstead or village.

Klarenz risked a small grumble. "You kept women out of my bed the entire time we stayed in Hammaborg, liege. Can't we at least enjoy one warm night and hay for our animals while we journey south?"

"You have every right to ask. Why do you think I subject Hammerfoot to this?"

"Liege, I cannot say."

"The reason, good my fief, is that your swords will become known. In hindsight I believe Euwart had a weak moment when he accepted them, and put them on display. I regret asking him to do that."

"On display—as trinkets? Because of their mirror-bright blades?"

"If he sets them anywhere within reach, someone will try the edge. With his finger."

Klarenz gave Ordowahl a surprised look; he understood. "Prince Euwart may send men-at-arms to retrieve both me and the swords."

"I pray they won't try to shed blood. You will stay with me, Klarenz. Your opportunity to woo Gnade Grace would have come to naught anyway."

Klarenz returned a nervous guffaw.

Hearing a sudden "Hallooo" in the distance, they turned to look. A lone rider, unarmed and looking no better than the poorest peasant, approached them on a good horse. The horse meant that their halloooer was not a poor peasant—perhaps he worked for someone wealthy.

"Herr Schlach?" they both said at once.

When the fellow reached them they could see his horse heaving in distress. "Have a care, man!" cried Klarenz. He took the horse's reins and led it off over the edge of the hill to a small rill that had ice in it. A fire would turn the ice into water soon enough. Perhaps the poor beast could break through to a trickle of water below.

Klarenz directed him. "You—make yourself useful by building a fire. We need one to melt ice."

The peasant picked up the small axe and flint Klarenz had laid out . He scrambled to pick up dead branches and twigs to shave small splinters from them.

"So, whoever you are, now that your horse is near death, how will you return to your master?" Ordowahl gave the man a disgusted look. "Who is your master?"

"Prince, my master is aware that you are beyond temptation. He overheard a most amazing tale. It is said that someone noticed, don't ask me how, two mirror-like swords mounted on the wall of Rechtmann Castle. Not just mirror-bright: sharp beyond human ability to hone an edge. A moth flew toward a candle's reflection, and lost half its wing. The next time he had a chance to see for himself, no swords were to be seen; Prince Euwart even claimed that the idea was preposterous. There never had been such swords anywhere—most certainly not in his possession."

The fellow built a small tent of twigs around the collection of shavings. He struck the flint onto the axe; on his second try the spark caught. He rose to his feet to add large sticks to the infant flame.

Ordowahl asked him, "If that is so, why did your master have you bring a horse near death to tell me? You rode that horse with skill. You therefore know proper care of horses. You also know what you did to this one."

Looking upward at Ordowahl in a best attempt at eye to eye, he said, "My master made it clear that both I and the horse meant less to him than his wish to invite you to his Haus."

"Because of two disappearing mirror-like swords? Did he say why he connects them to me?"

"If it please you, Prince, the tale already does that. When Prince Euwart first put them on display he gave you credit. I think it was to mollify the people who still felt deep insult from your refusal to support Gnade as mother of your child, as though your gift would atone in some small way."

"How necessary was that? She may have dropped her foal by now. It surely isn't mine. Does the infant resemble her substitute husband?"

"Prince, these things are far above my stature to know, much less discuss."

"Then perhaps Klarenz is a better man to talk to than I am. All the people of Hammaborg knew him as a master of all crafts, steel wright and sword maker. Ask him." *Father God in heaven, please lead me away from this man. Lead him away from me.*

The fellow went over the edge of the hill to see how Klarenz was doing with his horse. He retreated at once, walking backward. Klarenz led the horse, shouting heavy abuse at its rider.

"On second thought, Klarenz may not be ready to converse with you."

Klarenz handed the horse's reins to its abusive rider and went to gather larger wood for the fire.

"Your mount can forage here alongside our animals. Go back to the stream; bring us ice. Make sure it is clean since we'll be drinking it," Ordowahl told the man. Once from beyond the crest of the hill he could be heard breaking ice in the stream bed.

"Klarenz, while the rider is out of earshot, help me think of a story that will send this fellow back to his master with an excuse that he did not find us. Someone may already suspect that the swords leapt off the wall, minced a thousand fingers, then flew to a mountain cave where they await the Returning Christ and His angels. Would, in fact, that He would come today. Amen, Lord Jesus."

Klarenz dropped several heavy branches near the fire, where the aromatic odor of burning pine already rose. "Liege," he said while reducing the wood to suitable pieces for the fire, "His horse will not live, *if* it manages to get back to his master's Haus."

"In other words, he will demonstrate by the horse's death that his master sent him too late?"

"A gold coin should never be seen in his pocket. Silver will he easier for him to hide and spend."

"Cut some grass to help the horse forage. I'll send our messenger back in the morning. In our prayer tonight, help me give thanks to God that the fellow has a story of failure that his master will accept."

*__*__*__*

March had already come when they found the Scharz Valley. It nestled in the northwestern part of the Harz Mountains. Ordowahl said, "This is the place Egeno mentioned."

"Liege? I haven't learned of any famed mountain valleys other than much farther south. What is it about this one?"

"I must teach you to read, Klarenz. I need to address that. Learning your letters and how to read them takes time. I imagine you'll pick it up quicker than most."

"Thank you, Liege. I want that even more than a hot meal and a warm bed. What does that have to do with knowing where we are?"

"That inn over there. Does it have a sign?"

"Yes. It pictures a dog and a chicken."

"It also has letters on it."

"I see them—those squiggly, prickly things people read and draw."

"The letters say 'Hund und Hahn,' Klarenz. Or 'Dog and Rooster.' There are more letters on that other sign, the one on the large town hall."

With dawning understanding, Klarenz looked at them again, but they remained squiggles. "I see you've read them and they tell you we're in this place you called Scharz Valley."

"Not only that, Klarenz, this town is called Ermsleben. My pupil Egeno mentioned a sizable house overlooking the town. Try to help me locate it."

Neither of them could pick it out. Ordowahl led Klarenz into the inn.

"Bitte gebt mir und meinem Gefolgsmann fuer heute Nacht ein Schlafkammer und euch ein gutes Nachtmahl." ("Please, give me a room for the night for my fief and myself, plus a good supper.")

The innkeeper looked at Ordowahl with respect. He tugged on the barman's sleeve and whispered a command in his ear. "Prince," he said in a passable Hammaborgish accent, "I hope that you are Prince Ordowahl of Nordweg. Free Knight Egeno has heard that you may be traveling in this direction and hopes to find you here."

Klarenz suppressed a look of surprise. Best not to play the fool so soon. Later when he had some local people sized up— not now.

"Mr. Innkeeper, tell me about this fellow Egeno. Is he well liked in the Scharz Valley? Did he describe me accurately?"

"Prince, Egeno visits this tavern often enough. He tells tales of someone the size of two men together. He even told us, 'Hear me now and believe me later.' Egeno is not someone to doubt, because here you are!"

Ordowahl and Klarenz found seats at a table near the fire. Each held a mug of passable ale when Egeno himself came through the door. He saw Ordowahl and came over.

"Prince, please don't stand up for me. No, no, stay seated. May I join you?" Without waiting for an answer he waved at the barman and sat down.

"My good friend," he said, "I had heard about your leaving Hammaborg. And in the middle of winter! Then recently I heard you might be coming my way. Ordowahl, Prince, it is so good to see you!"

"Likewise, Egeno. It's good to find a well-known face. How are you getting by?"

Egeno made a polite cough. "Ahem, Ordowahl, I do more than 'get by.' The life of a free knight is not without intrigue and not without risk, but the business aspects are very good. A free knight is loved by all, especially to his face!"

Ordowahl smiled. He understood the lowest ranks of highborn men. The boundaries were porous and ill-defined. A man and his grandson might have very different lives and go in either direction.

Egeno had the brash energy of a newcomer and could be a "boon companion" as the saying was. He often left Ordowahl shaking his head.

"Egeno, my friend, there came a time when my purpose in Hammaborg was complete. God put His small finger by my ear and flicked it gently. He whispered that I must go south. Perhaps He was thinking of you at the time."

"I am to be honored by a flick of God's small finger. I *like* that, Ordowahl. I do indeed. Come, you can't stay here! The innkeeper is a good friend of mine. We help each other out all the time. You must come up to my house, both of you!" He trained a curious look at Klarenz. "Ordowahl, I hear so many contradictory things about your man, here. We must keep him with us, don't you think?"

From living in a palace with a host
whose mind was firm and manner always mild,
to here. And what is this? At very most
his host a prosp'rous knight and Ord exiled.
    Fief Klarenz has outdone himself, for sure—
    a race to arm the realm with deadly tools?
    Prince Euwart was afraid, and wanted pure
    deep secrecy from prying minds, from fools.
Yet beauty is as beauty does, and beauty
on a wall is only that. The prince
showed grace, to hang them in plain sight like loot
or treasure, with a tale, an "Ever since—"
    No worry crossed Ord's mind, since Euwart held
    more calm control than Ord had e'er beheld.

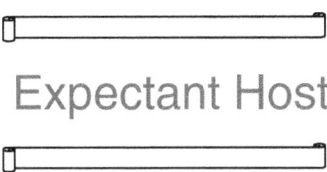

Expectant Host

Egeno's home sat on a hillside above the town. Tall trees down slope shielded it. "Here we are, my esteemed prince! Look through the trees, you can see the town below in the moonlight. I enjoy this sight often. When you are ready, come with me to the stable."

The bottom part of the house, half buried in the gentle hilltop slope, had foundation walls of broad stones set with care. On them stood a wide upper storey, of squared and fitted logs. The foundation walls enclosed storerooms, a workshop open to the outside, and a long enclosed stable housing chickens, goats, two pigs, three milk cows, a brace of mules and six horses.

"It's cozy. I'm sure your mount Hammerfoot—Ordowahl, he is an amazing animal indeed. Klarenz's horse and your mules will also have good shelter and forage."

After unburdening the animals and putting them in empty stalls with feed and water, they followed Egeno up a central stairway. Ordowahl looked back over his shoulder at Hammerfoot, whose ears flicked against floorboards between the joists above him.

"Hardly what you'll find in Hammaborg." Egeno had a point. While this wasn't Euwart's stone fortress, nor was it Herr Schlach's large stone house on the town square, it did have a rough-hewn air of prosperity.

Upstairs large timbers supported a vaulted ceiling. A few

windows of real glass provided some light, for a room large enough to set a feast for twenty or more. A door let onto a balcony half the length of the building.

"The part of the house over the storage and workshop area is divided into sleeping rooms. Here, let me get you situated. Mathilde!"

A pleasant female voice answered him. "Ja, Herr Egeno?"

"Liebchen, Prinz Ordowahl von Nordweg und sein Gefolgsmann Klarenz sind unsere Gaeste. Bitte bringt das Abendmahl fuer uns drei."

"Jawohl meiner Lieb. In zehn Minuten ist es bereit."

"We're in luck! By the time you're settled into your room supper will be on the table. Haensel, Franzel! Macht schnell! My prince, please allow my boys Hans und Franz to carry up your things."

Supper began with cold roast beef, sausages, pickled vegetables, bread, cheeses, and ale. The men ate near a substantial, freestanding fireplace; passageways on either side led to the cooking area. Through the fireplace they could hear family voices mingled with kitchen sounds. Soon a pleasant woman came around the fireplace with a tureen throwing off steam.

"Liebchen, hier ist eine kleine Schuessl Suppe," she said. A younger woman, perhaps a daughter, carried bowls and spoons. Then both of them, too shy to say anything more, went back out of sight behind the fireplace.

"Later on I'll introduce you to the rest of the family," Egeno said. "You've met my sons, Hans und Franz. Now I really must ask you more, my good friend, about this small finger of God you mentioned. Please don't treat me so badly as to withhold a simple description."

"How simple is that, Egeno? We came for a time, had an interesting brush with fate, trained a number of knights—you are very capable, Egeno. A fine ironmaster took Klarenz as apprentice. Did you know that, Egeno? After a time we chose to move on. There is only so much a fellow like myself can take of one place. I had to find a real fate. Hammaborg didn't seem to offer me a good one."

"Simple enough, I guess," said Egeno. "Yet I feel as though you are hiding something from me. No, I don't mean your dalliance with Gnade. 'Brood mare of Hammaborg', indeed! She has borne an infant for you and found a very likely-looking husband to raise it."

Ordowahl inferred from Egeno's wry grin that her infant resembled the husband so much he had been its father all along.

"Don't worry on my account, Ordowahl, my friend. You are a friend, I hope? I trust you with my home. Please trust me with at least a sliver of the truth."

Ordowahl was glad to see that Klarenz, maker of terrifying swords, maintained a blank expression.

"I need your help, Egeno. What could I be hiding? You must have heard gossip somewhere. What question would you like me to answer?"

"Tell me about the moth that lost its wing."

The question cemented the story they'd heard on the way here. "Is this some kind of riddle? Aesop told the tale of a thorn in a tiger's paw, or a stork offering a fox soup in a long-necked jar. I can tell you about those. I have no idea regarding a moth that lost its wing."

"So you tell me you weren't there when the moth lost its wing."

"Egeno, I've seen moths lose wings before, but not by themselves and not in Hammaborg."

"My moth flew too close to a sword."

At least no one lost a finger. Ordowahl pondered how not to lie, yet give this man an answer he would accept. *Do I place the blame on Euwart? No. Do I try to fool Egeno? No, at least not so soon. This is only the start of a decent visit thus requires room for respect between friends.*

"You're pausing in thought." Egeno smiled. "Surely this tale will be worth the listening. I wait upon you."

"Good my host, I will tell it better if I know it myself. Tell me the tale in your words and I will try to understand what you want to know."

Egeno nodded. "I see. I see. Yes, my friend, I'll share it with you as I heard it. A mutual friend, someone we trained with, someone whose understanding of arms is profound, noticed a very odd thing on the wall in Prince Euwart's library. He saw a pair of crossed swords such as not he nor I have ever seen. They seemed to be made of glass." He studied Ordowahl's face but found only simple curiosity.

Egeno continued, "When he looked more closely, they were steel, polished so wondrously that he could see his own eye looking back at him from the blade. He was about to touch one of the swords when Prince Euwart dragged him away on a pretext of some sort. Our friend thought the swords might possess a powerful magic. This man happened to visit the prince again the next day—the swords now raised above easy reach. While he gazed at them a moth departed from one of the lit candles in the chandelier near the ceiling. Light reflected by the sword drew it so near that its wing brushed against the sword's edge."

Ordowahl at last reacted. "I wonder what might have happened next."

Egeno looked at him with excitement in his eyes. "My prince, a sword that could sever a moth's wing, when the sword is still and only the moth's wing moves, would be an amazing thing. Our friend brought Euwart to the swords. He showed him the moth, flapping about with one wing much shorter than the other and the fragment there on the floor. Euwart looked at him as though he were daft. He objected to the nerve of this man, accusing his prince of keeping moths. Prince, the next day he again paid Euwart a visit; the swords had disappeared from sight. A few of the rich and noble remembered them and talked about how shiny they were. That's it. Gone. Out of sight. Vanished."

"That's quite a story, Egeno. What do you make of it, yourself?"

"Please! My friend! Your bondman Klarenz, sitting right here with the blank look on his face, he made those swords. Surely I don't have to lead you through the simple steps to show that! So I have to know more about them. What was going on? Why was Prince Euwart proud enough of them to mount them as trophies? Why did he suddenly deny them when my—our—friend discovered that one had severed the wing of a moth that flew too close? For that matter, why were they so shiny?"

Ordowahl said nothing.

"I can see you'll want time to think about this, my friend. I believe you hold a secret of unusual power. That is not a thing to be given lightly. I understand this. But mind you, my prince, we want to understand each other. You possess something of great power, and I will be looking for a way to exchange like for like, you do understand me. We, my prince, you and I," Egeno said with eyes riveted on Ordowahl, "can do amazing things together."

Ordowahl smiled and nodded at Egeno. Then he dipped bread into his soup. "Egeno, this is very good. I haven't had soup like this in some time!"

Egeno shrugged. "Ah! We get by."

The rest of the meal passed in small talk—weather, horses, jousting. No one mentioned swords again.

The next day, preparing for a morning of hard work in Egeno's training yard, Ordowahl praised Klarenz. "I congratulate you on controlling your face last night. You are known as a swordsmith hence Egeno reached his conclusion along with a host of others. By now all of Prince Euwart's realm plus most of the kingdoms, fiefdoms, and principalities bordering it have the story."

Ordowahl and Klarenz each made a reverent sign of the Cross.

"At least we left Hammaborg before the swords did. I do not believe Euwart will decide to send an army to bring us back and prove our deaths by a public spectacle, yet it must have occurred to him. So we'll have to bypass Hammaborg if I ever decide to return to Nordweg."

"Liege, everywhere I go something happens that gets me expelled. This is the first time, though, that it was for something I did to please a man not a woman."

"Ach. Good my fief, bondman, confidant, perhaps occasional companion. God above watches over us. We know that we are His workmanship, prepared by Him to do things that He himself has laid out before us. Didn't you survive the vinegar barrel? Didn't we both come through the Vikings' assault? That and more, Frau Klarenze? Go forward with God, Klarenz. To live is to face difficulties, hurts, sometimes humiliations. Trust His purpose. Persevere without regard for consequence. There is no other way."

Klarenz looked glum. "Yes, of course, Liege. I've heard that from many a priest. I've seen what looked like wonderful opportunities—"

"I've seen smiling faces, too, Klarenz. Don't you think our Father has many more ways to lead us than by inviting eyes? In fact here I am, training my bondman to handle himself when set upon. Let that become part of what leads you toward or away from taking action."

Three ordinary-seeming weeks went by as Egeno and Ordowahl became better acquainted. They trained outside in early spring's snow-blotched landscape. Even in the cold their winter clothing let them overheat.

Egeno said, "Come sit here on this snow chair, Prince Nordweg." Egeno patted a place on the snow bank piled up by shoveling winter's white gift out of the practice area. "We're too hot, I think. This will help to ice down a sore back or leg."

Ordowahl raised his boot to scuff out a flat seat and plopped down. "We do this in Nordweg, too, Egeno. In fact, we have a winter house, a very small one, with room for only a few to sit around a hardwood fire vented by a small hole in the roof. Inside it's very hot. We sprinkle water on a grill above the coals. Tossing cedar shavings into the fire adds aroma. We absorb the heat, naked, then dash outside to roll in the snow. After a moment in the snow we slap our bodies with fresh birch branches."

Egeno looked at Ordowahl. "Indeed, Prince, indeed! If you're still here at summer's end you may show me how to build such a thing."

"Yes, my host, if I am still here, no doubt I will. The discipline is priceless, and the effect afterward is hard to describe. I can't wait!"

"There is something else a man generally doesn't willingly wait for, my prince, and that is a woman in his bed."

"You do have a woman. I've seen your wife calling you Liebchen. She shows you open affection."

"I am a happy man, Prince. Are you?"

"Good my host, I am content. I've had the experience of women. I find them one of God's great gifts, if not abused."

"Prince, can I ask what constitutes abuse? Will you say that Gnade abused you?" he winked. "I am curious, good Prince Nordweg. I want to know your opinion on women in general and on a woman's company in particular."

"Hmmm. Egeno, this is what I think. Abuse, first: to alter a woman's life in a way that leaves her the worse off. It can range from murder, torture, rape, pillage—all of these are a stench to God. Or something as simple as bedding a lowborn girl, however willing she herself may be, without a thought that she might have to raise your bastard by herself. Gnade? Hear me, Egeno. Her bastard, so-called, will be reared by its true father. I owe him gratitude for the moist comforts of his child's mother."

"Prince, you seem to avoid the subject. Gnade we know about. She's no longer a concern."

"You are right, Egeno. Here it is. To take a woman without regard to a swain she may have, someone lowborn same as she, is impossible to respect."

"I see, Prince. I don't argue here. You speak plainly, even severely, but I see truth in your eyes. Now, please go on. What is your view of womankind?"

Ordowahl smiled. "Egeno, if I am to speak to that from now

until it's time to build the heat-house for you next fall, I will only be half done. I tell you what: I've said my mind on abuse. Now please make a short answer to your own question—no more than half an hour or so."

Egeno threw his head back and laughed. "I find you always a close guardian of your mind, Ordowahl. I will show you my own mind. Every eligible female, all their young married friends and, for that matter, every female past the age of ten, dreams of you. She whispers about you with her friends. Surely you've been aware of their interest? Yet you seem not to have acted on it. That pleases me. It also makes me fear that, at some point, you will choose. Your choice will become known. That means the woman you pluck may leave an emptiness behind her—you do understand me—dashed plans and relations that can bring fire down on my own head."

"Fire? How can I assure you, Egeno, that I will make no such choice? Well, in your place, my thoughts would be the same. So what is your answer to this?"

"Thank you for hearing me out, Prince. I don't want to do or say anything that would show disrespect. I am happy to have you as a guest in my house. I enjoy your company in the town. I love you as a brother. I hope for you to be as completely and as safely content as possible. So here is my mind in the matter. You are a man who has known the sweetness of a woman in the night. Or perhaps in broad daylight."

Egeno added an artless wink. "To bring peace to my heart, let me add a woman to your bed. Simple as that—a mistress, someone to keep you warm in bed. This will tell the women here that you have an outlet. It reduces the chance of confusion, do you know what I mean?"

"Egeno, she must be past childbearing age."

"Please, my prince, I don't find you taking me seriously."

"What about Klarenz?"

"He didn't learn from his noble victim fifteen years ago?"

"Learn? Yes, Egeno. Bear this in mind. That lesson only clubbed him over the head when he returned to Hammaborg.

Let's say he is the image of the trouble you imagine swirling about me. I've kept him out of harm's way, and at times it has been taxing to both of us. Get him a good woman past childbearing years to bring me peace."

"Then honor me, Prince Nordweg. Make it two-for-one. I place an older woman, past childbearing years, with Klarenz. How can I look my townspeople in the eye if I do that to you as well?"

Ordowahl smiled. "Then let her be a churchgoing woman—I mean that, Egeno—one who has no husband, jealous suitor, or the like. These things I will insist on."

Egeno paused in thought for a moment then leaped to his feet. "These chairs can freeze you to them if you sit for too long!" he blurted out. "By Satan's third butt cheek I am cold!"

*__*__*__*

Ordowahl had blown out the candle in the room he shared with Klarenz. "Good my fief, listen to me now. Let me tell you about older women. In the darkness after the candle dies, their beauty is hard to distinguish from any other's. An older woman is far less likely to be jealous. She's less temperamental. She is free from Venus's cycle, hence always available. She's probably a better conversationalist and may be more grateful than you can guess."

"Liege, you could be a merchant praising wool or tableware. I take your point."

"This will be important for us both, Klarenz. You will gain the freedom to walk the streets on your business without a guide. I will have the freedom to send you on an errand without worrying."

"Yah, Liege. We'll both like that."

"You simply must not let your winsome gaze catch or hold the eye of anyone female! If you see it coming your way you must pick your nose, or frown, or pretend not to see it."

"Liege, my poor nose will wear out."

"Then don't take it into harm's way, Klarenz. This is not a light matter. I command you in this: you'll have one woman.

One only. You will practice your wooing arts on her. You will persuade her that she has both your affection and your respect."

Klarenz said nothing.

"Do I ask the water to flow away from the sea?"

"Liege, I ..."

"Do I?"

Klarenz sighed. "Liege, I have never lied to a woman. I never work to woo or to court. Yes, I've felt both respect and affection for women—several at a time, in fact—but never have I tried to persuade a woman of something untrue."

"Good my bondman, my poet, my craftsman, you will discover that a small kindness may have a large effect."

"Indeed so! Liege, I've found this to be true with each of the several dozen women God has placed before me."

Ordowahl stared at him in the near dark. "Yes, and beneath you as well. Only trust me, Klarenz, that this will also be true when you and the woman come together by duller means than a wink from across the room."

"My Liege," sighed Klarenz.

Quotidian details, of who will sleep
with whom, with no precise morality,
reduce the toll on host Egeno's deep
concern they illustrate austerity.
    Prince Ordowahl has found a comfy place;
    now host Egeno wants to know the meat,
    what arm'rer's arts fief Klarenz might embrace?
    Two players read each other. They compete.
    The ev'ry-day routine's a welcome change.
Sour ostracism, then a winter slog
have given way to cordial exchange
of food and more, with Ord the pedagog.
    Such peace and ease, short winter days seem long.
    Prince Ord forgets to ask, "What could go wrong?"

Girly Metal

Shouts of child-men mixed with Klarenz's angry rasp came up from the ground-floor workshop area. Ordowahl arrived to discover Hans und Franz flailing about with two of Klarenz's mirror-shiny curved swords.

They were play fighting with them while Klarenz was doing his best to keep the two brothers from beheading each other.

"Aufhören!" commanded Ordowahl. The two boys stopped. Ordowahl glared at them with a raised eyebrow. "Was ist los? Haben meine Schwerter Euch gestört? Erklärt mir, bitte, warum Ihr mit Dingen spielt, die Euch nicht gehören!" ("What is this? Have you meddled with my swords? Explain why you're playing with things that aren't yours.")

The boys were not cowed by Ordowahl's fierce manner. Hans asked with a smirk, "Warum nennt Ihr dies weibische Stueck aus glänzenden Metall ein Schwert?" ("Why do you call this girly piece of shiny metal a sword?)"

"Weibsich? So sprechen Kinder. Ich höre den Klang der Unwissenheit. Lassen Sie jetzt!" ("Girly? This the way children speak. I hear the sound of ignorance. Leave now!")

The boys decided that Ordowahl's stupid-looking toy swords were his business, dropped them onto the workshop's earthen floor, and filed out.

"Klarenz? Tell me what happened."

"Liege, I found them in here playing, as you saw them."

"Tell me how they acquired those two swords, Klarenz."

Klarenz looked miserable. "Liege, I moved several items down here from that cramped room the four of us sleep in. I didn't suspect that they would pilfer our baggage."

"I see. Yes, our room has been slightly emptier for several days. I can't fault you, Klarenz, for so foolish an act as to place these swords where careless hands might find them unless I fault myself for not noticing they were gone. Klarenz, haven't you had any experience of the wild behavior of teenage boys?" Ordowahl paused for a moment and thought.

"No, I guess not. You haven't raised children yourself—for that matter neither have I—yet I can recall my brothers' and my own sense of mischief. And my nephews!"

"Liege, I—"

"It's done now, Klarenz. We'll have to do something with those swords before their true nature comes to light."

"Liege, I can hide them where nobody will ever find them. They'd have to burn this whole house to locate them."

"So how will that remove them from Egeno's conversation? No, when the cat is out of the bag, Klarenz, we need to kill and skin the cat."

"Liege?" Klarenz looked confused.

"Did I speak a riddle? Here it is. You will kill the cat by making these two beautiful swords into one. It must be plain. Then you will skin the dead cat by neglecting to bring the new sword up to your amazing state of lethal beauty. Make its edge sharp as a well-honed knife, Klarenz, straight, with a fuller and two edges."

Egeno confronted Ordowahl after the evening meal. "My prince, I have to insist. You must let me see what you've evidently brandished in front of my boys."

"How interesting!" said Ordowahl. "We won't argue over how your boys found things I thought were hidden. Clearly they weren't hidden well enough. I won't quibble with whatever tale they told. Instead, I've asked Klarenz to combine those two, er, 'girly pieces of shiny metal' into one real sword."

"Come now, Ordowahl! How do you expect me to believe that?"

"Egeno, good my host, my friend, do you still expect me to produce swords that can slice a moth's wing while hanging on a wall?"

Egeno held a level gaze. "In a word, yes. I do."

"Girly pieces? Or swords—which way will you have it? Take counsel with me, my friend. They will be telling their story to everyone, if they haven't already. Consider this: if those swords our friend spoke of, in Euwart's castle, appeared here, how long would it be before Euwart came looking for copies? There had to be something about them that made him remove them from his walls and deny they even existed."

"Yes, of course, Ordowahl! I taught my sons well regarding family secrets. They know that this is one. They will broach no word of it to anyone other than to me—that includes you and Klarenz, my friend, until such time as we can consider you family."

"So much as you've done so far, Egeno, is good. Do they have any thought about how lethal those 'playthings' might be? A sword capable of slicing a moth's wing could sever an arm or a neck just as easily."

"No, Ordowahl, they don't. I trust them with most secrets, but not that one. They're not yet fully men. I believe you when you speak of losing an arm to a sword Klarenz made."

"I see. Egeno, I will hide that secret in plain sight. I've told Klarenz to combine them into one large sword of the regular shape. He labored intensely to make them what they were—you can guess at the effort to achieve that polish. He is my bondman. His work is mine to dispose of. He is already heating the forge. Soon two shiny curved weapons will become one ordinary sword, of a size fit for my hand alone."

"Indeed, Ordowahl." Egeno smiled. "Yours, or two of anyone else's. With a sword of that heft and reach, you would be an even more dangerous opponent than you are now. Where there are two, might there not be more?"

"More than two hands?" Ordowahl lifted both eyebrows and tried to look innocent.

Egeno frowned then relaxed. "My honored guest, the power I sense in the two swords we know about isn't something you would surrender easily unless there were others. I'll avoid asking why they were so strange, so deformed, because you have a reason for everything you do. There have to be more. I am so excited, my prince. I must introduce you to my friend Schwarzknecht, the black knight."

Ordowahl didn't respond. Every time Egeno raised the subject of the black knight, disinterest was his only reply.

In the morning Klarenz labored at the forge in the ground floor workshop. The foundation wall gapped at that point to let smoke go out and cleansing air come in.

Bringing the two curved weapons to a workable heat had dulled their razor edge. Klarenz allowed himself to relax. He worked to remove the temper that quenching them had made, so they could be worked again.

By gradual steps Klarenz straightened the two pieces of metal, put them back-to-back, and pounded their thick sides together. Liberal use of burnt shell got them to weld cleanly in the forge. By day's end they would become one straight piece.

The boys were in and out for a while that day. With the luster and curve gone, they knew they were seeing only ordinary smithery. Nonetheless, professional interest held them. They would, as men, engage armorers to do work for them. They wanted to learn what they could first-hand.

Hans asked, "Klarenz, how is it that two pieces of metal become one?"

"They really don't like it, I'll tell you that. You have to soften them up first then make a real impression on them. After a while they tend to forget what they used to be."

Hans considered this. "I know that if you put a hot knife into a chunk of butter you'll get two chunks, and if you put them back together quickly they'll become one again."

"Careful here; if you're too slow about it with steel, rust will develop. If that happens, you're done! So slap them together quickly, sprinkle on some burnt shell, then move them back into the flame. It would be nice to have a hot knife to run between two pieces of steel, eh? I've never seen a knife that hot. You can only get the steel as hot as the fire you make—there are many arts to fire, believe me. Then you apply the weight of a hammer to it, again and again. Want to try it?"

He handed the hammer to Hans while younger brother Franz looked on. "Verdammt, I want to take a whack at it, too!" complained Franz.

"Franz, move it into the fire. Hans, you can work the bellows. That's it—"

Flame and sparks shot upward from the waist-high open furnace. Franz put on a heavy leather apron and plunged the sword awkwardly into the coals while turning away from the heat as best he could.

"Fine. You can let it go, the fire has it."

Franz relaxed his grip and went to help Hans pump at the bellows. After several minutes they began to sweat profusely despite the inrush of outside air.

Klarenz judged the fire hot enough. "Now move it from the fire to the anvil, here."

Hans didn't hesitate. He reached out with the tongs and grasped the sword as though it were a condemned prisoner and moved it to the anvil.

"Now hold it in place with one hand, take up the hammer in your other hand, and strike it hard. Be sure that you strike both fiercely and with good aim. Hitting it in the wrong spot or at the wrong angle can harm it!"

Hans looked at Klarenz, who acted out a series of hammer strikes from one end of the piece to the other, down the exact center where the two original spines had overlapped. Hans copied the gestures and struck the glowing metal many times, from end to end.

"Good!" said Klarenz. "Now, do this again and again, from

the morning meal to supper and you may have one blended bar."

The boys knew that the lesson was over. Klarenz was the Kraftmeister; they stood back to let him work. "This will go faster if you can spell each other on the bellows," suggested Klarenz. He was surprised at their willingness to take part. They didn't yet consider themselves to be "highborn."

By the end of the first day the two "girly pieces" had become one straight bar with a thick center and two finely tapering edges, mottled and wavy from a thousand hammer blows.

"Tomorrow, if you like, I'll show you how to make the fuller."

"Yah, the blood groove. Does it really make the sword stronger?"

"Indeed. With equal weights, the fuller makes a sword both wider and stronger. I have a special die, a pair of rounded bars linked by springy arms. With the blade aligned between the bars, hammering the top bar puts a blood groove, or fuller, on both sides. Take care to keep it centered. The blade will become wider not heavier, and gain strength."

"So," asked Hans, "what will you do with the metal?"

Klarenz winked back. "Push it around until the sword is longer. See, it has already become longer by half a foot."

The boys looked at it again, up close. It was cooling now; the dull red color was fading. "Jawohl!" said Franz. "It's bigger than anything Papa has ever had."

"Wait a bit," said Klarenz. "What size do you think my liege lord should use?"

They nodded, saying nothing.

A week later Ordowahl stood in the exercise yard. He showed Egeno his new sword, plain steel and with a knife's edge. "See this, my friend? Try it out."

The early spring morning glinted dully off the new weapon.

"My prince, now *this* is beautiful. This was once two girly pieces of shiny metal." The phrase had become a joke between them.

"Try it!"

"What balance! It feels somehow alive, Ordowahl, yet heavy in my hand. If I were to come onto the field of battle with this my opponent would be impressed, also very soon discover how slow I would be using it."

He handed it to Ordowahl, who set it aside. They began a set of conditioning and training drills.

One night at the end of April Egeno drank too much and spoke again of his friend the black knight. "In a day or two it will be May Day. A handful of weeks after that comes the first joust of the season and not far from here. It's to the west, but fear not—the family Klarenz diddled will not appear until the middle of summer. On the other hand you will meet my powerful friend, the black knight."

"You seem bent on telling me your tales." They were sitting at the dining table; Ordowahl had been drinking, too. He let his curiosity get the better of him. "Tell me about this black knight. Who is he? What is he known for?"

"He wears the raven on his breast."

Ordowahl's skin began to crawl.

"I've never seen the like of that before," continued Egeno. "He takes the color black because the bird has that color."

"What is he known for?"

"He is a hard man to defeat, Ordowahl. I've never seen him lose. I believe that you must challenge him. In fact, I think he will challenge you. I've told him a great deal about you. He always shows interest."

"Who are his family? Where did he prove himself a knight?"

"You know, Ordowahl, that is a mystery. He is from far away. He came amongst us as a roving knight and founded a small village. Over the past ten years or so he has become something of a fixture. He isn't accepted at any of the noble Hausen—they call him a gross intruder. I can understand that."

Ordowahl nodded. Acceptance for the lowest rank of nobility was never easy.

"Amongst the free knights he is a man with a following. You may or may not defeat him in a joust, Ordowahl, but by all means don't fail to respect his power. Those few free knights who have opposed him have suffered in very odd ways. I stay on his good side and suggest that, once the two of you have met and decided upon some contest, you should do the same. I say this as a friend."

Fief Klar'nz's curv'ed swords have put their host
upon the hunt. A sacrilege, to Ord,
to burn two glorious swords to lumpy toast.
Not easy come, not easy go—new sword.
   So what is this about the ebon knight?
   He's got Egeno in a curious hold.
   Egeno sees his role as acolyte
   to bishop, views black knight as finest gold.
   What's more the moth that had a severed wing,
the tale of "girly strips" now one great blade,
he hasn't shared these stories with his king.
He knows that Ordo feels it's his to trade.
   So what of peace and strategy and such?
   Can Prince foresee the Black Knight's master touch?

Power

MID-LATE SPRING

Ordowahl sat erect on Hammerfoot, looking out across Count Vergehlen's enormous hayfield. Several days prior a hundred serfs had cut the first short, sweet crop. Dried and raked haystacks along the field's far-flung edges framed the greening stubble. Fresh hay wafted its odor across the field.

This bright, sunny day he imagined the mock battle about to play out on it. He itched to gallop, his lance reaching out to strike the other knights like a cue striking balls on a table to scatter them. That was hardly a kind or temperate thought, and he felt no shame in it. All shared a common mind, all eager. Let it begin!

He whispered into Hammerfoot's ear. "Soo, soo, it's been a long winter. We want to have fun today, just have fun. Soo, soo, fine boy!"

"Liege, I was mastering iron at this point last year. You showed me well the duties of a knight's squire. Please have patience with me—I feel—fall—most strange today."

"Klarenz?" Ordowahl looked around at his bondman, who had been standing by the horse's left flank. "You look very much like your words. When have I ever heard the Great Frau Klarenze of Hammaborg misspeak?"

Instead of laughing Klarenz stumbled backward into a

haystack.

A voice said, "How odd!"

Ordowahl turned to see a knight approach, wearing all black and mounted on a fine black stallion. Nothing about him seemed impressive. The image of a raven worked into his tunic with threads of brass came as a shock. The fellow showed an inner, arrogant sense, as though he felt himself master of all he saw. At no time was a sneer far from his face.

"Yes?" inquired Ordowahl.

"Yes, indeed, how very odd. Your bondman, there, has gradually been losing his dignity all morning—now look at him!"

Ordowahl instead kept his gaze on Egeno's well-praised Schwarzknecht. "How odd might it be that the esteemed black knight tracks the morning rounds of a lowly bondman. Do you make me an offer for him?"

The black knight glowered. "Rather, you should make an offer for one of mine. I keep spares of everything. I'm surprised that your party is so small. Surely one of Egeno's sons could second your, er, second."

Ordowahl's gaze held steady on Schwarzknecht's face. He was difficult to read, though not due to a quietly guarded manner such as Prince Euwart. The man seemed to have none of Euwart's long training in the art of holding and confronting power. Instead he reminded Ordowahl of a working foreman back in Nordweg what was the man's name?—Wagnold!

A natural leader, yet he never seemed to say quite what he meant or mean quite what he said. Wagnold hid behind bravado. Perhaps this one did, also.

"So, Black Knight, how might I survey your set of spare bondmen? I could hardly place my preparation in the hands of someone whose heart I couldn't read or didn't trust."

The black knight's face went calm for a moment. "Right you are! I have one in mind, Heuermann. I'll send him over to you." Without waiting for a reply the smug black knight reined his horse about and loped away.

"Klarenz!" Silence. Ordowahl turned in his saddle to see his bondman slumbering against the stack of hay. Klarenz drooled. His chest and belly were shrunken in and not moving.

Ordowahl, wearing a full set of heavy leather-and-mail armor, dismounted as gracefully as only he could. He jumped to the side of his sole confidant.

"Klarenz?" He knelt and shook the slumbering form: nothing. He leaned close to test Klarenz's breath. He was breathing. His breath held an odd taint of something—Ordowahl searched his memory. Then he had it: King Ingvik's wine steward had served something that smelled like that, from his silver pitcher.

"Sleep well, Klarenz—don't let Schwarzknecht fool you— he's a fraud!" Klarenz's face wavered for an instant. His lips curled, then his face went slack. His color went from gray to grayish-pink. He grimaced a yawn and rolled onto his side. Ordowahl went back to Hammerfoot and leapt onto him, without a mounting block. The effort helped to settle his mind.

Not five minutes later Schwarzknecht's man showed up and identified himself.

"So, Heuermann, tell me the order in which you arm your master and get him up into saddle."

Heuermann paused, as though calculating whether Ordowahl would glean some key insight from a careless, thus very unfortunate, servant of the black knight.

"Indeed, Sire, every knight puts on his leathers first. His servant adjusts the straps until his knight agrees that everything is snug yet still gives freedom to move."

"You've seen this taking place yourself?"

"Sire, forgive me if I seem pert. I've done this myself many times, over long service."

"Very well then. Go on."

The man relaxed a bit and continued, "Then the knight raises his arms while the servant lowers the coat of chain mail over him."

"I already wear that mail, do I not?"

"Sire, yes, you do."

"Then?"

"Then, Sire, the servant brings a mounting block near to the horse and holds its reins carefully while the master mounts."

"Am I mounted, Heuermann?"

"Sire, yes, you are."

"And?"

"Then, Sire, the servant hands up the knight's mail cap. The knight usually holds it under his arm."

"Like this one under my left arm?"

"Sire, yes."

"Next?"

"Sire, then the servant picks up the knight's lance to place it upright, butt end on the ground, leaning on the horse."

"Show me; do that." Ordowahl observed the man and saw a hand dip furtively into a pocket. It came out and massaged the gripping spot on the lance. Then Heuermann placed the lance next to Ordowahl, on his left side.

"Heuermann."

"Sire?"

"Do all knights hold the lance in their left hand? In Nordweg every knight holds the lance in his right hand."

Heuermann played the passive servant. Nonetheless, Ordowahl saw a flicker of dismay dart across the man's face. "Sire?"

"I hold the lance with my right hand, a shield in my left. Did you imagine me leaning down, across to the left side? Or perhaps shifting the shield to my right hand, picking up the lance in my left and swapping the two in some clever fashion?"

"Sire? I truly don't catch your drift."

"No matter. You may carry the lance now. When I have a use for it you will place it on my right side, not my left."

"Sire! Yes, Sire."

Ordowahl donned his mail helmet, dismounted, and made his way back to the throng of knights waiting to compete when Egeno walked up to him.

"So, Ordowahl, how fare you today?".

"Egeno—it's a good day! How are you listed for the jousting?"

"I am highly ranked, so I will go early against someone with a quite low rank. And you, Prince?"

"I'm the special opponent of your friend Schwarzknecht."

"Oho! Then you have spared whoever has the lowest ranking from a brutish and early exit from the day."

"Egeno, jousting is always brutish. How have I spared the man at the lowest rank from that?"

"Well, Ordowahl, you may have put it together by now—Schwarzknecht is feared. In the joust he strikes with overwhelming force. It's as if his lance has the width of a small tree trunk. It hits like the whole tree. You've never seen him in action. I wager it will be a great surprise if your first look at him is head on."

"You saw me joust last summer in Hammaborg, did you not?"

"Not to offer any disrespect, Ordowahl, my friend and my guest, but if you strike like a wagon load of brick, Schwarzknecht strikes like two."

"How so? Is he sized like I am? He has decent size, yet not my match there. Is his horse that powerful? It is large, though not the equal of my own. Does he carry two lances then?"

Egeno shrugged. "You will only understand after seeing it with your two eyes, hearing the impact with your two ears—believe me, my friend, after you meet him in the joust, your ears will ring for a time."

The aged, solemn Count Vergehlen took his seat in the reviewing pavilion. It overlooked the center of the long jousting track. He wore bright green. The ladies and servants around him also wore green, diminishing in tone as befit the status of each.

A dozen or more courtiers, ladies, priests, and officers of the joust, each in their own colors, stood up when he did. The effect was as though blossoms in a garden grew sudden stems.

A trumpeter blew a long, solemn course of notes. The formal

mock-battle of the joust was ready.

A crier called out two names—one Schwarzknecht, the other Prince Nordweg. The ambient buzz of many dozen conversations amongst contestants, servants, and the assembled court gradually gave way to an expectant stillness. The single most exciting joust of the day was to be the first event. How had this come so soon?

The black knight and Ordowahl, freshly mounted, cantered out to stand side by side, facing the pavilion. Heuermann and the other squire trotted alongside them, bearing the lances.

Ordowahl observed that Schwarzknecht did expect his lance to be set down on the left side, and watched Schwarzknecht pick it up. There had to be some clue in all of this.

Schwarzknecht's other servant, like Heuermann, seemed to dip his hand again into a pocket. He applied a quick, subtle massage to the worn spot on the lance's handle.

Ordowahl picked up his lance in the usual manner, with a scarf between his glove and the lance.

Schwarzknecht pretended not to notice. He picked up his lance left-handed then threw the lance upward enough for the butt of it to clear his horse, swapped his shield from right hand to left, and caught the lance in his right hand. In all this he showed no effort.

As the black knight caught his lance, Ordowahl felt a slight tingle through the scarf, as though his lance had become subject to the other.

Some magic has to lie in Heuermann's and *the other servant's pockets. If Schwarzknecht has to use a servant to apply it to his own lance,* and *he used a servant to swab something on my lance, what is the meaning?*

On the way to his end of the jousting track Ordowahl let the facts dance in front of him; no pattern emerged. He reached the end and turned. *Something is about to go wrong. Father in heaven help me find a way to counter it!*

Schwarzknecht poised at the far end of the track on a prancing horse. Hammerfoot seemed listless. Ordowahl leaned forward to whisper in his ear. "Hei! Hai! Hau! Hoo! When you hear the horn, run!"

The horn blew. Hammerfoot lunged forward as though he had snapped a restraining rope. Ordowahl struggled to get into the jouster's three-point stance, two feet braced in the stirrups with his buttocks against the raised back of the jousting saddle.

Schwarzknecht approached, his lance steady. Ordowahl's lance, on the other hand, seemed to do the opposite of whatever he willed it to.

In his mind's eye he saw again how the black knight had touched his lance left hand first. Ordowahl moved his shield out of position to touch the lance with his left hand.

They were about to meet when the lance suddenly "found" Schwarzknecht's shield. The shock traveled back through his own lance. Ordowahl had felt great impacts before—each time he had knocked his opponent clean off his horse.

Ordowahl's shield flew out to meet and deflect Schwarzknecht's lance. The power of that lance doubled anything Ordowahl had felt before.

A "Whoooooaahh, whoa boy!" got Hammerfoot to slow to a canter. Using his knees to guide Hammerfoot, Ordowahl turned around to look for the black knight.

He was not at the far end of the track. His horse seemed to limp, riderless. The black knight lay in a heap in front of the pavilion.

Two ladies and a medicker had reached him. Four stout stretcher-bearers plodded out from the side of the pavilion. There was silence, except for an odd raven-like noise coming from the black knight.

Ordowahl stopped where Schwarzknecht lay. He dismounted outside the knot of people crouched around the crumpled body. A raven flew down to land on Schwarzknecht's chest and pecked at a bloody trickle oozing from under his mail cap. A well-dressed woman, on her knees beside Schwarzknecht, tried to shoo it away.

As though getting up from a brief nap, the black knight

rolled over onto hands and knees and stood up. The heavy mail affected him no more than a coat of feathers.

The stretcher-bearers and all who had gathered around him let out a collective gasp. Schwarzknecht gaped at them, as though their surprise was also his surprise. He stretched, shook himself, and turned to Ordowahl.

"Good my knight, I see your wits are very quick. You carry quite the punch—I am as good a man as any around here, yet you knocked me cleanly off my steed."

Ordowahl kept a smooth countenance. "I've been doing this since I was a lad. If you were to visit Nordweg, good my knight, you'd do well in the joust. It is hardly a diminishment to have Ordowahl, ninth son of Stegnwahl King of Nordweg, re-make your acquaintance with our mother the soil." He smiled and held out his hand.

Schwarzknecht looked closely at Ordowahl, as though searching for hidden mockery. "Truly, you are as Egeno said you would be. We must spend time together, Prince. I have much to teach and, I see now, some to learn." He ignored Ordowahl's gesture. Instead of the usual sneer his face went flat and lizard-eyed.

Hair stood up on the back of the prince's neck. He wondered what it was that the black knight had in store, what hidden magics, and how he planned to learn what Ordowahl did not want him to know.

Am I now a cynic? The scent on Klarenz's breath, the sly oiling of both lance handles, the left-handed touch—it looms darkly in my mind—not to mention the raven's effect on what should have been a broken body close to death. Ordowahl resolved to be on guard every moment he spent with Schwarzknecht.

"Yes, Black Knight. I agree that we should spend time together. I am eager to learn from you whatever you have to teach." Much more than that: both Heorald and Euwart had said it: *Keep your friends close, your enemies closer.*

*__*__*__*

Egeno and Schwarzknecht stood across from Ordowahl, who filled one side of a small table laden with ale, bread, pickles, cold slices of roast, and a pitcher of watered wine. The men had eaten their fill—except for Ordowahl, who was still young enough that "getting so full it hurts" took effort. Each time a server refilled his cup Ordowahl pretended to drink, sniffing first. He had a clear head, clear eye, and sound mind. He would keep it that way.

"Ordowahl," said Egeno, "no one will oppose you in the joust. This has never happened before. All the other knights and apprentice knights have agreed; none will challenge you. They have asked me, as your host and friend, to request that you desist from challenging anyone—that is, anyone other than their champion, the black knight.

"In fact," Schwarzknecht added, "I challenge you. Ordowahl, after losing to you so clearly—as you say, it's a long time since I've embraced our mother the soil! Ha ha!—I demand the opportunity to return that favor."

Ordowahl was beginning to read Schwarzknecht. He foresaw a lance that would suffer a bad break, or an injury to his stallion, or worse. "What happens, Black Knight, if a knight should die in a joust?"

"Why, a crowd of the dead knight's kin would each insist on meeting the victor until he either died or wished that he had. Is it any different in Nordweg?"

"It is the same in Nordweg. Jousting is fierce. We demand that our knights show their qualities as warriors. Injuries are accepted as acts of fate, yet when death does come, we require blood for blood."

"So," said Schwarzknecht, "you are casual about venturing so far away from your kin—knowing that your death could be unavenged, save perhaps by your host Egeno if he had a right reason. You seem not to worry about any damage to yourself?"

"Likewise, Black Knight, you also come from a far place. Who are the kin here to avenge harm done to you?"

A broad smile lit Schwarzknecht's face. "Egeno, here, would

be as aggrieved at my death as he would at yours—no, far more! I have many close friends, my prince of Nordweg. We've become even closer than brothers. Something stronger than a father's name or pizzle or mother's womb binds us together. Something much stronger."

Ordowahl had guessed this from the way Egeno deferred to the black knight, even honoring him as though he were royalty in disguise.

"In fact, Nordweg, there is a serious commitment—I say again, much more binding than simple blood and kin ties. I would like to see you cross over from being a stranger to being a True Brother, like my good friend Egeno."

A quotation from the Proverbs of Solomon came to him: 'Meliora sunt vulnera diligentis quam fraudulenta odientis oscula' or 'Better are wounds from a friend than deceitful kisses from an enemy.' *Father Ewald thinks far more highly of the proverbs than any prince of Nordweg, myself included. I understand the heft of this one. The black knight wears the correct color.*

With a nod and a smile Egeno said, "Ordowahl, my friend, my guest, there is much more to Schwarzknecht than any man can convey, or even comprehend, in so brief a span as a season. You are quick. Perhaps in a year or two you could become a true brother, as several of us are to Schwarzknecht."

A raven flew down from a nearby tree. It managed to hover near Egeno's head. It relieved itself behind Egeno then perched on his shoulder. Egeno's smile turned from enjoyment to bliss.

——*—*

Klarenz and Ordowahl stood at the edge of a small clearing in the woods. The sun, at the top of the sky, put everything not directly beneath a tree in bright light. The still, humid air emphasized their privacy. An hour would pass before the second round of jousting.

"Good my fief," Ordowahl said, "I understand that you dreamed a dream."

"Liege? Yes, I did. How you would know that? Are you

scolding me for falling sick?"

"No, I am not. Think back to this morning. I believe you ate or drank something unusual."

Klarenz scanned his memory. "Liege, I ate only common porridge and drank good water, no more."

"Did your porridge taste unusual? There's not much to remark about in your morning's porridge."

"Liege, there were almonds. Heuermann found me and offered a handful. I had forgotten those."

"Then?"

"Liege?"

"Think, Klarenz. You've prepared food often enough. Give me a close description of those nuts."

"Sire, they have a blunt end and a pointed end, are a bit longer than a fingernail, and brown. They also have white flesh."

"Klarenz, why is this becoming difficult?"

"Liege, I can only answer the questions you ask. I beg pardon if my answers are faulty."

"Then I will open my mind to you, Klarenz. You surely recall the Vikings who attacked Shortharbor."

"Liege, most certainly! If only we'd had some then!"

"I—what? What did Heuermann tell you about his handful of almonds?"

"Liege, he said they would help my digestion, and to eat only one. A raven swooped down and tried to steal one, so I threw all of them into the porridge pot and chased the bird away. When I came back there was, now that you mention it, an odd smell, like a new kind of spice, coming from the pot. I blew on it, the odor went away, and I ate my porridge."

"Then fell quickly asleep."

"Liege, it took an hour or more. I think I understand your question about the almonds."

"Let me explain more about Heuermann, his liege lord Schwarzknecht, and that odor coming from your pot. Then tell me about your dream."

Ordowahl listened to a jumbled tale that reminded him of his own dream contest with King Ingvik, especially the riddles. "Tell me again about your losing a contest with the black knight, Klarenz."

"Liege, I cannot. That was part of the rules we agreed to."

"So a rule you agreed to in a dream binds you against the command of your liege lord? Klarenz, before God, answer me."

Klarenz's face melted into tears. He could only manage a ragged sob. "Liege, even if you have me put to the question, if they break my bones, if they pluck out my eyes—Liege, I will not be able to answer."

"Peace, Klarenz, I believe you. *So like that time with Ingvik. Poor soul!* So in other words, I've lost your services. Perhaps now Egeno's master has a way to eavesdrop on us."

A raven hopped innocently down from a nearby oak tree, looking for insects crawling beneath the leaves. It cocked its head at the two men.

Ordowahl motioned with a finger; Klarenz slowly peeked around. When he noticed the bird he stooped down to caress it. The bird hopped onto his shoulder; Klarenz's face relaxed into a quietly happy smile.

"Stay standing, Klarenz."

The bondman sat down cross-legged. He and the bird looked lost in some rapt conversation.

Ordowahl was out of arm's reach of them. He squatted to be on their level. He crept gradually closer. The bird's eye never left him. He looked down at the dirt. After tense moments the bird's gaze drifted back to Klarenz's now blissful face.

Ordowahl closed his hand to scratch up a handful of debris. He lunged forward. Dust and leaves hit the bird. As it leaped into the air Ordowahl threw his other arm out over Klarenz and managed to swat the raven down then smash it flat.

Klarenz stood up; he looked at Ordowahl, sprawled now beside him. He might have kicked his liege in the ribs if Ordowahl hadn't rolled over and scrambled to his feet.

He slapped the side of Klarenz's head, with a hand still dirty with leaves and dust. His fief toppled backward.

"Klarenz!" shouted Ordowahl, near panic. "Klarenz! Don't leave me! Have I killed you? Father God in Heaven, please give him back to me."

The flattened raven wriggled under a bush then disappeared. Klarenz didn't move.

Ordowahl, aghast, paced in a tight circle for several minutes. Finally he knelt beside Klarenz's still form, sprawled akimbo on the ground.

Father God, I think now of your servant Job. If I continue to complain, don't scorn me. Your servant Job has said this:
A man is born of woman, to short days full of unhappiness. He rises up like a flower. He cannot stay the same, but goes back again like a shadow.
And again, he has said this:
Truly a man dies and returns naked to the dust, as the sea recedes or a riverbed runs dry.

Father God, I will become dust. I am of dust. I beg of you, let me have Klarenz beside me while I am not yet dust. Please, don't let him go to dust before he has fulfilled the promise I see in him. Father, according to Your perfect will. Amen, and Amen.

Ordowahl stood. Klarenz didn't seem even to breathe. Desolate, he turned back to the flattened raven. It was not there, and Ordowahl accepted that.

So it goes. Even if you slice such a bird open, it manages to crawl away. When the black knight seemed near to death a raven's beak, or the touch of a feather, let him rise up as though from a refreshing nap.

He recalled King Ingvik's last moment—the slicing of his neck. *Yes! He sliced himself open. Schwarzknecht won't be so kind. I'll have to accomplish that on my own.*

He heard a flutter of wings behind him. Yet another raven perched on the ground by Klarenz's leg.

"Shoo!" He flailed at the bird, and it flew up into the top of a nearby bush. *If you reclaim him, must I slice him open, too?* He heard Klarenz groan, and leapt back to crouch over the still form.

"Liege, I beg forgiveness. You were right to strike me down. I am so dizzy that I doubt I can stand by myself."

With one eye on the raven Ordowahl picked up Klarenz as though he were a child and sat with the bondman in his lap. "I could kiss you," he crooned and caressed the bloody cheek he had struck.

Klarenz tried to stiffen his body, testing his limbs. Ordowahl eased him up to a standing position, and stood with one arm around him to steady his swaying fief.

"Liege, kiss whom you will. Just keep me free of ravens."

The black knight used a magic on Ord's lance
and put a potion into bondman's mush.
Prince managed to outwit the one, but trance-
enraptured Klarenz? In the underbrush.
    Though Klarenz has recovered, still the prince
    has not the confidence he needs to feel.
    This lone trustworthy man cannot convince
    his liege that anything he says is real.
Go forward, Ordowahl? You know that God
has kept you whole for now, against a man
who wields a power like a demigod,
so if you trust in Christ, run t'ward the van.
    No life is worth the living, if in vain,
    so act the part you're made for, God's the gain.

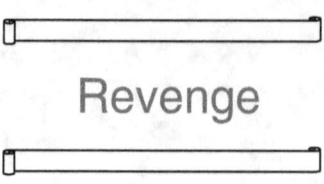

Revenge

Ordowahl sat next to bondman Klarenz on a log in the shade of a tall linden tree. "Klarenz, good my fief, you can tell me now. What was in your dream?"

Klarenz shook a cloudy head and nursed his bruised cheek with one hand. "Yes, Liege. I'm freed from Schwarzknecht's curse of death-but-not-death—I think, now, that the grain of truth in it was falling under your curse!"

"Klarenz, after I struck you I feared that I had taken your life. So yes, I nearly killed you—that shred of truth gave the sorcery its power. I've never studied with a black mage. My honored white mage Heorald, in Nordweg, once told me about such."

Klarenz showed aghast interest.

Ordowahl continued. "They exist, and thanks be to God they are far apart. My father's good white mage believes that the earth does not go on forever—much as it seems to when you try to find its limits—it even circles around to meet itself. Further, the distance you'd travel around that circle is vast. He gave me a number for it, huge beyond my imagining."

He looked at Klarenz to see whether his bondman had followed his train of thought. Was he alert? "The black mage, however! Heorald knows of one, who roams about over a piece of the earth that is much, much larger than the distance from

Nordweg to here. I dwell on that from time to time."

"Liege, in my dream there were riddles. No matter what I did or said, I wound up in some clever corner, until he owned my very life. He instructed me to tell no one about any part of the dream, or I would have an agonizing death that would come on me instantly, yet never let me die—in short, your hand!"

Hearing that, Ordowahl's face went grim.

"This morning when the black knight placed a raven on my shoulder I felt as though I was part of him, a new person yet also an old one, both at once. It was joy, yet it drained all the will from my soul."

"Then?"

"I woke up. While you were at the joust I saw a terrible thing."

"What was that?"

"The black knight, Liege Lord, fell—unhorsed and broken in body. I've never felt such death, such despair, or such a need to avenge him. Pardon me, Liege, I tell only a truth."

"Do you still feel a need for vengeance?"

"Liege, I do—on the black knight for the way he has bound up the souls of many, including our host Egeno. I spoke with him again, Liege, while that raven was on my shoulder just before you killed the foul thing."

"I see, Klarenz. Put peace in your heart. I hear your confession. I forgive you any wrong you may have felt against me. Now also rinse your heart from its darkness. The Lord God wreaks vengeance, for He is just while we, try as we might, are not."

"Liege?"

"I need you to focus on what is, on what may come. In no way can you dwell on how to shed blood or bring harm to Schwarzknecht. If God plans that, He may use me not you. It seems likely, no? Our Lord's strength perfects itself in weakness. Our own strength grows by surrendering to Him. I tell you true, when my bondman Klarenz has a quiet heart, when his mind focuses on his master's well-being and nothing else, only then will God's goodness affect the outcome. Tell me you understand this."

Klarenz struggled, and looked up at Ordowahl. "Liege, my head is full of bells clanging. My eyes see through a haze. Your open hand dazed me. Your fist would have meant death. Yet right now I fear no man nor hate any man and love only you. Guide me."

I am loath to give Klarenz my full trust, yet I must either trust him with my life or not at all. Father in heaven, I have chosen. I pray it is according to Your will.

From what Klarenz tells me, Schwarzknecht has great power to apply, and there is no way to foretell it. It will simply arrive. My lance, shield, armor, Hammerfoot, and saddle have all been where he can work on them while I've been retrieving Klarenz.

Yet black magery has darknesses within its own darknesses. How else could I have used the black knight's magic against him? It operates no matter who uses it. Father, guard me from becoming corrupt. Now I will know only that my own senses work. Everything else can fail. Father, let that much be true: let all my senses be truthful. Amen.

"Klarenz."

"Liege?"

"Did you bring a shiny sword?"

"Liege, a straight one. The black knight didn't think to ask me about it. It would've been an obvious question, which he may have been putting off until you were either dead or a slave."

"What did you learn?"

"Liege, he boasted. I can't understand his riddle in the dream. Once that first raven sat on my shoulder, he claimed that he would roast you with cold fire. He would also run you through with honey, or perhaps run you through with a spear made of cold honey—Liege, it was nonsense. I also believed it."

Ordowahl pondered Klarenz's scattered news, and asked Klarenz to test the coat of mail before putting it on him.

"Liege, it seems sound to me. It makes the same noise, has

the same heft. I don't know what magic is upon it. To joust without mail is to invite death."

"If it grows suddenly hot or cold, how will I fare? Reverse it, Klarenz, back to front and inside to outside."

"Liege, your face will bury itself in mail and leave your neck unguarded.

"Prepare to drop it over me."

"Liege, you stand next to me; standing on your mounting block I can, barely, hold it over your head."

"Yes—observe that I now turn around. This reverses front to back, doesn't it?"

Ordowahl gave Klarenz an odd look. "Now if you drop it on me, it'll have an in-side and an out-side."

"Yes, Liege. My arms tire. May I drop it now?"

Ordowahl reached overhead to take a side of the mail in each hand. "Now, Klarenz, while I have the weight of it, lift up one side."

"Yes, Liege." Klarenz hoisted one side of the mail, which was becoming a tangled mess.

"See now. When I switch hands, drop what you have onto my other hand."

"Yes, Liege." Klarenz pretended not to understand. He did what he was told, miming uncomprehending dutifulness.

"Now observe: what was to my left is to my right and the other way around; what was to touch a shoulder now faces the sky."

"Liege, you are as much a mage as any mortal."

Ordowahl sighed. "Klarenz, Klarenz. These are simple matters if one trains the mind. You, as master of all crafts of wood, metal, leather, and the like, should have been able to think through this on your own."

Klarenz rolled his eyes—he had feigned inability to comprehend a simple mechanical matter, and his liege fell for the joke. He could feel smug, a short hour after wearying pain had shrouded his head.

"Now let us look over the lance. Did Schwarzknecht have

much to say on that subject?"

"Honey—is it *your* lance which will become honey, Liege?—and will not run anyone through. No! Instead it will make a sticky mess that Hammerfoot will have to run through; it may stop him."

"Or he will have to leap it. How can I learn when the lance is about to do this?"

"There is no way, sire—simply hold it off to the side. That way it will dribble into the black knight's lane, not your own."

"Hmmmph. I see. What other riddles can you recall?"

"Liege, that is all of it. Your mount, shield, helmet, saddle— I have no idea whether he has done anything to those or not."

"So I will hold the sword alongside the lance and hope that sticky brown goo doesn't foul it. The shield will doubtless become feathers—"

"Liege! Yes!"

"—while the saddle and Hammerfoot will do whatever they're going to do. At least your liege lord will be alert. Perhaps the feathers will bind together with some of the honey?"

Klarenz rolled his eyes, this time in dismay. "Liege, God in heaven will help you choose rightly. I cannot."

*__*__*__*

At the far end of the jousting track Schwarzknecht sat on a fresh stallion, a dapple-gray. A blaring trumpet jolted the two opponents into an eager charge.

They would meet in six or seven rapid heartbeats. Ordowahl had checked his lance handle for odor—it had none. Neither did the glove on his hand. The lance drifted down to point exactly at Schwarzknecht, whose own lance, on the other hand, seemed to wobble to the side, as though the black knight had intuited Ordowahl's plan and was warning him away.

Ordowahl hefted his shield. It was heavy and very solid.

The black knight's lance still pointed askew, as though he wanted to swat Hammerfoot across the throat.

The crowd, which neither jouster could hear over thundering hooves and pounding hearts, had begun a dubious noise because they could see what was about to happen.

Ordowahl's mail was as it always was: heavy and familiar. His view went blank. He could not see Schwarzknecht and had to rely on instinct to put his lance where it always went—into the path of his onrushing opponent.

Ordowahl fell. His mail grew hot. His shield surrounded him. It had become a pile of splinters dusted with thousands of tiny feathers. His right shoulder was numb; a sticky brown-red mixture flowed from a deep wound. His right arm was useless.

"Get up! How dare you murder a horse?"

Ordowahl looked up to see the black knight coming toward him with a bared sword. Behind him the enormous grey charger thrashed in its final agony. His lance had gone into its chest and through the lungs. Its point emerged behind a stirrup.

"Rise! Ignoble wretch, impostor, false Christian, ignoramus, meet your death as though you were a man, which it's clear you cannot be."

The black knight was not rushing in! Ordowahl interpreted his verbal tirade as a ruse to wait for his magic to work. His mail began to smolder, charring his woven leather battle garment. The smoke was only visible to him and perhaps the black knight.

Speaking quietly so that only Ordowahl could hear him, the black knight said, "Now the cold mail grips you—I see the frost rising up! Freeze now and let the bees' treacle take you to a sweet and rigid death."

Ordowahl staggered to his feet. He bowed his torso to the ground. The ruse of reversing the mail had reversed cold to heat in the black knight's magic, making the honey flow. Now it lubricated the mail rather than freezing it into an immobilizing shroud. He began to shrug the mail off over his head.

The black knight stepped in. When he swung his sword caromed off the sizzling iron mail clumped at Ordowahl's neck, producing only a deep bruise and a burn.

Ordowahl breathed in. He got a strong smell of something aromatic, and acrid. *Father God, he uses a poisoned blade!*

He leaped back, leaving the mail on the ground between

them. It sizzled on the stubble of mowed hay. *My sword—* Ordowahl looked at his empty, useless right hand, dangling from the bleeding shoulder. His lance was gone, buried in the grey stallion. That blunt impact had sent Ordowahl to the ground as much as the deep puncture in his shoulder. He stood there weaponless.

The black knight stepped forward to behead a one-armed, defenseless giant. His boot slipped on the hot-honey-slicked mail—he flung out both arms to break his fall.

Ordowahl's good left hand seized the black knight's right forearm. He broke it; not letting go, he yanked the man into the air. He jerked him about the way a terrier shakes a rat, dislocating the black knight's right shoulder. He tossed him backward; the black knight fell on his other shoulder.

Ravens began to fly in from all directions.

Ordowahl looked around and noticed the glint of his sword. The black knight's sword was much closer. He stood over him; left-handed, he made trash of every raven he could.

Soon enough one of them reached the black knight, even though Ordowahl was standing over his body. When he sensed the man stir beneath him he flicked the sword down at the black knight's neck, and opened his throat.

A swarm of biting flies emerged. The remaining ravens attacked them; a tumbling melee of flies and hungry ravens flew away.

In moments both were gone. A ripe stench of fulsome rot wafted from the black knight's corpse; a tide of maggots gushed from the gaping throat.

Klarenz ran up to sheathe Ordowahl's mirror-bright sword while everyone else still gaped in shock.

"Lords and ladies!" the bondman raised his voice, to rasp at the throng of knights and nobles. The raw fire in his face held their attention. His rasping reedy tenor fell to baritone. "What have you had from the black knight? You've had trouble and lies. You've seen his friends go behind him doing every kind of evil. Now by the grace of God our Father in heaven, his time here is done. Tend to the wound of my master, Prince Ordowahl, ninth son of Stegnwahl, King of Nordweg."

A solitary jackdaw flew down. It lit on Ordowahl's shoulder and pecked at the wound, without noticeable effect. Ordowahl slumped to the ground. He lay still, bleeding, breathing shallow, hoarse breaths.

A wagon trip back to Ermsleben and Egeno's house carried a silent, huge body that refused to become a corpse. For the next several days, one or more jackdaws were always nearby.

What doesn't kill you makes you stronger? No,
how many crippled warriors have you seen
rise up and train for war again? Below
the jackdaws' eyes, does Ingvik intervene?
 That pudgy little man of blackened arts
 threw Ord a rope against the black knight's curse.
 What burden might that gift impose, what darts
 of debt pierce Ordo's soul? How reimburse?
The champion is down, his body torn.
He lies near death—Goliath, head still on—
but such a wound ought fester, and adorn
his corpse with curdling pus 'til life has gone.
 What God intended isn't clear to Ord;
 He lies asleep, en route to his reward.

Hale and Farewell

Ordowahl turned to see who approached his bed—Gelde, the second of the women Egeno had made part of the household to keep up appearances in the town, to show that the prince was not woman-hungry. He had companionship, so posed no threat to disrupt the town's own courtships. She, Gelde, had gone through menopause long since. Ordowahl had moved the "fresher" woman to Klarenz's bed . It was a secret, which two men and two women kept. The prince would never again risk an unplanned birth.

"How fare you now, O counterweight?"

"Ah, Gelde. You treat your prince with such familiarity!" Ordowahl rose up in the bed to a sitting position and levered his legs onto the floor.

She chuckled. "At least your sense of humor is coming back. Or did it ever leave?"

"I was once called imperturbable, also by someone I was deeply fond of. What has it been now, six or seven days since I fell off my horse? I dare say one or more of them passed without my permission."

"Ah, for one who thinks the sun rises and sets at his command, this must be a truth! Tell me now, you who press the bedding near to the floor, with me inbetweenst, what was that word you used, 'fond'?"

"Fond indeed, Gelde. I have a fondness for all sorts of things. You are at the front of the list. Shall I write it out for you? Put it on a parchment you can keep?"

"Prince, I do believe you mean that. No, I'll have no such that ties thee and me. Let God and Law forbid that. There will be a day, I know in my innermost parts"—she winked at him—"when you will leave this place. I see it coming."

She looked at him to see if he understood her. "Somewhere beyond this place, my too-honest, too-kind prince, you will encounter a woman who does not welcome you. She will require you to seek her. You must prove yourself to her. She will keep you on uncertain ground until in a moment she will turn. On the day you two first meet she will shy away from you. She will run, and run, until she overtakes you!"

Ordowahl looked at her in wonder. "Gelde, how do I read this?"

"Read!" she snorted. "Am I inked? Or am I only a person with a face, with a mind, with a Christian soul?"

"Why, now that you ask, dear woman, you are both and all. I read the parchment, the soft, wonderful set of lines and hollows across that plump face, as though your soul were writing them in ink that only my eye can parse. Of course you have a soul and a purpose. God made each of us as a work from His hands. We err to mistreat any soul."

She sighed. "Yet you play a ripe trick on Egeno. Instead of putting your seed into Philomeneke, you set her beneath Klarenz. The child she carries is his, and she deeply loves carrying it. Not only that, he is now morose at leaving behind yet one more fatherless infant. I take it that he has done this many times, and never by choice. What an oddity! That honking rasp of a voice, that odd-shaped head, that scrawny neck. Yet he has charmed and won her. Come to think of it, Ordi, you've been constantly sweet and kind to me, a *grandmother*."

"Then if so sweet, Gelde, we are twain. Having someone run hardened honey through your shoulder can accomplish that. Truly you can outrun me; I cower lest you strike me with your cane!"

"Ha-haa, you never cease. Cane, indeed. All I have to strike you with, Prince Ordi my kept lad, is my eyelashes. Shall I show you now?"

"Greedy girl, it has been a week since I visited your innermost parts. Would, indeed, that you were born later and differently. I could have held conversation with you such as none of the young women I left behind in Nordweg knew, nor cared to."

"Shush! Please don't let me hear you complain about any such young girl. Know you well, Ordi, that young folk are shallow vessels—perhaps not including you—not yet carved deep by fate and misfortune, thus with none of the polish that comes from years of handling." She looked at him carefully. "Prince-lad, in those early years of fertile bloom I was not a whit different from the lasses you managed to disappoint when you left Nordweg. I know the sort of woman you seek, Ordi. When you find one she will make conversation with you for a set purpose: to try you and test you. My masterful prince, you will not master her. She will rebut you, she will run away, until at last she turns to claim you."

Ordowahl stared at her.

She continued, "Believe me in this, Ordi. You must find your equal partner, one who will insist that you prove every bit of your worth, your reliability, your truth. Never show her a timid face, yet always, in all things, tolerate her whims in quietness. Humor her moods, bring her what she needs—in short, woo her. Now it's three times I've told you, so you will be sure to remember."

Ordowahl gave her his complete attention. This sort of schooling seemed to come from age's wisdom

"She will not show you a coy face or call you to her, only accept your right to continue courting her. Have patience, Ordi. You will find a partner worth every small agony, every tormenting doubt she might inflict you with. She will not be fair-minded toward you nor patient with you. You must shower her with complete trust and patience, for that is how she will plumb your depth. Then, when you least expect it, she will reverse and take you."

"Yes, Gelde, you've said that already."

She continued. "You won't know how or why she has done this, but in that moment, dearest Ordi, you will find the reward for all she will have made you suffer. You will be glad. If I live to hear of it, I will be glad also."

He nodded, trying to memorize this new wisdom.

"Now, Ordi, lean on my shoulder—a small lean, mind you! Yes, lean on me. Rise up to make your morning visit to the outhouse. I do look forward to not having your waste waking me in the middle night, even with a lid on the chamber pot."

Another week of healing, and Ordowahl regained basic mobility. "Egeno, it feels good not to be bed-bound. Tell me more about this black knight." They were on the balcony. Ordowahl sat down next to Egeno.

"Hallo, Ordowahl, good Prince. Ravens are suddenly skittish and few. The jackdaw on that limb not far from you has been keeping watch, however. The black knight, indeed. I and the other free knights who attached ourselves to him are diligent to extract ourselves from his memory. But you, receiving a wound such that you should have died in an hour's time! Here you are going up and down stairs, riding horses and I won't imagine what else," chuckling, "barely a fortnight gone. Come in, sit with me at table."

As they went back into the house Egeno called out, "Liebchen, bringst du uns Mittagessen. (Lovey, bring us lunch.)"

Ordowahl peered out the front window, marveling at the gift a decent piece of glass could make. He saw June's bright midday sun. He inferred a tiny breeze trying to sway the boughs of the pines rooted well down slope. Their branches made a patchwork across the view of Ermsleben, spread below them across the small valley.

"Egeno, my good friend, who chose the site for this house?

Who decided its construction, its proportion, its details?"

"Thank you, Ordowahl, for your attention. This house is my own handiwork. We've lived in it for enough years to make its age hard to guess, but it is in fact quite new. I expect it to last for many generations. This is a common design in the Scharz Valley area," he continued. "One day when I was a boy I was up here with some childhood friends. We imagined a castle on this spot. Through luck, hard work, and a knack for managing risk, I had this house completed before I was a married man."

"I see. From the size of your boys, many years have passed since then. How is it that you don't own ten more houses, all leased out to the nobility?"

"I see the wink, Prince Ordowahl. There is more to making a way in the world than turning money into housing."

"Cultivating a friendship with Schwarzknecht?"

"Prince, indeed you haven't lost your sharpness to a simple stab with hardened honey, through a shield reduced to pinfeathers and sawdust. Yes. He received much from my hand. I was happy to give it."

He paused to reflect. "Since the hour you opened him at the neck to release the rot that was his true self, I am left little better off than when I had a new wife with hopes of a child. I have wife, house and children, and not a great deal else. Yet that is not such a bad thing. We who fell under his control have much to do rebuilding trust and acceptance, but we strive."

"Egeno, it is twice now in the two years since I left home that a dark magicker has confronted me. The first one played at spells and potions. He opened his own throat. Schwarzknecht had much more capability and nearly got the better of me. I had to open his throat for him. I sense that, somewhere ahead of me, there is another, even greater threat. For the first—no, second— time in my life I feel genuine unease—what you might call fear."

Egeno nodded. He wore a small, rueful grin. "Fear. That coming from you is telling, Ordowahl. Yes, he sometimes spoke of a greater black mage, somewhere far to the south. He feared this other mage, yet honored him as a great teacher, the same as we honored the black knight. Indeed, Ordowahl, we feared our teacher. Greatly. Thank you, friend Prince, for ridding us of what could only have been a hideous fate at his hands."

He shuddered. "Ordowahl, you can't know the intense joy of that man's presence—what a cloak that was, to cover a wretched evil. I'm looking for a brave priest who will shrive me of what I heard and did under the black knight's spell. Could you smell it on me, sense it in any way, while I was in Hammaborg this past summer?"

"Egeno, I could not. I was naïve; I am, still. My friend, you seemed sane enough to me. I give you my peace on that, with my continued thanks for a place in your household."

Egeno raised his mug for a gulp, and looked across its rim at Ordowahl. "Prince, having you here, and with that most interesting fellow Klarenz, has been a joy. I would not choose to do this differently if the chance came again." A nearby birdcall punctuated his remark.

He turned from scanning the trees looking for the bird, to address Ordowahl face to face. "Speaking of hospitality, I think you've repaid me well in an earthy way. Philomeneke is with child. She will lie in near the start of January, quick work. Thank you, my friend, for bringing me the gift of your seed. I will treasure this child and raise it as my own, if need be."

Ordowahl looked at his hands then back at Egeno. "Did you say that Klarenz was an interesting fellow?"

"Yes, I certainly did. He can do almost anything! What a clever bondman you own. His company is so often amusing."

"Yes. Truth be known, Egeno, I put Philomeneke under Klarenz and took Gelde for mine, from the day you brought those women here. Philomeneke will swear that I am her child's father if you ask her. When you see the infant, you will know at once."

Egeno took the news calmly. "I see. Prince, you are always two steps ahead. One can never get you into a position you don't choose—or, in the case of the black knight, keep you there for long. Well done, my prince, well done. I don't welcome this change, but as sure as God makes sparrows in springtime, Philo's child will be a blessing even with Klarenz as its father."

"Who will raise the child, Egeno? I am certain that, once I am back to moderately good health, I will resume my search for the far side of somewhere. God's small finger, you know."

Egeno smiled back, this time with a rueful twist. "Prince, I understand. I have known for some time that nothing could root you here. Godspeed! Please tell me a couple of weeks prior so I can prepare a stoic face!"

They clasped hands, a gesture they seldom shared. is time it became a full embrace of friendship that would not diminish across time and distance.

Before summer's end Schwarzknecht's town would become a husk, uninhabited. A low mound in its crossroad was the knight's hasty grave, with no cross or stone to mark it.

Ordowahl's wound became a scab, then a scar. The scar itself faded away by early August.

Father God, perhaps when this life is over You will explain the temperance, even good will, that King Ingvik seemed to practice toward me, once I chased him out of that dream.

When You see fit, You will tell me whether you are healing me by the touch of an angel, whether the angel took the form of a jackdaw, and *perhaps one or two other things. Amen.*

$$*\_\_*\_\_*\_\_*$$

Healed and fully fit by the start of summer's most oppressive heat, Ordowahl and Klarenz left the Scharz valley. Klarenz's goodbye with Philomeneke began a week ahead of their departure. Those were the wettest days his shoulder had ever endured.

Ordowahl remarked on that. "Klarenz, is this the first time you've witnessed the tears of parting? Elspet, she who now is mother to one—or more!—youngsters, described the deep sorrows of the damsels you left behind after your visit to Nordweg."

Klarenz paused. A dawning understanding came over his

face. "Liege! Yes, Elspet, Verganeke, Gaelen—may the other forgive me for not keeping her name. My liege lord Ordowahl, thank you for taking me as bondman. If we ever go back to Nordweg, a child is there who is mine, just like the one I leave with Philomeneke to bear and nurture here in Ermsleben. Liege, my life has been under a curse for having too many women hence having no wife, for leaving offspring behind yet never seeing one born. Liege, I dread the morning, a day or two from now, when we—I—will leave a place yet one more time. My prince, I can't ask a favor. Yet, if I could, please let it be that, until you take me to a place where I can make a permanent home, protect me from having a fertile woman in my bed."

Ordowahl looked closely at Klarenz. "Good my bondman, I hear the ache in you. Saint Paul in his letter to Philemon pleads for gentle treatment of a runaway bondman named Onesimus, when he sends the man back to his master. How can I consider my own very loyal fief in a lesser light? It does no one any good now. Still, hear me in this, Klarenz. I regret requiring you to make a sacrifice that I refused to make myself. I confess it to you as a brother in Christ. It was wrong."

That final morning came. With sobbed goodbyes echoing behind them, Ordowahl and Klarenz set out on two horses, with two mules.

"Liege, what do you expect ahead?"

Ordowahl was silent for a moment. "Klarenz, when I told of God's small finger flicking my ear I had no idea, and still don't, of what might lie ahead. I hope that what we did, are doing, is God's intent."

"Liege? Ridding Ermsleben of the black knight looks that way to me."

"Yes, Klarenz. I'm sure of that. I don't look ahead hoping to see some larger, darker bird or a stronger, nastier black mage wearing its image. I know that once a thing is accomplished it is a privilege to rest for a time then go forward to the next work God has prepared."

He paused for a moment. "Do I boast to say that I am as I

am?—able to outwit most, outfight all, yet strongly aware of my debt to our heavenly Father. You, Klarenz? God has made you to be exactly as you are. He put us together at the appropriate time. Thus far the cost to you has included any chance at a peaceful life. Yet we, you and I, love God. We must understand that His will is even more important for us than anything we can imagine on our own."

Klarenz mulled over what Ordowahl had said. "Liege, did He invent Black Magic?—or merely step in with His perfect will to wrest good from that evil?"

"I believe you know that answer, Klarenz. Do you recall the wretched raven sitting on your shoulder? Klarenz, the hand of God on a man's heart is, over the span of his life, also a joy, and a pure one. I seek it, Klarenz. I believe that you are my gift from God, as perhaps I might even be yours, whether or not you can believe that. We go where the road leads us. We will recognize our next task when we come to it. We will begin to understand what is wanted of us when we see what is in a place."

Klarenz looked closely at Ordowahl. "Liege, I've listened to your stories about leaving Nordweg, jousting with Vikings, sailing the sea with them—I saw what you did in that fishing village whose name I no longer care to recall. You captured me there, Liege, and I try to understand all that you say."

"Klarenz, St. Paul writes in his letter to the Ephesians that we are God's workmanship. He tells us that Almighty God has prepared tasks in advance to be done by those He loves. In effect Paul says that we are Christ's tools, if you want to think of it that way. What we accomplish, as long as we keep Him in our thoughts, is His doing, not ours—no more ours than a craftsman's work belongs to his awl or hammer."

"Liege, I sense a risk of doing wrong in God's name. Or doing wrong not in His name for that matter—some day I hope to learn more of what good the Father has done for you via Gnade Grace and you for her."

"Klarenz, you understand. Yes, someday I will have to find the explanation for my behavior with Grace. Whatever God has reaped there, He plainly did not sow it. Because we are God's tools, we should not work for what we imagine. Instead let us discover the work that God has planned. Many such things are easy to understand—clothing the naked, feeding the hungry, giving shelter to those who lack it."

"Liege, that includes nearly everyone we meet!"

"That's why it's work, Klarenz." Ordowahl smiled. "Everyone who wants to do God's will needs to step back from his own planning. Did I fight the black knight because it would bring me glory? No, it was because a great opponent confronted me—one that shouted its evil. God decided the outcome, no matter jackdaws or ravens or sorcerer's honey."

Klarenz kept silent for a while, pondering the black knight and his own peril.

Ordowahl watched his fief and broke the silence. "Klarenz, what do you think of baked apples, cream, and a slice of cheese?"

Klarenz sighed. He turned to look at the prince. "Liege, I know where we ate them last winter."

In the humid warmth of early August the two men followed a descending road, leaving the Harz Mountains. They traveled toward the south and west at the speed of a walking horse. Ordowahl was careful to stay far from Rigomonde's native city of Bremen, thus also Haus Tannhaueffig.

Klarenz had a different problem on his mind. "Liege, I have often left a place, but never before in such a calm state. The feeling is strange. Why do I fear what lies hidden somewhere down the road?"

Ordowahl answered, after a moment's thought. "Klarenz, you have served me for two years. You were fourteen years absent from Hammaborg even then. If that leaves you fearing what is strange, well, I don't find that strange." He gave Klarenz a wry look.

Klarenz said nothing; he crossed himself. His liege was noble, also barely able to grow hair on his chin, not yet twenty years of age. He whispered a prayer for protection against whatever challenge might lie ahead, and no matter how subtle its disguise.

So as all does, those soft days go to dust.
Prince Ordowahl, now healed, still seeks God's touch
and takes poor Klarenz back to wanderlust.
Importance, his—his fief's child? Not so much.
He hears no call, no cause for him to stir.
    Ermsleben's evil knight has been interred.
    Lax boredom's sin for our adventurer.
    His plan at surface is, research God's word.
    Here deviate from Ordowahl, now cast
adrift. He's handled all the men he's met,
though very few—he's young. How will he last
'gainst femme who'll use his head to play croquette?
    Prince Ordowahl, a scholar of God's Book
    picks up and leaves without a backward look.

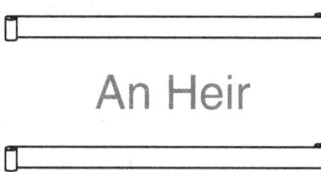

An Heir

(pronunciation guide, vowels, with letters j, v, w)

Based on	Jakop	YAH kawp	
modern	Janalei	YAHN a lye	(Jana, YAHN nee)
Dutch	Joop	YOPE	(Joopi, YOPE ee)
pronunciation	Rappje	ROPP yeh	
	Rutelyn	ROOT eh lin	
	Vendink	FEN deenk	
	Wegjulde	veg YOOL deh	

ANNO DOMINI MXLVII (1047)

Outside, moonlight glimmered in the late August evening. Rappje, Count Vendink, now so old that once-gray hair had gone to wispy white, drank ale with his son Jakop after the rest of the family had gone up to sleep. In that privacy he revealed his anguish. "Jakop, I am old. I will die soon. If it is tomorrow, you will be cast out."

The frank remark froze Jakop's face in mid-swallow. He gulped "Father?"

"I have named someone else as my heir." His face became stoic.

Jakop's stunned disbelief caromed off his father's stony gaze like a mouse's panic off a cat's striking paw.

259

"What age have you reached, son? More than fifty years? Are you a grandfather yet?—Don't answer that—you are many times over. Yet what heir do you supply me?"

"Papa, I am of course the heir you ask for."

"What of your heir? Since growing a beard and a real dick you've plowed the women of this and every neighboring county. You've cuckolded a hundred husbands, left them to give your bastards Christian names and raise them as their own."

"Papa, am I the only one who does this?"

Rappje's face clouded in anger. He whispered to keep his voice from carrying. "What sort of example have I given you? You excuse yourself by others' vices? Verdoemte, Jakop!"

The count's son went pale.

Rappje took three deep, slow breaths to calm himself. He exhaled three times through clenched teeth. "God intervene to keep your sons and daughters, all of them unknowing half-brothers or half-sisters, from marrying each other." He glared at Jakop, indicating the moral stench of engendering such scandal and without a second thought. "This is nobody's secret. The cross-hatch of scars on your face reminds everyone of duels fought by the braver of those men."

Jakop could think of nothing to say. Life as the son of a powerful, respected count gave him easy access to both sins and forgiveness. He'd never been one to hold back. Now two years past fifty, he still played the carefree, vagabond lover, albeit one with a grudging understanding of a count's demanding role.

Rappje, once possessing a vigor that commanded fear—and through that respect—had faded to a dignified yet still-forceful elder, and from there to a man who commanded respect on memory alone. The count spoke only truth. His yes was yes, his no was no. Rappje Count Vendink had no favorites and a single vice—his son Jakop.

"I near my end. I have decided this much—thirty years too late, in my frank opinion. I require you to become an honorable man. Your word to man and woman alike must be your bond, lest you be turned out with nothing once I die."

Jakop paused before he answered. "Father, I won't ask which of my several cousins you've groomed to succeed you as count. Rumors are like leaves on a tree while truth lies hidden as heartwood."

Rappje leaned closer to his son. "Jakop," he said in a conspiratorial whisper, "I have loved you more than you may ever know. Thereby I also shielded you from the need to grow up."

Jakop searched a face that could still freeze any other man where he stood. His father did not blink.

"Here is my command. Marry. Get your wife with child. Name a child born to you by your wedded wife, not a village-full of other men's wives."

"Yes, Papa." Jakop used the voice of a chastened boy.

"Even if your firstborn is female, Jakop, on that day I will restore you as my heir. Then you will inherit at my death—only then."

Jakop knew the other, less spoken half of the bargain. He would become a man of honor in his father's mold else there could be no marriage, for lack of his father's blessing.

Jakop spent a month paying careful attention to unmarried women—hardly a change. He attended every ball, party, or celebration. His list narrowed within a week to a half-dozen. By month's end Jakop knew the one.

October began. Tall, red haired, with a dazzling smile and robust health, she had already toppled many hearts. The miracle of her single state let Jakop hope. He realized that the only way to traverse this sudden tightrope, his strange new vulnerability, lay in open pursuit of the spectacular, strong-willed Rutelyn, daughter of Carlamt, Baron Wegjulde. Her father had not married her off, and no one knew why—Jakop wondered at that and fell into rapt fascination.

Ever the wooer, he found himself assessing the fact that, at his level of the nobility, personal relationships mattered far less than families' political and economic interests. Surely Wegjulde would leap at the chance. They had been close friends for decades. Yet he remained patient.

After two months of closer and closer approach he told Rutelyn that he was considering how to approach her father.

"Grandfather Jakop?" she smirked at him, "My father has often told me how he looked up to you, when you were both young. In fact, I think you are senior to my father by two years."

She spoke as to a casual acquaintance, regarding some off-hand fact.

"Yes?" he said.

"Please have your father speak to mine—that is, if he hasn't gone too far into his dotage to handle weighty matters."

Her nominal agreement so punctured his formal dignity that he bit down to stifle a happy shout. He had fixated on her. He feared that her choice in the matter could overpower her father's.

Despite her solemnity, a tiny crinkle at the eyes hinted that she was merely testing him. Hearing "grandfather" stung more than the casual disrespect for his father the count. Receiving her mercy exposed his vulnerable state.

Looking at him in the moment, she said, "Grandfather, do I see terror in those ancient eyes?" In a whisper to herself she added, "And beneath it, courage?"

"Child," he said back. He ignored her unsubtle dig. "Yes, I'm older than your father. I am also far wiser than any of the young men you've turned aside. Also I am still a great force to be reckoned with." The crinkle in his own eye showed that he felt like a young man toward her.

Rutelyn took a second look at her suitor. Jakop was infamous for "feeling like a young man" toward any female who had passed menarche, including many that were quite old. She turned and stalked away. For a month she refused to sustain eye contact with him. No one overheard her other, repeated, whisper, "I fear becoming, post-marriage, bored with lonely nights."

She turned aside each of his attempts to converse. Every time he saw her at a ball, or party, or picnic, she would flirt with one or two of the handsomest, most desirable, unwed young men. She stared at him at those moments—that is, when there was room to catch his eye through the ring of fascinated bachelors.

At last, early one frosty morning at the turn of the new year, a Wegjulde footman knocked at the grand entry door of Castle Vendink. He bore an invitation to receive a visit from Lord Jakop the next morning. Jakop had already gone out for the day. The head servant knew at once what the request would entail. He replied that Jakop would call on the baron at his earliest convenience.

The day passed, night fell. That servant found Jakop in the stables as he was handing his tired steed to a groom. "My Lord Jakop," he said formally.

Jakop turned to look at him, knowing something important had happened. "What is it?"

"My Lord Jakop, Carlamt Baron Wegjulde has asked that you call on him. I have already taken the liberty of telling him that you would do so at your earliest convenience. Pardon me if I have erred."

There was no chance of that. Still, the polite demurrer satisfied servant-master protocol. "You have done well!" Jakop said. He turned to the groom and said, "What luck! I will leave before first light."

At dawn the next morning, the head servant held open the door to the Wegjulde mansion. "Welcome, Lord Jakop. My master, Carlamt Baron Wegjulde, is pleased that you have come." He led Jakop into a small room off the vestibule. In too little time to be coincidence the baron strode in. "My lord," he began in a formal voice, "we can speak in private here," as though privacy were possible in a well-staffed house.

"My daughter has spoken to me of your pursuit." His face held no expression to guide Jakop one way or the other. Their long-ago man-to-man relationship held many fond memories. Three intervening decades and the risk to his jealously guarded daughter restrained the baron the way a stone wall in mid-collapse can restrain someone eager to repair it.

Jakop, on the other hand, wondered whether Rutelyn had accused him of an impropriety—or might he find a better sort of conversation?

"Yes, my friend Carlamt, what do you wish to tell me about your daughter? If I can speak, pertinent to the subject on your mind, she is a most amazing young woman."

"Yes," said the baron. He held back the normal "thank you."

"Yes. She asked me whether you have spoken with me. I cannot recall any recent conversation. I have nothing to say to you. Can you speak to me about my daughter?"

"Yes indeed, my friend, I can."

"Friend Jakop, I love my daughter like my own life. Her happiness is important to me in ways that you, who haven't raised a daughter to womanhood, cannot comprehend."

Jakop studied the baron's very serious expression. Count Rappje's protective regard for his son may trouble the baron; Jakop saw that its converse moved Baron Wegjulde just as deeply. "My honorable friend, Baron, since discovering the joys of the flesh I have abused the hearts of too many women to count. I confess this with no pride and full penance."

Carlamt frowned. Jakop's incorrigible resort to all the seductive arts made "penance" hard to visualize.

"I must find a wife and have considered a hundred young women. Your daughter's good will controls me. I offer my loyalty—to you, to her, and to your family. Please accept me as a future son-in-law."

The baron's face didn't change. He waggled a finger at someone standing outside the room. Rutelyn came in, dressed as though for a grand ball.

She regarded Jakop as though sizing up a horse at an auction. Making a pirouette, she showed a slow, tentative smile.

"Better judgment be damned, Grandpa," she said while looking him in the eye. "I accept your twin pledges of loyalty and honor. Papa, choose my fate now, lest I change my mind."

Another half-pirouette, and she walked away with starchy, erect posture. At once the baron stood. Jakop also rose to his feet.

The baron paused.

Jakop held his old friend with a thoughtful gaze. *This matter is difficult for him to settle. He knows it may never fully settle in his daughter's mind. She has asked her father to award me, his childhood companion and the count's son, the formality of beginning to settle on a dowry. Before we negotiate the details of inheritance, titles, and such, he grants me the mere right to approach her.*

"Carlamt, I am an old dog," Jakop said. "I do not promise to change, except for one thing. Your daughter has changed me. I do not want to go back."

Baron Wegjulde sighed and extended his hand. "Lord Jakop, I hope for the best from our future bond as father-in-law and son-in-law."

Jakop realized that he had been holding his breath. For a dizzy moment he steeled himself to stay upright. He inhaled with a loud rasp as he accepted Carlamt's hand. "Dear future father-in-law, even though you are a younger man than I, you have my full respect. Thank you."

*__*__*__*

No one bothered to count back 40 weeks to conception, a time when Rutelyn, daughter of Carlamt Baron Wegjulde, was not yet wife to Lord Jakop, son of Rappje Count Vendink. Arrival of a healthy child mattered, nothing else. Jakop watched his father's smile. In that era the birth of a titled heir overrode modesty. Rutelyn's audience—although in her deep fatigue she didn't notice—watched the midwife extract an infant from her spread loins.

Dangled upside down, the baby wore a crown of her mother's red hair. She rebelled at the midwife's tender swat. Her fury and her size almost made grandfather Rappje sit on the floor. He ran out of the room, Jakop on his heels, to shout to the rest of the Haus that a child was born. Her name was to be Janalei.

Toddler Janalei's curiosity overflowed, every day and all day, except when she gave her nanny Joop the respite of a shared nap. Because Joop loved men not women he was ideal as Lady

Janalei's caregiver. Some of her lasting memories from childhood involved sleeping either alongside Joop or nestled in his arms. On one such summer afternoon she woke, stretched, and touched Joop's groin.

"Joopi, when I get bigger like Mama and Papa, will we be naked and make sex?"

"Child, where do your ideas come from?" He stretched slowly away from her pudgy fingers.

"Well, I watch them!"

"Jana, you watch them? How do you do that?"

She looked at him as though he were daft. "Joopi, I see them all the time I am awake. Right now Mama is telling Cook what to buy tomorrow morning from farmers in the square."

"Hmmm," said Joop, "what will she buy?"

With a grownup's precise diction Janalei gave word-for-word the countess's instructions to a trusted lowborn subordinate. "See, Joopi? We're out of lamb and Papa loves it so much. He even calls Mama his leg of lamb when he licks her cunt. Mama wonders, "Why that?" She loves it so much she doesn't care."

Joop said nothing. He gave Janalei a thoughtful look. Finally, when she looked a question at him, as if to say, "What? What are you thinking?" he said, "Jana, people feel very private about those parts of their bodies."

"Yes!" she said. "Mama and Papa always make sure no one else can see them."

"So?" he asked.

"So," she said, "I should not talk about Mama and Papa's all-alone times. Can I still talk about them with you?"

"You can, but then someone other than your Mama and Papa will know about those. Do you think they would like that?"

Janalei's little face fell. "There is so much happiness all over their bodies when they do that. I love it!"

Joop said nothing.

By the time Janalei had reached her fifth birthday, midafternoon naps had shrunk to a lazy half hour in whatever shade they could find, watching clouds. Janalei's casual acceptance of that constant awareness of her parents — in a few small ways understanding them better than they did themselves — challenged Joop. He'd become inured to it. Then she surprised him.

"Joopi," she said, turning to look up into his face, "I will meet a bad, bad man,"

He gave her a serious look. "Tell me about that, Jana."

"I will be a grown woman. My greatest happiness in life is to become Countess once Daddy passes away. Some huge, strong man will come, from far far far away to the north."

"Is the north bad?"

"Joopi! It isn't bad or good, it just isn't County Vendink. How can I be countess if he takes me back to where he was born?" Her skeptical frown accused Joop of clear stupidity.

Joop decided to believe that she not only had constant second-sight into her parents, she even knew things that would affect her future. "Jana, we trust in God. We pray to God every day. When evil comes, we resist it, and trust that God's love will keep us safe."

"Yeah," she said, and sat up.

In time Joop forgot the matter. She was too prone to such pronouncements for him to take any of them seriously.

*__*__*__*

Trees had begun to leaf out in the first temperate days of spring. They remained mostly sticks. Janalei, not yet eleven and already very tall, rode out into the countryside with Joop, to a place where the land wasn't tillable. They found an apple orchard with a small stream running beside it.

"Joopi, climb a tree with me!" She halted her horse and hopped off.

Joop dismounted, tied both horses to the closest tree, and asked her, "Do you want an old man, past thirty years like me, to climb like a child?"

"Joopi," she said with a grin, "Don't you ever like fun?"

She doesn't know anyone other than her parents – I haven't told her what is most fun to me. And I'm not sure she would care. Alas, I worry over the opinion of a ten-year-old! "Jana, watching you have fun is the closest thing, for me. Just don't fall and hurt yourself."

He instantly regretted saying that. She turned away from him, missed her grip on a limb, sat down on a broken-off twig— a large one—and screamed in pain. "Joopi, the tree has killed me!"

He moved to stand beneath her and held his arms up, making a basket to catch her. She dropped into his arms, weeping with pain. Indeed, she had been injured. He saw blood.

"Put me on the ground," she said. Once down, she laid back, lifted her skirt, and moved her legs apart.

"Child, your pantaloons have a tear, and right where it is not fatal." He found it difficult to suppress a laugh. "It would seem that the tree deflowered you."

"It hurts like all hell! That didn't happen to Mama when Papa deflowered her."

"Well, you father had something a lot more suited to the purpose." He lifted her up, she still holding the hem of her skirt around her shoulders, and sat her down in the stream.

"Good God in heaven that's cold!"

'It won't kill you. Wash yourself as best you can, rinse the blood from your pantaloons, then I'll dry you with my tunic."

My own God in heaven she curses like her father, reacts to injury like him   I can't wait to tell my beloved Endru next time I can get away to see him.

"Well," Janalei said with a philosophical sigh, "It's up to me to remain a virgin in spirit if not in body. I tell you three times, Joop, I will never take a husband."

Red-headed, tomboy, always in command
because she knows far more than what is good,
her gift of second sight a mult'plicand
that makes her parents' lives too understood.
    She knows that Ord will visit her one day
    and that, once there, he'll switch her life around.
    His name's unknown, and once he's sent away,
    she'll still wear pants, and ne'er be wedding-gowned.
Today she starts to practice for her role
as virgin countess, 'til the day she die.
Jan aims to exercise complete control;
forewarned, she's sure that naught can go awry.
    She, two years older than this lummox threat,
    e'en so must wait to see who wins the bet.

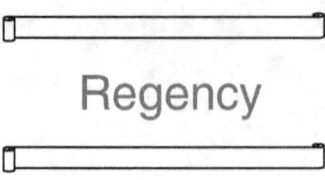

Regency

ANNO DOMINI MLXVI (1066), 9 MAY

"Lady Janalei, my daughter," said Count Jakop, "this day is your seventeenth birthday. Today I name you Regent."

The remark didn't seem to surprise her in the slightest. Had she said, "Yes, Daddy, I knew this beforehand. I have awaited it," her father also would have felt no surprise.

What she did say was, "I adopt this city's name, Utrecht, for my given name as vice-count. Know me as Vice-Count Utrecht of Vendink. Do men exercise authority?" she asked. "I'll exercise a vice-count's authority in public. To substantiate the role, I will wear a man's garb."

He had in fact asked the abbot at St. Martin's Church whether a woman could wear a man's clothing.

The abbot knew her with a confessor's insight. "Count," the abbot replied, "she has already asked me the same. I gave her permission to dress as a man while pursuing a man's duties."

That didn't make the idea pleasant. Jakop raised an eyebrow.

"Daddy, I located a very surprised tailor who has already completed my wardrobe. He is also very circumspect." She crinkled her nose at him. "I delight in surprises."

Jakop sighed.

She continued. "He made up numerous pantaloons, tunics, and coats for each season—without sleeves in spring and fall, with sleeves in winter."

"Daughter, While I am still able to conduct the county's business, I will rely on you, by degrees, to assume my duties. In a scant two or three years I may need you, Vice-Count Utrecht, my heir and assign, to become my face and my voice." *I am more certain than ever that you have been able to peer inside my mind,* and *your mother's, from your first breath. Yet I still have your love* and *respect!*

She gave him a sincere smile.

1070 END OF AUGUST

"Liege," said Klarenz, can we find shade? Our horses and mules bear the sun's heat on this hot, moist day." He put a hand to his brow to scan both the lane ahead and the flat cropland far to either side.

Ordowahl smiled. "Yes, bondman, my livestock perspire and are weary. All five of you. Yet we've seen longer, warmer days than this."

"True enough, liege, yet we draw near to the ocean and that makes the air much more, well, wet. I give thanks to God that our destination, Utrecht, is close at hand."

"Then why worry about a bit of shade now, Klarenz? Simply keep on and let the road take us to more than shade and water, to a city."

"See ahead, Liege, someone not quite large enough to give shade comes our way."

Ordowahl looked forward. Perhaps two hundred yards distant he spied a horse. *Lovely animal, and with glistening tack. Its rider appears smallish. Even from this distance I can see that he is very self-assured.* "What do you think, Klarenz? Who comes?"

"Liege, I have heard that the count seated in Utrecht has a daughter as his heir. She's said to be the equal of any man you care to mention. Not you! Liege, not you. *She* is formidable. Furthermore she is said to receive court from nobles far and wide, and soon enough rejects each one."

"Her position as heiress would guarantee a stream of

suitors."

"Yes, Liege. She is also said to have a face which inflames a man's heart with Cupid's fiery arrow."

Within minutes the three faced each other. The other rider proved female, as Klarenz had predicted.

She spoke. "News of you has reached me, and I am greatly displeased. Are you not the man who slit another man's throat while he was down?" She waited for Ordowahl to respond.

"That is beyond dispute. I believe I see a woman dressed against Scripture, in a man's garments. So we are each highly suspect."

Her face twitched, as though her nose itched; her eyes didn't smile. "In other words you state a fact and make it into an insult. Since I have not made it known that I am Vice-Count Utrecht, Regent of County Vendink, I will ignore that. Be sure to know your place hereafter." This time her nose didn't twitch.

"And I am Ordowahl, Prince of Nordweg, ninth son of King Stegnwahl. I received the same, a fact misconstrued as an insult. I surely know my place, and have told you what it is." He could not put a scowl on his face when looking at her. *Klarenz, you are too poor a poet.*

"I will be the judge of what my words mean, Prince – if indeed what you say is true. I've never heard of you, or your father, and don't look forward to any sort of acquaintance. I am regent of this county. Whatever business you have here is my concern. State it."

"As you will, Vice-Count. Being the final son of many, my place in God's world has no set definition. I don't expect it to take a shape for years, if then. For the time being I seek instruction amongst Utrecht's community of religious scholars. During my childhood, study of the Vulgate of Saint Jerome left a great deal of it living within my memory. It yearns for scholars to stimulate it."

"Do you seek novitiate status, perhaps to become a monk or even priest?"

She seems to enjoy that idea. "No, Vice-Count Utrecht, I

have my father's command that I must return to Nordweg and expand the royal family there. I make no plan. In fact, God in heaven seems to have led me to each of the places I so far have gone. I do not doubt He put me here. As yet the reason hides from me. I am here, and I plan to study. Past that, or what I will have to eat in the morning, are unknown."

She scoffed, "You believe God in heaven has used you to slit a defenseless man's throat." She coughed up phlegm and spat at Hammerfoot's front hoof. "Please keep your presence from galling mine." She spurred her horse and brushed past him. Ordowahl could hear Klarenz doing his best to stifle a guffaw.

Nothing about her asked Ordowahl to consider Gelde's remarks regarding the woman he would find for himself; any such lay in a distant future. Yet this one indeed had a compelling presence and maddening beauty.

The main square contained a hum of mid-morning traffic. An alehouse lay just off it, close by the castle gate. It held Vice-Count Utrecht. She took her usual place in deep dimness at the back of the foul-smelling, windowless room. She appeared there often, usually in late afternoon, to "hear gossip." Many of the gabbier sort would bring her tales of who did what, how, to whom—she always gave wife beatings a sympathetic ear. Which noble family had done something friendly, or inimical, toward another. Underhanded practices in the market. Who had been seen on the roads coming toward the city. And so on.

The vice-count found it pleasing to retreat from her formal, stern male persona there. In the dimness she could relax her posture. If the information sounded useful she would often buy her news bringer a mug of ale as a token gift. At this moment, however, she shut out the outside world—the day's details had been trivial—and relived yesterday's encounter with the ill-omened man from far to the north.

How well I can bring to mind Mother's first encounters with Daddy. He had a male aura that roused a tingling in her female parts. No one has ever done that, God help me, to my female

273

parts. I give thanks to You, Father in heaven. I have had no trouble remaining virgin, thus future Countess.

Yet! Meeting that giant on the east road took me close to surrender! Father God in heaven, hear my plea. Save me from this man. And not only did I meet him as he came in, I circled around to watch his arrival from a place not fifty feet from here – and felt that pull all over again. I plead with you. Mother Mary and all the saints, guide me! Help me to live out my life in County Vendink. Help me die old, never wed, and very, very happy!

Under her breath she muttered, "So, whoever you are, too-young man, brutish intruder, northern giant, I care not that you might have killed an evil knight. Fare you well. Visit if you must; then get you gone."

He lives from day to day and trusts that God
will guide his footsteps—then he makes a plan!
He'll study in a famous place. Applaud
his choice or not, Ord's not a welcome man.
    She's feared for years the brutal man who'd drag
    her, callously, away from home and life.
    His servant, bondman? Randy scalawag
    who, legend has it, made a sword-sized knife.
While mysteries rise up like waves before
a seaward eye, there's nothing dim 'bout him.
She's seen him coming, her pet minotaur,
and hers the lab'rinth, his the horns she'll trim.
    Two strangers meet upon the roadway, and
    each notices the other's self-command.

Back Story

Ordowahl's extended family

Stegnwahl b. 1009   King of Nordweg

Clothilde	b. 1011		queen, deceased, 1042
Frenkowahl	b. 1031,	17 October	
Dinnowahl	b. 1035,	3 March	
Ennowahl	b. 1037,	12 September	
Gerdowahl	b. 1039,	15 August	
Heinowahl	b. 1042,	7 January	
Vibeke	b. 1021		queen, deceased, 1049
Leowahl	b. 1044,	14 March	
Adennowahl	b. 1046,	12 November	
Meldowahl	b. 1049,	8 March	
Magnhild	b. 1027		Queen
Ordowahl	b. 1051,	26 May	
Ruta	b. 1053,	17 June	
Marget	b. 1055,	27 November	
Maryon	b. 1058,	3 February	

Other Nordwesh characters, in order of appearance:

Mage Heorald

Father Ewald

Elspet, daughter of the town's thane; "Auntie El"

Vronken, smith

Brohonna, town lass

Rohondelinde, a distant cousin

Mehrwal, first cousin

Behrwal, Khetwal, sons of Mehrwal

Marthe, sent by Mehrwal

Dahnekin, wife of Mehrwal

Lonny, an innkeeper

Vlowohl, first cousin

Marien, Anne and Marthe, housemaids to Vlowohl

Kleywehl, second cousin

Ordwehl, son of Kleywehl

Jonwehl, a child

Blunhetle, Frennete, Nanneke: daughters of Kleywehl

Jonquil, wife of Kleywehl

I sing of Ordowahl of box-boned face.
In time of absent moon his mother birthed
him; 'neath a darkened star began life's chase,
Prince Ordowahl the huge, ne'er overgirthed.
  Full straight and strong he grew. Though featured ill
  his inward parts held honor's holy spark.
  Three mothers bore nine sons, but not until
  this last did one appear with kingship's mark.
From early on his purposed, patient way,
his study, caught his father's wond'ring eye.
But quickest mind and pow'rful martial sway
had made each brother's ill-will multiply.
  What started with an infant's outraged squall
  became a quest to meet then master all.

Dark Skies, Early Years

The king stared into a setting sun. It glared mute farewell, and sank through the bottom of a dim sky, gray as ancient lead. *Eight children, all sons, and I lament that each is or will be drunk on inherited power. No son of mine old enough to assess understands honor beyond fearlessness in combat. Real strength knows how to be gentle and kind, yet I have failed to instill this. Dear God, please let me have one child to be truly proud of. Amen.*

Royal mage Heorald stood near him. "Sire, an overturned moon set near an hour ago, poured out and invisible to all but a tutored eye. Scarce an hour after sunrise a new one will appear, frail and ready to fill."

The king looked at his mage, and nodded. *Heorald means more than he says. What can the sky tell me now?*

Soon, perhaps this night, new Queen Magnhild, tall and raw-boned, would bear her first child. She came to the kingdom large and plain as a field ox; now her belly bloomed larger than any the king had ever seen. She waddled the palace halls; contralto complaints filled stone corridors the way a trumpeter's note swells out through the instrument's bell. Her protests made it impossible to conduct the business of Nordweg.

The king wondered, *did she carry a child or a troupe?* Two other queens had carried his get. Clothilde bore him five, all sons. He had mourned her while cradling her last infant, Heino, beside a mound of fresh earth. Soon enough his best-beloved, Vibeke, had died birthing her third, son Meldo. Eight children, eight heirs. Would Magnhild finally give him a daughter to dote upon? He felt torn – yes to the girl, and no to the face this wife would likely give her.

The queen ate no supper; no one in the palace found sleep. The king's sons gathered around him by a smoky hearth. Frenkowahl, eldest, was over two years into his Manhood. In brief silences between echoing protests they tried out various names – *I beseech You, dear God, a girl, and a clean birth.*

Magnhild came from warrior stock and was rightly a queen. Her noise grew, and increased again. It did not quaver; she was fierce, not anxious. At last in a dark hour of middle night an infant cried. The king snorted out of a half-slumber, leapt from his place at the hearth, and rushed past protesting midwives to look upon the bloody birthing bed, to see what he had.

A son.

He growled. He saw why her belly had been so large. The midwives tied off the umbilicus and washed the child as the king looked on; they dandled him, naked and squalling, to be inspected. His supine queen rose up and propped herself onto her elbows: "A man not a boy! Look, he's so big he might stand on his own. King, Stegnwahl my lord and beloved, give me his naming. Have I not earned it?"

The king smiled at his ox-plain, badger-proud queen. "I had a girl in mind, and have run through the list for boys. I invite you to name my ninth son."

"Ordeal! A joy beneath my heart, but oh, such a rumpus he's raised, these months banging about inside me; let him be called Ordo."

Morning came; the king kept a royal discipline and rose to greet the sun. He and mage Heorald stood in the chill courtyard and thought they could see, at the eastern horizon beneath the sun's fierce hello, the faint empty cup of a new moon. "Sire," said Heorald, "This moon passed from old to new at the same deep hour that Ordo came forth from his mother to seize first milk from her breast."

Neither King nor mage mentioned that morning again, yet the signs spoke plainly. The sky had blanked the stars and held no moon. They followed the Book and paid heed to Father Ewald's reading from it: fate always hid and God had stated his intent in the heavens once only, and that time He had sent a angels to sing the announcement.

They could not forget the oddness of this birth. The mage was heir to training that far predated Priests and Book, and he mumbled something in an ancient tongue. The king thought he heard hope, and terror, and awe – Heorald stayed locked in silent struggle and said no more.

"Papa, I smack it!" Four-year-old Ordo, half a head taller than six-year-old Meldo, held a small spade in one hammy fist and a bent rabbit in the other.

The king turned from his stroll along Magnhild's herb garden and stopped to see; "Tell me about the rabbit."

"I watch where they go, and I get a shubble, and wait for one. And I smack it!"

"And what will you do with your prize?"

"I gib it to cook!"

"Indeed; a man who hunts his own food stands a better chance of eating." He smiled; no prince of Nordweg would ever starve. Ordo's size suggested that. The king mused; what other son at this, nay, at any age had spent himself in close study of ordinary things? Or had surprised and harvested game with his hands?

Which one, while still learning to speak clearly? And then see the carcass as more than a windfall to brandish, see that it had a purpose?

Small distinctions, perhaps; but the king noted that his oversized ninth son might have a mind as robust – and, God willing, as quick – as his body. *What was his Baptismal verse? - yes! – from the twenty-seventh Psalm: "Wait on the LORD: be of good courage and He shall strengthen thine heart: wait, I say, on the LORD." My son, you have learned the waiting part.*

"Here, what's this?!" King Stegnwahl had walked into a gravel paved side yard of the castle, and confronted a stair-stepped ring of sons, ages ten to fifteen, surrounding eight-year-old Ordo. Each showed some sign of recent combat - a scrape, a bruised face, and so on. Ordowahl, in the middle, was a mess, yet stood as tall as he could. Meldo was shorter, Adenno about the same, Leo taller.

"You see, Father," said Leo, "We're teaching our youngest brother to stand his ground and fight. He seems to be catching on."

"And, of course, you're doing so in a way that emphasizes nobility of heart, fairness of equal combat, and, oh, I'm sure you can name two or three more of the primary concerns that one brother should show another."

Leo was silent.

"Father, let me defend Ordo," spoke up Adenno, who was approaching twelve.

"Go then, Adenno. Go stand beside him," said the king. "I will take your spot in the ring of challengers and do my best to enlarge your experience as a fighter."

"Sire! What I meant to say was that Ordo agreed to be in the ring, and that he has been very capable, for his size and age."

"Don't smirk at me, boy! Get into the ring, and fight with me. When I have instructed each of you to my satisfaction, we will consider this lesson complete. I insist that all of you reach adulthood - so I will be gentle with you now - Becoming an adult also means to achieve wisdom and tact. Perhaps I can fight some of that into you as well."

"Papa, fight with me first!" shouted Ordo.

What have I created? Here is a son to be proud of; what

have I not done with his brothers that I did with him? He sighed. "My sons, I've seen more of an adult in your youngest brother than from any three grown men I can choose at random. Not to mention courage. Ordo, what did your brothers tell you, to get you to agree to this?"

"Papa, they didn't tell me, you did. A man is always ready to fight, no matter what. I asked 'Denno to fight with me, and the others came to help. I am a man!"

"Yes, Ordo, you are. I see that you have done well. Now, the rest of you sons of mine, clean yourselves up, and take care to clean Ordo before his mother sees him. She lives by the Holy Book, yet might forget herself.

"And since you want to learn to fight, Ordo, I will tell Engtzohn, our fightmaster, it is time to tutor you." He looked directly at his three sons from beloved Vibeke, one by one, to let them know he included them in particular: "Engtzohn is a good and effective teacher."

What was his Baptismal verse? - yes! – from the twenty-seventh Psalm: "Wait on the LORD: be of good courage and He shall strengthen thine heart: wait, I say, on the LORD." My son, you have shown me the good courage part, and your heart is very, very strong. Now Father in Heaven, I recommit myself to waiting on You, and ask that all of my sons witness and learn it themselves.

Four boys, Leo down to Ordo, sat on straight-backed chairs in the dim, candle-lit library. Each had a small table in front of him with a slate and chalk. While their lessons with mage Heorald were always one-on-one and his training was diverse, this was Father Ewald's class, and he taught them all at the same time. They learned the Christian faith and Latin. These were the chief curricula for all educated men. Those who earned the trust of a priest might read from Holy Scripture. Regular study included lesser things such as legal contracts, records of the nobility, and correspondence between this kingdom and the rest of Christendom. King Stegnwahl insisted that Father Ewald also teach them the classics of Roman literature.

At their thirteenth year the king's sons also began to study Greek. The king gave them Aristotle, Homer, Epictetus, and Sophocles to read, alongside Pliny, Josephus and Virgil.

King Stegnwahl's sons despised Greek. Their father spoke it at the midweek supper. Before leaving table each son of Greek-learning years had to use it to describe something new that he had read during the past seven days, preferably something he had read in Greek. They learned in their early, Latin years not to disappoint him.

Father Ewald began a lesson in Greek vocabulary.

Ordo stood, slate in hand, and asked, "Father Ewald, may I begin to learn Greek?"

"Ordo, sit down," said Father Ewald. "Find a book and study silently whilst I instruct your brothers. Be quiet now."

Ordo managed to look shocked; "Yes, Father Ewald, if you say I must."

"You must. You are a year too young for Greek. Do you want to rush on to Athens?"

"Good my teacher, Father Ewald, I do not know where that is. How could I want to go in haste to an unknown kingdom such as, what you say, Athens?"

Father Ewald smiled, something he usually avoided. One showed kindness to the weak, and even though the King's sons were under his tutelage, they needed no indulgence. "Good my pupil, you may take the Holy Book, the Vulgate of Saint Jerome, and content yourself by reading from the Proverbs of Solomon."

A week later before starting the Greek lesson Father Ewald asked Ordo, "Youngest prince, what have you taken from Solomon?"

"Father, he is diverse and tends to repeat a given lesson, each time with new terms. With respect to what subject would you like me to recite?"

The priest knew that Ordo worked harder and retained more than anyone else in his extensive experience, including any student at the great schools in which he'd been the pupil not the master. Even so, Ordo could still surprise him. "Quote for me, if you will, three proverbs of Solomon which address keeping silent while others learn."

Ordo suppressed a smile; Father Ewald was challenging him to justify using his older brothers' Greek lesson time.

"Yes, baby brother, teach us well! You act as though you are already king-in-waiting!" taunted sixth-born Leo. Five princes had reached manhood, including Heino, last son of Clothilde. Four remained under Father Ewald's tutelage.

Vibeke's three sons sneered; "Well, half brother, you with a Mama at your beck and call, speak up!"

Ordo put a finger to his lips and made a thoughtful frown; the room was silent for a moment. Then he recited five proverbs of Solomon which happened to deal with circumspect behavior in the presence of wiser men.

"Well done, child," said Father Ewald. "Keep King Solomon in mind, and I will call on you here and there during the study of Greek."

——*—*

The king and a subordinate stood in a counting-room in the interior of the castle. Their quiet conversation ceased when Leo stepped into the room. Blood leaked through fingers pressed against his nose and spotted his battle apron.

"So! Has someone pinked you in arms practice? What is it, my boy?"

"Sire, it's that hog's-breath Ordo! He -"

"Leo!" said the king, his voice calm. Leo knew its meaning.

"Sire, he is a menace! What am I to do? Might I refuse a challenge? – No. Must I give kinder treatment to one so young? – Yes. But, Sire, does this bounding bullock, seven years younger than I am, show respect for arms? He leapt upon me while I was taking a Ready Position and struck a full blow as though I were a straw target, or a townsman, or someone low."

The king frowned. Ordo was thirteen and had started the change from child to man. His voice was doing what man-boys' voices did; the sound of him speaking could make the king struggle not to laugh.

At first glance he also made a fair partner for Leo. They stood to equal height, and after subtracting Ordo's baby fat, *Dear God, let it be baby fat!* they carried equal weight. Wile Leo could reach a bit farther, his two feet together would make only one of Ordo's.

The king sighed. Ordo felt himself invincible, and had only begun to learn the protocols of manly arts "I'll have a word with him," he said.

Leo half-hid a smirk and turned to leave. At that moment Ordo dove through the door like a bird of prey in full stoop, horizontal in mid-leap. His shoulder took Leo right at the breastbone. For a silent moment the boys lay in a heap together in front of the king and his clerk, who tried to be inconspicuous.

The king nodded to the clerk and each bent down, pulled a royal son off the floor, and held him in a bear hug. Ordo struggled, helplessly. A bleeding cut above his eye had painted half of Ordo's face.

"Boys!" The king still sounded calm, although with shrinking patience. The boys both went slack and were released. The king watched Ordo very closely. He knew from eight prior sons that the year of changing from boy to man threw both mind and heart into wooly confusion. He glared, until Ordo realized he had to keep silent and use great care.

"Leo, I sense that you may have omitted some points."

Leo, nursing a growing lump where his head had hit the stone floor, looked confused. The king could see him thinking, trying to construct a story that his father might accept. The king was fond of Leo yet knew this sixth son mixed moderate love for truth with great finesse at coloring it.

Leo composed himself and spoke: "Sire, it is as I said; Ordo leaped in before I was ready and struck a full blow. Did I return a blow of my own? Yes, of course I did. I hope that I did not put out an eye." The smirk threatened to creep back.

"I see that you did not. I wonder whether, in the grip of anger, you may have let yourself try, and only added a 'hope' afterward." He gave Leo an odd look – love showed, as well as disappointment.

Life demanded self-governance, and Leo's seven extra years required him to succeed better at it than to strike so carelessly close to a brother's eye. The king was half-sure that missing Ordo's eye was what Leo regretted. If so, that would make Leo even less useful a son – to venture a thing and not accomplish it. He turned to the brash, homely youngest.

"Ordo, speak. Give me only facts, in the order in which they occurred. Recite them as you recall them, once and plainly. I will interpret. Omit nothing."

Ordo had been standing erect and at ease; he stiffened his shoulders, set his face into an expressionless mask, and spoke formally. His gaze bored through a spot six inches above the king's head.

"Sire! I came into the practice area, armed myself with a practice sword and shield, and challenged Leo. I did not see him respond. I stepped closer to him and challenged a second time.

"He suddenly turned toward me with sword and shield at the ready. I raised my shield to parry his sword and struck him; you see my mark on him from that. I stepped backward, but not far enough. He engaged me, and managed to put me on my back. He extended a hand as though to help me rise, but instead struck me with the hilt of his sword, which he had concealed in his grip.

"He gave a goodly blow, but not one I expected from a brother. I rolled away and started to chase him, but Leo had the jump on me, and I paused to clear the blood from my eye. Sire, Leo, I apologize to you both."

The king was bemused. He saw Ordo struggle to maintain discipline, and succeed – and at such an age! Leo's face had shifted slightly while Ordo spoke, and the king recalled that Ordo had been challenging Leo more and more often. A son well past his Manhood – moreover a son increasingly tried, harried, and once or twice handily bested by his youngest brother, three

286

rungs down the ladder of age and inheritance – he saw Leo losing faith in himself, and hating Ordo for it. His disappointment deepened.

"Leo and Ordo! You will avoid each other in martial training. If either challenges the other I will be displeased – hear me well. Go now and clean yourselves."

A troubled Ordo sat himself beside
his auntie. "Why so glum?' she says, but Ord
replies, "Should I discuss my manly side?
No issues may I own save anger, joy and sword.
 "Instead," he asks, "Why failed you, Auntie El,
 to share your own beleaguered soul with me?"
 "Because, my pet, you would have good and well
 done harm to him who loved a girl like me."
"Yet if you must, dear Elspet, here's the meat:
all girls are sweet until I speak, and then
they pout, and run away on frowny feet."
"Because you ask for wit from what's a hen.
 "A maid sees she's unfit, and you're the cur.
 Take from me now this thong, my sorrow's spur."

Frowning

"Young Prince, come sit by Auntie Elspet and empty your heart."

Ordo turned to see Elspet, eldest daughter of the town thane, sitting on a small bench under a shade tree. She beckoned to him, and made room for him to sit beside her.

"Thank you, Auntie El. Why do you think I should want an empty heart?" He winked at her, although she could see it took some effort.

"Sometimes I have a heart that is too full, and it helps to speak it to another caring soul. Have you ever been like that?"

Ordo looked sheepish. "I am not supposed to have, or show, any feelings beyond joy, anger, and the heat of combat. All of these fill my heart, as you say, but I don't recall ever needing to sit down under a quiet tree and empty it before my best girl in the whole town, Auntie El; never once."

She tsk'd at him. "Ordo, don't play word games. I know you're always too far ahead to catch. This time you must come to Auntie. I can see that you are feeling some fourth thing, and it isn't cousin to joy, rage, combat, or anything else you trivialize as 'manly.'"

"Ah! It is my turn, dear Auntie, to tsk! at you. Manly is as manly does, and is never trivial. Well, sometimes when a man relaxes he may tell stories or boast or tease. Those things are manly because a man does them, thus they are not trivial."

She sighed. "Have I offended the single most imperturbable male in Nordweg? Forgive me, please. In fact I'm sure you have already forgiven me. But really, Ordo, I see little cracks in your composure. Tell me now, or tell me later; just tell me!"

Ordo looked at her carefully, as though trying to read each soft, sweet edge of her face, dappled as it was by spots of sunlight that flowed with the breeze. Elspet remained single at an age where most young women have a husband plus at least one child to show for it.

"Are you staring?" she asked.

Ordo continued to stare, as though he hadn't heard her. He was looking for places where the tinker who had come through the town last fall may have left a kiss; did it burn?

"So, Elspet, does it burn?"

"What?!"

"All the places, your cheek I am sure, your lips . . does it still burn where the tinker showered you with kisses?"

Elspet was astonished, and her lip quivered.

"When your heart was full, Auntie El, did you come to me to empty it?"

She looked back at him with wide, open eyes, and the same stare.

"No, young Prince Ordo, I did not. Do you know why? Clearly you knew I had a full heart, when the tinker left town. He had filled the hearts of three young women in this town, perhaps one in the village down the South Road, and at least one belly. In fact, we drove him away.

"So, do you know why none of us told you about it? I'll say it now, Ordo my pet. Your father and your brothers would have thought us fools, and we knew that already. They would have forgotten the matter then and there. But you, Ordo? You would have gone after him, brought him back, and Heaven only knows what harm your kindness would have done to him. No, Ordo, we all loved him, and all miss him to this day."

"Yet, Elspet, beloved Auntie, your heart was filled with its breaking. Today it still makes your lip quiver."

"Ah, Prince my pet, you have understanding that is much older than your years. So we have emptied my heart; now tell me, you of great wisdom in the hearts of women, what has filled up your young and manly-manly heart?"

He thought for a moment. "Wisdom, you say? That is what I do not have, Elspet. The young girls around here are, as my brothers say, 'As available as ripe wheat is golden, as ready as a brown rabbit is furry.' They say, 'Take in hand the brown and gold fur of the young women, boy; take and enjoy.'"

Elspet smiled at him; "Ordo, you call me Auntie, but if I had been ten or even five years younger, I would have been one of those happy, eager girls. So what is your problem, exhaustion?" She smiled innocently.

"Elspet, I am confused! Priest and Book are very clear on this: to fornicate, to loosely couple with any willing partner, is contrary to God's wish. Yes, there is much of a young woman's ways that I do not know, and their hearts?! By all that is gracious, Elspet, I cannot make conversation with any of them.

"Whatever I say, they reply that I am unguessably wise. Well, what is that to me? I want to hear something that answers what I have said, yet nothing returns How am I to choose a sweetheart -" he stopped in mid sentence and stared at her -

"Elspet, you are the only female, other than my mother and sisters, who can hold my attention for more than two heartbeats. And my sisters are, shall we say, children?"

Elspet laughed aloud. "Forgive me, pet, my Prince, but I know your sisters well, and they bring great pride to their mother and, yes, their father. I will not share your view of them with anyone."

"Thank you. Yes, they are all younger than I. Ruta is beginning to be womanly, and is, er, rather turbulent to be around. Mother just smiles, and Father is getting used to what often amounts to abuse from her; he dotes on her, and on Margeth, and on Maryon."

Elspet waited; he had more to say.

"Auntie, here is my overflowing, the leakings from my manly-manly heart. Yes I yearn for kisses and cuddles and for naked furry intimacy. When I try to talk to one girl or another, she quickly sobers, closes her soul to me, and with it her body. Can you see the failure I have created in myself?"

Elspet sat in silence. She wanted to caress him in some way. She didn't, because she knew he would only pull back. After a pause she said, "Failure, is it? I believe, Ordo, that you want them to be something they cannot. When they realize there will be nor kissing nor cuddling coming from you, due to their apparent lack, they feel disdained.

Ordo continued to look morose.

"Can you tell me, pet Prince, how an offended woman behaves?"

"That, Elspet, is something I am still studying. I have no answer."

Her voice soared into laughter. "You at fifteen regard women the way your father's mage Heorald regards black magic! You know that he is renowned, as far as anyone can travel, as the White Mage of Nordweg, and your father shields him sternly. No one can take up his time without a very, very important question.

"And he absolutely abhors gaining any familiarity with Black - or brown or golden - magic." She winked broadly at him.

Ordo smiled to let her know she was partly correct. "Mage, eh? How like I am to a mage, yet how far from understanding. Is that it?"

"Here, my pet - do you see this trinket on my necklace?"

The necklace dangled deep inside her dress. She undid several buttons and opened her blouse, exposing a breast - looking at him to be sure he didn't miss the effect.

"Look closely at my heart, Ordo." She tugged and the bottom part of the necklace appeared. She refastened the buttons, smiling rather pertly at him, and showed him a curious bangle on the leather thong.

"This was the tinker's gift to me; it was the prettiest of all the gifts he gave to his many loves. See that it shows skill in leather, in tinkering with pot metal, with silver, and with agate stone. He was an artisan who mastered many things beyond foolish hearts, Ordo. Now I make this a gift to you. I am done with his memory, so you hold it for me."

Ordo looked at it closely. The trinket itself was far too frilly for a young man to possess. It if were all silver or gold, or a fine gem, that would be one thing. This was a tinker's boast, no more. He smiled and accepted the gift, tucking it into a pocket.

"My Ordie, please don't fall, lest tending to
your injuries I kneel and stain my dress!"
Ord smiles at Ruta's jest and asks anew,
"Who wrestles here, this grass-green plot to mess?"
    Smith Vronken had the size last year, but length
    has gone to Ordo in the nonce. "Young Prince,
    let age and guile tie knots in youth and strength."
    Yet when it's done, it's smith who wears the wince.
The village lasses come to give a kiss;
"You've won this right!" They all line up and smile.
"Just so," says Ord, "I'll hug and kiss each miss
that's here; I'll give! Line up in single file.
    They grew fair frank, when Ruta brought a friend;
    their laughing shrieks brought matters to an end.

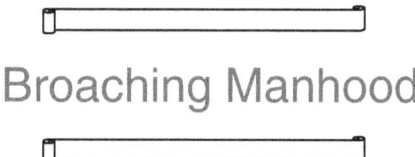

Broaching Manhood

Summer's hot glare baked the freshly cut and mown hayfield. Serfs had raked and stacked the hay along the two longer sides of the field, leaving room for a jousting track. A roofed platform looked upon its midpoint.

King Stegnwahl occupied the center chair, a temporary throne. Beside him sat matronly Queen Magnhild, and on the other side fourteen-year-old Ruta, eleven-year-old-Margeth and nine-year-old Maryon. Ruta, tall and self-possessed, coolly looked over the proud, poised young men about to joust, race, wrestle, duel with dulled swords, and throw the axe.

She stood and called to her brother, "Ordo! Yoo hoo, Ordie! Watch yourself, big brother! I'd hate to get mud on my knees tending to my downed hero!"

Ordo looked up and smiled. He waved at her, and continued removing his tunic; it was time to wrestle. "Who will try a fall with me?" he asked the group of men who had gathered on a grazing area next to the hayfield.

"My prince, I will come and try you!" It was Vronken, the blacksmith, a man of about thirty, in the prime of life. Half a head shorter than Ordo, he was very strong. His arms and hands seemed carved from oak, and his chest was prodigious. "I promise your father to keep you from harm."

Smiling, Ordo replied, "Well said, Vronken, and I promise your wife and children the same. Shall we begin?"

The prior year Vronken had pinned Ordo after a stout battle. Over the winter the story had grown, and now Vronken needed to live up to it. He leaned low in a wrestler's crouch, arms outspread above the green grass.

"We've cleared away most of the meadow muffins, but first round always finds one or two!" came a voice from the crowd.

"A moist landing for one of us, eh, Prince?" said Vronken, as he began to weave back and forth looking for an opening. "Now that you've grown past me, I have the advantage of coming from below," and made a sudden upward lunge into Ordo's chest.

Ordo swept his right arm up into Vronken's left elbow and dodged around him. "Good smith, I am over here!" he said.

Vronken smiled. "Prince, shall you win by running away?" and tried the move a second time.

Ordo twitched his right arm then swept his left arm up into Vronken's right elbow, which made the smith stumble. Ordo leapt behind Vronken and drove him face first into the grass.

An "Oooooff!" came out of Vronken, and he scrambled to his feet. Standing as tall as he could, the smith walked toward Ordo with an outstretched hand, as though to congratulate him for the move. Ordo took the hand, appearing not to notice Vronken's intent to yank him off his feet.

Vronken leaned backward, hard, trying to pull Ordo with him. To his surprise, the prince not only went with him, he also pushed. Vronken fell flat on his back, and Ordo plastered himself across the huge chest.

Vronken shrugged him off and rolled into an all-fours crouch. Again, Ordo seemed to anticipate the move; he was up and behind Vronken in time to flatten the smith and press him to the ground again, with his left arm under Vronken's and his left hand up on the burly neck.

The smith pushed against the ground with his right arm, stretching it outward to make it impossible for Ordo to get underneath it, and heaved himself up onto his knees. Ordo again moved with him, shot his right arm under Vronken's now-available right arm, and had him in a full headlock.

Ordo stood up: Vronken's feet dangled. His toes clutched madly at the grass. Ordo heaved the smith up and launched him to the left side. The smith rolled on the grass. He was back on his feet and charging at Ordo so quickly the crowd cheered him.

Again the prince anticipated his move, and was able to push the smith over onto his back. A second time Ordo pushed Vronken's shoulders into the green meadow grass, and once again the smith shrugged and heaved his body up.

This time Ordo moved with him, and came right back onto the smith, who had already begun to sweat. The smith bucked, fell back, bucked again, fell back again, and realized that he was in trouble. He reached behind the prince's head to grab a handful of rich brown hair, and pulled Ordo off his chest.

Vronken's elbow hit the green, stubbly grass, and Ordo was now belly up next to the smith. What a predicament. Vronken tried to roll onto the flat, firm sixteen-year old torso; Ordo used the smith's momentum to move him one more turn, so that Vronken was down and Ordo was up; and now each man had a good grip on the other man's hair.

"Next year, my good smith, if you become bald, please remind me to shave my head! This year I see that you have a goodly mane. Now let me remind you that your handful of my hair has put your shoulder on the grass. What might I do about the other one?" His voice was that of a calm teacher leading a pupil through an exercise in thought.

Vronken snorted in laughter and tried to repeat the move. With his shoulder already on the ground, he could not move Ordo drove his head against the smith's downed shoulder and threw his body across the man's other side, shoulder and all.

The smith heaved and writhed for several tense moments, with the crowd shouting him encouragement. One of them acted the referee and pressed his face down for a clear view of Vronken's shoulders. "One! - - - Two! - - - THREE!" he shouted, and the wrestlers let go of each other and got to their feet.

Ordo wrapped the smith in a firm bear hug. Vronken exhaled, then wrapped his own arms behind Ordo, and squeezed back, very hard.

He got a small "Ooof" from the prince, who then applied all his strength. Neither could breathe and both began to turn purple in the face, when the smith broke his grip. Ordo released him, and stepped back. With a huge smile, Vronken gave the prince a resounding slap on his shoulder, which the prince returned. Then arm in arm they went over to where ale was set out.

A gaggle of town and village lasses had come to watch the two wrestle. When Vronken and Ordo went away to drink they urged to boldest one, Brohonna, to go after them.

Soon she returned with a still shirtless Ordo trailing behind her. The prince's lean and very large form awed the lasses. They clustered around him. Brohonna organized the girls into a single line.

"Now, Prince, darling Ordo, we ask the right to give the victor a winner's kiss!"

He drained the drinking cup and set it on the grass. He looked them over, in a way that made them feel like ladies he wanted to know better. "As your prince, I will set the terms. These kisses, and a hug with each, are my gift to you this afternoon. Brohonna, please join the line. Since you should be first, come hither."

He stooped down to each lass and wrapped her in a tender hug, then stood up and kissed her. His kissing was not expert; a few managed to make him, briefly, a pupil, and each time he set a lass down, she seemed giddy to have been picked up bodily and then kissed, all the while pressed against a warm, hard, male body.

"We thank you, Prince Ordo, for your gift," said Brohonna. Winking at some of her friends and using her hands to lift and emphasize her breasts, she turned to Ordo. "Dear prince, please judge between us. Each girl thinks her figure is best for nursing a child. Please settle our little dispute, by telling us who is best formed."

The other girls giggled, and made a circle around Ordo. Ruta and a third cousin, also highborn, broke into the line behind him and gestured at the other girls to keep their secret.

"Since each of you certainly has the means to nurse a child," he said nervously, it won't be necessary to undress." He looked at Brohonna to be sure she knew he was serious. He carefully considered each of the several bosoms in his line of sight, when Brohonna made herself clearer.

"Dear Prince, we are asking for more, perhaps, than you are willing to perform." Her arched eyebrow made several of the girls snicker. "Please examine each of us; weigh in your hand, test for contour, and, if you are very careful, even tweak a nipple to feel its firmness of purpose."

Feeling somewhat out of his element, Ordo paused to think this over, and then proceeded carefully to fondle each pair of breasts. He worked his way around the circle until he noticed that the next bosom belonged to Ruta.

"Aye, Ordie, do you wish to kiss your sister or judge her flesh same as the town lassies? Or perhaps skip over me, as I'm barely fourteen, and pass judgment on our far-cousin Rohondelinde."

The ring of lasses sang out a cascade of feminine hoots. Ruta and Rohondelinde tsk-ed at him and shook their heads.

"My prince," said a nearby village lad, "I will gladly take on your duties! May I complete the round?" He looked admiringly at Ruta and Rohondelinde.

Ordo silenced him with a blank-faced stare. He shrugged, then picked up his tunic and outer belt and went toward the axe-throwing contest.

Though homely, Ord was calm and always kind.
Aside from brothers, all he knew were friends.
His wink and wit made "grumpy" undefined
where'er he went, no matter what his ends.
    Which, word or weapon, showed his greatest skill?
    Outdoing elder brothers brought him strife.
    Ninth son, though first in wit, and arms, and will,
    he went away to find, and keep, his life.
The king his father sent him, thus: "Erase
yourself from Nordwesh lands, for doubt I all
your brothers' love for one with half your grace.
Bestride some other place; there let fate fall."
    The feasting-day that saw him counted man
    begot the day his legend quest began.

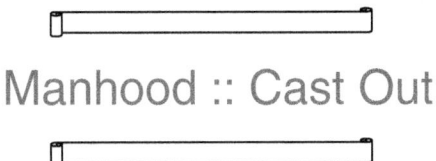

Manhood :: Cast Out

"Nine sons, and the last ends his seventeenth year. This day he enters into Manhood." The king spoke from a raised platform in the great courtyard of the castle. "Today, Ordowahl, I deem you a man. You may marry, you may come and go without let or hindrance, you may buy and sell lands and houses, you may do all that is lawful for a man to do." The solemn phrases of the Manhood ceremony rolled out.

The king, still a proud and fearsome warrior, had gone from gold to ash at the temples. Gray dimmed his beard. Piercing blue eyes shone below bushy brows. The sunlight of the cloud-dappled May afternoon turned the deep lines on his weathered face into a craggy map.

Eight sons stood in an arc behind him. All save Vibeke's last, Meldowahl, were husbands and fathers. *Last year I honored my fourth grandson. Now, my final son.* He looked out over the large gathering of daughters-in-law, grandchildren, nobility, thanes, and town folk.

The king was a hard man, yet always fair. The qualities he valued highest had not passed down to the eight heirs grouped behind him. This plagued the king. He could do nothing now about the adults he had so far given the world.

Here is my last, Ordowahl. Three daughters have come after, and Magnhild is very much their mother. Each has the height of a man and can match a man in grip and gait. And. a huge blessing, all are passably fair.

Their brother was not. Ordowahl's cheeks and jaw had the angles of a tree stump; his eyes twinkled with mischief and wit. A collection of pink scars ran from neck to scalp, such as all highborn men accumulate while sparring – each of these marks remembered well by the man who had put it there, including Leo.

"My son," said the king, "Give me the Latin of this. 'The Father of the righteous shall greatly rejoice; and he that begetteth a wise child shall have joy of him.'"

"Father, certainly. it is in the Proverbs of Solomon: exultat gaudio pater iusti qui sapientem genuit laetabitur in eo. Father, while none are completely righteous, I strive toward this standard. Thank you, Father, for my teachers; you have been first amongst them, whether or not you know it."

Stegnwahl nodded. His point became clear—he had laid a second name on Ordowahl, "Solomon." The moment did not let him smile, and the knowledge that his teaching had not affected his first eight sons disquieted him, behind a sober countenance.

Ordowahl stood a full head taller than his father the king, and a butcher looking at them might have guessed Ordowahl at twice his father's dressed-out weight. No one could outrun him in a dead sprint, although a few might pass him in a moderate race, say from the town center, up to the castle, around its walls, and back.

Still, despite plain advantages in size, and wit, and prowess, this day dropped Ordowahl into mortal danger. A full year had passed since anyone dared compete with him in any martial art. *Yet today I am counted an adult, and therefore also a friendless pauper. The season is fair, yet the future seems bleak. Any hope for lands and wealth will have scant connection with Nordweg.*

The Manhood rite stripped him of a child's protections. He posed a direct challenge to each of his brothers, and their open enmity burnished a deadly truth. Eight scornful and keenly jealous older brothers laid the guarantee on his deep peril.

The king, like David choosing Solomon, would choose a son to succeed him. Exactly which? Clearly now, Ordowahl. Those eight grimly agreed that the ninth and last would never, could never be their father's choice.

I am unsure whether Ordowahl can survive a week, and what is worse, I am unsure of what damage he might do to those who dare attack him.

The feast moved indoors and dwindled to a drunken, belching cadre, perhaps a dozen nobles, several brothers, Father Ewald, three carefully less drunken town elders, and deeply grayed mage Heorald. In a quiet moment the king pulled Ordowahl aside.

"Tell me your love for your brothers."

"Papa, I have seen my brothers reach Manhood. Most have wives and children – many of those children seem more like cousins than nieces or nephews. I love all men as Jesus commands and I have a special love for my father, mother, and all their offspring.

"Yet, and I tell a truth, each brother makes loving him a hard thing. I sense that each fears me in a way I cannot undo, and shows me none of the kindness we are taught to pass between men, much less brothers, born to the same father. Do I love them? Not well, Papa. Earnestly, though not well."

"Ordowahl, do not spar with me."

"Papa, teach me how to answer your question. My brothers do not love me. They do not open their conversations to me. They want me gone and care not how. With effort, Father, I suppress such a mood in myself. Although we are many strong men, after you the kingdom will need, and be the stronger for, each of us.

I am as I am. I fear no one by light of day, and I ask God to guard me when I cannot see. I love Nordweg, Father. I do not love this place."

The king nodded slowly. "God sets your fate before you, Ordowahl. If it's here it is also brief. I know your heart well and love you as much as any of my sons. I know your brothers' hearts. Final son, you are my last chance to give Nordweg a proud and righteous king. I command you to leave. Your brothers quarrel; no surprise there. They unite for one aim, to end the threat they fear from your coming of age.

"Your mother and I must lose you. Please make it a kind loss by giving us your farewell. Tell me that you will obey out of love more than fear."

Ordowahl felt surprise. His brothers' intent and plotting gave him a curious apprehension, and he felt his father's fear. He took hold of his father's hands and knelt. He kissed the royal signet ring, rose and went to his bedchamber. Ordo did not bother looking to left or right. He did keep his ears and other senses sharp.

Priest Ewald shrove the prince and gave him grace.
"My son, before you go we'll say the Mass.
Now say it with me; 'tis not out of place
for one who's taught his tutor, class by class.
    Old Heorald the mage found Ordowahl
    whilst he was packing Hammerfoot and mule.
    "Young prince, go lean and wary, yet withal
    here's meager gold. Spend little! That's the rule.
With parting gift of two gold coins, his horse
and pack mule loaded, Ordowahl went south.
The kingdom's love bedewed him. His remorse?
Eight brothers' hate was arid, like a drouth.
    A jackdaw eyed his progress down the road;
    Each peasant's friendly wave made light his load

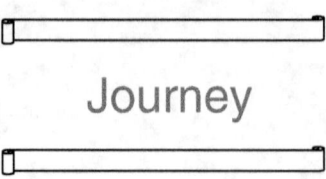

Journey

In the morning he ate broke bread in quiet with his mother, father and sisters, plus Father Ewald and mage Heorald.

"Ordowahl," his father said, "We have given some thought to the best way for you to leave this place."

"Father? Isn't it enough just to ride away?"

"No, it is not. We, Father Ewald, Heorald and I, believe that your brothers are planning to see that you do not come back here, and in our very educated opinions, that becomes a matter of not allowing you to live long enough to go far, much less return."

"Yes, I suppose so, Father. You asked me last night not to make my departure difficult. If I should wind up defending myself against my brothers, perish the thought, some of them might die. Forgive me, Mother, Father, for speaking so baldly."

"Ahem." Mage Heorald had something to say, and needed permission from the King and Prince.

"Yes, Heorald, speak to this new Man," said the king.

"I believe they have decided -- God only knows why." He continued with an air of innocence, "They believe you will be going to the northeast. Since the only reasonable course is southward, they decided, quite on their own," again looking as innocent as possible, "that you would never do something so obvious. I managed not to show them how silly their idea was, and this morning, despite their heavy drinking last night, six of them have ridden to the northeast. Frenkowahl, as eldest, has stayed behind to intercept any unusual event, and your next-older brother Meldowahl – he is the slyest of them, Ordowahl, which you know well – is Frenkowahl's second pair of eyes. He stands ready to race after the others if you are seen going anywhere odd, such as to the south. Frenkowahl is at home, placidly enjoying the day with his family.

Father Ewald spoke next. "Even if he is sly, Meldowahl must do penance for his drunkenness and loose behavior last night with two of the more pliable chambermaids. I have sent him to a windowless room with a candle, and instructed him to do penance by reading in the Proverbs of Solomon, regarding chastity. It appears that he does not know them well enough."

"There it is, my son," said the king. "We have allowed one of those chambermaids to discover him in the midst of his penance, and carry a message from us, that we saw you leave to the northeast a short while ago, and warn him not to follow you. She doesn't know the ruse, so cannot betray it."

"Father, good my tutors, Mother, Ruta, Marget, Maryon, I see I must go quietly, and soon. God be with all of you, as I trust He will be with me. Forgive my haste; goodbyes are difficult, and the sun is above the horizon."

They rose from the table; Prince Ordowahl bent down to shed childhood's final tear on his mother's shoulder. He gave each sister a tender embrace, kissed each cheek, and exchanged blessings with the good priest. He wrapped his father in a final manly hug, and set out to find his fortune in a far land.

In the hallway to the stables Father Ewald called to Ordowahl, "Young prince! If you can honor an old man, a parting word!"

"What is it, Father? Time with you is always well spent."

"Can we go into the chapel? My son, let me hear what may be the last confession you give me, and I will say the Mass."

Yes, Father. Can I confess on the way to the chapel? – in which case, my first sin is speed, for nothing should perturb a sinner's quiet repentance."

Father Ewald smiled; "Yes, my son. I also make haste. I am happy to hear you wherever you are. Bless you, my son; what are your other sins, since your last confession?"

The hallway leading to the chapel was short, and they were scant steps from it. "Father, I have failed to love my brothers. Their love for me is none of my concern, for I must love all of God's children, and so much more my own kin. I have tried to silence angry thoughts, and have failed."

"Yes, my son; and what else? Have you harbored doubts of God's grace, or impure thoughts, or lusts toward any worldly pleasure?"

"Father, doubt is foreign to me, and ordinarily I would say that I have selfish impulses. Yet since my confession to you yesterday noon, before the Manhood Day ceremony, I have had little time to think of pleasures, foolish or otherwise. I drank a goodly amount, and ate well past a full belly. These were as much duty as indulgence, eh?"

He got a chuckle from that. "And dalliance with the very willing young women? They dote upon you, you know, with hopes of a kiss or cuddle."

"Father, you've heard me address temptations often – yet not today. I have been preoccupied with plans to move forward into adulthood, and away from here."

"I understand; your thoughts have been focused. Yet you tell me that they have wandered away from the light of God and the love commanded you by our Lord and Savior Jesus Christ."

Ordowahl had knelt in a pew at the front of the chapel and the priest stood in front of him. It was the first time in years that he could recall gazing at Ordowahl eye to eye outside of class. "Yes, Father – the loss of time to prepare my thoughts wounds me as much as my own sin."

Father Ewald chuckled a second time. "My son, I absolve you of your sin. Your penance will be to say the Mass with me; I will keep an eye over your shoulder whilst we do that. We will forgo a homily; and I grant you as co-celebrant, this one time, to partake of the cup as well as the bread. Tut! Do not blush, or I'll suspect you of unwillingness to carry out your act!"

Stumbling only once or twice, speaking the Mass for the first time after more than six thousand daily morning Masses, Ordowahl went through it with Father Ewald, and rang the bell at the appropriate moment to alert the congregants – in this case, only Father Ewald and himself – that the elements were about to be consecrated. They broke the host between them and ate it, shared the cup; Ordowahl's eye seemed to glisten. Father Ewald calmly shook his head, very slightly, and went on until the final Amen.

"Go now, my son; your heart is once again shriven, and clean. Go and keep watch on that errant heart. Now I will keep watch for an errant brother or three, eh? Come, let me go with you as far as the stables."

——*—*

The day's rotation of serfs had harnessed the draft horses and taken them out to work the king's lands, leaving the stable half-empty, if still full of the odors of hay and warm livestock. Ordowahl heard a quiet step, and turned. His cherished magery-tutor Heorald approached with arms wide. One hand held a small leather pouch.

"Let me embrace you one more time, Ordowahl. I fear the day of your return, if I even live to see it. In fact, God have mercy on an old man to let me see your children and give them their first lessons in life skills, Arabic numbering, and nature's subtleties."

"Master Mage, you always draw me past the immediate; you see things that lie farther off. Your prayers are mine too, Old tutor. I would be overjoyed to see you gather my children and teach them, as you taught me." He embraced his teacher, as gently and warmly as he could.

"Ooof – I hope your mind can some day match your arms and back!" The mage shook himself and smiled. "Here,

Ordowahl, is a parting gift. The king knows nothing of this, nor should he – and in fact if he did, his own gift would burden your mule.

This one is better, my new Man. It will keep you coined, if thinly. The privileged life of a royal son is gone, and very unlike what you will find when you leave your father's realm. Learn to live lean, and by your wits and arm alone."

As though my brothers haven't shown me that already! "Of course, Master Heorald; you have always taught me this. If your student missteps, it is his fault and none of yours. I can recite for you endlessly, Sir; now God will watch me, and perhaps prompt me, at a time of need, which lesson He finds right."

"See this, Ordowahl." The mage gestured toward a mule. On a shelf next to the mule lay a traveling kit that outdid any Ordowahl had seen before. His two best suits of mail armor, cooking gear, sundry clothing, a blanket, flour, bacon, herbs, salt, cooking utensils, skillet, pot – Ordowahl smiled to see the collection.

"Load it up, new man; load it well. The mule is sturdy, and your jousting stallion Hammerfoot stands ready with his own load. Struvardekel, the king's armorer, packed a useful set of tools behind the saddle an hour ago. These animals will be your caravan. Keep them well. See to their rest, water, shade, and good forage. Your life is theirs, for if they die or are lost, your safety dwindles."

"Yes, I know these things well. A larger loss hangs behind me. I suffer the forfeit of my brothers' love, and now I pay that price. I am shamed to have won only their hatred, and twice shamed by the price that has cost Mother and Father."

"Speak not of that! Do not carry such a thought with you; it is unworthy. I taught all nine of you, and you are the one I love. Life is always in front of you, not behind."

"Yes, Heorald; lesson five, age six. I have held that in conscious view ever since."

310

"Now, one last embrace, Ordowahl – gently! I cannot abide the sight of your back, and your horse's tail, leaving and unlikely to return. I go."

Ordowahl bundled all the gear onto the mule, tied it expertly – how many times his brothers had made him do this for them! He was grateful for their inadvert gift of expertise. Holding the mule's lead in one hand he mounted the enormous stallion, and rode into the stony courtyard and out through the castle gate. He did not look back.

The mage stood in a shaded corner of the courtyard because he also could not abide missing what might be his last glimpse of Ordowahl.

An odd thing caught his eye; a jackdaw, an agricultural pest, sat on a pine bough watching the prince's departure. *A crow, now, a crow flying overhead would be a sign of good fortune – no matter the priest's interpretation of God's Creation, He put crows in it as signs. This stupid, thieving jackdaw, acting the spy – what might it mean? Probably nothing.*

The mage muttered something in the ancient tongue and threw a pinch of white powder into the air; it made a small, misty cloud that covered his view of Ordowahl. For the rest of the day anyone who did see him would immediately forget.

I pay a price in clouding what might be the last glimpse of Ordowahl I'll ever get; and no one else will even report seeing him.

————*——*

Ordowahl knew this road from life-long use. It split, and split again into other roads he'd visited often, and beyond them terrain he'd traveled and hunted. Bees buzzed. Birds sang among the trees all around him in this long, humid late May morning.

Occasionally the road passed broad fields of green hay or wheat, quiet except for a whisper of breeze to move the surface this way or that. Other times, when he saw peasants they would pause and call out to him. Their affection was so different from his brothers'—he was no threat to them. Today they waved, then ignored him. Ordowahl put that out of his mind and went on to the south.

First cousin Mehrwal welcomed him; "I'm glad
to see you, cousin, be a guest. I hear
your father's sent you forth. You're just a lad
and need some space, some air, some cheer.
　　"Come plow a field (an elbow in the ribs) –
　　I've sev'ral lasses waiting for your oats.
　　Next spring I'll see which woman got first dibs."
　　(A brisk young widow cornered all the votes.)
A week of martial arts and hunting stags
put Ordowahl in better state of mind.
Rough manly humor shared, and manly brags
erased the pall of kinfolk left behind.
　　Another set of sad goodbyings. All,
　　this time, gave grace and smiles to Ordowahl.

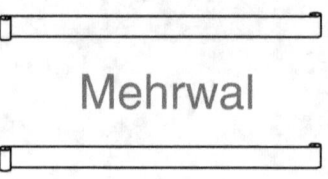

Mehrwal

Late the second afternoon he reached the estate of his cousin Mehrwal.

"Ordowahl! I've only this day returned from your Manhood feast. What a joy that was, my boy – no, Man! Come spend a while here; we're happy to have you to ourselves."

"Cousin Mehrwal, it is my honor to visit with you. Do you know the reason for my coming this way?"

"Yes I do, Ordo, I do indeed. Your father explained it all to me, and I see his wisdom. You'll never become the great man we each expect you to become if you stay in the shadows beneath your <u>eight</u> older brothers. So he sent you away to unfold the full nature of yourself, to grow wise in the wide world.

"He doesn't want you to end up like a seedling in the deep forest, never seeing broad daylight, and neither do I. The summer is young, and this makes a great time to dry off behind the ears, don't you think?"

Ordowahl smiled at Mehrwal's friendly jest. He had unhorsed his older cousin many times while jousting, and had not met him lance to lance for at least three years. "We shall see what a dry ear can do, eh? I recall wet ones being fairly useful."

Mehrwal guffawed and slapped Ordowahl hard across the shoulder blades, which made Ordowahl's grin grow wider, and they went into the grand stone manor house.

For a nobleman such as Mehrwal and even a king such as Stegnwahl, each day demanded hours of focused exertion. Nobility did not tend land or animals; the lowborn did that. Instead they trained for battle with each of many kinds of weapon.

They attacked dummy and post endlessly in set drills; they jumped or danced in complex rote maneuvers. They sparred with each other, and did this as though life depended on it, because it did. Power and right, right and law, law and power were interwoven in ways that made both honor and fierce courage as important as anything else in life.

"Ooof! We are sparring, cousin, aren't we?" Mehrwal staggered back from Ordowahl's assault.

"Pardon me, cousin; I realize that two days on horseback have left me pent up. Let me go back to the post and dummy; I'm sure your workmen will enjoy making new ones tomorrow!"

"They'll do it, and I hope their love of you will get them smiling, after you've destroyed their best," and Mehrwal waved Ordo back to the practice yard. "Hallo00! Behrwal, Khetwal, stand back. Guard yourselves against flying splinters!"

The next day was a Sunday. After Mass they sat down to a grand mid-day dinner. Mehrwal and wife Dahnekin sat at opposite ends of a large table, full of handsome sons and daughters, with Ordowahl at the center of one side. Servants carried plates of steaming mutton, breads, cheeses, and raisin pudding to the table. Other servants stood quietly behind them, and kept water, ale, and wine goblets brimming.

After a brief grace and a few bites, Mehrwal spoke his mind. "Ordo, lad, wild oats are something every highborn man your age should sow. I would smile to see infants in the town next spring showing your likeness, with size and heft to match. I'll keep watch, in fact, to see how many lasses you've warmed."

315

"Mehrwal! Please, husband, leave talk of breeding and stud service to the farmyard. I must apologize, Ordo, my husband is blunt at the best of times."

"Yes, Dahnekin, Mehr is merry and more, eh? Mehr, I'm a student of private discipline, and have not left my home villages any such, as you say, gift. I am very much a man. Up 'til now, yes, I have lived as a boy. Say what you will, I also take seriously the Book and its lessons."

Mehrwal stifled a sudden laugh. He saw Ordowahl's deadpan expression and wiped a flat hand down his own face. "Cousin, you are all the man a man could want to be, and your company here is all the gift I can ask. A fellow can hope, eh? As I hear the priest tell it, stay away from the married ones, and let the rest look out for themselves," he ended with a wink and a nudge.

Ordo raised an eyebrow at Mehr, smiled, and said nothing.

——*—*

That evening, after the household had gone to sleep, a quiet tap hit his bedchamber door. He opened it to see a sturdy looking woman with pale blue eyes set in a plain, open face, dressed in a simple brown woolen dress, and about five years older than he.

Her manner was direct, and pleasant. "May I come in?" she asked.

"Who are you, and why have you come? I am about to retire for the night. Can this wait until morning?"

Her laugh sounded low and earthy. "I think not, Sir. I am Marthe, a recent widow, and I have the pleasure of being your host's gift. You'd honor this gift by servicing me same as I you."

He stared; no clear meaning came to mind. He could not let himself stray from the chivalrous and polite.

"Oh, Mehr said you'd be thick. My land sake, Prince, every man has a first woman, and it seems my luck to be first with you! Now you quiet your big sweet mouth, sit down on that bed, and do what Mama Marthe says."

Ordowahl stared in disbelief: a peasant had spoken a command to the king's son. He felt astonished more than offended. She pushed lightly on his abdomen and walked him back toward the bed. One foot pushed backward to shut the door behind her. She pulled a pin from her hair, which cascaded around her shoulders.

Bewildered and suddenly aroused, Ordowahl felt helpless to do anything else, so he sat on the bed.

"My land sakes you're massive. So here's what we're going to do, Honey." She climbed into his lap and used both hands to push him onto his back.

Ordowahl had a new tutor, again a practiced instructor. She presented a frank, leisurely lesson in the ways of women and men. Before they finally slept, she realized she'd taken him from novice to moderately savvy adult. God willing, he'd taken her from manless widow to happy mother-to-be, which had been Mehr's real intent. She wondered what it would be like to bear the get of someone this huge, yet looked forward to enjoying that massive weight on her frame each of the next several nights.

Does Mehr want this boy-man, this awkward giant, to scatter his seed on several women? No, Marthe is making that plain; she will keep this one to herself!

When it was clear that the evening's business was well and truly finished, he knelt beside the bed, asked her to kneel with him, and recited his evening prayer.

My God in heaven, let this man surprise me again, but not soon! I've never seen the like. My own dear Erik did so with me once, or was it twice; and here the king's son invites me to share his prayers as though it were usual. Bless him, and bless us – I'm sure You know how! Amen.

——*—*

The next day Mehrwal staged a hunt, and asked Ordowahl to ride a hunting horse instead of the enormous Hammerfoot. "You or your horse or the both of you will likely fall and die, jumping through the forest when we pursue a stag. Ordo, honor me by taking Jumping Bill. Your heft will be a surprise to him, and he

317

is the best hunting mount you'll find anywhere in five days' travel."

The dogs sprinted into the leafing-out, newly green forest, and soon began to bay. The other five hunters galloped off. "Tilf, Behr, they have him going up Margul's Canyon!" "No, Khet, you're off by one, it's Blenbo's Draw; race you there!" Mehrwal chuckled and set out after them, at a more reasonable pace. Jumping Bill carried Ordowahl alongside, and soon began to lather and breathe heavily.

"Mehr, we'll follow you; I'd rather have a live horse at the end of the day than go on foot just to view a dead stag."

"Indeed, Ordo – you're more than even Jumping Bill can carry. How does that steed of yours get you and your metal up to a gallop?"

Ordowahl grinned; "I tell him sweet lies, and he believes them. Hard to start is hard to stop, eh?"

Mehrwal grunted a respectful assent, and spurred his horse to overtake the others.

Ordowahl let Jumping Bill amble toward a stream and drink. In fact the horse knew even better than the hunters how the hunt would unfold. Ordowahl gave him a slack rein. A simple "Sksk!" set Jumping Bill off at an easy gait.

For a time the stag gave the dogs and men the slip. The dogs regained its scent and caught up. Jumping Bill and Ordowahl came across the dogs in a small clearing where they had cornered the heaving stag.

Mehrwal had called an unusually early hunt specifically to honor Ordowahl, his guest, at a time when antlers were at most velvet stumps. The stag, still lean from winter, put its rump between high boulders and struck out repeatedly with hooves that flashed in and out of the sunlight falling through the branches of trees standing close behind the boulders.

Its strength visibly ebbed; even if they let the stag go its life would soon end.

"My host!" called out Ordowahl.

"Honored guest! This amazes me. How is it you have found the stag right where we ran it to ground?"

"It is Jumping Bill, Mehr: he hunts better than dog or man, eh? May I claim the stag's life, good my host, to honor the day's best hunter?"

The men by this time all dripped with sweat. Their horses lathered in sweat and stood panting. The men cheered for Jumping Bill. "Ordo, how will Jumping Bill take a stag's life?" one of them called out.

"This way," said Ordowahl; he pulled a short bow from beside his saddle, nocked a broad headed hunting arrow, and let fly. The stag leaped high, shuddered, and fell on its side.

"Ordowahl, good my guest, everything around you smiles – even yon jackdaw. See, how intently it gazes at you."

A week had passed. After breakfast, Ordowahl stood in the manor's dooryard to face the entire household, from Mehrwal, Dahnekin, Behrwal and Khetwal, down to the youngest children and the household staff, and endured a new sad set of goodbyes. He'd not be likely to see these kin for an unguessable time, and could not keep the gloom from his face. "What!" Mehrwal exclaimed. "What? Have I gifted you so shabbily that you must leave me with a face as long as that? Weren't the gifts of my house well received?"

Ordowahl struggled to find a smile. "Yet another goodbye, Cousin, and an unknowable one at that."

Mehrwal's eye twinkled. "Go with God, Cousin. I'll look after whatever of yourself you may have left behind."

A nose-full of brass pennies and a single
silver coin got Ordowahl the royal
quarters at the inn. Past there the king
must use the forest, for the road went coy.
    He came to Vlowohl, cousin once removed.
    Another hunt, this time with less success;
    another round of manly jests disproved
    his sense of kinfolk judging him the less.
Host Vlowohl cautioned him to be discreet.
"No household's happy when its serving maids
wax jealous. Son, if pressed, you must retreat" –
The lot of them sang nightly serenades.
    Almighty, was I wrong? Your gift of Eve
    exceeds – how can I thank and not receive?

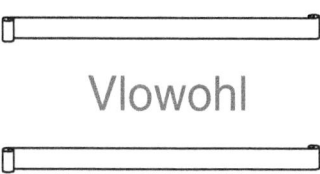

Vlowohl

A day's journey brought him to a small village at the end of the road. One house was slightly larger; its owner used the extra space as an inn.

Ordowahl dismounted and tied his horse and mule to a post set in front of it. A man, the innkeeper, came out to see what the disturbance was, when half the village seemed to gather by his door..

"I say," said the innkeeper. "One look at you says you'll eat double and your stallion the same. I trust you've got funds, my good Noble?"

The innkeeper was not the same fellow who'd had this place the last time Ordowahl had been there, and several village folk standing behind the man gave Ordowahl small "hello" waves and grins.

"Indeed, my fine innkeeper, fare for two and forage for three – don't forget the mule! That should come to five, eh, six brass pennies, no?"

The fellow grinned, and stood his ground. "Pennies might do for a child and its pony; but I'll play at the game with you. I believe adequate payment for the night requires silver; one coin for you, and one for your animals."

Snickering erupted behind the innkeeper, who turned around. "Oy, the lot of you, I trade fairly with everyone who passes by; leave me to my bargaining!"

"Lonny, hey nonny nonny, that one's the king's son Ordowahl. He'll give you silver; but take care you don't have to pluck it from a nostril!" Someone laughed aloud.

Lonny turned back to stare up at Ordowahl, whose odd, placid face seemed to flutter delicately. *Was that a giggle pounding on the inside?* "Aha, so it's not only Noble, but Prince. I am honored to be Royal Provider to the King of Nordweg, my lord Prince Ordowahl. Whatever has been customary is more than enough for the night."

Ordowahl gravely counted out ten pennies, then added a small silver coin. "We are at a bargain, then?" asked Ordowahl. "And this will include three mugs of your best ale, as usual. Now please show me to the Royal Chamber."

With a dawning sense of having been played, Lonny the innkeeper escorted Ordowahl to his own quarters, shooed out his wife and children, and had them carry in supper and ale.

For years afterward the village folk would ask to see the Royal Chamber – and no matter which sort of answer Lonny gave, they always rolled with laughter. Eventually he took over the tale and claimed the Royal Chamber was his own idea.

*__*__*__*

Setting out the next morning Ordowahl caught sight of a jackdaw flying overhead. It would perch on a tree limb then flutter off. The bird appeared to be tracking him, but after a while flew away into the forest.

A day-long trek across empty hill country brought Ordowahl to a more distant cousin, Vlowohl.

Vlowohl also accommodated Ordowahl with diligent weapons practice, and with a hunt. Vlowohl's horse struggled to bear Ordowahl all the way to the stag, and arrived after the beast had been hung up, drained and quartered.

"Hollo, is that Ordowahl? My good prince, we believed that you had scorned us! We salute you, arriving calmly and in good spirits. Now take up the task of Last to Arrive."

Vlowohl was serious; Ordowahl, for coming last, had to shoulder the carcass and carry it home. There was a background of commentary:

"Egads, man, the blood running down your mount's flanks! Have a care!"

"We worked hard to drain and quarter the beast, and save its blood for a pudding – and now you dribble out what we left you to guard – see the mess!"

"You couldn't keep pace with us coming – can you do the job going back? Shall we walk our horses to make them slow enough for you?"

Ordo took his ribbing with good humor. Compared to what his brothers would dish out, it was musical.

"Yes, my good fellows – as Prince of the Realm I must tell you that when I hand this off to the cook, my own share may exceed half the animal. A slow ride brings on a great hunger, and you'll have to plead an artful case if you want much of this meat."

He managed to look very hungry and very possessive, and stared them down – until Vlowohl caught a sly wink, and laughed.

"Hand the man a flagon! Perhaps when his thirst wanders off his hunger will chase it!"

Ordowahl could not express the thought, and would not if he could; exchanging his brothers' disdain for this easy banter was priceless balm. Hunting with Mehrwal and Vlowohl would return to his thoughts many times over the span of his life. These weeks were his taste of the fresh, green years that filled so many young male lives.

*__*__*__*

Vlowohl imagined that this king's son, one as personally kind as Ordowahl, might not take customary advantage of his position by spreading manly attention to as many local girls as he could get to wink back – which was, all things considered, roughly all the unmarried, and many with husbands. Yet, he wanted to be sure. The second afternoon, after a particularly strenuous battle drill, he pushed aside the pine cones and sat down in the soft brown layer of needles beneath a tall pine to sweat and breathe, and Ordowahl came over to sit beside him.

Vlowohl looked over at him; "Good Prince, Cousin, I have a particular request to make, and hope that you will understand both my reasoning and my love for you."

"Of course, Cousin. What would you ask of me?"

"We are somewhat remote from the center of Nordweg; there are fewer of us, and so the more tightly knit. It may be common for a highborn man to take a local woman with little thought for any after-effect. Here, I must ask you to tread lightly. Any maid in this small fiefdom of mine, especially if she is comely, will have a devoted young man lined up to wed her. This happens early here. Do you take my meaning?"

"Cousin, I do. It would burden my conscience to take a thoughtless pleasure yet know that it might break someone's happiness. While I stay here I will not wink, as you might say, at local women."

"Oh, and anyone living under my roof; we're at peace on that, Cousin? As Prince you always have my loyalty. If you also want to keep my love and affection, please strive to be circumspect. At night you may hear a muted giggle outside your bedchamber door; you and I know very well what that means, and what can come from thoughtless invitations?"

"I have heard soft giggles before, Vlo." Ordowahl smiled. "I do not want to make one or the other unhappy, and as yet I am a beginner where women's feelings are concerned."

"It is good that you see this now," replied his host. "I am still a learner myself; dwell on that. Whatever you do, you must remain discreet. I beg you to keep to yourself; the women of the household staff seem very happy the way things are."

Ordowahl smiled to himself. *Oh, Vlo, if you only knew the why of that, and how well they share! Discreet? Surely.*

324

————*——*

A third night; as before, he heard a small cough outside the door to his room, plus a hushed giggle; Ordowahl opened it. Two of the household maidservants had visited him. He had not had a night alone. Each had passed childbearing age; when the candles went out that hardly mattered. Tonight the entire complement of the house's maids stood there, all three of them.

"I am content with your visits," Ordowahl began politely. "Please give me your name," he asked the one who had not been there before.

"Sir, I am Marien," she said.

"And your husband?"

"Sir, I will never have one again; I am barren, and no man will take me. But, Sir, it appears that if I wish to have of you once or twice, my friends have said they would share."

Ordowahl looked closely at the other two. "Forgive me," he said to them, "I have neglected the courtesy of asking your names, and your master Vlowohl will not speak them."

The older one curtsied and said, "If it please you, Sir, I am Anne; and she is Marthe."

At the mention of that name Ordowahl smiled. "Yes, I have encountered the name before; the last I knew who had it was a remarkable woman. We must close the door; I do not want my host to think I am keeping special company."

Anne closed the door quietly and quietly. She said, "Sir, Prince Ordowahl, whatever choice the royal house may propose, it will be our pleasure to provide it."

"Then let all of us wear a smile tomorrow. Marien, you may leave your gown over there. Anne, Marthe, if I become fatigued, then remind me tomorrow night where it was I left off."

Marien looked at Anne and Marthe, in the dim glow of the flickering candle. "Dear younger sister," said Anne, "We are not impatient to share; it will be a while before this stallion tires."

————*——*

A week had passed, and Ordowahl was alone on his final night. He looked forward to deep slumber, and got into bed thinking of travel. In the morning he would again face an entire household, from Vlowohl down to the youngest staff, to endure yet another set of goodbyes. *If only Vlowohl knew his servants the way I've come to. Father in Heaven, thank You for the gift of carnal conversation. I know you place limits, and I ask forgiveness if I have trespassed. I have a better understanding of my brothers' casual talk regarding women. These are dear, sweet women. I feel a doting fondness toward them. Thank You, in Adam's name, for the gift of Eve!*

The way grew steep; Prince Ordo thought it brief.
He found the lofty valley 'neath the pass
to Viking lands, and Kleywehl's tiny fief.
"Come, Prince! Be welcome – help us raise a glass!"
   Because they were so few the social ties
   were close. "My Prince, I'm loyal through the worst,
   yet will withhold my love if you make prize
   of maidens here; they all have beaus who'd burst.
It was a final time to speak at length
of purpose, right and wrong, and noble grace.
What chose twixt high and low? Each had a strength
that served the realm, yet some were high, some base.
   The priest, and she of vi'let eyes, they each
   were loath that he should travel past their reach

Kleywehl

For two days Ordowahl saw no one. At mid-morning of the third day he ascended a familiar creek-drained slice carved in the lush, green mountainside. It began in a valley high above. He paused often to rest the animals and let them graze wherever the creek widened or a small meadow appeared. No jackdaw was in sight; he had become wary of the irregular visits, and when one did appear it put him slightly on edge.

Ordowahl broached the rocky lip of the high mountain valley. It held Kleywehl, his family, and a small community that worked the land. The feudal bonds between landholder and serf were loosely informal, and Ordowahl had always felt a special pleasantness there.

"Halloo, halloo the manor!" called Ordowahl, while he was too far away for the sound to carry. On impulse he reached into his saddlebag and removed a small hunting horn – Struvardekel had supplied it, yet one more act of foresight. It wasn't an instrument he'd learned well, yet after a few clumsy toots he managed a piercing sound.

In a few minutes he heard an answer, far deeper in tone; this sound should carry from end to end down at least a league of valley. Ordowahl cantered forward and found a cart track running beside a hay field. In short order a dim profile the size of a mouse at the far end of the track expanded to cat, hound, horse, then horse and rider.

"Halloo, halloo the manor!" Ordowahl repeated himself, and got a "Halloo, Welcome" in return. When the rider came closer he recognized Ordwehl, second son of third-cousin Kleywehl.

"Ordwehl, my how you've put on size! What are you now, nineteen?"

"Ordowahl, you've put on size yourself. Yes, nineteen – and I learnt that you've become a Man and search for the far corner of the world! In fact you're half way there now. Welcome."

The manor and nearby fields had poured out at least twenty people, from toddler to grandparent, and more were coming. Visitors were rare and exciting in the isolated high valley. In the hubbub of their conversation Ordowahl could hardly hear himself think. *Quiet up here, isn't it?*

"Look, a jackdaw!" shouted a ten-year-old. One of his responsibilities was to control pests, and the jackdaw was a bane bird. It ate seed in the spring, wheat at harvest time, and generally worked against the farmer. Sling and a stone slipped out of a pocket; a whirl, and the bird fell out of a cloud of feathers. It managed to crawl under a bush.

"Good one, Jonwehl," said a grandpa. The boy ran to collect his prize, and could not find it. "We saw it fall. It's robbed its last, boy."

Kleywehl took Ordowahl's hand; "You've only visited, what, every fourth year? Yes, your father the king comes by about that often to drink our ale, slay a stag, wink at our women, and joust with us. It is good, Ordowahl, to see you on your own. We can get to know you better; in fact, you could do worse than to stay right here."

"I'll certainly be here long enough to drink my way through your best keg and down a stag, Kleywehl. It honors me to find you well and receive your welcome."

"Ah, the diplomat! You render the phrases correctly, Ordowahl, Prince of Nordweg; now get off your high horse, and be informal with us," Kleywehl said with a friendly grin.

——*—*

The next-to-last day was again a Sabbath. An aging priest served the tiny congregation. Ordowahl tried to compare him to Father Ewald. This fellow knew his office, heard confession with kindness and dignity, and said the Mass as well as any. He seemed otherwise a dull sort. Keeping this tiny parish seemed to use him up.

The day's homily showed care; he addressed humility and peace. The priest "could not pretend to offer counsel to those of Noble heart." He merely assaulted the conscience of a young man far from home. "Is it right to test God? Is it right to enter into the fiery lions' den after Shadrach, Meshach and Abednego, even with no Nebuchadnezzar to command you?"

Ordowahl paid closer attention than usual, because the priest preached directly to him, and at him. *I understand the inference, mixed as it is. My father sends me to light, not to fire. He sends me away not because I have violated his command. He sends me to help me keep it. My brothers would end me. No, the fire is at home. Where I go I might find both heat and cool.*

More than that, there was an Angel in the furnace; so God may send an Angel where I go, to guard me as long as I stay true to Him. That was good enough; Ordowahl decided that he and the priest simply did not understand each other. A priest, after all, even if called to the Word, is no less human and no less fallible than anyone else.

The quiet and rest of the Sabbath surrendered in late afternoon to Kleywehl's three younger daughters. They ranged from Blunhetle, a slender brown-haired girl, an imp with a saucy smile, to yellow haired Frennete and eldest Nanneke, eighteen and with bright red hair. They brought out a lute, a harp, and pan pipes. Their concert was simple, and they seemed proud to show off for the prince. They blushed when he applauded at the end.

"Now, daughters, that is very good, and also quite enough," said their father, and he shooed them out. Blunhetle, only twelve, already had begun to change from tomboy to a slender, pretty pre-woman. Her sisters were fifteen and eighteen, and an older sister was already married. The girls obeyed their father, and managed to throw Ordowahl careful smiles on their way out.

"You have sisters somewhat like these, eh?"

"Yes, Kley, not exactly the same ages. Seeing your girls makes me homesick for my sisters." When the girls had gone down the hall and out of sight Ordowahl broached a difficult subject.

"Kinsman, on the one hand a man, a true man, shields the weak, and that includes women. Every man I've met is prone to brag about conquering a woman, or treating her with less than purity and kindness. One host told me he'd like to see my likeness pop up all over his village next spring – and another encouraged me to take my wild oats and sow them, just not under his roof."

Kley smiled thinly; "You aren't asking for the company of any of my girls, eh?"

Ordowahl snorted. "Talk to me about treating a woman one way because she is highborn, and treating a lowborn woman another. Doesn't she still enjoy a man's protection?"

Kleywehl paused to think. "High and low birth are part of God's Order. Your father and I command the people beneath us for their ultimate good, with authority if persuasion falters. The people living within this strong wooden palisade built it, and keep it strong. Their houses are here inside it, all around mine. When the Vikings come over the mountain, we survive together because we could not survive without each other.

"As I was saying, God's Order includes both high and low birth, and lowborn women serve highborn men in particular ways the same as lowborn men do in other ways. We do not consider it good breeding to discuss such things. They are as they are. Highborn men, for good or ill, often take casual carnal use of lowborn women and think little of it."

"I understand as much. What I do not understand is how the strong use the weak; that part still escapes me. A low man serves the high with his strength, and together both are the stronger. So, does a high man's casual use of a low woman do anything to make her stronger? Often she will bear a child that has no father to raise it, or a cuckolded one. What part of the exchange leaves her stronger, better able to live?"

Kley chuckled. "Such an active conscience you have, Ordowahl. Your questions touch things I have seldom given a thought. Let us say that a high man's attention to a lowborn woman often includes gifts – clothing, jewelry, a silver coin. It keeps peace when both gain, eh?"

"Yes, I suppose so, as long as the strong behave gently toward the weak. That is close to God's command, isn't it?"

"I suppose so. That is the sort of thing you notice, without having to tell your sons. If you are kind toward the weak yet still strong toward the strong, your sons will be the same. Is not that so?"

"Yes. My father is like that, and I try to be the same. My brothers…"

"I know your brothers well. These things are a mystery, eh? I know your father very well; perhaps they found other models to draw on when they were young. Be thankful that you chose the right model, Ordowahl. It will guard you. Respect belongs to those who show character and sound judgment. Everyone sees it in your father."

Kleywehl's wife had come into the room to hear their discussion, and Kleywehl had not minded her presence; she had been sitting quietly on the arm of his over-stuffed chair.

Ordowahl turned to her and said, "Dear Jonquil, beloved hostess, I am sad this evening. Tomorrow I will continue my journey."

"Surely, Ordowahl, you jest. Those wild, murderous people, what are they called, Vikings, they are scum and will eat you!"

"Sweet Jonquil, I have been to the edge of this valley and looked over. I saw only rock, snow, and some gentle grass. Far below there may be other people. Whatever their name or their habits, I trust to God's provision. I have heard of these Vikings, as you call them. Like all people they admire strength and will as soon welcome a warrior as exhaust themselves trying to block or slay him."

Kleywehl added to his wife's remarks. "Ordowahl, please hear me. I understand that you have never been in danger here; no one in the Nordwesh realm would or could offer you any harm. We have long and hard experience with these folk. Certainly you will pass among them, and may find peace. Be wary, my Prince. Be wary. These Vikings consider war and plunder to be part sport, part privilege, part duty, and all business. So long as you are with them you will be amongst murder and theft."

"Thank you, Host and Hostess; I take to heart everything you have said tonight. My way is clear. I will guard myself against any sort of pagan corruption, and hope some day to come back the same way I left. We shall see each other again, I am sure of it."

As Ordowahl bent down to blow out his candle someone opened the door to his room. He pulled up his breeches and there, in a modestly flowing sunflower yellow nightgown, with a candle holder and lit candle, stood Kleywehl's eldest unwed daughter, Nanneke, she with the red hair and violet eyes. Ordowahl raised an eyebrow.

"Surely I can have a quiet word with you, Sir? I have heard you speak about gentleness toward the weak, and I am far too weak to push you aside. So keep true to your word and allow me to enter!"

"And what if I stay in this spot?"

"Why, I'll rip my nightdress, strike my own face – I will certainly do that! – and scream."

"Yes, you could do all those, Nanneke. What then?"

"Why, you'd pay a price, and not I. It will be much simpler, don't you see, to let me come in?"

Ordowahl smiled and stepped aside. "I think you are showing me that there are other strengths, and ungentle ways of using them. I pray for mercy."

She snorted and pushed herself against him. He let her get far enough into the room to close the door with a backward thrust of one foot. *What is this? Who was the last woman to press her way in at bedtime, using her foot to close the door?* She set the candle on a table, pulled the gown over her head, sat on the bed and coyly slid her feet – perhaps a little of one calf too – under the bedcovers. Red hair spilled over the pillow, red hair shone beneath one up flung arm; tangled red hair covered her virginity.

"Quietly, my good lass; it happens best when you are asleep. You must trust me on this; we do not say, 'They slept together,' and not mean it. Hss, now, relax in my arms. Feel our two bodies nestle quietly. In the morning you will awaken to a wonderful surprise."

"Humph! I know much better than that! The scullery maids talk incessantly. I'll guess they've been up here each night since the day you arrived."

"Dear girl, they have not. When you say 'Any scullery maid knows it,' do you choose scullery maids to do your knowing? I am a truth teller if nothing else and I say that you must lie with me, quietly as a kitten, and sleep alongside me. Then in the morning there will be a great surprise."

She could not believe him, neither could she disbelieve him. He seemed so calmly gentle, so quietly matter-of-fact. If she had seen him playing cards with her brothers she might have understood that seeming innocence. Even after toying with the hairs on his chest, and nibbling awkwardly at his face, and trying desperately to tickle him, she could only sleep.

In the morning Kleywehl pushed the door open; his entire immediate family stood behind him. Ordowahl moved to throw off the covers; the girl beside him shrouded herself in them with strength born of panic.

"Ordowahl! Why have you outraged your host like this? My heart breaks. And Nanne, daughter, why did you not cry out in the night?"

She began to babble; Ordowahl simply sat up on the other side of the bed, pulled on his trousers, and stood to face the family.

"Dear ones, she was awake in the night and needed comfort. She is clearly too old to go to her parents' bed, so she came to a brother's, in this case to mine. I ask you to examine the sheets, nay, the entire room. She came here a virgin – how else? Then it is easy to learn whether her purity has survived a night of quiet sleep."

Kleywehl saw through his daughter's performance. "What did you have to gain? Thoughtless woman-child! Showing your nakedness to a man, and spending the night thigh to thigh with him?

"Ordowahl, I appreciate your wit, and your kindness. Nanneke can be willful, eh? I pity whichever man gets her; she will drive him crazy. In fact you've managed her so well you'd be a very handy husband."

It hung in the air; Ordowahl kept silence, to avoid nay saying his fond host. Then the girl turned her violet eyes to the floor and picked up her nightgown from beneath a cascade of long, silky red hair. She struggled to get under the gown and pull it over her head without too much of herself showing, then rose and stormed out of the room. Her mother, Jonquil, ran after her, pleading to salvage some peace and calm. One by one her sisters and brothers shook their heads and left, not trying to hide smirks.

Kleywehl continued to look grim,. He finally relaxed. "Children! God gives them. Sometimes it isn't God who moves them!" He reached up a hand to pat Ordowahl's still bare shoulder and left, closing the door behind him.

Silence settled over the house, and continued through breakfast. Ordowahl went out to stand in front of the house and say his goodbyes.

"Good my host, good my hostess, good my borrowed brothers and sisters, I pray God continues to give you peace and health. I will enjoy a happy smile each time I remember your house and all who are in it. Thank you. Now God keep you, and fare you well." He made a half-leap onto Hammerfoot and set off to ascend the pass. All the farming folk, household staff, Kleywehl, Jonquil, and their sons and daughters had gathered, and as he left they waved sadly – all save Nanneke, who tossed her red hair and stalked back into the house.

Across a rocky pass, down icy steeps,
to find a pagan hut and trampled lea,
a pond, a stream that trickles, grows and keeps
descending 'til a river meets the sea.
    The first to see him ran at full attack,
    yet when he showed his strength, and peace, they smiled,
    passed time in idle chat. From maniac
    to slumber, then to parting unbeguiled.
A pagan folk they were, and all who met
him spoke a murky tongue. No nobles bid
him "Hail". Those jackdaws lurked; they would not let
the people speak aloud, with mind unhid.
    From lonely ice and rock to river's mouth,
    Prince Ordowahl observed, and traveled south.

Viking Folk

The morning sun shone obliquely across the land and filled the prince's eyes. The slope was gradual enough, and winter's ice long gone. The sun had gone halfway up the sky before the track found a gravelly gap between granite crags of the mountain. It looked un-trod and nearly flat. Each winter's melt washed it gently, and something had pushed away the larger rocks. A few sparse plants grew in the thin soil, and no clear trail disturbed them.

Ordowahl descended the far side. The sun now threw bright light on the land. It took a deep slope away from the pass. Ice lay packed behind the bases of trees and boulders. He dismounted and led the pack mule. The stallion picked its own way gingerly in the track of the more confident mule.

An hour's walk brought Ordowahl to what could only be a campground. A stone hut stood in the center, with open windows and an empty doorway. Ordowahl glimpsed objects of bone, horn, and woven leather strips hanging on one wall. Nearby sat an altar of piled rock.

The campground showed years of trampling. Tendrils of hardy spring grass defied the chill of departing winter. While the animals grazed he examined perhaps fifteen stone fire pits. The surrounding forest lay bare, picked clean of downed wood. He

338

wondered about these people, and how often they had beset Kleywehl. Ordowahl crossed himself and left that place. He saved a memory of it.

A small creek skirted one edge. He followed it to a tarn. At its far edge it leaked through a dam of broken rock and splashed down toward foaming water rushing through the steep, chilly, noisy canyon. Ordowahl led Hammerfoot and mule slowly down the crumbled rock wall of the tarn to a place that had a footpath, soil and shrubs, where he remounted.

The entire day he followed a filigree of paths that slowly grew wider and less steep. Downed wood lay akimbo among the trunks of pine and fir. Saplings, a few hardy shrubs, and pine needle covered soil hid most of the jumbled mountain rock. Out of the corner of his eye he might catch sight of a squirrel, or the sudden color of a mountain jay. One such bird looked oddly like a jackdaw. It ducked behind a thick fir bough before he could make sure.

Near dusk he stopped to water the stock and fill his water bag. Then Ordowahl carefully led the animals over bare rock and away from the path. When he judged they were well out of earshot through the thick forest, he halted and made a light camp.

At sunup he loosed the hungry animals to find forage, broke camp, and when they had fed he continued. Yesterday's trails had been sketchy at best. When he found the trail this time, it was clearly defined. By mid-morning it became wide enough for mounted riders to pass each other, although he met no one trekking upward. There were occasional sunlit patches of grass and flowers. The slope was gentle, the canyon wider and the stream somewhat slower, and occasionally easy to ford.

At midday he reached a small valley with tilled land and a cluster of huts. A young child saw him first, and ran screaming into an open door. A man came at a dead sprint from a small animal shed, armed with both a knife and a fierce expression.

Hardly what you'd think of as hospitality. Ordowahl halted his mount and observed the man, as he came closer. *Not slowing down any – he seems bent on using that knife.* Ordowahl dismounted to meet the man on foot. *Nobody fights with a knife that way in Nordweg – does he know something I don't?* A simple feint and trip put the man on his face. Ordowahl hadn't unsheathed his own blade.

With a knee lightly placed on the fellow's shoulder blades and a powerful grip pressing two calves into the dirt, Ordowahl looked up to see who else might be coming. A single jackdaw flew out of the hut the child had run into, then paid quick visits to the others. In moments at least fifteen peasants of all ages also came at a run. The able-bodied had armed themselves with pitchfork, scythe, and spade; the women held knives and one also gestured with a meat tenderizing mallet.

Ordowahl stood up and dangled the first attacker in front of him like a talisman of good luck. He drew his own knife. Viking speech was cousin to his own: "<u>Etstanden ealle, elles ic cwelle thhess byad'rink!</u> (Stop, you-all, else I kill the warrior!)" he said, and they seemed to understand that he would exact harm on the first man who had attacked him if they came much closer.

They stopped in shock, then laughed. "<u>Beahdurinc!</u>" one of them said with a derisive snort.

Ordowahl more or less carefully put the man down on his feet. With a knife in each hand he gave the man back his own small weapon. "<u>Thhu acwellst meh? Elles freond?</u> (You kill me? Or friends?)"

The fellow looked grumpy and rubbed several bruises. He would ache for days. Looking at his knife, then at Ordowahl's, he grinned. Gravely putting his knife back into a crude sheath at his waist, he turned around and reached back to Ordowahl with one hand.

"<u>Kynn follc, ic giefan eovh meen niwe gheselda.</u> (Kinfolk, I give you my new companion)" and tugged Ordowahl to stand beside him. In a quiet whisper he asked, "<u>Hwelk ees eower nama?</u> (What is your name?)"

"Ordowahl."

"Or-r-r Dou Vahlll!" Turning aside to Ordowahl he added, with a polite expression, "Vee vil kalda demm Vahllij. (We will call you Wally.)"

With solemn aplomb Ordowahl bowed deeply to the small crowd. They carefully laid down their implements and ran up to hug him, shake hands, reach as high as they could to slap him on the back, and generally make him understand that he was welcome. *Must not get many visitors. I wonder what's in store after this place?*

The women, Meatmallet in the lead, hustled back, evidently to cook something worthy of an honored guest. They didn't mind that his speech had a terrible Nordwesh accent; that was no matter. They agreed that he was both a master warrior, and a friend. Work ceased for the afternoon.

An older man, a grandfather and probably clan elder, went to the animal shed and brought out a calf. He slaughtered it, and in short order skinned, gutted and quartered the animal. A favored grandson had held a leather bag beneath the calf's severed jugular. Soon its hide lay on the grass with the cleaned carcass resting on it. The tied-off bag of blood sat next to it. A pile of innards also had its place on the hide. Nothing would be wasted. Grandfather and grandson took the results – carcass, bag, and loaded hide – into Meatmallet's hut and returned to the men's gathering. Once seated they casually wiped their hands on the short, recently grazed grass.

While the Grandfatherhad been processing the calf, two men lugged out a wooden tub. Everyone old enough to hold a cup went to grab one, and returned to drink up. What these Vikings considered ale wasn't, in Ordowahl's kindest opinion, much better than a tub of cracked grain soaked and left outside to fester. At least it had fermented, had energy.

The ale gradually became tolerable, and the conversation grew louder and happier.

At a lull in the talking Ordowahl asked, "Havvor langt er det teel byenn? Havvor langt er det teel lahnt? (How far is it to a city? How far is it to the shore?)"

341

They suddenly looked pained; "<u>Vee er ikka megget kend-scob</u> (We're barely acquainted,)" and "<u>En friggtellig kongen liv ved kysten</u> (A terrible king lives on the shore,)" and "<u>Tak teel træ spreetahs hahn aldreeg komma soh langt</u>! (Thank the tree sprites he never comes this far!)"

Ordowahl looked at them sternly and said that he was the son of a king, and a very wise king at that; how was it that theirs was, as they said, "frightful?"

Silence; he could see them thinking this over. At last grandfather said the jackdaws always came as a warning. That was their reason to attack Ordowahl in the first place. The king kept hundreds of jackdaws in a special cage the size of ten houses. They considered the king secretive and suspicious, and not Viking-like.

Christians use the sign of the Cross to guard themselves; pagans, or at least these Vikings, pinched their left ear with their right hand, spat three times rapidly on the ground, and blinked. The effect might have pushed Ordowahl's sense of princely decorum into laughter, if it weren't done with such sincere lament.

The mood fell, as though rain had started to fall. Soon enough, the women came out of a smoky hut and hooted musically. The men rose, patted their bellies *another ritual?* and walked toward a common area at the center of the circle of huts.

A crude trestle table held the food. Wordlessly, each took a piece of flatbread and used it as a wrapper to pluck meat sliced off the steaming carcass. Then all sat on the ground with legs folded, and ate. More ale came out, and a cauldron of soup – small bits of heart, kidney, liver, and who knew what else, garden greens, thickened with cracked grain plus a lot of onion. It served as sauce for the meat. Ordowahl was not amazed at how well they could eat; gluttony was no sin at feasting time. They ate in dedicated silence.

The sun sat low in the sky; everyone drifted into one hut or another. At length one woman was left, and four children, plus Ordowahl.

"Yeg er enn ennka; komma ee seng. (I am a widow; come to bed.)" She got to her feet and took Ordowahl's hand. The children ran giggling into one of the huts, and Ordowahl followed, stooping very low to enter.

There was one sleeping pallet, more or less big enough for the woman and her children. "Geev mee et barn, (Give me a child,)" she said. She shooed the children away from the pallet, and they hunkered down on another piece of floor. It was summer, so it was no hardship.

"Oonska dee ott goora stooy? (Do you want to make noise?)" She at first thought he was asking her to cry for her dead husband. Shortly he figured out his real intent.

"Lahd verden hoora, hvad shoft vee vil ahnda! (Let the world hear what fun we're having!)"

*__*__*__*

In the morning all shared a communal breakfast. The women frankly appraised Ordowahl and lasciviously fondled him; he was oddly amused. The men didn't seem to mind, and in fact sent him many winks and nudged him in the ribs, man to man.

And then, as though Ordowahl were a casual part of everyday life, each adult and all the older children got up and went off to begin their daily work.

Again only his hostess remained. "Meet navn er oor-r-rsoola," she said.

"Ursula, I am named Ordowahl. I see that you are keeping the young children, and hope that, this time next summer, you will have another one to watch over."

She dimpled shyly, slapped him across the kidneys with surprising strength, and herded the children out to a vegetable garden. Ordowahl watched them chasing grasshoppers and picking weeds. When one or another would turn and stare, Ursula kept them busy tending the garden.

Leaving without a good-bye felt crudely impersonal, but Ordowahl was ready to go on. The sun, even low in the eastern sky, lit his trail toward the sea.

——*—*

Day by day the farms and villages got larger, and the people less suspicious; Ordowahl felt lulled. Jackdaws seemed to pop up everywhere. No one minded. At one midday stop he thought he overheard a guarded reference to "the king's spies" - they sat on every branch, and left no man free to his own devices. *How odd is that? Everyone works at something all the day. In fact I've grown rusty myself! Devices, indeed: what are they, all of them tinkers and clockmakers?*

Each afternoon the prince went away from the sight and sound of other people. He made early camp in a small clearing. For the rest of a long and very tiring afternoon he drilled. He practiced parries and thrusts, leaps and counter spins, tumbling moves, calisthenics, and wind sprints. When he'd done a whole set, Ordowahl drank deeply from the nearest small creek, paused long enough to calm his racing heart, then began again. At the end of these afternoons he was often too tired to cook a hot meal. A journey cake, a chunk of summer sausage, a handful of cheese, and night came.

——*—*

The waning moon would not be up until the middle of the night. The bright, sparkling sky gave enough light to make out the jagged tree line of the meadow's edge. *How many times before have I slept alone, with no one around? Before leaving Nordweg, none that I recall. Now I give you, Heavenly Father, my prayers in Your company, and no one else's. Please bless my sleeping, Father, and watch me through the night. I ask Your pardon for sins I have not confessed – I have no priest to confess them to. I ask pardon for what can only be fornication – and while I did confess that to Vlowohl's and Mehrwal's priests, I have not turned away from women. Please guide me, Father; I am willing to abstain, yet the flesh is so strong!*

Bless, Father in Heaven, my father and mother, my brothers and their families, and all in the kingdom of Nordweg. Especially, Almighty Father, bless Father Ewald and my dear mage Heorald. They have made me into a contest between themselves, which I hope has amused You. Each of them has trained me well, and I thank You for the gifts You have sent me through those two diligent and holy men.

Amen.

Through each long afternoon he felt an audience, as rows of silent jackdaws would line the branches of a nearby tree. He never saw them come. While he labored to re-train sloppy eyes and hands and maintain his body's strength and endurance, the feathered audience sat rapt, intent. He never saw them leave. When he awoke in the morning, they seemed to filter in from somewhere, and await his next move.

Unknown to Ordowahl, his next move would enmesh him in a Viking context.

Other Titles:
  Joel Hinrichs
An Adult's Garden of Verses   (2017)
Ordowahl : Mate   (2021)
Genesis and Creation   (2024)
Ordowahl : Mourner   (Coming)
Ordowahl : Monarch   (Coming)
Ordowahl : Mage   (TBD)
Ordowahl : Martyr   (TBD)

  Jody Glittenberg
SAVING MOTHER EARTH   (2018)
  THE PROMISE SEED

Words With a Mission (wordswithamission.com)

oh-and-another-thing.blog